"Balogh can always be depended on to deliver a beautifully written Regency romance."　　　*—Publishers Weekly*

"I loved this book. I read it in one sitting and it made me smile a lot and cry a little."　　　—Smart Bitches Trashy Books

"Balogh always crafts stories that are powerful, poignant, and romantic, but what makes them extraordinary is how she beautifully balances emotional intensity with sensuality."
　　　—RT Book Reviews (4½ stars, top pick)

Praise for the Westcott series

Someone to Care

"A love story nearly perfect in every way."
　　　—Booklist (starred review)

"A story that is searing in its insight, as comforting as a hug, and a brilliant addition to this series. Another gem from a master of the art."　　　*—Library Journal* (starred review)

Someone to Wed

"With her signature voice and steady pace, Balogh crafts a thoughtful, sweet Regency-era love story to follow *Someone to Hold*."　　　*—Publishers Weekly*

"Balogh's delightful ugly duckling tale may be the nonpareil Regency romance of the season."

—*Booklist* (starred review)

SOMEONE TO HOLD

"Written with an irresistibly wry sense of humor and graced with a cast of unforgettable characters, the second in Balogh's exceptional Westcott series, following *Someone to Love*, is another gorgeously written love story from the queen of Regency romances."   —*Booklist* (starred review)

"This 'Cinderella' reversal story seethes with desire, painted paradoxically in the watercolor prose that is the hallmark of this author."   —*Kirkus Reviews*

"This Regency romance dives deeper than most and will satisfy fans and new readers alike."   —*Publishers Weekly*

"Balogh is, and always will be, a grand mistress of the genre."   —RT Book Reviews

A VERY SPECIAL CHRISTMAS

Including *A Christmas Bride* and
Christmas stories from *Under the Mistletoe*

MARY BALOGH

JOVE
New York

A JOVE BOOK
Published by Berkley
An imprint of Penguin Random House LLC
375 Hudson Street, New York, New York 10014

🐧

A Christmas Bride copyright © 1997 by Mary Balogh;
Epilogue for *A Christmas Bride* copyright © 1997 by Mary Balogh
Under the Mistletoe copyright © 2003 by Mary Balogh; "A Family Christmas"
copyright © 2003 by Mary Balogh; "The Star of Bethlehem" copyright 1989 by Mary
Balogh; "The Best Gift" copyright © 1994 by Mary Balogh; "Playing House" copyright ©
1990 by Mary Balogh; "No Room at the Inn" copyright © 1993 by Mary Balogh

A JOVE BOOK, BERKLEY, and the BERKLEY & B colophon
are registered trademarks of Penguin Random House LLC.

ISBN: 9781984802170

A Very Special Christmas First Omnibus Edition: October 2018

A Christmas Bride Signet mass-market edition / November 1997
Epilogue for *A Christmas Bride* marybalogh.com / 1997
A Christmas Bride/Christmas Beau Dell mass-market edition / November 2015
Under the Mistletoe New American Library trade edition / November 2003
Under the Mistletoe Signet mass-market edition / December 2013

Printed in the United States of America
1 3 5 7 9 10 8 6 4 2

Cover photographs: woman by Richard Jenkins; winter night
by Vitallii Bashkatov / Shutterstock Images
Cover design by Katie Anderson
Book design by Laura K. Corless

Contents

A CHRISTMAS BRIDE

Chapter One

❖

Mr. Edgar Downes had decided to take a bride.
Doubtless he should have made up his mind to do
so long before he did, since he was six-and-thirty years old
and had both a high respect for matrimony and a fondness
for family life. But the truth was that he had procrastinated.
He had felt caught between two worlds. He was not a gentleman. He was the son of a Bristol merchant who had
grown enormously wealthy over the years and had eventually purchased and renovated a grand mansion and estate
near Bristol and retired to live there like a gentleman.
Edgar had been educated at the best schools, had become a
respected and successful lawyer, and then had taken over
his father's business.

He was hugely wealthy in his own right. He had received
a gentleman's education. He spoke and dressed as a gentleman. He would inherit Mobley Abbey on his father's death.
He was extremely eligible. But he was not a gentleman by
birth, and in certain circles that fact made all the difference
in the world.

He had thought about marrying someone of his own
kind. At various points during his adulthood he had even
singled out a few daughters or sisters of his middle-class
acquaintances as possible wives. But he had never felt that
he quite belonged in their world—not when it came to
something as personal and intimate as marriage. He would
have been hard put to explain exactly why that was so.

There were certain almost puritanical attitudes in the class, perhaps, or a certain vulgar preoccupation with money and possessions for their own sake. Though neither explanation quite accounted for his discomfort.

He had thought of marrying a lady. But there had been obvious arguments against that. And they all narrowed down to one simple fact—he was not a gentleman. It was true that Cora, his sister and only sibling, had married a younger son of a duke seven years before and had become Lady Francis Kneller as a result. It was true, too, that Edgar got along remarkably well with his exceedingly elegant brother-in-law and with those of their aristocratic friends he had met. But though Cora's marriage appeared to be bowling along very nicely indeed and had produced four bouncing children, Lord Francis would not in the normal course of events have wed her. It was her disastrous tendency to play heroine without pausing for one hundredth part of a second to consider the wisdom of her actions that had forced him on more than one occasion to her rescue and to compromising circumstances at the same time. Finally, poor fellow, he had had no choice—as a *gentleman*— but to take on a leg shackle and Cora all at the same time.

Lord Francis Kneller and his friends—the Earl of Thornhill, for example, or the Marquess of Carew, or the Duke of Bridgwater—might be quite prepared to treat Mr. Edgar Downes, Lady Francis's brother, as a friendly acquaintance. But would they be happy to watch him woo and wed their sisters or cousins if he so chose, and if there were any such females available? It was a question Edgar could not answer with any certainty since he had never posed it to any of the gentlemen concerned, but he could make an educated guess.

Some lesser gentleman with a daughter difficult to fire off in a more acceptable manner—due to impoverishment or lack of beauty or a shrewish nature, perhaps—might be very willing to ally her to a cit, to a lawyer-turned-merchant who also happened to be as wealthy as all but a few of the bluest-blooded lords in the land and with as much more wealth again to inherit on the death of his father. That lesser gentleman, however, would believe in his heart—and all the genteel world would believe with him—that he had stooped low indeed for the mere satisfaction of seeing his daughter wed.

But at the age of six-and-thirty Edgar Downes had decided to take a bride. A bride of good birth. A lady, no less. And he was going to do it soon. By Christmastime he would either be betrothed or have fixed his choice firmly and confidently enough that he would invite the woman and her family to Mobley Abbey for the holiday and a celebration of the betrothal. It was a promise he had made his father, and he always kept his promises.

The elder Mr. Downes had celebrated his sixtieth birthday at the beginning of September. And though it would be difficult to find a healthier, more robust, more mentally agile man of his age anywhere in the kingdom, he had chosen on that occasion to remember his mortality and to declare himself an old man. An old man with a dying wish. Cora had shrieked when he had put it thus, doubtless imagining all sorts of hidden and deadly ailments, and Lord Francis had pursed his lips. Edgar had rocked back on his chair. The dying wish was to see his son wed. Perhaps he would even be spared long enough to see a son of his son in the nursery . . . A man longed for an heir to his heir.

And since Mr. Downes had achieved almost every goal that any man could possibly set himself in the course of his lifetime—including a lamentably short but blissfully happy marriage, the birth and survival of the best son and daughter a man ever had, not to mention a challenging and successful career and the acquisition of the abbey—he had only one more thing to wish for, apart from the marriage of his son, of course, and that was the birth of a son to his son. He could wish that his son would marry well, that he would finally ally the Downes name to one of undoubted gentility.

"You are a gentleman, my son," he said, nodding his head in Edgar's direction, his eyes beaming with pride and affection. "Your dear mother was a lady in every sense that mattered to me. But for my son I want a lady by birth. You have deserved such a wife."

Edgar felt embarrassed, especially since these words had been spoken in the presence of Lord Francis Kneller. He also felt suspiciously damp-eyed. His father meant more to him than almost anyone else in this world.

"And it is high time you married, Edgar," Cora said. "It is all very well for the children to have an uncle who spoils them dreadfully every time he crosses paths with them, but cousins would be of more practical value to them. And an aunt."

Lord Francis chuckled. "You must confess, Edgar," he said, "you have had a good run of it. You are six-and-thirty and only now is your family laying siege to your single state."

"That is quite unfair, Francis," Cora said. "You know that every time Edgar has come to Sidley since our marriage I have thrown the most eligible young ladies in his way. You know that I have tried my very best."

Lord Francis chuckled again. "You are as successful as a matchmaker, my love," he said, "as you are at your swimming lessons."

"Well," she said crossly, "whoever says that the human person—*my* human person anyway—is not heavier than water and will not sink like a stone when laid out on top of it must have windmills in his head and that is all I have to say."

"For which mercy may the Lord be praised," Edgar said, provoking outright laughter from his brother-in-law and a glare followed by a rueful chuckle from his sister.

But his father was not to be diverted from what he had clearly planned as the mission of his sixtieth birthday. Edgar was to marry and to marry a lady. A duke's daughter could not be too good for his son, he remarked.

"What a pity it is that Francis's sisters are married," Cora commented. "Is it not, Francis?"

"Quite so, my love," he agreed.

But any lady of breeding would do nicely, Mr. Downes continued after the interruption. Provided Edgar could like and respect her—and feel an affection for her. That, it seemed, was of greater importance than almost anything else.

"She does not have to be a lady of fortune, my boy," Mr. Downes said. "She can come to you penniless, provided she has the birth and breeding and can love you."

A penniless lady of *ton* would probably love his money a great deal, Edgar thought cynically. But he could not argue with his father, who looked as if he would live until the age of one hundred with all his energies and faculties intact, but who was, when all was said and done, sixty and aging. It was understandable that his father should need the assurance that all he had worked for through his life would descend to more than just an unmarried son.

And so Edgar found himself agreeing that it was indeed time he took it upon himself to find a bride and that if it would please his father he would choose one who had some distinction of birth. And there was nothing to be served by delaying, he suggested without waiting to be prompted by his father. He had some business in London, a city he hated and avoided whenever it was possible to do so. He had a few connections there who would effect some introductions. He would undertake to choose himself a bride, perhaps even to be affianced to her by Christmas. He would bring her down to Mobley Abbey for Christmas—or at least invite her parents to bring her. By his father's sixty-first birthday he would be married and be in a fair way to getting his first child into the nursery.

Cora shrieked and clasped her hands to her bosom.

"You are conceiving an idea, my love?" Lord Francis asked, sounding amused. He was frequently amused, having decided long ago, it seemed, that it would be far more comfortable to laugh his way through life with Cora than to grimace his way through all her excesses and disasters. Wise man.

"Francis was not able to have his month in London during the Season this year," she said. "First we were in the north with Jennifer and Gabriel and then we went with them to Stephanie and Alistair's, and we were all having such a marvelous time and so were the children—were they not, Francis?—and Stephanie has the most *adorable* baby, Papa. He even had me dreaming of number five, but Francis insists in that most odious voice he uses when he wants to pretend to be lord and master that four is quite enough, thank you very much. What was it I set out to say?"

"That since I was not obliged to spend a month of the Season in town," Lord Francis said, "I should be encouraged to take you and the children there for the autumn. I do believe that was where your verbal destination lay, my love."

She favored him with a dazzling smile. "What a splendid idea, Francis," she said. "Jennifer and Gabriel and Samantha and Hartley were talking about going there for a month or so after the heat of the summer was over. We could have a wonderful time. And we could take Edgar about with us and see to it that he meets the right people."

"With all due respect, my love," Lord Francis said, "I do not believe Edgar is a puppy who needs our patronage. But certainly we will give him the comfort of having some familiar faces to greet at whatever entertainments are to be found during the autumn. And you will stay with us if you please, Edgar. The Pulteney Hotel may close its doors and go into a permanent decline when they discover that they are not to have your business, but we can offer some rowdy nephews and a niece for your entertainment. Who could possibly resist?"

"Edgar will spoil them and make them quite unmanageable," Cora said.

"Their maternal grandfather has spoiled them for the past two weeks as well as their uncle. *We* spoil them, my love," her husband said. "Yet we manage them perfectly well when it is necessary that they be managed. Their rowdiness and exuberance do not denote lack of all manners and discipline."

Between them they sealed Edgar's fate. He was to go to town by the end of September, it seemed, and stay at his brother-in-law's town house. He was to involve himself in the social life of the capital as it was lived in the autumn. There would not be all the balls and huge squeezes for which the spring Season was so renowned, but there would be enough people in residence in the grand houses of Mayfair to allow for a fair sprinkling of social entertainments. Lord Francis would see to it that Edgar was invited to a goodly number of them, and Cora would undertake to introduce him to some likely matrimonial prospects.

He needed their help. Despite the courteous tact of his brother-in-law's words, Edgar felt no doubt about that. He might have managed it himself, but with far more effort than would be needed if he simply relied upon the fact that Francis was a member of the upper echelons of the *ton*. Edgar was resigned to forcing his way into ranks from which his birth would normally exclude him. He was prepared for some coolness, even some rejection. But he knew enough about the world to believe that his wealth and his prospects would open a number of doors to him, especially those of people who felt themselves in need of sharing in his wealth.

He did not doubt that it was within his power to win himself a bride by Christmas. Someone of birth and breeding. Someone who would not look upon his own origins with contempt or condescension. Someone pretty and personable. Someone of whom he could be fond, it was to be hoped. He came from a family that set much store by that elusive something called love. He loved his father and his sister and was loved by them in return. His parents had enjoyed a love match. So did Cora and Francis, though the marriage had not appeared too promising at the start. Edgar rather thought that he would like to make a love match, too, or at least a match of affection.

He had until Christmas. Three months.

He was going to choose himself a bride. He traveled up to London at the end of the month, a little chilled by the thought, a little exhilarated by it.

After all, he was enough his father's son to find a challenge stimulating.

L ord Francis Kneller's friends were indeed in London. The Earl and Countess of Thornhill and the Marquess and Marchioness of Carew had come down together from Yorkshire with their six children for the purpose of shopping and seeing the sights and socializing at a somewhat less frantic pace than the Season would have allowed. Even the Duke and Duchess of Bridgwater had come up with their new son, mainly because their other friends were to be there. The duke's sister and Cora's special friend, the Countess of Greenwald, was also in residence with her husband and family. And they all decided to be kind to Cora's brother and to take him under their collective wing.

It was all somewhat daunting. And rather embarrassing. And not a little humbling to a man who was accustomed to commanding other men and to thinking himself very much master of his own life and affairs. His first social invitation, to what was termed an intimate soirée, came from the Countess of Greenwald. The affair was termed "intimate," Edgar guessed, to excuse its lack of numbers in comparison with what might have been expected during the Season.

But when his sister informed him that quite one hundred people had been invited and that surely all but a very few would make an appearance, Edgar felt absurdly nervous. He had never forgotten how the other boys at school had made him suffer for his birth. He had never complained to his father, or to any of the masters, who had undoubtedly shared the sentiments of the bulk of their pupils anyway. He had learned how to use his fists and his tongue, too, with blistering effect. He had learned endurance and pride and self-respect. He had learned that there was an invisible barrier between those men—and boys—who were gentlemen and those who were not. He had vowed to himself that he would never try to cross that barrier.

As a very young man he had scorned even to want to

cross it. He had been proud of who he was and of what he had made of himself and what his father had made of *him*-self. But Cora had married Francis. And the bridge had been set in place. And then his father had expressed his dying wish—surely thirty years before he was likely to die.

Edgar dressed carefully for the soirée. He wore a plain blue evening coat with gray knee breeches and white linen. He directed his valet to tie his neckcloth in a simple knot rather than fashion one of the more elaborate and artistic creations his man favored. His only jewelry was a diamond pin in the folds of the neckcloth. His clothes were expensive and expertly tailored. He would allow the tailoring to speak for itself. He would not try to put on any show of wealth. He certainly would not wear anything that might suggest dandyism. The very thought made him shudder.

Cora and her friends would doubtless introduce him to some young ladies. Indeed, he had been quite aware of them going into a huddle after dinner at the Carews' the evening before. He had been painfully aware from the enthusiastic tone of their murmurings and the occasional furtive and interested glance thrown his way by one and another of them that he had been the subject of their con-versation.

He hoped they would not introduce him to very young ladies. He was thirty-six. It would be most unfair to expect a young girl straight from the schoolroom to take him on. And he did not believe he would find appealing a girl al-most young enough to be his daughter. He should have told Cora that he wanted someone significantly past the age of one-and-twenty. Such ladies were deemed to be on the shelf, of course. There had to be something wrong with them if they had not snared a husband by the age of twenty. And perhaps it really was so. How would he know?

"I would lead you in the direction of a congenial game of cards, old chap," Lord Francis said to him as they arrived at the Greenwalds' town house. He clapped a hand on his brother-in-law's shoulder and grinned. "But Cora would have my head and your purpose in coming to town would not be served. I shall allow her to go to work as soon as she emerges from the ladies' room. But no, you will not have to wait that long. Here comes our hostess herself, and from the look in her eye, Edgar, I would guess she means business."

And sure enough, after greeting them both with a gracious smile, Lady Greenwald linked one arm through Edgar's and bore him off to introduce him to a few people he might find interesting.

"Everyone is starved for the sight of a new face and the sound of new conversation, Mr. Downes," she said, "especially at this time of year when there are so few people in town."

It seemed to Edgar that there was a vast number of people in Lady Greenwald's drawing room, but the fact that almost all of them were strangers might have contributed to the impression.

He was introduced to a number of people and conversed briefly with them about the weather and other such general topics until Lady Greenwald finally led him to where he guessed she had been leading him from the start. Sir Webster Grainger shook him heartily by the hand instead of merely bowing, and laughed just as heartily for no apparent reason. Lady Grainger swept him a curtsy that looked deferential enough to have been made in the queen's drawing room. And Miss Fanny Grainger, small, slight of figure, fair of hair, rather pretty, blushed rosily and directed her gaze at the floor somewhere in the vicinity of Edgar's shoes.

It had been planned, he thought. As both an experienced lawyer and a businessman he was canny at interpreting tone and atmosphere and the language of the body. Words were not always necessary for the assessment of a situation. It was very clear to him from the first moment that Sir Webster Grainger and his lady were in search of a husband for their daughter, that they had heard of his availability, and that they had determined to fix his interest. He did not doubt that Lady Greenwald would have done her job well. The Graingers would be well aware of his social status.

"You are familiar with Bristol, I understand, Mr. Downes,"

Sir Webster said as Lady Greenwald excused herself to greet some new arrival at the drawing room door.

"I live there and conduct my business there, sir," Edgar said very deliberately. Let there be no possible mistake.

"We invariably spend a day in Bristol whenever we go to Bath for Lady Grainger to take the waters," Sir Webster said. "She has an aunt living there. At Bristol, that is."

"It is an agreeable place in which to have one's residence," Edgar said. Good Lord, the girl could be no more than eighteen. He must have been her present age when she was born. Her mother must be of an age with him.

"Fanny always particularly enjoys the days we spend in Bristol," Lady Grainger said. "You must tell Mr. Downes what you like best about Bristol, Fanny, to see if he agrees with you."

There could have been no suggestion better calculated to tie the girl's tongue in knots, Edgar could see. She lifted her eyes to his chest, tried to raise them higher, failed, and blushed again. Poor child.

"Whenever I have been to London and return home," he said, "I am invariably asked what I liked best about town. I am never able to answer. I could, I suppose, describe the Tower of London or Hyde Park or a dozen other places, but I can never think of a single one when confronted. In my experience, one either likes a place or not. Do you like Bristol, Miss Grainger?"

She shot him a brief and grateful glance. She had fine gray eyes in a rather thin face. "I like it very well, sir," she said. "Because my great-aunt lives there, I believe, and I like her."

It was not a profound answer, but it was an endearingly honest one.

"It is the best reason of all for liking a place," he said. "I grew up in Bristol with a father and a sister whom I loved and still love, and so for me Bristol will always be a more pleasant place than London."

The child had almost relaxed. She even smiled briefly. "Is your mother d— Is she not living, sir?"

"She died giving birth to my sister," he said. "But I remember her as a loving presence in my life."

"And your sister is Lady Francis Kneller, Mr. Downes," Sir Webster announced, just as if Edgar did not know it for himself. He rubbed his hands together. "A fine lady. I remember the time—it was before her marriage, I do believe—when she saved Lady Kellington's poodles from being trampled in Hyde Park."

"Ah, yes." Edgar smiled. "My sister has a habit of rushing to the rescue."

"She saved some dogs from being *trampled*?" Miss Grainger's eyes were directed full at him now.

It needed Francis to tell the story in all its mock-heroic glory. But Edgar did his best. It appeared, though, as if he failed to convey the humor of Cora's heroism in endangering her life to save some dogs who had been in no danger except from her rescue. Miss Grainger looked earnestly at him, her mouth forming a little O of concern. A very kissable little mouth—in rather the way that Cora's children's mouths were kissable when they lifted them to him on his visits to the nursery.

. He must be getting old, he thought. Too old to be in search of a bride.

And then he glanced across to the doorway, where another new arrival stood. A woman alone, dressed fashionably and elegantly in a high-waisted, low-bosomed dress of pure scarlet silk. A woman whose magnificent bosom more than did justice to the gown. Her whole figure, in fact, was generous. It might even be described as voluptuous more than slender. But then it was a mature woman's figure. She was not a young woman, but well past her thirtieth year if Edgar's guess was correct. Her dark hair was piled high and dressed in smooth curls rather than in more youthful ringlets. She looked about her with bold eyes in a handsome face, a half smile on her lips, which might denote confidence or contempt or mere mocking irony. It was difficult to tell which.

Before Edgar could realize that he was staring and proving himself to be indeed less than a gentleman—Sir Webster was saying something complimentary about Cora—the woman's eyes alit on him, held his own for a moment, and then moved deliberately down his body and back up again. She lifted one mocking eyebrow as her eyes met his once more and pursed her lips into something like the O that had just made Miss Grainger's lips look kissable. Except that there was nothing this time to remind him of his niece and nephews. He felt heated, as if there had been a hot hand at the end of her eyebeams that had scorched its way down the length of his body and back up again.

If he had not been standing in the Earl of Greenwald's drawing room, he would have been convinced that he was surely in the presence of one of London's more experienced and celebrated courtesans.

"Ah, yes, indeed," he said to Sir Webster, feeling that it was the correct response to what had just been said, though he was not at all sure.

Sir Webster seemed satisfied with his answer. Lady Grainger smiled and Miss Grainger lowered her gaze to the floor again.

The scarlet lady had moved into the room and was being greeted by the Earl of Greenwald, who was bowing over her hand.

Chapter Two

Helena Stapleton was invited everywhere. She was quite respectable, even though the general feeling seemed to be that she was only just so. She had been a widow for ten years, yet apart from the first four of those years, when she had gone to stay with cousins in Scotland, she had adopted neither of the two courses that were expected of widows. She had not retired to live quietly as a dowager on the estate of her dead husband's son, and she had not shown any interest in remarrying.

She had gone traveling. Her husband, more than thirty years her senior, had been besotted with her and had left her a very generous legacy. This she had conserved and increased through careful investments. She traveled to every corner of the British Isles and to every country of Europe, the wars being long over. She had even been to Greece and to Egypt, though she would tell anyone who cared to ask that she thought too highly of her creature comforts to repeat either of those two experiences. Sometimes she rested from her travels and took up temporary residence in London, where she proceeded to amuse herself with whatever entertainments were available. This was one of those occasions. She almost always avoided the crush of the spring Season.

She was always careful to travel with companions, with congenial female acquaintances and with gentlemen to serve as escorts. She always set up house in London with a female companion, usually an aunt, whom she sent into the country to visit a nephew and a brood of great-nephews and great-nieces as soon as respectability had been established. And so she almost always arrived alone at entertainments, making her aunt's excuses to her hosts. There never had been such a sickly aunt.

Ladies—even those of six-and-thirty with independent means—were not expected to move about town or about *ton* parties alone, even when they had the misfortune to have female companions who were always catching chills or suffering from headaches. And ladies of six-and-thirty were not expected to dress as they pleased, unless it pleased them to wear such colors as purple or mulberry and to cover their hair with large turbans decked out with waving plumes. They were certainly not expected to favor scarlet gowns or emerald green or sunshine-yellow ones—or to go bareheaded into society.

Lady Stapleton did all that a lady of six-and-thirty was not expected to do. But there was a confidence and a self-assurance about her that seemed excuse enough for the absence of escorts or companions. And she had a beauty and arrogance of bearing, coupled with an impeccable taste for design and elegance, that made one hesitate about describing her appearance as vulgar or even inappropriate to her age.

She had few, if any, close friends. There was an air of aloofness, even of mystery, about her, even though she conversed quite freely about her travels and experiences. Everyone knew who she was—the daughter of a respectable but impoverished Scottish gentleman, the widow of Sir Christian Stapleton of Brookhurst. She was amiable, charming, sociable—and yet she gave the impression that there was a great deal more to be known about her than she had ever revealed.

She was invited everywhere. Gentlemen found her fascinating despite the fact that she was long past her youth. Ladies were secretly envious of her, though her age protected her from their jealousy. Yet the feeling was—though

no one could quite explain it—that she hovered dangerously close to the edge of respectability.

She knew it. And cared not the snap of two fingers. She
had decided long ago—six years ago, to be precise—that
life was to be lived and enjoyed, and live it and enjoy it she
would. She had earned her enjoyment. She had been
snatched from the love of her life—or so she had thought
with the foolish sensibilities to which very young people
were so prone—at the age of nineteen in order to be forced
into marriage with the wealthy, fifty-four-year-old Sir
Christian Stapleton. She had lived through seven years of
marriage to him with bright smiles and determined affection and feigned eagerness in the marriage bed. She had
lived through—but she would not remember what else she
had lived through during those years. She had punished herself after her husband's death for her widowhood and her
youth and her human frailties by retiring to a quiet life in
Scotland, where she had seen her former love himself married with five children and an eagerness to begin an affair
with her. Although she had longed to give in, she had resisted and had in general become a dull and abject creature,
as if she believed that she deserved no better.

She deserved better. She deserved to live. Everyone deserved to live. No one owed anyone else anything. She
owed no one anything. And if she did, then she had more
than paid with eleven years of her life—seven with Christian and four after his death.

At the age of thirty—perhaps it was the nasty shock of
that particular number—she had thrown off the shackles.
And though she was always careful to cling to the sem-
blance of respectability, she did not care that she hovered
close to its edge. Indeed, she rather enjoyed the feeling of
being almost, but not quite, notorious.

Helena arrived rather late at Lady Greenwald's soirée,
as was customary with her. She liked to arrive after
everyone else so that she could look about her and choose

the group to which she wished to attach herself. She hated to be caught among people who had no conversation beyond the weather and the state of their health. She liked to be with interesting people.

She was acquainted with most of the people, she saw, standing in the doorway, looking about her. But then one usually was at *ton* events in London. And it was even more true of events outside of the Season. There were not a great many families in residence at this time of the year. Inevitably, all who were, were invited everywhere. Equally inevitably, all who were invited attended every function.

The Marquess of Carew was there, she saw, in the midst of a group of his particular friends. She had met the marquess for the first time just the week before. She had not sought out the introduction since he was a very ordinary-looking man with a slightly crippled hand and foot and a smiling placidity of manner that usually denoted dullness. He had spoken to her about his passion, landscape gardening, a dull topic indeed. And unexpectedly he had held her fascinated attention. The extremely elegant, almost foppish Lord Francis Kneller was part of the same group. Whenever she saw him, Helena felt regret that he was a married man. He had married a cit's daughter, who went with him almost wherever he went. She was with him now, laughing with quite ungenteel amusement at something someone had said. What a waste of a perfectly lovely man.

And then her eyes, moving on to another group, alit on a man whom she did not know—and paused on him. At first she looked only because he presented the novelty of being a stranger. And then she looked because he looked back and she would not glance away hastily and in apparent confusion. Though in reality there was more reason to look at him than stubbornness. He was a very tall and very large gentleman. Large not in the sense of fatness. She doubted that there was one spare ounce of fat on his frame. But he was certainly not a slender man. It was a perfectly proportioned frame—she looked it down and up again in leisurely fashion, noting at the same time the simple yet very expen-

sive elegance of his clothing. And he had a head and face
worthy of such a body. His brown hair was short but expertly styled. His face was strikingly handsome. He gave
an impression of strength and power, she thought. Not just
physical power. He looked like a man who knew exactly
who he was and what he was and was well satisfied with
both. Like a man who knew his own mind and was comfortable with his own decisions and would not be easily
moved by anyone who opposed him.

She felt a wave of pure lust before he looked away to pay
attention to the Graingers, with whom he stood, and the
Earl of Greenwald arrived almost simultaneously to greet
her. She explained that her aunt had been persuaded to stay
at home to nurse a persistent cough.

Who was he? she wondered. She would not ask, of
course. It was not her way to signal so direct an interest in
a man. But she set about maneuvering matters slowly—
there was no hurry—so that she would find out. And not
only find out who he was. She was going to meet him. It
was quite soon obvious to her that the man was not married, even though he must be very close to her own age.
There was no strange lady in the Greenwalds' drawing
room. And it was unlikely that he had a wife who was absent. The Graingers took much of his time, and it was an
open secret that they had brought their daughter to town in
the hope of finding her a husband before Christmas. They
were not wealthy. They could not afford to bring their
daughter to town during the Season, when there would be
the exorbitant expenses of a court dress and innumerable
ball and party gowns. And so they had come now, hoping
that there would be a single gentleman of sufficient means
to be snared. The girl was twenty and perilously close to
being on the shelf.

The unknown gentleman must be both single and rich.
He certainly *looked* rich—wealthy and self-assured enough
not to have to make an obvious display of his wealth. He
was not bedecked with jewels and fobs and lace. But his

tailor doubtless charged him a minor fortune to fashion coats such as the one he wore tonight.

She talked with Lord Carew and Lord Francis Kneller and their wives for a while, and then sat with elderly Lord Holmes during a musical presentation. She told Mr. and Mrs. Prothero and a growing gathering of other people about some of her more uncomfortable experiences in Egypt while they all refreshed themselves with a drink together afterward and then accepted Sir Eric Mumford's invitation to join him at the supper table. He did not even realize that she led him rather than submitting to being led once they were inside the dining room. She seated herself beside the still-unknown gentleman, but turned her head immediately away from him to speak with her partner.

She was an expert at maneuvering matters to her own liking. Especially where men were concerned. Men were so easily manipulated. She laughed with amusement at something Sir Eric said.

Her low laugh shivered down his spine. It came straight from the bedchamber, even though she was sitting in a crowded dining room beneath brightly lighted chandeliers.

She had seated herself in the empty chair beside his and was reacting to something her supper companion had said to her. She was totally unaware of him, of course, Edgar thought, as she had been all evening after that first assessing glance. She had not once looked his way after that. She was Lady Stapleton, widow of Sir Christian Stapleton of Brookhurst. Brookhurst was not so very far from Mobley Abbey—not above twenty-five or thirty miles. But she did not live there now. Sir Gerald Stapleton, the present owner, was only her stepson.

Edgar had been introduced to three marriageable ladies during the course of the evening, all of whose parents had clearly been informed of his own possible interest and had acquiesced in allowing their daughters to be presented to a man whose immense wealth would perhaps compensate for the fact that he was not a gentleman. All three ladies were amiable, genteel, pretty. All three knew that he was a prospective bridegroom and they appeared docile and accepting. His sister and her cohorts had done a superlative job in so short a time, he thought. They had gone about things in the correct way, choosing with care, preparing the way with care, and leaving him choices.

There was only one problem—well, two actually, but the second was not in the nature of a real problem, only of an annoyance. The problem was that all three ladies appeared impossibly young to him. It struck him that any one of them would be a perfect choice for just that reason. All three had any number of breeding years ahead, and breeding was one of his main inducements to marry. But they seemed alarmingly young to him. Or rather, perhaps, he felt alarmingly old. Did he want a wife only so that he might breed her? He wanted more than that, of course. Far more.

And the problem that was not a problem was his constant awareness—an uncomfortable, purely physical awareness—of the lady in scarlet. Lady Stapleton. His mouth had turned dry as soon as she seated herself beside him and he smelled her perfume—something subtle and feminine and obviously very expensive.

And then she turned his way, leaned forward slightly, ignored him completely, and spoke to the young lady at his other side.

"How do you do, Miss Grainger?" she said. "Allow me to tell you how pretty you look in blue. It is your color."

Her bosom brushed the top of the table as she spoke. And her voice was pure warm velvet. Edgar could see now that he was close that the red highlights he had noticed in her dark hair were no reflection of her gown. They were real. He could not make up his mind whether her eyes were hazel or green. They had elements of both colors.

"Why, thank you," Miss Grainger said, blushing and

gratified. "It is my favorite color. But I sometimes wish I could wear vivid colors as you do."

Again that low bedroom laugh.

"Oh," Miss Grainger said, "may I present Mr. Downes? Lady Stapleton, sir."

Her eyes came to his. She did not move back, even though she was still leaning forward and was very close to him. He resisted the urge to move back himself. She looked very directly at him, a faint mockery or amusement or both in the depths of her glance.

"Ma'am," he said, inclining his head.

"Mr. Downes." She gazed at him. "Ah, now I remember. Lady Francis Kneller was a Downes before her marriage, was she not?"

"She is my sister," he said.

"Ah." She made no immediate attempt to say anything else. He could almost sense her remembering that Cora was the daughter of a Bristol merchant and realizing that he was no gentleman. That half smile deepened for a moment. "You are from the west country, sir?"

"From Bristol, ma'am," he said. And lest she was not quite clear on the matter, "I have lived there all my life and have worked there all my adult life, first as a lawyer and more recently as a merchant."

"How fascinating," she murmured, her eyes moving to his lips for a disconcerting moment. He was not sure if it was sincerity or mockery he heard in her voice. "Pardon me. I am neglecting Sir Eric quite shamefully."

She turned back to her companion. Obviously it had been mockery. Lady Stapleton had found herself seated beside a cit and conversing with him before realizing who he was. She would not repeat the mistake.

He set himself to making Miss Grainger feel comfortable again. He felt quite protective of her. She so clearly knew why she was in London, why she was here tonight, and why she was spending a significant portion of the evening in his company. The Graingers, he guessed, were going to be more persistent in their attentions to him than either of the other two couples. Miss Grainger's pretty blue gown, he noticed, was neither new nor costly. Nor was it in the first stare of fashion.

Helena sat with Mr. Hendy and a few other guests after supper. The others mainly listened while the two of them exchanged stories and opinions about the land-crossing from Switzerland to Italy. They both agreed that they were fortunate indeed to have lived to tell of it.

"I admire mountains," Mr. Hendy said, "but more as a spectator than as a traveler crawling along a narrow icy track directly above a sheer precipice at least a mile high."

"I do believe I could endure crawling with some equanimity," Helena said. "It is riding on the back of one of those infernal mountain donkeys that had me gabbling my prayers with pious fervency."

Their audience laughed.

Mr. Downes had left his group in order to cross to a sideboard to replenish the contents of his glass. There was no one else there. Helena got to her feet and excused herself. She strolled toward the sideboard, her own empty glass in hand.

"Mr. Downes," she said when she was close, "do fill my glass with whatever is in that decanter, if you please. One becomes mortally sick of drinking ratafia merely because one is female. I would prefer even the lemonade at Almack's."

"Madeira, ma'am?" He looked uncertainly at the decanter and then at her with raised eyebrows.

"Madeira, sir," she said, holding out her glass. "I suppose you do not know about the lemonade at Almack's."

"I have never been there, ma'am," he said.

"You have not missed anything," she told him. "It is an insipid place and the balls there are insipid occasions and the lemonade served there is insipid fare. Yet people would kill or do worse to acquire vouchers during the Season."

He half filled her glass and looked into her eyes. She had

the distinct feeling that if she ordered him to fill her glass he would refuse. She did not issue the order. He was a law-yer and a merchant. He had freely admitted as much. A prosperous merchant if her guess was correct. But a cit for all that. If his sister had not had the good fortune to snare Lord Francis Kneller, he would never have gained entry to such a place as the Earl of Greenwald's drawing room. But she understood now the aura of confidence and power he exuded. He was a wealthy, powerful, self-made man. She found the idea infinitely exciting. She found *him* exciting.

Sexually exciting.

"I am tired of this party, Mr. Downes," she said. "But I am a single woman alone, alas. My aunt, my usual compan-ion, is indisposed, my manservant and maid walked home rather than stay in the kitchen with my coachman, and will not return for another hour at the earliest. Yet I will be scolded by aunt and servants alike if I return unaccompa-nied."

He was not sure he understood her. His eyes shrewdly regarding her told her that. She raised her eyebrows, half smiled at him, and sipped her madeira. It was a vast im-provement on ratafia.

"I would offer my escort, ma'am, if I thought it would be welcomed," he said.

"How kind you are, Mr. Downes," she said, mocking him with her eyes. "It would be accepted."

"Shall I have your carriage called around, then?" he asked. "Shall I have a maid accompany us?"

She allowed herself to laugh softly. "That will be quite unnecessary, Mr. Downes," she said, "unless you are afraid of me. We are both adults."

He inclined his head to her without removing his eyes from hers, set down his glass, and slipped quietly from the room.

She found flirtations exhilarating, Helena admitted to herself as she sipped from her glass and looked about the room without making any attempt to rejoin any group. She indulged in them whenever she felt so inclined—always in private. She scorned the appearance of propriety for its own sake, but how could one conduct a satisfactory flirtation in the sight of others? She did not care if people noticed her disappearing alone with a certain gentleman and thought her promiscuous.

She was not. She had never desired the distastefulness of full physical intimacy—she had endured enough of that during her seven-year marriage. Though of course there had been a time during that marriage . . . no! She shuddered inwardly. She would not think of that now—or ever if she could help it.

She had never sought to enliven her widowhood with affairs—or even with *an* affair. But then she had rarely met a man with as great a physical appeal as Mr. Downes.

She would take him home and lure him up to her drawing room. She would find out more about him. She suspected that he might be a fascinating man—perhaps he could fascinate her for an hour or more of the night. Nights were always interminably long. She would flirt with him. Perhaps she would even allow him to steal a kiss—there was definite appeal in the thought, though she normally avoided even kisses.

Perhaps he would not be satisfied with a mere kiss. But she was not afraid. She had never found herself unable to deal with amorous men, though she had known her fair share.

She smiled as her eyes found the Countess of Greenwald.

She set her glass down in order to go bid her hostess a good night.

And perhaps *she* would not be satisfied with a mere kiss, she thought a few minutes later as she allowed Mr. Downes to hand her into her carriage and climb in beside her.

She had never felt quite so tempted.

How would it feel *with him?* she wondered, turning her head to smile half scornfully at her companion, though he was not necessarily the object of her scorn. With a handsome, virile, powerful, doubtless very experienced man.

She felt a twinge of alarm at the direction her thoughts had taken. And more than a twinge of desire.

She would talk sense into herself before she arrived home, she told herself. She might even dismiss him on the pavement outside her door and send him back to the soirée.

But she knew she would not do that.

Sometimes loneliness was almost a tangible thing.

Chapter Three

Edgar was not really sure he understood the situation. Or believed her story. Why would two servants have walked home after accompanying her to the Greenwalds'? And she did not seem the sort of person to tire early when she was at a party. She had been the center of attention in every group gathered about her all evening.

And why him?

He sat beside her as close to his side of her carriage as he could so that she would not think he was taking advantage of the situation. She sat with her back half across the corner at her side, looking at him in the near-darkness, talking easily and quite without malice about the people who had attended the party. She spoke in that low, velvety voice, the half smile of mockery or something else on her lips every time a street lamp lit her face.

He would help her to alight at her door, he thought, see her safely inside her home, and then walk back to Greenwald's house. It was not very far. He would refuse the offer—if she made it—of a ride back in her carriage. He would go back to the soirée rather than straight home. He had not told Cora he was leaving.

But when the lady had stepped down from the carriage to the pavement and had removed her hand from his, she did not lift her skirt with it the more easily to ascend the four steps to the front door. She slipped it through his arm.

"You must come inside, Mr. Downes," she told him, "and have a drink before returning."

Presumably the aunt she had mentioned was inside the house. But was it likely that an ailing lady would be out of her bed at this time of night—it must be well past midnight—and sitting in the drawing room with her embroidery on the chance that she would be called upon to play chaperone? He was not being naive. He was merely unwilling to accept the evidence of his own reasoning powers.

A manservant had opened the front door even before the steps of the carriage had been set down. He took Edgar's hat and cloak from him, after favoring him with a level, measuring look—he was as tall as Edgar and even broader, and as bald as a polished egg. He looked more like a pugilist than a butler, an impression enhanced by his crooked, flattened nose.

"You need not wait up, Hobbes," Lady Stapleton said, taking Edgar's arm and turning him in the direction of the stairs.

"Very well, my lady," the servant said in a voice one might expect a man to use if he had a handful of gravel lodged in his throat.

The lady paused on the first landing as if in thought, appeared to come to some decision, and climbed on to the second. Edgar would have had to be an innocent indeed if he had expected to find a drawing room beyond the door at which she stopped, indicating with an inclination of the head that he might open it. This was not the living floor of the house. Even so it was something of a shock to find himself entering a very cozy bedchamber. There was a soft carpet underfoot. The curtains were looped back from the large canopied bed. The bedcovers were neatly turned back. There were lit candles on the dressing table and bedside table. A fire burned in the hearth.

Edgar closed the door behind his back and stayed where he was. It was a very feminine room, warm and comfortable and clean. That subtle perfume she wore clung to it. It was, he thought, the room of a very expensive courtesan.

He found himself wondering if he would be presented later with a quite exorbitant bill. He did not much care.

"Well, Mr. Downes." She had walked into the room and turned to him now, one hand resting on the dressing table. There was a look almost of defiance on her face. She raised one mocking eyebrow. "Shall I ring for tea?"

"That seems hardly necessary." He walked toward her until he was a foot away from her. But why him? he wondered. Because of her discovery that he was not a gentleman? Would a gentleman have offered his escort? Would he have come inside the house with her? Ascended that second flight of stairs with her?

To hell with what gentlemen would have done or would do. She had made her choice. She would live with it for tonight. He set his hands on either side of her waist—not a slender waist, but an undeniably shapely one. He drew her against him, angled his head to one side, parted his lips, closed his eyes, and kissed her.

And felt that he had landed in the very midst of a fireworks display—not as a spectator but as one of the fireworks.

She moved against him. Not just to bring herself closer to him but to—move against him. He became hotly aware of everything—her warm and shapely thighs, her generous hips, her abdomen rubbing against his almost instant erection, her breasts, her shoulders. One of her arms had come about his waist, beneath his coat. The fingers of the other hand twined themselves in his hair. Her mouth opened beneath his own and moved against it. He found himself doing what he had not done since his youth, having found it distasteful then. He pressed his tongue deep into her mouth.

And then she withdrew and he withdrew and they stood gazing at each other, still touching from the waist down, their breathing labored. That strange smile lingered about her lips. But her eyes were heavy with passion and excitement.

"I do hope you live up to early promise, Mr. Downes," she said.

"I shall do my very best, ma'am," he said.

And then she turned and presented him with a row of tiny pearl buttons down the back of her gown. He undid them one at a time while she lifted her arms and withdrew the pins from her hair. She held it up until he was finished and then let it fall, long and dark and wavy, with its enticing reddish tints. He nudged the gown off her shoulders with the straps of her shift and she let them fall to the floor before turning and removing her undergarments and her stockings while he watched.

She had a mature figure—firm, ample, voluptuous. She was incredibly beautiful. He felt his mouth go dry again as he shrugged out of his coat and reached for the button of his waistcoat.

"Ah, no," she said, brushing his hands aside and laughing at him with that throaty laugh that now seemed to be in its proper setting. "You have had the pleasure of unclothing me, Mr. Downes. You will not deny me the pleasure of doing the like for you."

She undressed him while he listened to his heartbeat hammering against his eardrums and concentrated on controlling and mastering the urge to tumble her back onto the bed so that he might the sooner explode into ease. She took her time. She was in no hurry at all.

Not until they were finally on the bed. Then she became passion unleashed. There was no shyness, no shrinking, no ladylike modesty, no taboos. Her hands explored him with frank interest and wild demand while his did the like to her. Her mouth participated in the exploration, moving over him, kissing, licking, sucking, biting. He devoured her with his own mouth, tasting perfume and sweat and woman.

He had never been a man for rough sex. Perhaps because of his size he had always been careful to leash his passions, to touch gently, to mount slowly, to pump with control. But he had never before been with a woman whose passion could equal his own—and perhaps even outstrip it. When he rolled her nipples between his thumbs and the bases of his forefingers, she spoke to him.

"Harder," she begged him. "Harder."

And when he squeezed and she gasped with pain and he would have desisted, her hands came up to cover his, to press his thumbs and forefingers together again. She gasped with pain once more.

"Come to me," she was saying then, her body in frenzied motion. "Give it to me. Give it to me."

He moved between her thighs, felt her legs lift to twine about his, felt her hands spread hard over his buttocks, positioned himself, and thrust hard and deep. She cried out. He settled his weight on her—his full weight. He knew what she wanted and what he wanted. Neither of them would have it if he allowed her to buck and gyrate beneath him. And he was very aware that she had led the way thus far. It was not in his nature to allow a woman to dictate his every action and reaction.

She urged him on with frenzied words and clawing hands and with the muscles of her thighs and the muscles inside, where he worked. But he took her without frenzy, with deep, methodical, rhythmic strokes. His heart felt as if it must burst. With every inward thrust he felt as if he must surely explode into release. But he would not let a woman master him.

She was pleading with him. She was swearing at him, he realized in some surprise. And then she lost her own control and came shuddering and shattering about him. He continued to stroke her while it happened and then, when she began to relax, he drove to his own release, growling out his pleasure into her hair.

He was not quite sure he was going to survive, he thought foolishly, relaxing downward onto her damp and heated flesh. He felt her legs untwine themselves from about his and somehow found the energy to lift himself off her and draw her against him before closing his eyes and sinking into sleep.

She did not sleep. She lay relaxed against the heat of his body. She tried to summon the energy to wake him and dismiss him. She would have to dismiss him. She needed to be alone.

She needed to digest what had just happened—what *she* had caused to happen. She had not even taken him as far as the drawing room. She had scarcely even paused on the first landing.

She had seemed to be led by a power quite beyond her will to control. A ridiculous notion—*though it had happened before. She* had chosen to bring him to her bed, just as she had chosen that other time. . . .

She breathed in slowly—a mistake. She breathed in the smells of his sweat and his cologne, of his maleness.

Her earlier curiosity at least had been satisfied. She knew now how it felt with him.

It had felt frightening. The pleasure—oh, yes, there had been an overabundance of that—had got far beyond her control. It had been in his control and he had held it from her—quite deliberately, she would swear—with his weight holding her immobile and with his insistence on setting the pace himself. Having made the decision she had made, she had at least wanted to command the situation. She had wanted to protect something of herself. He had not allowed it.

She had been frightened. All she had was herself.

He had the most magnificent body she could ever have imagined. It seemed all massive, solid muscle. And that part of him . . . She closed her eyes and inhaled slowly. She had been stretched and filled. For one foolish moment she had felt the terror of a virgin that there could not possibly be room. She rather believed she had screamed.

He was a man who expected and got his own way. He was a businessman. Clearly a very successful and wealthy one. A man did not achieve success in the business world unless he was firm and controlled and even ruthless, unless he was well able to make himself undisputed master of any situation. She had sensed that on her first sight of him, of course. It was not his looks alone that had prompted that rush of lust and the growing temptation. And then she had had her intuition confirmed at supper when he had told her, a look of cool defiance on his face, that he had been a lawyer and was a merchant. Lustful words. She wondered if he had realized that she found them so.

She should not have chosen to break her own—and society's—rules with him of all people.

She wanted him again, she thought after a while. She could feel her breasts, her womb, her inner thighs begin to throb with need. She wanted his weight, his mastery. No, she did not. She wanted to be on top. She wanted to master him. She wanted to ride him at her own speed, to drive him mad with desire, to have him shatter past climax so that she could feel she had avenged what he had done to her.

She wondered if she would be able to master this man if she woke him and aroused him and got on top of him. Would she win this time? Or would he merely resume that alarmingly controlled stroking and endure long enough to send her headlong again into release and happiness—and weakness? It would be humiliating to have that happen twice.

And wonderful beyond belief.

She did not want anything wonderful beyond belief.

And then, while she was still at war with herself, the decision was taken out of her hands. She had not noticed that he was awake again. And aroused again. He turned her onto her back and came on top of her. She found herself opening her legs to him, lifting to him, letting her breath out on a sighing moan as he came, hard and thick and long, sliding into her wetness. And she found that she had his full and not inconsiderable weight on her again and that she did not fight either it or him. She lay under him rather as she had always lain beneath Christian—but no, there was no comparison. None whatsoever.

She observed their coupling almost like a spectator. Almost. There was, of course, the throbbing desire she had felt even while he still slept, and the crescendo of desire that built *there,* where he stroked relentlessly, and spread upward in waves, through her womb, up into her breasts, into her throat, and even behind her nose. He found her mouth with his and she opened to his tongue and did not even try to fight the total invasion of her body—or even the frightening sensation that it was her whole person that was being invaded.

She was, she thought a moment before she burst past control to another of those intense moments of something that felt deceptively like happiness, though it was not that at all—she was a little frightened of Mr. Downes, Bristol merchant and cit. And that was perhaps a large part of the attraction. She had never felt frightened of any other man. His own climax came a few moments after hers, as it had the first time. He was, then, in perfect control of himself, even in bed.

She had made a mistake. *Of course* she had made a mistake.

They lay beside each other, panting, waiting for their heartbeats to return to normal. The backs of their hands touched damply between them. She wondered if he had set out to make a fool of her, or if mastery came so naturally to him that he did not even think of her as a worthy adversary. She hated him in that moment, quite as intensely as she had earlier lusted after him.

She got off the bed, crossed the room unhurriedly on legs that shook slightly—the candles, though low, were still burning—picked up her night robe, which her maid had set out over the back of a chair, and drew it about her as she went to stand at the window, looking out on the deserted street below. She drew a deep, silent breath and released it slowly.

"Thank you, Mr. Downes," she said. "You are superlatively good. A master of the art, one might say. But I daresay you know that."

"I can hardly be expected to reply to such a compliment," he said.

She looked over her shoulder at him. He was lying on the bed, the covers up to his waist, his hands clasped behind his head. Even now, sated as she was, he looked magnificent.

"It is time for you to leave, sir," she said.

"Past time, I believe," he said, throwing back the covers and coming off the bed with remarkable grace for such a big man. "It would not do for me to be seen slinking from your house at dawn, wearing evening clothes."

"No, indeed," she agreed. And she stood watching him dress. She had never thought of any other man as beautiful—*oh, yes, she had.* Yes she had. She clenched her hands unconsciously at her sides. But he had been youthful, slender, sweet. . . .

She turned back to the window.

She shrugged her shoulders when his hands came to rest there, and he removed them.

"Thank you," he said. "It was a great pleasure."

"I daresay you can see yourself out, Mr. Downes," she said. "Good night."

"Good night, ma'am," he said.

She heard the door of her bedchamber open and close again quietly. A minute or so later she watched him emerge from the front door and turn right to walk with long, firm strides along the street. She watched him until he was out of sight, a man quite unafraid of the dark, empty streets of London. But then he had probably known a great deal worse in Bristol if his work took him near the dock area. She would pity the poor footpad who decided to accost Mr. Downes.

What was his first name? she wondered. But she did not want to know.

She stood at the window, staring down into the empty street. Now, she thought, her degradation was complete. She had brought home a total stranger, had taken him to her bed, and had had her pleasure of him. She had given in to lust, to loneliness, to the illusion that there was happiness somewhere in this life to be grasped and to be drawn into herself.

And she was to be justly punished. She already knew it. Her bedchamber already seemed unnaturally quiet and empty. She could still smell him and guessed that the enticing, erotic smell, imaginary though it doubtless was, would linger accusingly for as long as she remained in this house.

Now she was truly promiscuous. As she always had been, though she had never lain with any man except Christian—until tonight. Now her true nature had shown itself. She closed her eyes and rested her forehead against the cold glass of the window.

And she had enjoyed it. Oh, how she had enjoyed it! Sex with a stranger. She heard herself moan and clamped her teeth hard together.

She was awash with the familiar feeling, though it was stronger, rawer than usual—self-loathing. And then hatred, the dull aching hatred of the one man who might have allowed her to redeem herself and to have avoided this. For years she had waited patiently—and impatiently—for him to release her from the terrible burden of her own guilt. But finally, just a year ago, he had plunged her into an inescapable, eternal hell. She felt hatred of a man who had done nothing—ever—to deserve her hatred or anyone else's.

A hatred that turned outward because she had saturated herself with self-hatred.

She could feel the rawness in her throat that sought release through tears. But she scorned to weep. She would not give herself that release, that comfort.

She hated Mr. Downes. Why had he come to London? Why had he come to Lady Greenwald's soirée? He had no business there, even if his sister was married to a member of the *ton,* even if he was something of a nabob. He was not a gentleman. He had stepped out of his own world, upsetting hers.

But how unfair it was to hate him. None of what had happened had been his fault. She had seduced him. His only fault had been to allow himself to be seduced.

For one moment—no, for two separate moments—the loneliness had been pushed back. Now it was with her again, redoubled in force, like a physical weight bowing down her shoulders.

She must never again—not even by mild flirtation—try to dislodge it. She must never again so much as see Mr. Downes.

* * *

Edgar felt shaken. What had just happened had been a thoroughly physical and erotic thing, quite outside his normal experience. He had been caught up entirely in mindless passion.

Lady Stapleton. He did not know her first name. It somehow disturbed him that he did not even know that much about her. And yet he knew every inch of her body and the inner, secret parts of her with great intimacy.

He had had women down the years. But except for his very early youth, he had never been led to them from lust alone. There had always been some sort of a relationship. He had always known their first names. He had always bedded women with the knowledge that the act would bring him more pleasure than it brought them. He had always tried to be gentle and considerate, to make it up to them in other ways.

He had never known a truly passionate woman, he realized—until tonight. He was not sure he wanted to know another—or this one again. There had been no doubt about her consent, but still he felt vaguely guilty at the way in which he had used her. He had not been gentle. Indeed, he had been decidedly rough.

He felt distaste at what he had done. He felt dislike of her. She had clearly set out to lure him to her bed. If there was a seducer in tonight's business, it was she. He did not like the idea that he had been seduced. If she had had her way she would have dictated every move of that first encounter, including, he did not doubt, the moment and manner of his climax.

He had come to London, he had gone to that soirée, in order to find himself a bride. And he had been presented with three quite eligible prospects. He would perhaps choose to pay court to one of them. He would betroth himself to her before Christmas or perhaps at Mobley Abbey during Christmas. He would wed the girl soon after and in all probability have her with child before spring had turned into summer. He had promised his father, and it was high time, even without the promise.

And yet on the very evening he had met those three young ladies, he had allowed himself to be drawn into a scene of sordid passion with a stranger, with a woman whose first name he did not know.

She was a lady, not a courtesan. A beautiful lady, who was accepted by the *ton*. Obviously tonight's behavior was not typical of her. If it were, she would be unable to keep it hidden well enough to escape the sharp eyes and gossiping tongues of the beau monde. Clearly, then, he was partly to blame for what had happened. He had stared at her when she had first appeared, and she had caught him at it. He had freely admitted his origins and present way of life to her at supper and had thus revealed to her that he was a man outside her own world.

Somehow he had tempted her. He understood that young widows—and perhaps those who were not so young, too— could feel loneliness and sexual frustration. One of his longer-lasting mistresses had been the widow of a colleague of his. He might eventually have married her himself if she had not suddenly announced to him one day that she was to marry a sea captain and take to the sea with him.

He had done Lady Stapleton a great wrong. It would not be repeated. He wondered if he owed her an apology. Perhaps not, but he owed her something. A visit tomorrow. Some sort of an explanation. He must make her aware that he did not hold her in contempt for what she had allowed tonight.

He did not look forward to the visit.

Lord Francis came out of his library as Edgar let himself into the house. He lifted the cup he held in one hand. "The chocolate is still warm in the pot," he said. "Come and have some."

Edgar had hoped everyone would be safely in bed.

"Waiting up for me, Francis?" he asked, entering the library reluctantly and pouring himself a cup of chocolate.

"Not exactly," Francis said. "Waiting for Cora, actually. Annabelle woke up when we tiptoed into the nursery to kiss the children, and Cora lay down with her. I daresay she has fallen asleep. It would not be the first time. Once Andrew came to *me* for comfort and climbed into bed beside me because his mama was in his own bed fast asleep and there was no room left for him."

"That sounds like Cora," her brother said. He felt some explanation was necessary. "I escorted Lady Stapleton home because she had no other escort. And then I decided to walk about Mayfair and get some fresh air rather than return to Greenwald's. A few hours at such entertainments are enough for me."

"Quite so," Francis said. "Firm up the story for Cora by breakfast time, old chap. She will wish to know about every post and blade of grass you passed in your nocturnal rambles. You do not owe me any explanation. She is a woman extraordinarily, ah, well-endowed with charms."

"Lady Stapleton?" Edgar said carelessly, as if the idea were new to him. "Yes, I suppose she is."

Lord Francis chuckled. "Well," he said, "I am for my lonely bed. You look as if you are ready for yours, too, Edgar. Good night."

"Good night," Edgar said.

Damnation! Francis knew all right. But then, he would have to be incredibly dim-witted to believe that story about the walk and fresh air.

Chapter Four

Helena was usually from home in the mornings. She liked mornings. She loved to walk in the park early, when she was unlikely to meet anyone except a few tradesmen hurrying toward their daily jobs or a few maids running early errands or walking their owners' dogs. Her own long-suffering maid trotting along behind her or, more often, the menacing figure of Hobbes, the one servant who traveled everywhere with her, made all proper. She liked to go shopping on Oxford Street or Bond Street or go to the library to look at the papers or borrow a book. She also liked to visit the galleries.

Mornings were the best times. The world was fresh and new each morning, and she was newly released from the restlessness and bad dreams that oppressed her nights. Sometimes in the mornings she could fill her lungs with air and her body with energy and pretend that life was worth living.

But on the morning after Lady Greenwald's soirée, she was at home. She had not found the energy nor the will to go out. The clouds were low and heavy, she noticed. It might rain at any moment. And it looked chilly and raw. In reality, of course, she rarely allowed weather of any type to divert her when she wished to go abroad. This morning she was tired and listless and looking for excuses.

She would send for her aunt, she decided. Aunt Letty liked town better than the country anyway, and would be quite happy to be summoned. She was, in fact, more like a friend than an aging relative—and therein, perhaps, lay the problem. Helena had numerous friendly acquaintances and could turn several of them into close friends if she wished. She did not wish. Friends, by their very nature, knew one intimately. Friends were to be confided in. She preferred to keep her acquaintances at some distance. She certainly did not need a friend in residence. But, paradoxically, her friendless state sometimes became unbearable.

She procrastinated, however, even about writing the letter that would bring her aunt home. She stood listlessly at the drawing room window, gazing down on the gray, wind-blown street. She was standing there when she saw him coming, walking with confident strides toward the house just as he had walked away from it last night. He wore a greatcoat and beaver hat and Hessian boots. He looked well-groomed enough, arrogant enough, to be a duke. But that firm stride belonged to a man who had all the pride of knowing that he had made his own way in his own world and was successful enough, rich enough, confident enough to encroach upon hers.

She hated him. Because seeing him again, she felt a deep stabbing of longing in her womb. What she had allowed last night—what she had initiated—was not so easily shrugged off this morning. Her hands curled into fists at her sides as she saw him turn to approach her front door. She stepped back only just in time to avoid being seen as he glanced upward.

So he thought he had acquired himself a mistress from the beau monde, did he? As a final feather in his cap? She supposed that a mistress from her class might be more satisfactory even than a wife, though perhaps he thought to acquire both. The Graingers would not have shown such interest in him last evening if they had not heard somewhere that he was both eligible and available.

He thought that because he had given her undeniable pleasure last night she would become his willing slave so that she could have more. She swallowed when she remembered the pleasure. How humiliating!

The door of the drawing room opened to admit her butler. There was a card on the silver tray he carried. She picked it up and looked at it, though it seemed an unnecessary gesture.

Mr. Edgar Downes. *Edgar.* She had not wanted to know. She thought of Viking warriors and medieval knights. *Edgar.*

"He is waiting below?" she asked. It was too much to hope, perhaps, that he had left his card as a courtesy and taken himself off.

"He is, my lady," her butler told her. "But I did inform him that I was not sure you were at home. Shall I say you are not?"

It was tempting. It was what she wished him to say, what she intended to instruct him to say until she opened her mouth and spoke. But it was not to be as simple as that, it seemed. She was on new ground. She had done more than flirt with this man.

"Show him up," she said.

She looked down at the card in her hand as she waited. Edgar. Mr. Edgar Downes.

She felt very frightened suddenly—again. What was she doing? She had resolved both last night and this morning never to see him again. He posed far too great a threat to the precarious equilibrium of her life. She had spent six years building independence and self-assurance, convincing herself that they were enough. Last night the glass house she had constructed had come smashing and tinkling down about her head. It would take a great deal of rebuilding.

Mr. Edgar Downes could not help. Not in any way at all.

She could no longer possibly deny that she wanted him. Her body was humming with the ache of emptiness. She wanted his weight, his mastery, the smell of him, his penetration. She wanted him to make her forget.

But she knew—she had discovered last night if she had been in any doubt before that—that there was no forgetting.

That the more she tried to drown everything out with self-gratification, the worse she made things for herself. She should not have told Hobbes to send him up. What could she have been thinking of? She must leave the room before they came upstairs.

But the door opened again before she could take a single step toward it. She stood where she was and smiled.

A t each of his professions in turn Edgar had learned that there were certain unpleasant tasks that must be performed and that there was little to be gained by trying to avoid them or put them off until a later date. He had trained himself to do promptly and firmly what must be done.

It was a little harder to do in his personal life. On this particular morning he would have preferred to go anywhere and do anything rather than return to Lady Stapleton's house. But his training stood him in good stead. It must be done, and therefore it might as well be done without delay. Though he did find himself hoping as he approached the house that she would be from home. A foolish hope—if she was out this morning, he would have to return some other time, and doubtless it would seem even harder then.

He knew that she was at home when he turned to climb the steps to her door and looked up and caught a glimpse of her at a window, ducking hastily from sight. She would not, of course, wish to appear overeager to see him again. His irrational hopes rose once more when that pugilist of a manservant who answered the door informed him that he thought Lady Stapleton might be from home. Perhaps she would refuse to see him—that was something he had not considered on his way here.

But she was at home and she did not refuse to see him. He drew deep breaths as he climbed the stairs behind the servant and tried to remember his rehearsed speech. He should know as a lawyer that rehearsed speeches scarcely ever served him when it came time actually to speak.

She looked even more beautiful this morning, dressed in a pale green morning gown. The color brought out the reddish hue of her hair. It made her look younger. She was standing a little distance from the door, smiling at him— that rather mocking half smile he remembered from the evening before. The events of the night seemed unreal.

"Good morning, Mr. Downes." She was holding his card in one hand. She looked beyond his shoulder. "Thank you, Hobbes. That will be all."

The door closed quietly. There was no sign of the aunt or of any other chaperone—an absurd thing to notice after last night. He was glad there was no one else present, necessitating a conversation about the weather or the social pages of the morning papers.

"Good morning, ma'am." He bowed to her. He would get straight to the point. She was probably as embarrassed as he. "I believe I owe you an apology."

"Indeed?" Her eyebrows shot up. "An apology, sir?"

"I treated you with—discourtesy last evening," he said. Even in his rehearsed speech he had been unable to think of a more appropriate, less lame word to describe how he had treated her.

"With discourtesy?" She looked amused. "*Discourtesy,* Mr. Downes? Are there rules of etiquette, then, in your world for—ah, for what happens between a man and a woman in bed? Ought you to have said please and did not? You are forgiven, sir."

She was laughing at him. It had been a foolish thing to say. He felt mortified.

"I took advantage of you," he said. "It was unpardonable."

She actually did laugh then, that low, throaty laugh he had heard before. "Mr. Downes," she said, "are you as naive as your words would have you appear? Do you not know when you have been seduced?"

He jerked his head back, rather as if she had hit him on the chin. Was she not going to allow him even to pretend to be a gentleman?

"I was very ready to take advantage of the situation," he said. "I regret it now. It will not be repeated."

"Do you?" Neither of them had moved since he had stepped inside the room. She moved now—she took one step toward him. Her eyes had grown languid, her smile a little more enticing. "And will it not? I could have you repeat it within the next five minutes, Mr. Downes—if I so choose."

He was angry then. Angry with her because despite her birth and position and title she was no lady. Angry with her because she was treating him with contempt. Angry with himself because what she said was near to truth. He wanted her. Yet he scorned to want what he could not respect.

"I think not, ma'am," he said curtly. "I thank you again for your generosity last night. I apologize again for any distress or even bodily pain I may have caused you. I must beg you to believe that whenever we meet again, as we are like to do over the next few weeks if you plan to remain in town, I shall treat you with all the formal courtesy I owe a lady of your rank." There. He had used part of his speech after all.

She took him by surprise. She closed the gap between them, took his arm with both of hers, and drew him toward the fireplace, in which a fire crackled invitingly. "You are being tiresome, sir," she said. "Do come and sit down and allow me to ring for coffee. I am ready for a cup myself. What a dreary morning it is. Talk to me, Mr. Downes. I have been in the mopes because there is no one here to whom to talk. My aunt is on an extended visit in the country and will not be back for a couple of days at the earliest. Tell me why a Bristol merchant is in London for a few weeks. Is it for business, or is it for pleasure?"

He found himself seated in a comfortable chair to one side of the fire, watching her tug on the bell pull. He had intended to stay for only a couple of minutes. He was feeling a bit out of his depth. It was not a feeling he relished.

"It is a little of both, ma'am," he said.

"Tell me about the business reasons first," she said. "I

hear so little that is of interest to me, Mr. Downes. Interest me. What *is* your business? Why does it bring you to London?"

He had to wait while she gave her instructions to the crooked-nosed servant, but then she looked back at him with inquiring eyes. They were not rhetorical questions she had asked.

He told her what she wished to know and answered the numerous other questions she asked—intelligent, probing questions. The coffee was brought and poured while he talked.

"How satisfying it must be," she said at last, "to have a purpose in life, to know that one has accomplished something. Do you feel that you have vanquished life, Mr. Downes? That it has been worth living so far? That it is worth continuing with?"

Strange questions. He had not given much thought to any of them. The answers seemed, perhaps, self-evident.

"Life is a constant challenge," he said. "But one never feels that one has accomplished all that can be done. One can never arrive. The journey is everything. How dull it would be finally to arrive and to have nothing else for which to aim."

"Some people would call it heaven," she said. "Not being on the journey at all, Mr. Downes, is hell. It surely is, is it not?"

"A self-imposed hell," he said. "One that no one need encounter for any length of time. It is laziness never to reach beyond oneself for something more."

"Or realism," she said. "You must grant that, Mr. Downes. Or are you so grounded in the practicalities of a business life that you have not realized that life is ultimately not worth living at all? Realism—or despair."

He had been enjoying their lively discussion. He had almost forgotten with whom he spoke—or at least he had almost forgotten that she was last night's lover, to whom he had come this morning in some embarrassment. But he was jolted by her words. The smile on her lips, he noticed now, was tinged with bitterness. Was she talking theoretically? Or was she talking about herself?

She gave him no chance to answer. She took a sip from her cup and her expression lightened. "But you came to town for pleasure, too," she said. "Tell me about that, Mr. Downes. For what sort of pleasure did you hope when you came here?" Her smile was once more pure mockery.

To his mortification Edgar felt himself flush. "My sister and brother-in-law were to be here the same time as me," he said. "They have insisted upon taking me about with them."

"How old are you, Mr. Downes?" she asked.

She had a knack for throwing him off balance. He answered before he could consider not doing so. "I am six-and-thirty, ma'am," he said.

"Ah, the same age as me," she said. "But we will not compare birthdays. I was married at the age of nineteen, Mr. Downes, to a man of fifty-four. I was married to him for seven years. I have no wish to repeat the experience. I have earned my freedom. But it is an experience everyone should be required to have at least once in a lifetime. You have come to London in search of a wife?"

He stared at her, speechless. Did she really expect him to answer?

She laughed. "It is hardly even an educated guess," she said. "Sir Webster Grainger and his lady were determinedly courting you last evening. They are in desperate search of a wealthy husband for poor Miss Grainger. I daresay you are very rich indeed. Are you?"

He ignored the question. "*Poor* Miss Grainger?" he said. He was feeling decidedly irritable again. How dare she probe into his personal life like this? Would she be doing so if he were a gentleman? "You believe she would be pitied if she married me, ma'am?"

"Very much so," she said. "You are sixteen years her senior, sir. That may not seem a huge gap in age to you and me—we both know that you are vigorous and in your prime. But it would appear an enormous age difference to a very young lady, Mr. Downes. Especially one who has a prior attachment—but a quite ineligible one, of course."

He frowned. Was she deliberately goading him? He could not quite believe he was having this conversation with her. But was it true? Did Miss Grainger have an attachment to someone else?

"You need not look so stricken, Mr. Downes," she said. "It is a common thing, you know. Young ladies of *ton* are merely commodities, you see. Sometimes people make the mistake of thinking that they are persons, but they are not. They are commodities their fathers may use to enhance or repair their fortunes. Unfortunately, young ladies have feelings and an alarming tendency to fall in love without sparing a single thought to the state of their fathers' fortunes. They soon learn. That is one thing women are good at."

This, he thought, was a bitter woman indeed. And doubtless an intelligent woman. Too intelligent for her own good, perhaps.

"Is that what happened to you?" he asked. "You loved another man?"

She smiled. "He is married now with five children," she said. "He was kind enough to offer me the position of mistress after I was widowed. I declined. I will be no man's mistress." Her eyes mocked and challenged him.

He got to his feet. "I have taken too much of your time, ma'am," he said. "I thank you for the coffee. I—"

"If you are going to apologize again for your discourtesy in bedding me without saying 'please,' Mr. Downes," she said, "I beg you to desist. I should then feel obliged to apologize for seducing you and that would be tiresome since I do not feel sorry. But you need not fear that I will do it again. I never seduce the same man twice. It is a rule I have. Besides, in my experience no man is worth a second seduction."

"Ah," he said, suddenly more amused than angry, "you will have the last word after all, will you? It was a magnificent set-down."

"I thought so, too," she said. "You are a superior lover,

Mr. Downes. Take it from someone who has had some experience of lovers. But I do not want a lover, even a very good one. Especially perhaps a very good one."

He despised himself for the satisfaction her words gave him.

"I would prefer a friend," she said.

"A friend?" He looked at her.

"Life can be tedious," she said, "for a widow who chooses not to burden her relatives with the demand for a home and who chooses not to burden herself with another husband. You are an interesting man. You have more to talk of than health and the weather and horses. Many men have no knowledge of anything beyond their horses and their guns and their hunting. Do you kill, Mr. Downes?"

"I have never been involved in gentlemanly sports," he said.

She smiled. "Then you will never be properly accepted in my world, sir," she said. "Let us be friends. Shall we be? You will alleviate my tedium and I will ease you into my world. Do you enjoy wandering around galleries, admiring the paintings? Or around the British Museum, absorbing history?"

"I am, I believe, a tolerably well-educated man, ma'am," he said.

She looked at him measuringly. "You are not perfect after all, are you?" she said. "You are sensitive about your origins. I did not imply that you are a clod, sir. But you do not know London well?"

"Not well," he admitted.

"Take me somewhere tomorrow," she said. "I shall decide where between now and then. Let me have someone intelligent with whom to share my observations."

He was tempted. How was he to say no? He must say no.

"You are afraid of ruining your matrimonial chances," she said, reading his hesitation aright. "How provincial, Mr. Downes. And how bourgeois. In my world it is no matter for raised eyebrows if a gentleman escorts a lady about who is not his wife or his betrothed or his intended, even when there is such another person in existence. And no one is scandalized when a woman allows a man to escort her who is not her husband or her father or her brother—even when she is married. In my world it is considered somewhat bad *ton* to be seen exclusively in the company of one's spouse."

"I daresay, then," he said, "that my sister is bad *ton*. And Lord Francis Kneller, too."

"Oh, those two." She waved a dismissive hand as she got to her feet. "I do believe they still fancy themselves in love, sir, though they have been married forever. There are other such oddities in the beau monde, but they are in the minority, I do assure you."

"You were right," he said. "I came to London in search of a bride. I promised my father that I would make my choice by Christmas. I rather think I should concentrate upon that task."

"My offer of friendship is rejected, then?" she said. "My *plea* for friendship? How very lowering. You are no gentleman, sir."

"No," he said with slow clarity, "I am not, ma'am. In my world a man does not cultivate a friendship with one woman while courting another."

"Especially with a woman whom he has bedded," she said.

"Yes," he agreed. "Especially with such a woman."

Her smile this time was one of pure contempt. "And you were right a minute or two ago, Mr. Downes," she said. "You have stayed overlong. I tire of your bourgeois mentality. I would not find your friendship as satisfying as I found your lovemaking. And I do not desire lovemaking. I use men for my pleasure occasionally, but only very occasionally. And never the same man twice. Men are necessary for certain functions, sir, but essentially they are a bore."

Her words, her looks, her manner were all meant to insult. He knew that and felt insulted. At the same time he sensed that he had hurt her somehow. She had asked for his friendship and he had refused. He had refused because he would not be seduced again and knew beyond a doubt that any friendship with Lady Stapleton would inevitably lead eventually back to bed. She must surely know it, too.

He did not want a thirty-six-year-old mistress. *Rationally* he did not want her. Irrationally, of course, he wanted her very much indeed. He was a rational being. He chose to want a wife who was below the age of thirty, a wife who would give him children for his contentment, a son for Mobley Abbey.

"I am sorry," he said.

"Get out, Mr. Downes," she said. "I shall be from home if you call again, as I would have been today if I had had any sense. But I daresay you will not call again."

"No," he said, "I will not call again, ma'am."

She turned away from him and crossed the room to the window. She stood looking out of it while he let himself out of the room, as she had looked from the window of her bedchamber the night before.

She was a strange woman, he thought as he left the house and made his way along the street, thankful for the chilliness of the air. Confident, independent, unconventional, she appeared to be a woman who made happiness and her own gratification her business. Other women must envy her her freedom and her wealth and her beauty. Yet there was a deep-seated bitterness in her that suggested anything but happiness.

She must have had a bad marriage, he thought, one that had soured her and made her believe that all men were as her husband had been.

He had, it seemed, been one of a long string of lovers, all of whom had been used and never reused. It was a lowering and a distasteful thought. She made no secret of her promiscuity. She even seemed proud of it. His brief involvement with her was an experience he would not easily forget. It was an experience he was very glad was in the past. He was relieved that he had found the strength to reject her offer of friendship—he had certainly been tempted.

She was not a pleasant woman. A beautiful temptress of a woman, but not a pleasant one. He did not like her.

And yet he found himself regretting that he would not see her again, or if he did, that he must view her from afar. She could have been an interesting and an intelligent friend if there had never been anything else between them.

Chapter Five

Helena summoned her aunt from the country and felt guilty when she arrived for having encouraged her to leave just a few weeks before. She was uncomfortably aware that her aunt was not a person who deserved to be used.

"How very thoughtful you are, Helena, my dear," Mrs. Cross said as she stood in the hallway, surrounded by her rather meager baggage. "You know that I find life with Clarence and his family trying, and you have invited me back here, where I am always happy. Have you been enjoying yourself?"

"When do I not?" Helena said, hugging her and linking her arm through her aunt's to draw her toward the stairs. "Hobbes will have your bags attended to. Come to the drawing room and drink some tea. There is a fire there."

She let her aunt talk about her journey, about her stay in the country, about the snippets of news and gossip she had learned there. Sometimes, she thought, it felt good to have a companion, someone who was family, someone who loved one unconditionally. Often it was annoying, confining. But sometimes it felt good. Today it felt good.

"But here I am going on and on about myself," her aunt said eventually. "What about you, Helena? Are you looking pale, or is it my imagination?"

"The wind has not stopped blowing and the sun has not once peeped through the clouds for days," Helena said. "I have stayed indoors. I *feel* pale." She smiled. "Now that you are here, I shall go out again. We will go shopping tomorrow morning. I noticed when you arrived that there was a hole in the palm of your glove. I daresay there were no shops of note in the village close to Clarence's where you might have bought new ones. I am glad of it. Now I have an excuse to buy them for you as a gift. I was still in Switzerland at the time of your birthday, was I not?"

"Oh, Helena." Her aunt was flustered. "You do not need to be buying me presents. I wore those old gloves because they are comfortable and no one would see them in the carriage."

Helena smiled. Mrs. Letitia Cross was a widow, like herself. But Mr. Cross had not left her with an independence. Her meager stipend barely enabled her to keep herself decently clothed. She had to rely on various relatives to house her and feed her and convey her from place to place.

"I need gloves, too," Helena said, "and perhaps a muff. I need a warm cloak and warm dresses for a British winter. Ugh! It seems to be upon us already. Why can no one seem to build up the fires decently in this house?" She got up and jerked on the bell pull.

"But Helena, my dear." Her aunt laughed. "It is a magnificent fire. One would need a quizzing glass to be able to detect the fires in Clarence's hearths, I do declare. Though I must not complain. They were kind to me. The children and the governess were not allowed fires in their bedchambers either."

"I shall have one built half up your chimney tonight," Helena said. And then she turned to speak irritably to Hobbes, who looked expressionlessly at the roaring fire and said he would send someone immediately with more coals.

"I think I may go to Italy for Christmas," Helena said, throwing herself restlessly back onto her chair. "It will be warmer there. And the celebrations will be less cloying, less purely hypocritical than they are here. The Povises will be going at the end of November, I daresay, and there is always a party with them. I shall make one of their number. And you will make another. You will like Italy."

"I will not put you to so much expense," Mrs. Cross said with quiet dignity. "Besides, I do not have the wardrobe for it. And I am too old to be jauntering around foreign parts."

Helena clucked her tongue. "How old *are* you?" she asked. "You speak as if you are an octogenarian."

"I am fifty-eight," her aunt replied. "I thought you planned to stay here for the winter, Helena. And for the spring. You said you longed to see an English spring again."

Helena got restlessly to her feet and walked over to the window, although it was far from the fire, which a maid had just built up. "I am bored with England," she said. "The sun never shines here. What is the point of an English spring, Aunt, and English daffodils and snowdrops and bluebells when the sun never shines on them?"

"Has something happened?" her aunt asked her. "Are you unhappy about something, Helena?"

Her niece laughed. "Of course something has happened," she said. "Many things. I have been to dinners and dances and soirées and private concerts and have seen the same faces wherever I go. Pleasant faces. People with pleasant conversation. How dull it is, Letty, to see the same faces and listen to the same conversation wherever one goes. And no one has been obliging enough to do anything even slightly scandalous to give us all something more lively to discuss. How respectable the world has become!"

"There is no special gentleman?" her aunt asked. It was always her opinion that Helena should search for another husband, though she had never done so herself in twenty years of widowhood.

Helena did not turn from the window. "There is no special gentleman, Aunt," she said. "There never will be. I have no wish for there to be. I value my freedom far too much."

The street outside was quite busy, she noticed, but there was no tall, broad gentleman striding along it as if he owned the world. It was only as the thought became conscious that she realized she had spent a good number of hours during the past five days standing just here watching for him, waiting for him to return to apologize again. Had she really been doing that without even realizing it? She was horrified.

"And yet, my dear," Mrs. Cross said, "all husbands must not be condemned because yours made you unhappy."

Helena whirled around, her eyes blazing, her heart thumping with fury. "It was *not* an unhappy marriage," she said so loudly that her aunt grimaced. "Or if it was, the fault was mine. Entirely mine. Christian was the best of husbands. He adored me. He lavished gifts and affection on me. He made me feel beautiful and charming and—and lovable. I will not hear one word against him. Do you hear me? Not one word."

"Oh, Helena." Her aunt was on her feet, looking deeply distressed. "I am so sorry. Do forgive me. What I said was unpardonable."

Helena closed her eyes and drew a deep breath. "No," she said. "The fault was mine. I did not love him, Letty, but he was good to me. Come, let me take you up to your room. It should be warm by now. I am in the mopes because I have not been out in five days." She laughed. "That must be something of a record. Can you imagine me not going out for five whole days?"

"Frankly no, dear," her aunt said. "Have there been no invitations? It is hard to believe, even if this is October."

"I have refused them," she said. "I have been suffering from a persistent chill—or so I have claimed. I do believe it is time I recovered my health. Do you fancy an informal dance at the Earl of Thornhill's tomorrow evening?"

"I always find both the earl and the countess charming," Mrs. Cross said. "They do not ignore one merely because one is past the age of forty and is wearing a gown one has worn for the past three years and more."

Helena squeezed her arm. "We are going shopping tomorrow morning," she said. "I feel extravagant. And I feel so full of energy again that I do not know quite what to do with it." She stopped at the top of the stairs and hugged her aunt impulsively. "Oh, Letty, you do not know how good it is to have you here again." She was surprised to find that she had to blink her eyes in order to clear her vision.

"And *you* do not know," Mrs. Cross said, "how good it is to be here, Helena. Ah, the room really is warm. How kind you are to me. I feel quite like a person again, I do declare. And how ungrateful that sounds to Clarence. He really was very good to me."

"Clarence," Helena said, "is a sanctimonious, parsimonious bore and I am very glad he is not *my* relative. There. I have put it into words for you so that they will not be upon your conscience. I am going to leave you to rest for a while. There is nothing more tiring than a lengthy journey."

"Thank you, dear," her aunt said with a grateful sigh.

Had she really not been out for five days? Helena thought as she made her way back downstairs. Had she really convinced herself that the weather was just too inclement? And that the company of those of the beau monde who were at present in London was too tedious to be borne?

Her lip curled with self-mockery. Was she afraid to face him? Because he had rejected her? Because he had refused her offer of friendship and declined her invitation to escort her to one of the galleries? Was she so humiliated that she could not look him in the eye?

She *was* humiliated. She was unaccustomed to rejection. No man had ever rejected her before—oh! Her stomach lurched uncomfortably. Oh, that was not true. She realized something else suddenly about the past five days. She had hardly eaten.

To have been rejected by a cit! To have been rejected by any man—but by a man who was not even a gentleman. And a man to whom she had *given* herself. She had offered to make him better acquainted with London. She had offered her—patronage, she supposed was the word she was looking for. And he had said no for the purely bourgeois reason that he was about to pay court to some young girl.

How dared he reject her! And how petulant that thought sounded—and was.

She should, of course, never have asked for his friendship. She wanted no one's friendship, especially not any man's. Most especially not his. She could not imagine what she had been thinking of. She should not even have received him. And he had not even come to beg for further favors, but to apologize for his lack of *courtesy*. If it were not so lowering, it would be funny. Hilarious.

She certainly was not going to avoid him. Or show him that his rejection had meant anything to her. The very idea that she should mope and hide away just because he had refused to give her his escort on an afternoon's outing! She wished him joy of his young girl.

She was going to the Earl of Thornhill's informal ball tomorrow evening and she was going to dance and be merry. She was going to be the belle of the ball despite her age or perhaps because of it. She was going to wear her bronze satin gown. She had never worn it in England before, having judged it far too risque for stodgy English tastes. But tomorrow night she was going to wear it.

She was going to have Mr. Edgar Downes salivating over her—if he was there. And she was going to ignore him completely.

She hoped he would be there.

Edgar was uncomfortable with Fanny Grainger's age. It seemed that she was twenty, at least two years older than she looked. But even so she seemed a child to him. Lady Stapleton had been wrong when she had said that the age gap must appear nothing to him, that it would be apparent only to the girl herself. He was uncomfortably aware that he was well past his youth, while she seemed to be just embarking upon hers.

The other two young ladies he had met at the Earl of Greenwald's appeared equally young. And less appealing in other ways. Miss Turner, whom he had met two evenings later, was noticeably older—closer to thirty than twenty at a guess—but she was dull and lethargic and totally lacking in conversation. And she had a constant dry sniff, an annoying habit that grated on his nerves when he sat beside her for half an hour.

Miss Grainger, he rather suspected, was going to be the one. He had imagined when he came to London that he would be able to look about him at his leisure for several weeks before beginning a serious courtship of any lady in particular, almost as if he had thought he would be invisible and his intentions undiscernible. Such was not the case, of course. And Sir Webster Grainger and his lady had begun to court him. They were quite determined, it seemed, to net Edgar Downes for their daughter.

She was sweet and charming in a thoroughly youthful way. If he had been ten years younger, he might have tumbled head over ears in love with her. At his age he did not. He kept remembering Lady Stapleton's saying that the girl had a previous, ineligible attachment. He did not know how she had learned that. Perhaps—probably—she had merely been trying to make him uncomfortable. She had succeeded. The thought of coming between a young lady and her lover merely because he happened to be almost indecently rich was not a pleasant one.

He wondered if the girl disliked him, was repulsed by him. Whenever he spoke with her—and her parents made sure that he often did, always in their presence—she was polite and sweet, her deeper feelings, if she had any, quite hidden from view.

Cora was pleased. "She is a pleasant young lady, Edgar," she announced at the breakfast table one morning, "and will doubtless be a good companion once she has recovered from her shyness, poor girl, and her awe at your very masterful bearing. You could try to soften your manner, you know, but then it comes naturally enough to you and soon she will realize that behind it all you are just Edgar."

"You do not think I am too old for her, Corey?" he

asked, unconsciously using the old nickname he had tried to drop since her marriage.

"Oh, she will not think so when she comes to love you," his fond sister assured him. "And that is bound to happen very soon. Is it not, Francis?"

"Oh, quite so, my love," Lord Francis said. "Edgar is eminently lovable."

Which remark sent Cora off into peals of laughter and left Edgar quite unreassured.

The promise he had made to his father seemed rash in retrospect. Perhaps at the Thornhills' ball, he thought, he would dance with the girl and have a chance to converse with her beyond the close chaperonage of her parents. Perhaps he would be able to discover the answers to some of his questions and find out if Cora was right. Could Miss Grainger be a good companion?

Was there something in his bearing that other people, particularly young ladies who were facing his courtship, found daunting, even overbearing? Lady Stapleton had not been daunted. But he did not particularly wish to think of Lady Stapleton. He had not seen her since that ghastly morning visit. He hoped that she had left town.

He realized she had not when he was dancing with Miss Turner, feeling thankful that the intricate patterns of the dance took away the necessity of trying to hold a conversation with her. It was not a great squeeze of a ball. Lady Thornhill had been laughingly apologetic about it and had insisted on calling it a small informal dance rather than a ball. To him the ballroom seemed crowded enough, but it was true that it was possible to see almost all the guests at once when he looked about him. He looked about him—and there she was standing in the doorway.

He did not even notice the older lady standing beside her. He saw only her and found himself swallowing convulsively. She wore a gown that might have appeared indecent even in a boudoir. It was a bronze-colored sheath that shimmered in the light from the chandeliers. To say that it was

cut low at the bosom was seriously to understate the case.
It barely skimmed the peaks of her nipples and dipped low
into her decolletage. The gown was not tightly fitted and
yet it settled about her body like a second skin, revealing
every shapely and generous curve. It left little if anything
to the imagination. It made Edgar remember with unwilling clarity exactly how that body had looked and felt—and
tasted—beyond the thin barrier of the bronze satin.

She stood proudly, looking about her with languid eyes
and slightly mocking smile, apparently quite unaware of
any impropriety in her appearance. But then she somehow
looked too haughty to be improper. She looked plainly
magnificent.

The lady beside her must be the aunt, Edgar decided,
noticing the woman when she turned her head to address
some remark to Lady Stapleton. She was gray-haired and
pleasant looking and dressed with neat propriety.

Edgar returned his attention to the steps of the dance.

She had been late to the Greenwalds' soirée, too, he remembered. Clearly she liked entrances. But then she had
the looks and the presence to bring them off brilliantly.
Thornhill was hurrying toward her.

Edgar returned his partner to her mother's side at the
end of the set, bowed to them both, and made his way in the
direction of his sister. There was to be a waltz next. He
would dance it with Cora, who was closer to him in height
than almost any other lady present. He felt uncomfortable
waltzing with tiny females. But the Countess of Thornhill,
one of Cora's close friends, hailed him as he passed and he
turned toward her with a sinking heart.

"Mr. Downes." She was smiling at him. "Have you met
Lady Stapleton?" It was a rhetorical question, of course. She
did not pause to allow him to say that, yes, he had met the
lady at Lady Greenwald's soirée the week before and had
escorted her home and stayed to bed her two separate times.

"And Mrs. Cross, her aunt," Lady Thornhill continued.
"Mr. Edgar Downes, ladies. He is Lady Francis Kneller's
brother from Bristol."

Edgar bowed.

"I am pleased to make your acquaintance, Mr. Downes," Mrs. Cross said.

"How do you do, Mr. Downes?" He had forgotten how that velvet voice could send shivers down his spine.

"Lady Francis is a very pleasant lady," Mrs. Cross said. "She is always very jolly."

Yes, it was an apt description of Cora.

"And quite fearless," Mrs. Cross continued. "I remember the year the Duchess of Bridgwater—the dowager duchess now, of course—brought her out. The year she married Lord Francis."

"Ah, yes, ma'am," he said. "The duchess was kind enough to give my sister a Season."

"The next dance is a waltz," the Countess of Thornhill said. "I have promised to dance it with Gabriel, though it is perhaps vulgar to dance with one's own husband at one's own ball. But then this is not a real ball but merely an informal dance among friends."

"I think one need make no excuses for dancing with one's husband," Mrs. Cross said kindly.

Edgar could feel Lady Stapleton's eyes on him, even though he looked intently at her aunt. He could feel that faint and characteristic scorn of her smile like a physical touch.

"Ma'am." He turned his head to look at her. "Will you do me the honor of dancing with me?"

"A waltz, Mr. Downes?" She raised her eyebrows. "I believe I will." She reached out one hand, though there was no necessity of taking to the floor just yet, and he took it in his.

"Mrs. Cross," the countess was saying as Edgar led his partner onto the floor, "do let me find you a glass of lemonade and some congenial company. May my husband and I have the pleasure of your company at the supper table when the waltz is at an end?"

Edgar's senses were being assaulted by the heady mixture of a familiar and subtle perfume and raw femininity.

* * *

"Well, Mr. Downes," she said, turning to face him, waiting for the music to begin, "in your school for budding merchants, did they teach you how to waltz?"

"Well enough to keep me from treading on your toes, I hope, ma'am," he said. "I was educated in a gentleman's school. They allowed me in after I had promised on my honor never, under any circumstances, to drop my aitches or wipe my nose on my cuff."

"One can only hope," she said, "that you kept your promises."

She was alarmed by her reaction to him. She felt short of breath. There was fluttering in her stomach, or perhaps lower than her stomach, and a weakness in her knees. She had vowed, of course, to ignore him completely tonight. But then she had not planned that very awkward introduction Lady Thornhill had chosen to make. Strange, that. It was just the sort of thing she would normally maneuver herself. But not tonight. She had not wanted to be this close to him again. He was wearing the same cologne. Though it seemed to be the smell of the very essence of him rather than any identifiable cologne. She had fancied even as recently as last night that there was a trace of it on the pillow next to her own.

He danced well. Of course. She might have expected it. He probably did everything well, from making love on down—or up.

"Are congratulations in order yet, Mr. Downes?" she asked to take her mind off her fluttering nerves—and to shake his cool air of command. "Have you affianced yourself to a suitably genteel and fertile young lady? Or married her? Special licenses are available, as you must know."

"Not yet, ma'am," he said, looking at her steadily. He had been looking into her face since the music began. Was he afraid to look lower? But then he had seen all there was to see on a previous occasion. "It is not like purchasing cattle, you know."

"Oh, far from it," she agreed, laughing, "if by *cattle* you mean horses, Mr. Downes. I would not have asked you so soon if I must congratulate you if it were a horse you were choosing. I would know that the choice must be made with great care over an extended period of time."

He stared at her for so long that she became uncomfortable. But she scorned to look away from him.

"Who hurt you?" he asked her, jolting her with surprise and even shock. "Was it your husband?"

The same assumption in two days by two different people. Poor Christian. She smiled at Edgar. "My husband treated me as if I were a queen, Mr. Downes," she said. "Or to be more accurate, as if I were a porcelain doll. I am merely a realist, sir. Are your riches not sufficient to lure a genteel bride?"

"I believe my financial status and my personal life are none of your concern, ma'am," he said with such icy civility that she felt a delicious shiver along her spine.

"You do that remarkably well," she said. "Did all opposing counsel crumble before you in court? Were you a very successful lawyer? No, I will not make that a question but a statement. I have no doubt you were successful. Do all your employees quiver like jelly before your every glance? I would wager they do."

"I treat my employees well and with respect," he said.

"But I will wager you demand total obedience from them," she said, "and require an explanation when you do not get it."

"Of course," he said. "How could I run a successful business otherwise?"

"And are you the same in your personal relations, Mr. Downes?" she asked. "Am I to pity your wife when you have married her—after congratulating you, of course?" With her eyes she laughed at him. Her body was horribly aroused. She had no idea why. She had never craved any man's mastery. Quite the opposite.

"You need feel nothing for my wife, ma'am," he said. "Or for me. We will be none of your concern."

She sighed audibly. "You are naive, Mr. Downes," she said. "When you marry into the *ton*, you will become the concern of the *ton*. What else do we have to talk about but one another? Where can we look for the most fascinating scandals but to those among us who have recently wed? Especially when the match is something of a misalliance. Yours will be, you know. We will all look for tyranny and vulgarity in you—and will hope that there will not be only bourgeois dullness instead. We will all look for rebellion and infidelity in her—and will be vastly disappointed if she turns out to be a docile and obedient wife. Will you insist upon docility and obedience?"

"That will be for me to decide," he said, "and the woman I will marry."

She sighed again and then laughed. "How tiresome you are, Mr. Downes," she said. "Do you not know when a quarrel is being picked with you? I wish to quarrel with you, but I cannot quarrel alone."

For the first time she saw a gleam of something that might be amusement in his eyes—for the merest moment. "But I have no wish to quarrel with you," he said softly, twirling her about one corner of the ballroom. "We are not adversaries, ma'am."

"And we are not friends either," she said. "Or lovers. Are we nothing, then? Nothing at all to each other?"

He gave her another of those long stares—even longer this time. He opened his mouth and drew breath at one moment, but said nothing. He half smiled at last—he looked younger, more human when he smiled. "We are nothing," he said. "We cannot be. Because there was that night."

She almost lost her knees. She was looking back into his eyes and unexpectedly had a shockingly vivid memory of that night—of his face this close, above hers. . . .

"Do you understand the etiquette of such sets as this, Mr. Downes?" she asked. "It is the supper dance. It would be unmannerly indeed if you did not take me in to supper and seat yourself beside me and converse with me. What shall we converse about? Let me see. Some safe topic on which people who are nothing to each other can natter quite happily. Shall I tell you about my dreadful experiences in Greece? I am an amusing story-teller, or so my listeners always assure me."

"I believe I would like that," he said gravely.

She almost believed him. And she almost wanted to cry. How absurd! She felt like crying.

She never cried.

Chapter Six

It was amazing how few choices could be left one some-times, Edgar discovered even more forcefully over the following month. He tried very hard not to fix his choice with any finality, simply because he did not meet that one certain lady of whom he could feel confident of saying in his heart that, yes, she was one he wished to have as his life's companion, as his lover, as the mother of his children.

Miss Turner was of a suitable age, but he found her dull and physically unappealing. Miss Warrington was also of suitable age, and she was livelier and prettier. But her conversation centered almost entirely upon horses, a topic that was of no particular interest to him. Miss Crawley was very young—she even lisped like a child—and had a tendency to giggle at almost any remark uttered in her hearing. Miss Avery-Hill was equally young and very pretty and appealingly vivacious. She made very clear to Edgar that she would accept his courtship. She made equally clear the fact that it would be a major condescension on her part if she stooped to marry him.

That left Miss Grainger—and the Grainger parents. He liked the girl. She was pretty, modest, quiet without being mute, pleasant-natured. She was biddable. She would doubtless be a good wife. She would surely be a good mother. She would be a good enough companion. She would be attractive enough in bed. Cora liked her. His father would, too.

There was something missing. Not love, although that was definitely missing. He did not worry about it. If he chose a bride with care, affection would grow and even love, given time. He was not sure quite what it was that was missing with Miss Grainger. Actually there was nothing missing except fortune, and that certainly was of no concern to him. He did not need a wealthy wife. If there was something wrong, it was in himself. He was too old to be choosing a wife, perhaps. He was too set in his ways.

Perhaps he would even have considered reneging on his promise to his father if matters had not appeared to have moved beyond his control. He found that at every entertainment he attended—and they were almost daily—he was paired with Miss Grainger for at least a part of the time. At dinners and suppers he found himself seated next to her more often than not. He escorted her and her mother to the library one day because Sir Webster was to be busy at something else. He went driving in the park with the three of them on two separate occasions. He was invited one evening to dinner at the Graingers', followed by some informal musical entertainment. There were only four other guests, all of them from a generation slightly older than his own.

Cora spoke often of Christmas and began to assume that the Graingers would be coming to Mobley. She was working on persuading all her particular friends—hers and Francis's—to spend the holiday there, too.

"Papa will be delighted," she said at breakfast one morning after the topic had been introduced. "Will he not, Edgar?" Francis had just suggested to her that she write to her father before issuing myriad invitations in his name.

"He will," Edgar agreed. "But it might be a good idea to fire off a note to warn him, Cora. He might consider it somewhat disconcerting to find a whole gaggle of guests and their milling offspring descending upon him and demanding a portion of a lone Christmas goose."

Lord Francis chuckled.

"Well, of *course* I intend to inform Papa," Cora said.

"The very idea that I might neglect to do so, Edgar. Do you think me quite addle-brained?"

Lord Francis was unwise enough to chuckle again.

"And everyone knows that my main function in life is to provide you with amusement, Francis," she said crossly.

"Quite so, my love," he agreed, eliciting a short bark of inelegant laughter from his spouse.

"And I daresay Miss Grainger will be more comfortable with Jennifer and Samantha and Stephanie there as well as me," Cora said. "She is familiar with them and they with her. But she *is* rather shy and may find the combination of you and Papa together rather formidable, Edgar."

"Nonsense," her brother said.

"I did, Edgar," Lord Francis said. "When I dashed down to Mobley that time to ask if I might pay my addresses to Cora, I took one look at your father and one look at you and had vivid mental images of my bones all mashed to powder. You had me shaking in my Hessians. You might have noticed the tassels swaying if you had glanced down."

"And what gives you the idea," Edgar asked his sister, "that Miss Grainger will be at Mobley for Christmas? Have I missed something? Have you *invited* her?" He had a horrid suspicion for one moment that perhaps she had and had forced his hand quite irretrievably.

"Of course I have not," she said. "I would never do such a thing. That is for you to do, Edgar. But you will do it, will you not? She is your favorite and eligible in every way. I love her quite like a sister already. And you did promise Papa."

"And it is Edgar's life, my love," Lord Francis said, getting to his feet. "We had better go up and rescue Nurse from our offspring. They are doubtless chafing at the bit and impatiently awaiting their daily energy-letting in the park. Is it Andrew's turn to ride on my shoulders or Paul's?"

"Annabelle's," she said as they left the room.

But Cora came very close that very evening to doing what she had said she would never do. They were at a party in which she made up a group with the Graingers; Edgar; Stephanie, Duchess of Bridgwater; and the Marquess of

Carew. The duchess had commented on the fact that the shops on Oxford Street and Bond Street were filled with Christmas wares already despite the fact that December had not even arrived. The marquess had added that he and his wife had been shopping for gifts that very day in the hope of avoiding any last-minute panic. Cora mentioned Mobley and hoped there would be some snow for Christmas. All their children, she declared—if she could persuade her friends to come—would be ecstatic if they could skate and ride the sleighs and engage in snowball fights.

"There are skates of all sizes," she said, "and the sleighs are large enough for adults as well as children. Do you like snow, Miss Grainger?"

Edgar felt a twinge of alarm and looked pointedly at his sister. But she was too well launched on enthusiasm to notice.

"Good," Cora said when the girl had replied that indeed she did. "Then you will have a marvelous time." She reacted quite in character when she realized that she had opened her mouth and stuffed her rather large slipper inside, Edgar noticed, wishing rather uncharitably that she might choke on it. She blushed and talked and laughed. "That is, if it snows. If it snows where you happen to be spending Christmas, that is. That is, if . . . Oh dear. Hartley, do tell me what I am trying to say."

"You are hoping there will be snow to make Christmas a more festive occasion, Cora," the Marquess of Carew said kindly. "And that it will fall all over England for everyone's delight."

"Yes," she said. "Thank you. That is exactly what I meant. How warm it is in here." She opened her fan and plied it vigorously before her face.

Sir Webster and Lady Grainger, Edgar saw, were looking very smug indeed.

And then at the very end of November, when the noose seemed to have settled quite firmly about his neck, he discovered the existence of the ineligible lover—the one Lady Stapleton had mentioned.

Edgar was walking along Oxford Street, huddled inside his heavy greatcoat, avoiding the puddles left by the rain that had just stopped, wondering if the sun would ever shine again and if he would ever find suitable gifts for everyone on his list—he had expected London to make for easier shopping than Bristol—when he ran almost head-long into Miss Grainger, who was standing quite still in the middle of the pavement, impeding pedestrian traffic.

"I do beg your pardon," he said, his hand going to the brim of his hat even before he recognized her. "Ah, Miss Grainger. Your servant." He made her a slight bow and re-alized two things. Neither of her parents was with her—but a young man was.

She did not behave with any wisdom. Her eyes grew wide with horror, she opened her mouth and held it open before snapping it shut again. Then she smiled broadly, though she forgot to adjust her eyes accordingly, and proceeded to chatter.

"Mr. Downes," she said. "Oh, good morning. Fancy meeting you here. Is it not a beautiful morning? I have come to change my book at the library. Mama could not come with me, but I have brought my maid—you see?" She gestured behind her with one hand to the young person standing a short distance away. "How lovely it is to see you. By a very strange coincidence I have run into another acquaintance, too. Mr. Sperling. May I present you? Mr. Sperling, sir. Jack, this is Mr. Downes. I-I m-mean *Mr. Sperling,* this is Mr. Downes."

Edgar inclined his head to the slender, good-looking, very young man, who was looking back coldly. "Sperling?" he said.

A few things were clear. This particular spot on Oxford Street was not between the Grainger lodgings and the li-brary. The doorway to a coffee shop that sported high-backed seats and secluded booths was just to their right. The maid was not doing a very good job as watchdog. Jack Sperling was more than a chance acquaintance and the meeting between him and Miss Grainger was no coincidence. Sperling knew who he was and would put a dagger through his heart if he dared—and if he had one about his person. Miss Grainger herself was terrified. And he, Edgar, felt at least a century old.

He would have moved on and left his prospective bride to her clandestine half hour or so—he doubted they would allow themselves longer—with the slight acquaintance she happened to call by his first name. But she forestalled him.

"Jack," she said. She was still flustered. "I m-mean *Mr. Sperling*, it was pleasant to meet you. G-good morning."

And Jack Sperling, pale and murderous of countenance, had no choice but to bow, touch the brim of his hat, bid them a good morning, and continue on his way down the street as if he had never so much as heard of coffee shops.

Fanny Grainger smiled dazzlingly at Edgar—with terrified eyes. "Was not that a happy chance?" she said. "He is a neighbor of ours. I have not seen him for years." Edgar guessed that beneath the rosy glow the cold had whipped into her cheeks she was blushing just as rosily.

"May I offer my escort?" he asked her. "Are you on your way to or from the library?"

"Oh," she said. "To." She indicated her maid, who held a book clasped against her bosom. "Y-yes, please, Mr. Downes, if it is not too much trouble."

He felt like apologizing to her. But of course he could not do so. He should be feeling sternly disapproving. He should be feeling injured proprietorship. He felt—still—a century old. She took his arm.

"Mr. Downes," she said before he had decided upon a topic of conversation, "p-please, will you—? That is, could I ask you please— Please, sir—"

He wanted to set a reassuring hand over hers. He wanted to pat it. He wanted to tell her that it was nothing to him if she chose to arrange clandestine meetings with her lover. But of course it *was* something to him. There was one month to Christmas and he had every intention—he had thought it through finally just last evening and had come to a firm decision—of inviting her and her parents to Mobley

Abbey for the holiday, though he had thought he would not make his offer until they had all been there for a few days and he could be quite sure before taking the final step.

"I believe, my dear," he said, and then wished he had not called her that, as if she were a favored niece, "my size and demeanor and—age sometimes inspire awe or even fear in those who do not know me well. At least, I have been told as much by those who do know me. I have no wish either to hurt or distress you. What is it?"

He noticed that she closed her eyes briefly before answering. "Please," she said, "will you refrain from mentioning to Mama and Papa that I ran into Mr. Sperling by chance this morning? They do not like him, you see, and perhaps would scold me for not giving him the cut direct. I could not do that. Or at least I did not think of doing it until it was too late."

"Of course," he said. "I have already forgotten the young man's name and indeed his very existence."

"Thank you." Some of the terror had waned from her eyes when she looked up at him. "Though I w-wish I had done so. It was disagreeable to have to acknowledge him. I was very relieved when you came along."

"It is a quite impossible situation?" he found himself asking when he should have been content to play along with her game.

There was fright in her eyes again. She bit her lip and tears sprang to her eyes. "I am sorry," she whispered. "Please do not be angry with me. It was the last time. That is— It will not happen again. Oh, please do not be angry with me. I am so frightened of you." And then the fright escalated to terror once more when she realized what she had said, what she had admitted, both about him and about Jack Sperling.

This time he did set his hand over hers—quite firmly. "That at least you need not be," he said. "What is the objection? Lack of fortune?"

But she was biting hard on her upper lip and fighting both tears and terror—despite his words. The library was before them.

"I shall leave you to your maid's chaperonage," he said, stopping on the pavement outside it and relinquishing her arm. "We will forget about this morning, Miss Grainger. It never happened."

But she did not immediately scurry away, as he rather expected she would. She looked earnestly into his face. "I have always been obedient to Mama and Papa," she said, "except in very little things. I will be obedient—I would be obedient to a husband, sir. I would never need to be beaten. I—Good morning." And she turned to hurry into the library, her maid behind her.

Good Lord! Did she imagine—? Did he look that formidable? And what a coil, he thought. He could not possibly marry her now, of course. But perhaps it would appear that he had gone rather too far to retreat without good cause. There was excellent cause, but nothing he could express to another living soul. He could not marry a young lady who loved another man. Or one who feared him so much that she imagined he would be a wife-beater.

Whatever was he going to do?

But he was not fated to think of an answer while he stood there on the pavement, staring at the library doors. They opened and Lady Stapleton stepped out with Mrs. Cross.

He forgot about his problem—the one that concerned Miss Grainger, anyway. He always forgot about everything and everyone whenever his eyes alighted on Lady Stapleton. They had avoided each other for the past month. They attended almost all the same social events and it was frequently necessary to be part of the same group and even to exchange a few words. But they had not been alone together since that evening when they had waltzed and then taken supper together. The evening when he had told her they could be nothing to each other because there had been that night.

That night. It stayed stubbornly in his memory, it wove itself into his dreams as none other like it had ever done. Not that there had been another night like that. Perhaps, he thought sometimes, he would forget it sooner if he tried less hard to do so. He did not want to remember. The memories disturbed him. He was not a man of passion but one of cool reason. He had been rather alarmed at the passionate self that had emerged during that particular encounter. He looked forward to returning to Mobley and then Bristol. After that, he hoped, he would never see her again. The memories would fade.

He made his bow and would have hastened away, but Mrs. Cross called to him.

"Mr. Downes," she cried. "Oh, Mr. Downes, might we impose upon you for a few minutes, I wonder? My niece is unwell."

He could see when he looked more closely at Lady Stapleton that she was leaning rather heavily on her aunt's arm and that her face and even her lips were ashen pale and her eyes half closed—and that until her aunt spoke his name, she had been quite unaware of his presence.

Her eyes jolted open and her glance locked with his.

The Povises had already left for the Continent with a group of friends and acquaintances. They intended to wander south at a leisurely pace and spend Christmas in Italy. Helena might have gone with them. Indeed, they had urged her to do so, and so had Mr. Crutchley, who had had designs on her for a number of years past, though she had never given him any encouragement. It was sure to be a gay party. She would have enjoyed herself immensely if she had gone along. She would have avoided this dreariest of dreary winters in England—and it was still only November. She could have stayed away until spring or even longer. Perhaps she could even have persuaded her aunt to go with her if she had set her mind to it.

But she had not gone.

She did not know why. She was certainly not enjoying London. There were almost daily entertainments, and she attended most of them for her aunt's sake. The company, though sparse, was congenial. She was treated with respect and even with warmth wherever she went—even on that evening when she had worn her bronze satin and Lady Francis Kneller had quite frankly and quite sincerely commended her bravery. Being in one comfortable home was certainly preferable to moving from one inn to another. And coach travel day after day could be tedious and even downright uncomfortable. She should be happy. Or since happiness was not a possible state for her, contented. She should be contented.

She felt lethargic and even ill. Her aunt had a bad cold soon after returning to town, but Helena did not catch it from her. It would have been better if she had, she thought. She would have suffered for a few days and then recovered. As it was, she felt constantly unwell without any specific symptoms that she might treat. Even getting out of bed in the mornings—her favorite time of day—had become a chore. Sometimes she lay late in bed, awake and bored and uncomfortable, but lacking the energy to get up, only to feel faintly nauseated and unable to eat any breakfast when she did make the effort.

She knew why she felt that way, of course. She was living through an obsession—and it was no new thing. If it had been, perhaps she would have been better able to deal with it. But it was not new. She had been obsessed once before and just the memory of it—long suppressed but never quite hidden below consciousness—could have her poised with her head hanging over the close stool, fighting to keep the last meal down.

Now she was obsessed again. Not in any way she could explain clearly to herself. Although she saw him almost daily, she never again felt the urge to seduce him—though the knowledge that it would not be an easy thing to do a second time was almost a temptation in itself. She just could not keep her eyes off him when he was in a room with her. Though that was not strictly accurate. She rarely looked directly at him. She would scorn to do so. He would surely notice. Other people would. She kept her eyes off him. But every other part of her being was drawn to him as if to a powerful magnet.

She was not even sure that it was just a sexual awareness. She imagined sometimes being in bed with him again, doing with him the things they had done on that one night they had spent together. But though the thoughts were undeniably arousing, she always knew that it was not that she wanted. Not just that anyway. She did not know what she wanted.

She wanted to forget him. That was what she wanted. She hated him. Those words they had spoken while waltzing would not fade from her mind.

Are we nothing, then? Nothing at all to each other?

We are nothing. We cannot be. Because there was that night.

There was a deep pit of emptiness in her stomach every time she heard the echo of those words of his—and she heard it almost constantly.

She should go away. She should have gone with the Povises. She had stayed for her aunt's sake, she had told herself. But when had she ever considered anyone's feelings except her own? When had she ever had a selfless motive for anything she had ever done—or not done? She should go away. She should go to Scotland for Christmas—horrid thought. But *he* would be going away for Christmas. He would be going to his father's estate near Bristol. She had heard Lady Francis Kneller talking about it. The Grainger girl would doubtless be going there, too. They would be betrothed—and married by the spring. Perhaps then she would know some peace.

Peace! What a ridiculous hope. Her last chance for any kind of peace had disappeared over a year ago with the marriage of another man.

She decided to accompany her aunt to the library one morning, despite the fact that she felt not only nauseous but even dizzy at breakfast, and even though her aunt urged her to go back to bed for an hour. She would feel better for a little fresh air, she replied.

She did not feel better. She sat with a newspaper while her aunt chose a book, but she did not read even the headlines. She was too busy imagining the humiliation should she vomit in such a public place. She mastered the urge as she had done on every previous occasion, even in the privacy of her own rooms.

But a wave of dizziness took her as they reached the door on their way out. It was so strong that her aunt noticed and became alarmed. She took Helena's arm and Helena unashamedly leaned on her for support. She drew a few deep breaths of the cold outside air, her eyes half closed. And then her aunt spoke.

"Mr. Downes," she called, her voice breathless with distress. "Oh, Mr. Downes, might we impose upon you for a few minutes, I wonder? My niece is unwell."

Helena's eyes snapped open. There he was, tall and broad and immaculately groomed and frowning at her as if he were quite out of humor. He of all people! There was suddenly another wave of nausea to be fought.

Chapter Seven

❖

She pushed away from her aunt's side and stood upright. "I am quite well, I thank you," she said. "Good morning, Mr. Downes."

The effect of her proud posture and brisk words was quite marred by the fact that she swayed on the spot and would perhaps have fallen if Mrs. Cross had not grasped her arm and Edgar had not lunged forward to grab her by the waist.

"I am *quite well*," she said testily. "You may unhand me, sir."

"You are not well, Helena," her aunt insisted mildly. "Mr. Downes, *may* we impose upon you to call us a hackney cab?"

"No!" Lady Stapleton said as Edgar looked back over his shoulder toward the road. "Not a hackney cab. Not a carriage of any sort. I shall walk home. The fresh air will feel good. Thank you for your concern, Mr. Downes, but we need not detain you. My aunt's arm will be quite sufficient for my needs."

She was attempting her characteristic mocking smile, but it looked ghastly in combination with parchment white face and lips. The foolish woman was obviously trying to defy an early winter chill.

"I shall summon a hackney cab, ma'am," he said and turned away from her in order to hail one.

"I shall vomit if I have to set foot inside a carriage," she said from behind him. "There. Is that what you wanted, Mr. Downes? To hear me admit something so very ungenteel?"

"My dear Helena," her aunt said, "Mr. Downes is just being—"

"Mr. Downes is just being his usual overbearing self," Lady Stapleton said. "If you must offer your assistance, sir, give me your arm and escort me home. I can lean more heavily on yours than I could on Letty's."

"Helena, my dear." Mrs. Cross sounded shocked. "Mr. Downes probably has business elsewhere."

"Then he can be late," her niece retorted, taking Edgar's offered arm and leaning much of her weight on it. "Oh, I do wish I had gone to Italy with the Povises. How tiresome to be in England when it is so cold and sunless and cheerless."

"I have no business that cannot be delayed, ma'am," Edgar told Mrs. Cross. "I shall escort you home, Lady Stapleton, and then go to fetch a physician if you will tell me which. I suppose you have not consulted him lately." It was a statement rather than a question.

"How kind of you, sir," Mrs. Cross said.

"I do not consult a physician every time I am subjected to an overheated library and half faint from the stuffiness," Lady Stapleton said. "I shall be quite myself in a moment."

But she was very far from being herself even five minutes later. She continued to lean heavily on his arm and walked rather slowly along the street. She did not speak again, even to contradict Mrs. Cross, who proceeded to tell Edgar that her niece had not been in the best of health for some little while. By the time they came in sight of her house, her eyes were half closed and her footsteps lagged more than ever.

"Perhaps, ma'am," Edgar suggested to Mrs. Cross, "you could go ahead to knock on the door and have it open by the time Lady Stapleton arrives there." And without warning to his flagging companion, he stopped, released her arm, and scooped her up into his arms.

She spoke then while her one arm came about his neck and her head dropped to his shoulder. "Damn you, Edgar," she said, reminding him of how she had sworn at him on a previous occasion. "Damn you. I suppose you were waiting outside that library for the express purpose of humiliating me. How I hate you." But she did not struggle to be set down.

"Your effusive expressions of gratitude can wait until you are feeling more the thing," he said.

The flat-nosed pugilist was in the hall and looked to be bracing himself to take his mistress in his own arms. Edgar swept by him with hardly a glance and carried his burden upstairs. She was certainly no light weight. He was thankful when he saw Mrs. Cross outside Lady Stapleton's bedchamber, holding open the door. Had she been ascending the stairs behind them, he might have forgotten that he was not supposed to know where the lady's bedchamber was.

He set her down on the bed and stood back while her aunt removed her bonnet and a maid, who had rushed in behind them, drew off her half boots. She was still terribly pale.

"Who is your physician?" he asked.

"I have none." She opened her eyes and looked up at him. Some of her hair had come loose with the bonnet. The richness of its chestnut waves only served to make her face look more colorless. "I have no need of physicians, Mr. Downes. I need a warm drink and a rest. I daresay I shall see you at Lady Carew's musical evening tonight."

"Oh, I think not, Helena," Mrs. Cross said. "I will send a note around. The marchioness will understand."

"You need a physician," Edgar said.

"And you may go to the devil, sir," she said sharply. "Might I expect to be granted the privacy of my own room? It is not seemly for you to be standing there looking at me here, is it?" The old mockery was back in both her face and her voice. It was the very room and the very bed, of course . . .

"When you are feeling better, Helena," Mrs. Cross said with gentle gravity, "you will wish to apologize to Mr. Downes. He has been extraordinarily kind to us this morning, and there is no impropriety with both Marie and me here, too. We will leave you to Marie's care now. Sir, will you come to the drawing room for tea or coffee—or something stronger, perhaps?"

"Thank you, ma'am," he said, turning toward the door, "but I really do have business elsewhere. I shall call tomorrow morning, if I may, to ask how Lady Stapleton does."

Lady Stapleton, he saw when he glanced back at the bed before leaving the room, was lying with her eyes closed and a contemptuous smile curling her lip.

"I am worried about her," Mrs. Cross said after he had closed the door. "She is not herself. She has always had so much restless energy. Now she seems merely restless."

"Would *you* like me to summon a physician, ma'am?" he asked.

"Against Helena's wishes?" she said, raising her eyebrows and laughing. "You do not know my niece, Mr. Downes. She was unpardonably rude to you this morning. I do apologize for her. I am sure she will do so for herself when she feels better and remembers a few of the things she said to you."

Edgar doubted it. "I understand that Lady Stapleton prides herself on her independence, ma'am," he said. "She was embarrassed to have to accept my assistance this morning. No apology is necessary."

They were in the hall already and the manservant, looking his usual surly self, was waiting to open the door onto the street.

"You are gracious, sir," Mrs. Cross said.

He wished she would see a physician, Edgar thought as he strode along the street in an effort not to be quite impossibly late for a meeting he had arranged with a business associate. She was not the type of woman to be always having the vapors and relying upon men to support her to the nearest sofa. She had hated having to accept his help this morning. She had even damned him—and called him by his first name. Her indisposition was very real, and it had been going on for some time if her aunt was to be believed.

He was worried about her.

And then he frowned and caught the thought. *Worried* about her? About Lady Stapleton, who meant nothing to him? How had they expressed it between them during that evening when they had been waltzing? They were not adversaries or friends or lovers. They were nothing. They could be nothing, because there had been that night.

But there had been that night. He had known her body with thorough intimacy. He had known exhilarating and blazing passion with her.

Yes, he supposed she was *something*. Not anything that could be put into words, but something. Because there had been that night.

And so he was worried about her.

She had allowed Marie to undress her and tuck her into bed. She had allowed her aunt back into her room to draw the curtains across the window and to send for a hot drink of weak tea—the thought of chocolate or coffee was just too nauseating. She had allowed them both to fuss— though she hated people fussing over her.

And now she had been left alone to sleep. She felt as far from sleep as she had ever felt. She lay staring up at the large silk rosette that formed the peak of the canopy over her bed. She could not believe how foolish she was. She was stunned by her own naivete.

Although her husband had been fifty-four when she married him and sixty-one when he died, he had been a vigorous man. He had had her almost nightly for the first year and with frequency after that, almost to the end. She had never conceived. She had come to believe that the fault was in herself. Although Christian had had only the one son, she had been told that his first wife had had an appalling number of stillbirths and miscarriages.

The possibility of conception had not occurred to her when she had lain with Edgar Downes—either before or during or after. Not even when she had begun to feel persistently unwell.

She was careless about her own cycle. Her monthly flow, that great nuisance to which all women were subjected, almost always took her by surprise. She had no idea if she was strictly regular or not. She was one of the fortunate women who were not troubled by either pain or discomfort or a heavy flow.

And so for a number of weeks she had allowed symptoms so obvious that they were like a hard fist jabbing at her chin to pass her by unnoticed. Even now, when she set her mind to it, she could not remember when her last flow had been. She was almost sure there had been none for a while—none since that night, anyway. She was almost sure enough to say that she was quite certain. Oh, yes, of course she was certain. And that had been well over a month ago.

She had been feeling lethargic and nauseated—especially in the mornings. Her breasts had been feeling tender to the touch.

As she stared upward, strong suspicion turned unwillingly to certainty—and to a mindless, clawing terror. She closed her eyes as the canopy began to swing about her—and then opened them again. Dizziness was only worsened when one closed one's eyes. She drew deep breaths, held them, and released them slowly through her mouth.

At the age of six-and-thirty she was with child.

She was pregnant.

She was going to swell up to a grotesque enormity just like a young bride. And then there was going to be a baby. A child. A person. For her to nurture.

No.

No, she could not do it. She could not face the embarrassment. Or the shame. Though she did not care the snap of two fingers for the shame. But the embarrassment! She was six-and-thirty. She had been a widow for ten years. If the *ton* suspected that she occasionally took lovers—and her carelessness of strict propriety had made that almost inevitable—then they would guess, too, that she was worldly-wise and knowledgeable enough to take care of herself. It was unpardonably gauche to allow oneself to be impregnated, especially when one did not have a live husband upon whose paternity to foist the love child.

She would be the laughingstock.

She did not care about that. Why should she care what people thought about her? She had not cared for a long time.

Her terror had little to do with either shame or embarrassment. It had everything to do with the fact that there was going to be a *baby*. A child who was half hers and would come from her body. A child she would be expected to nurse and to love and to teach.

She had involved someone else, drawn someone else into her own darkness. A child. An innocent.

Her mind reached frantically about. If she searched carefully for a good home, if she gave the baby up at birth, if she was careful never to see it again, never to let it know who or what its mother was, would the child have a chance?

But she could not think clearly. She had only just realized the truth, though it had been staring her in the face for some time. He had stopped a short distance from the house and taken her totally by surprise by picking her up and carrying her the rest of the way. She had felt the strength of his arms and the sturdiness of his body—and she had known in a blinding flash the nature of her obsession with him. Her body had been speaking for a few weeks but her mind had not been listening. She had this man's child growing inside her.

And so she had damned him and would have used worse language on him if she had had the energy.

Where would she go? She closed her eyes and found to her relief that the dizziness had gone. Scotland? Her cousins were respectable people. They would not appreciate the notion of entertaining a pregnant woman whose husband had died ten years ago. Italy? She could find the Povises and their party. If she told the story well enough, they would be amused by it. They were worldly enough to accept that such things happened.

She could not tell this story amusingly. There was a *child* involved. An innocent.

Where, then? Somewhere else in Europe? Somewhere here in England?

She could not think straight. She needed to sleep. She was mortally tired. If she could but sleep, she could clear her head and then think and plan rationally. If she could but sleep . . .

But she kept seeing Edgar Downes standing beside her bed, looking even more massive and forbidding than usual in his caped greatcoat, his booted feet set apart on her carpet, his face frowning down at her as he suggested fetching a physician.

And more alarmingly, she kept seeing him above her on the bed, his weight pressing her down, his hot seed gushing deep inside her. She kept feeling herself being impregnated.

She hated him. She did not blame him for anything. It had been all her fault. She had seduced him and had taken no precautions to avoid the consequences. But she hated him anyway.

He of all people must never know the truth. She would never be able to live with that humiliation. He would probably proceed to take charge, to send her somewhere where she could bear the child in comfort and secrecy. He would probably find a home for it. He would probably support it until it was adult and he could find it suitable employment. He would see her as just a weak woman who could not possibly manage alone.

He must never find out. He was not going to organize the life of *her* child. He was not going to take her child away from her or lift from her shoulders the responsibility of caring for it. It was her child. It was inside her body. Now. And not *it*. He. Or she. A real person.

She was biting her upper lip. After a while she tasted blood. She did not sleep.

* * *

Lady Stapleton and Mrs. Cross were not at the Carews' musical evening. Mrs. Cross had sent a note making their excuses, the marchioness explained when someone noted their absence. Lady Stapleton was indisposed.

It was only surprising that most of them remained healthy in such dreary weather, someone remarked.

Fanny Grainger had mentioned seeing Lady Stapleton at the library looking quite ill, Lady Grainger reported.

She had been looking not quite herself for a few weeks, the Countess of Thornhill said. Poor lady. Some winter chills were very hard to shake.

But look at the gowns she wore, Mrs. Turner remarked— or rather did not wear, her tone implied. It was no wonder she took chills.

No one picked up that particular conversational cue.

"I must pay her a call," Cora Kneller announced in the carriage on the way home. "I wonder if she has seen a physician. At least she is fortunate to have Mrs. Cross to tend to her. Mrs. Cross is a very amiable and sensible lady. I like her excessively."

"I shall come with you, Cora," her brother said.

"Oh good." She looked only pleased and not even mildly suspicious, as Lord Francis did. "I will not need your escort then, Francis. You may take the children to the park."

"They will probably take me, my love," he said. "But I shall allow myself to be dragged along."

And so Edgar made his promised morning call in company with his sister. He hoped that Lady Stapleton would have kept to her bed so that they might make their inquiries of Mrs. Cross and spend just a short while in conversation with her. But when they were shown up to the drawing room, it was to find both ladies there.

Lady Stapleton was looking more herself. There was little color in her cheeks, but she was looking composed and was dressed with her usual elegance. She even favored Edgar with her usual mocking smile as she greeted him. He and Cora were invited to have a seat and Mrs. Cross rang for tea.

"I was quite disturbed to hear last evening that you were indisposed," Cora said. "I can see for myself this morning that you are still not quite the thing. I do hope you have consulted a physician."

Lady Stapleton smiled at Edgar. "I have not," she said in her velvet voice. "I do not believe in physicians. But thank you for your concern, Lady Francis. And for yours, sir."

Edgar said nothing. He merely inclined his head.

"Letty tells me that I owe you an apology," she said. "She tells me I was rude to you yesterday. I cannot remember saying anything I did not mean, but perhaps I was feeling ill enough to say something to offend. I do beg your pardon."

"Yesterday?" Cora said with bright curiosity. "Did you see Lady Stapleton yesterday, Edgar, and said nothing last evening when we were discussing her absence? How provoking of you!"

"Ah, but doubtless Mr. Downes was too modest to admit to his own gallantry," Lady Stapleton said, her eyes mocking him. "I leaned heavily on his arm all the way home from the library, and he actually carried me the last few yards and all the way upstairs to my bedchamber. My aunt was with us, I hasten to add. Your brother has amazing strength, Lady Francis. I weigh a ton."

"Oh, Edgar." Cora looked at him curiously. "How thoughtful of you. And you did not say a word about it. I am not surprised that you wished to come to pay your respects today. But *you* are quite well, ma'am?" She turned her attention to Mrs. Cross.

The two of them proceeded to discuss Lady Stapleton's health almost as if the lady herself was not present. Mrs. Cross was worried because her niece had been under the weather for a week or more—yes, definitely more—but refused to seek a cure. She was ill enough each morning to be quite unable to eat any breakfast and her energy seemed to flag several times each day. She had come near to fainting on more than one occasion. And such behavior was quite unlike her.

Lady Stapleton kept her gaze on Edgar while they spoke, a look of mocking amusement in her eyes.

"I know just what it is like to be unable to eat breakfast," Cora said. "I sympathize with you, Lady Stapleton. It happened to me during the early months when I was expecting all four of my children. And yet breakfast has always been my favorite meal."

Lady Stapleton raised both eyebrows, but continued to look at Edgar. "Goodness me," she said. "We will be embarrassing Mr. Downes. I do believe he is blushing."

He was not blushing, but he was feeling remarkably uncomfortable. Only Cora would speak so indelicately in mixed company.

"Oh, Edgar will not mind," Cora said. "Will you, Edgar? But of course in my case, Lady Stapleton, it was a natural effect of my condition and passed off within a month or two. So did the dreadful tiredness. I do hate being tired during the day. But in your case such symptoms are unnatural and should be confided to a physician. It is unmannerly of me to press you on the issue, however, when I am not a relative or even a particularly close acquaintance. I am a concerned acquaintance, though."

"Thank you," Lady Stapleton said. "You are kind."

The conversation moved on to a more general discussion of health and by natural progressions through the weather and Christmas and some of the more attractive shops on Oxford Street.

Edgar did not participate. His discomfort had turned to something more extreme, though he was trying to tell himself not to be so foolish. She was his age, she had once told him. As far as he knew, she had never had children, though she had been married for a number of years and had admitted to numerous lovers since her widowhood. Was it possible for a woman to have a child at the age of six-and-thirty? Foolish question. Of course it was possible. He knew women who had borne children at an even more advanced age. But a first child? Was it possible? After years of barrenness or else years of careful guarding against such a thing?

It surely was not possible. How she would laugh at him if she knew the suspicions that were rushing their course through his brain. Just because Cora had compared the early months of her pregnancies with Lady Stapleton's illness. What an absurdity for him to take the extra step of making the direct comparison.

But then Cora did not know—and in her innocence would not even suspect—that the lady had had a lover just over a month ago. Neither would her aunt suspect it.

"And what are your plans for Christmas, Mr. Downes?" Mrs. Cross asked him suddenly.

He stared at her blankly for a moment. "I will be going down to Mobley Abbey, ma'am, to spend the holiday with my father," he said.

"There will be quite a house party there," Cora said. "Francis and I and the children will be going, of course, and several of our friends. I am looking forward to it excessively."

"And Mr. Downes's future bride will be there, Letty," Lady Stapleton said, looking at Edgar as he spoke. "Did you not know that he has come to town for the express purpose of choosing a bride from the *ton*? He is to take her to Mobley Abbey to present her to his father for approval. A Christmas bride. Is that not romantic?" She made it sound anything but.

This time Edgar really did flush.

"Now you are the one to have embarrassed Mr. Downes, Helena," Mrs. Cross said reproachfully. "But there is nothing to be embarrassed about, sir. I wish you joy of your quest. Any young lady would be fortunate indeed to be your choice."

"Thank you, ma'am," he said and noticed with some relief that Cora was getting to her feet to take her leave. He stood up and the other two ladies did likewise. He made his bow to them and then waited while Cora thought of something else she must tell Mrs. Cross before they left. He looked closely at Lady Stapleton, who smiled back at him.

Are you with child? he wanted to blurt out. But it was a ridiculous notion. Bizarre. She was a thirty-six-year-old widow. With whom he happened to have had sexual relations—twice—just over a month before. And now she was suffering from morning sickness and unusual tiredness and fainting spells when she tried to push on with her usual daily activities. And she was unwilling to see a physician.

He felt dizzy himself for a moment.

He could not imagine a worse disaster. It could not possibly be. But what other explanation could there be? Morning sickness. Tiredness. Even he was aware of those two symptoms as very characteristic of pregnancy in its early stages.

He followed his sister downstairs with some longing for the fresh air beyond the front door—even if it was chilly, damp, windblown air. He had to think. He had to convince himself of his own foolishness. But was it more foolish to think that it might be or to imagine that it could not possibly be?

Was she pregnant?

By him?

Chapter Eight

⁕

Helena had decided to stay in town over Christmas. After a few days of suppressed terror and near panic, she calmed down sufficiently to decide that she had to plan carefully, but that there was no immediate hurry. She was a little over one month pregnant. Soon the nausea and the tiredness would pass off. Her condition would not be evident for a few months yet. She need not dash off somewhere in a blind panic. There was time to think and to plan.

Soon most of her acquaintances would disperse to their various country estates for the holiday. Some would remain and others would arrive, but the people she most wanted to be rid of would be gone. Edgar Downes would be gone and so would that bold, curiously appealing sister of his and her family. They were taking a number of other people with them to Mobley Abbey—the Carews, the Bridgwaters, the Thornhills, the Greenwalds. And very probably the Graingers, too.

She felt sorry for Fanny Grainger, though it was not normally in her nature to feel sorry for people. Perhaps she pitied the girl because she was reminded of herself at that age, or a little younger. So unhappy and fatalistic. So very obedient. Like a lamb to the slaughter, to use the old cliché. Fanny would be quite suffocated by Edgar Downes.

She forced herself to attend most of the social functions to which she was invited—and she was invited everywhere—while she was careful to curtail her morning activities and to keep most of her afternoons free so that she might rest.

She succeeded in feeling and looking a little better than she had with the result that her aunt, though not quite satisfied, stopped pressing her to consult a physician.

Sooner or later, Helena thought, she was going to have to see a doctor. How embarrassing that was going to be. But she would think of it when the time came—after Christmas. By then she would have decided where to go and exactly what to do with the child. Perhaps she would keep it, she thought sometimes, and live somewhere on the Continent with it, thumbing her nose at public opinion. Probably she would give it up to a carefully chosen family and disappear from its life. She was not worthy of being a mother.

She took care to think of the child as *it*. Terror could return in a hurry when she began to think of its personhood and to wonder about its gender and appearance. Would it be a boy who would look like *him*? She would shake off the speculations. She could not imagine a real live child, born of her own body, in helpless need of her arms and her breasts and her love.

She was incapable of love. She knew nothing of nurturing.

Oh, yes, she rather thought she would give up the child. *It.*

She saw Edgar Downes frequently. They became very skilled at avoiding each other, at sitting far from each other at dinner and supper tables, at joining different conversational or card-playing groups, at sitting on opposite sides of a room during concerts. They never ignored each other—that might have been as noticeable to a society hungry for something to gossip about as if they had been constantly in each other's pocket. When they did come face-to-face, they smiled politely and he asked about her health and she assured him that she was quite well, thank you.

They watched each other. Not with their eyes—a strange notion. They were *aware* of each other. She was sure it worked both ways. She felt that he watched her, though whenever she glanced at him to confirm the feeling, she was almost always wrong. When he asked about her health, she sensed that the question was not a mere courtesy. For days after he had carried her to her bed and then called on her with his sister, she had half expected him to return with a physician. It was just the sort of thing she would expect him to do—take charge, impose his will upon someone who had no wish to be beholden to him in any way, do what he thought was best regardless of her feelings.

And she was always aware of him. She could not rid herself of the obsession and in the end stopped trying. Soon he would be gone and she would not have daily reminders of him. Within eight months his child would be gone— from her womb and from her life. She would have her own life, her own particular hell, back again.

She thought of him constantly—not sexual thoughts. They would have been understandable and not particularly disturbing. She kept thinking of him escorting her home, his arm solid and steady beneath her own, his pace reduced to fit hers. She kept thinking of him lifting her into his arms and carrying her into the house and up two flights of stairs as if she weighed no more than a feather. She kept thinking of his near-silence when he had called with Lady Francis, of that frowning, intent look with which he had regarded her, as if he were genuinely worried about her health. She kept imagining herself leaning into his strength, abandoning all the burdens of her life to him, letting him deal with them for her. She kept thinking of herself sleeping in his arms. Just sleeping—nothing else. Total relaxation and oblivion. Safety. Peace.

She hated the feeling. She hated the weakness of her thoughts. And so she hated him even as she was obsessed by him.

By the middle of December she was impatient for his departure. He had come to choose a bride. He had chosen her long ago. Let him take her to his father, then, and begin a grand Christmas celebration. She could not understand why he delayed. She resented the delay. She wanted to be free of him.

She wanted desperately to be free. And she laughed contemptuously to herself whenever she caught herself in the thought. Had she forgotten that there would never be freedom, either in this life or the next? Had hope somehow been reborn in her even as she knew that despair was the only end of any hope? She had dulled her sensibilities to reality before that dreadful evening when desperate need had tempted her to seduce Edgar Downes. Perhaps, she sometimes thought, she would have fought the temptation harder if she had had even an inkling of the fact that he would not be easily forgotten. That he would impregnate her.

She waited with mingled patience and impatience for him to be gone.

Edgar had always thought of himself as a decisive man, both by nature and training. He had never been a procrastinator—until now.

He delayed in making his intentions clear to Miss Grainger and her parents. And he delayed in speaking with Lady Stapleton and putting his suspicions into words. As a result, with only two weeks to go until Christmas, he suddenly found himself in a dreadful coil indeed.

He was at a dance at Mrs. Parmeter's—she and her husband were newly arrived in London to take in the Christmas parties. He had just finished dancing a set of country dances with the Duchess of Bridgwater and had joined a group that included Sir Webster. The conversation, inevitably he supposed considering the date, centered about Christmas and everyone's plans for the holiday.

"Your father is to entertain quite a large house party at Mobley Abbey, I hear, Mr. Downes," Mrs. Parmeter said, smiling at him with marked condescension. As a new arrival she was not as accustomed as most of her other guests to finding herself entertaining a mere merchant.

"Yes, indeed, ma'am," he said. "He is delighted that there will be such a large number, children included. He is passionately fond of children."

Sir Webster was coughing against the back of his hand and shifting his weight from foot to foot. "I must commend you on the number of guests with whom you have filled your drawing room, ma'am," he said.

"Yes." Mrs. Parmeter smiled graciously and vaguely. "And Sir Webster was telling us that he and his lady and *Miss Grainger* are to be among the guests, Mr. Downes," she said, placing particular emphasis on the one name. She raised her eyebrows archly. "Is there to be an interesting announcement during Christmas, sir?"

"Oh, I say." Sir Webster sounded suitably mortified. "I was merely saying, ma'am—"

"I am certainly hoping that Sir Webster and Lady Grainger and their daughter will be among my father's guests," Edgar said, aghast at what he was being forced into—as a businessman he had perfected the art of avoiding being maneuvered into anything he had not pondered and decided for himself. At least he had the sense to leave the woman's final question alone.

"I am sure you are, sir," Mrs. Parmeter said. "You know, I suppose, that Lady Grainger's father is Baron Suffield?"

"Yes, indeed, ma'am," Edgar said.

She turned her conversation on other members of the group and soon enough Edgar found himself with Sir Webster, a little apart from the rest of them.

"I say—" that gentleman began. "Mrs. Parmeter totally misunderstood me, you know. I was merely saying—" But he could not seem to remember what it was he had been merely saying.

Perhaps, Edgar thought, it was as well to have his hand forced. He had only two weeks left in which to keep his promise. There was no one more suitable—or more available—than Miss Grainger. There was that young man of hers, of course—he should have found a way of dealing with that problem by now. And there was that other problem, too—but no. She appeared to have recovered from her indisposition whatever it had been, though she still seemed paler than he remembered her to have looked. He could not do better than Miss Grainger—not in the time allowed, at least. And perhaps he had carried the courtship rather too far to back off now without humiliating the girl and her family. Certainly the father seemed to expect a declaration.

"But my father would be delighted to entertain you and your wife and daughter at Mobley, sir," Edgar said, releasing the man from his well-deserved embarrassment. "And my sister and I would be delighted, too, if you would join us and other of our friends there for Christmas. If you have no other plans, that is. I realize that this is rather short notice."

"No," Sir Webster said quickly, "we have no other plans, sir. We were thinking of staying in town to enjoy the festivities. That was our plan when we came here. We were undecided whether to stay, too, for the Season. Fanny would enjoy it and it is time to bring her out, I suppose. It is difficult to part with a daughter, Mr. Downes. Very difficult. One wants all that is the best for her. We will accept your gracious invitation, sir. Thank you. And we will decide later about the Season."

There would be no Season if he came up to scratch, Edgar understood. And probably no Season if he did not, either. The Graingers were said to be too poor to afford such an expense. But he was not going to pick up the cue this time. He merely smiled and bowed and informed Sir Webster that Cora would write to their father tomorrow.

His father would read eagerly between the lines of that particular letter, he thought. Or perhaps not between the lines either. Cora would surely inform him that Miss Grainger was the one, that he might prepare to meet his future daughter-in-law within the fortnight.

Edgar felt half robbed of breath. But it was a deed that must be done. It was time to stop dragging his feet. Young Jack Sperling could not be helped. This was the real world. And the girl's age could not be helped. Young ladies were married to older men all the time. He would be kind to her and generous to her. He would treat her with affection. So would his father and Cora. She would be taken to the bosom of their family with enthusiasm, he did not doubt. She would learn to settle to a marriage that could be no worse than thousands of marriages that were contracted every year. And he would settle, too. He would enjoy having children of his own. Like his father, he was fond of children.

Children of his own. There—that thought again. That nagging suspicion. His eyes found out Lady Stapleton. She was at the other side of the room—without ever looking at each other for any length of time, they always seemed to maneuver matters so—talking and laughing with Mr. Parmeter and the Earl of Thornhill. She was wearing the scarlet gown she had worn that first night—the one with all the tiny buttons down the back. It must have taken him all of five minutes. . . .

She looked healthy enough and cheerful enough. She looked pale. She did not look as if she felt nauseated. But this was the evening rather than the morning. Besides, Cora had said that the feeling passed after a couple of months. It was two months since . . . Well, it was two months. She did not look larger. But it was only two months.

It could not possibly be. Beautiful and alluring as she looked, it was a mature beauty and a mature allure. But she was only six-and-thirty. She was still in her fertile years. She had never had a child before—at least he did not believe so. Why would she conceive now? But why not?

Such conflicting thoughts had teemed in his head for the past two weeks. They had woven themselves into his dreams—when he had been able to sleep. They had kept him awake.

He caught her eye across the room, something that rarely happened. But instead of looking away from each other, both continued to look as if daring the other to be the first to lose courage. She raised one mocking eyebrow.

He despised indecisiveness. If there was one single factor that could keep a man from success in the business world, he had always found, it was just that—being indecisive, allowing misplaced caution and unformed worries to hold one back from action that one knew must be taken. He knew he must talk with her. And time was running out. He should already have left for Mobley. He must do so within the next few days.

He must talk to Lady Stapleton first. He did not want to—he would do almost anything to get out of doing so if he could. But he could not. Not if he was to know any peace of mind over Christmas. He walked across the center of the drawing room, empty now between sets, and she smiled that smile of hers to see him come. She did not turn away or even look away from him.

"Ma'am?" He bowed to her. "May I have the honor of dancing the next set with you?"

"But of course, Mr. Downes," she said. That low velvet voice of hers always jolted him, no matter how often he heard it. "It is a waltz, and I know you perform the steps well." She set her hand in his. It was quite cold.

"And how do you do, ma'am?" he asked her when they had taken their positions on the floor and waited for the music to begin.

"Very well, thank you, Mr. Downes." Her perfume brought back memories.

There was no dodging around it, he decided as the pianist began playing and he set his hand at the back of her waist and took her other in his own. And so he simply asked the question.

"Are you with child?" His voice was so low that he was not sure the sound of it would carry to her ears.

Clearly it did. She mastered her surprise almost instantly and smiled with brutal contempt. "You must think yourself one devil of a fine lover, Mr. Downes," she said. "Is it the factor by which you measure your success? Have you peopled Bristol with bastard children?"

But not quite instantly enough. For the merest fraction of a second—had he not been looking for it he would certainly have missed it—there had been something other than contempt in her eyes. There had been fright, panic.

"No," he said. "But I believe I have got you with child." Now that the words were out, now that he had seen that fleeting reaction, he felt curiously calm. Almost cold.

"Do you?" she said. "And do you realize how absurd your assumption is, sir? Do you know how old I am?"

"You told me once," he said. "I do not believe you are past your childbearing years. Are you?"

"You are impertinent, sir," she said. "You dare ask such a question of a lady, of a virtual stranger?"

"A stranger whom I bedded two months ago," he said. "One who is to bear my child seven months from now, if I am not much mistaken."

She smiled at him—a bright social smile, as much for the benefit of the other dancers and watchers as for his, he guessed. "You, Mr. Downes," she said, "may go to hell."

"But I notice," he said, "that you have not said no, it is not true. I notice such things, ma'am. I have been and still am a lawyer. Is it that you are afraid to lie? Let me hear it. Yes or no. Are you with child?"

"But I am not on the witness stand, Mr. Downes," she said. "I do not have to answer your questions. And I scorn to react to your charge that I am afraid to answer. I will not answer. I choose not to."

"Have you seen a physician?" he asked her.

She looked into his eyes and smiled. "You are a divine waltzer, Mr. Downes," she said. "I believe it is because you are so large. One instinctively trusts your lead."

"Do you still suffer from morning sickness?" he asked.

"Of course," she said, "it is not just your size, is it? One cannot imagine enjoying a waltz with an ox. You have a superior sense of rhythm." Her smile turned wicked.

"I shall find out for myself tomorrow," he said. "You once invited me to escort you to one of the galleries. I accept. Tomorrow morning will be the time. We have arranged it this evening. You may tell Mrs. Cross that if you will. If you will not, I will tell her when I come for you that I have come to discuss your pregnancy."

"Damn you, Mr. Downes," she said sharply. "You have the manners of an ox even if not the dancing skills of one."

"Tomorrow morning," he said. "And if you have any idea of bringing your aunt with you, be warned that we will have our frank talk anyway. I assume she does not know?"

"Damn you to hell," she said.

"Since we are dancing for pleasure," he said, "we might as well concentrate on our enjoyment in silence for the rest of the set. I believe we have nothing further to say to each other until tomorrow."

"How your underlings must hate you," she said. "I am not your underling, Mr. Downes. I will not be overborne by you. And I will not be blackmailed by you."

"Will you not?" he said. "You will tell Mrs. Cross the truth, then, and have that servant of yours refuse me admittance tomorrow morning? I believe I might enjoy pitting my strength against his."

"Damn you," she said again. "Damn you. Damn you."

Neither of them spoke after that. When the music drew to an end, he escorted her to her aunt, stayed to exchange civilities with that lady for a few minutes, and then took himself off to the other side of the room.

He felt rather as if he had been tossed into the air by that ox she had spoken of and then trodden into the ground by it after landing. It was true, then. He could no longer lull himself with the conviction that his suspicions were absurd. She had not admitted the truth, but the very absence of such an admission was confirmation enough.

She was with child. By him. He felt as dizzy, as disoriented, as if the idea had only now been planted in his brain.

What the devil were they going to do?

And why the devil did he need to pose that question to himself?

She damned him to hell and back throughout a sleepless night. She broke a favorite trinket dish when she picked it up from her dressing table and hurled it against the door. She considered calling his bluff and telling her aunt the truth—though she had hoped to go away somewhere alone so that no one need know—and then instructing Hobbes to deny him entry.

But he would come tomorrow morning even if she told her aunt and even if Hobbes tried to prevent him. She had great faith in Hobbes's strength and determination, but she had a nasty feeling that neither would prevail against Edgar Downes. He would come and drag the truth from her and proceed to take charge of the situation no matter what she did.

She would not dance to his tune. Oh, she would not. She did not doubt that he would plan everything down to the smallest detail. She did not doubt that he would find her a safe and comfortable nest in which to hide during the remainder of her confinement and that he would find the child a respectable home afterward. He would do it all with professional efficiency and confidentiality. No one would ever suspect the truth. No one would ever know that the two of them had been more to each other than casual social acquaintances. And he would pay for everything. She did not doubt that either. Every bill would be sent to him.

She would not allow it to happen. She would shout the truth from the rooftops before she would allow him to protect her reputation and her safety. She would keep her child and take it with her wherever she went rather than allow him neatly to hide its very existence.

And yet, she thought, mocking herself, she did not even have the courage to tell her aunt. She would go out with him tomorrow morning, two acquaintances visiting a gallery together, a perfectly respectable thing to do, and she would allow herself to be browbeaten.

Never!

She would fight Edgar Downes to the death if necessary. The melodramatic thought had her lip curling in scorn again.

She mentioned to her aunt at the breakfast table that Mr. Downes would be calling later to escort her to the Royal Academy. He had mentioned wanting to go there while they had danced the evening before and she had commented that it was one of her favorite places. And so he had asked to escort her there this morning.

"I have promised to show him all the best paintings," she said.

Mrs. Cross looked closely at her. "Are you feeling well enough, Helena?" she asked. "I have become so accustomed to your staying at home in the mornings that I have arranged to go out myself."

"Splendid," Helena said. "You are going shopping?"

"With a few other ladies," Mrs. Cross said. "Will you mind?"

"I hardly need a chaperone at my age, Letty," Helena said. "I believe Mr. Downes is a trustworthy escort."

"Absolutely," her aunt agreed. "He is an exceedingly pleasant man. I was quite sharp with Mrs. Parmeter last evening when she remarked on his background as if she expected all of us to begin to tear him apart. Mr. Downes is more the gentleman than many born to the rank, I told her. I believe he has a soft spot for you, Helena. It is a shame that as his father's only son he feels duty bound to marry a young lady so that he may set up his nursery and get an heir for that estate near Bristol. The Grainger girl will not suit him, though she is pretty and has a sweet enough nature. She has not had the time or opportunity to develop enough character."

"And I have?" Helena smiled. "You think he would be better off with me, Letty? Poor Mr. Downes."

"You would lead him a merry dance, I daresay," Mrs. Cross said. "But I believe he would be equal to the task. However, he must choose a young lady."

"How lowering," Helena said with a laugh. "But I would not be young again for a million pounds, Letty. I shudder to remember the girl I was."

She would gain one advantage over Mr. Edgar Downes this morning at least, she thought while she began to talk about other things with her aunt. She would confront him on home ground. Her aunt was going out for the morning. That would mean that she and Mr. Downes need not leave the house. She would not have to be smilingly polite lest other people in the streets or at the gallery take note. She could shout and scream and throw things to her heart's content. She could use whatever language suited her mood.

Only one thing she seemed incapable of doing—at least she had been last night. She could not seem to lie to Edgar Downes. She could get rid of him in a moment if only she could do that. But she scorned to lie. She would withhold the truth if she could, but she would not lie.

She went upstairs after breakfast to change her dress and have her hair restyled. She wanted to look and feel her very best before it came time to cope with her visitor.

She waited for an hour in the drawing room before he came. She had instructed Hobbes to show him up when he arrived.

Chapter Nine

Edgar was rather surprised to be admitted to her house without question. The manservant, his face quite impassive, led the way upstairs, knocked on the drawing room door, opened it, and announced him.

She was there alone, standing by the fireplace, looking remarkably handsome in a dark green morning gown of simple, classic design. Her chin was lifted proudly. She was unsmiling, the customary mocking expression absent from her face. She was not ready for the outdoors.

"Thank you, Hobbes," she said. "Good morning, Mr. Downes."

Her face was pale. There were shadows beneath her eyes. Perhaps, he thought, she had slept as little as he. The thought that this proud, elegant woman was pregnant with his child was still dizzying. It still threatened to rob him of breath.

"I suppose it was too much to expect," he said, "that you would not somehow twist the situation to impose some sort of command over it. We are not to view portraits and landscapes?"

"Not today or any other day, Mr. Downes," she said. "Not together at least. My aunt is from home. I would have had Hobbes deny you admittance but you would have made a scene. You are so ungenteel. If you have something to say that is more sensible than what you were saying last evening, please say it and then leave. I have other plans."

He could not help but admire her coolness even while he was irritated by it. Most women in her situation would be distraught and clinging and demanding to know his intentions.

"Thank you for offering," he said, walking farther into the room after removing his greatcoat—the servant had not offered to take it downstairs—and tossing it onto a chair. "I believe I will sit down. But do have a seat yourself, ma'am. I am gentleman enough to know that I may not sit until you do."

"You are impertinent, Mr. Downes," she said.

"But then I am also, of course," he said, gesturing toward the chair closest to her, "quite bourgeois, ma'am."

She sat and so did he. She was furious, he saw, though she would, of course, scorn to glare. She sat with her back ramrod straight and her jaw set in a hard line.

"You are with child," he said.

She said nothing.

"It is a reality that will not go away," he said. It had taken the whole of a sleepless night finally to admit that to himself. "It must be dealt with."

"Nothing in my life will be dealt with by you, Mr. Downes," she said. "I deal with my own problems, thank you very much. I believe this visit is at an end."

"I believe, ma'am," he said, "it is *our* problem."

"No!" Her nostrils flared and both her hands curled into fists in her lap. "You will not treat this as a piece of business, Mr. Downes, to be dealt with coldly and efficiently and then forgotten about. I will not have a quiet hideaway found for me or a discreet midwife. I will not have a decent, respectable home found for the child so that I may return to my usual life with no one the wiser. You may be expert at dominating your subordinates with that confident, commanding air of yours. You will not dominate me."

Good Lord!

He leaned back in his chair, set his elbows on the arms, and steepled his fingers beneath his chin. He stared at her for a long time before speaking.

"You realize, I suppose," he said at last, "what you have admitted to me." If there had been one thread of hope left in him, it was gone. On the whole, he was glad of it. He liked to have issues crystal clear in his mind.

There was a flush of color to her cheeks. But her expression did not change. She did not speak.

"You have misunderstood my character," he said. "There will be no hideaway, no decent home for the child away from his mother, no resumption of your old way of life, no sweeping of anything under the carpet. We will marry, of course."

Her head snapped back rather as if he had punched her on the chin. Her eyes widened and her eyebrows shot up. And then she laughed.

"Marry!" she said. "We will marry? You jest, sir, of course."

"I do not jest," he said. "Of course."

"Mr. Downes." All the old mockery was back in her face. No, it was more than mockery—it was open contempt. "Do you seriously imagine that *I* would marry *you*? You are presumptuous, sir. I bid you a good morning." She was on her feet.

"Sit down," he told her quietly and sat where he was, engaging in a silent battle of wills with her. He never lost such battles. This time, after a full minute of tension, he tacitly agreed to accept a compromise when she turned and crossed the room to the window. She stood with her back to him, looking out. He remained seated.

"I thank you for your gracious offer, Mr. Downes," she said, "but my answer is no. There. You have done the decent thing and I have been civil. We are even. Please leave now."

"We will marry by special license before going down to Mobley Abbey for Christmas," he said.

She laughed again. "Your Christmas bride," she said. "You are determined to have her one way or another, then? But have you not already invited Miss Grainger in that capacity? Do you have ambitions to set up a harem, Mr. Downes?"

He dared not think of that invitation to the Graingers. Not yet. Experience had taught him that only one sticky problem could be dealt with at a time. He was dealing with this one now.

"Better still," he said, "we could take the license with us and marry there. It would please my father."

"Your father would be quite ecstatic," she said, "to find that you had brought home a bride as old as yourself. He wants grandchildren, I do not doubt."

"And that is exactly what he will have, ma'am," he said.

He could see from the hunching of her shoulders that she had only just realized her mistake. Although she must have known for a lot longer than he, although she was carrying the child in her own womb, he supposed that the truth must seem as unreal to her as it did to him.

"It will be easier if you accept reality," he said. "If we both do. We had our pleasure of each other two months ago without a thought to the possible consequences. But there have been consequences. They are in the form of an innocent child who does not deserve the stigma of bastardy. We have created him or her. It is our duty to give him parents who are married to each other and to nurture him to the best of our ability. We have become rather unimportant as individuals, Lady Stapleton. There is someone else to whose whole life this issue is quite central—and yet that person is at the mercy of what is happening in this room this morning."

"Damn you," she said.

"Which would you prefer?" he asked her briskly. "To marry here or at Mobley? The choice is yours."

"How clever you are, Mr. Downes." She turned to look at him. "Giving the illusion of freedom of choice when you have me tied hand and foot and gagged, too. I will make no choice. I have not even said I will marry you. In my world, you know—it may be different with people of your class— a woman has to say that she does or that she will before her marriage can be declared valid. So I do still have some freedom, you see."

He got to his feet and walked toward her. But she held up both hands as he drew close.

"No," she said. "That is far enough. You are too tall and too large, Mr. Downes. I hate large men."

"Because you are afraid you will not have total mastery over them?" he said.

"For exactly that reason." Her voice was sharp. "I made a mistake two months ago. I rarely make mistakes. I chose the wrong man. You are too—too *big*. You suffocate me. Go away. I have been remarkably civil to you this morning. I can become ferociously uncivil when aroused. Go away." Her breathing was ragged. She was agitated.

"I am not going to hurt you," he told her. "I am not going to touch you against your will." He clasped his hands behind his back.

She laughed. "Are those the sentiments of an ardent bridegroom, Mr. Downes?" she said. "Do you speak only in the present tense or do your words have a more universal meaning? You would never touch me against my will? You would be facing an arid, celibate life, sir, unless you would take your ease with mistresses."

"I have a strong belief in marital fidelity," he said.

"How bourgeois!" She laughed again.

"Yes."

"Mr. Downes." Her arms dropped to her sides. Both the agitation and the contempt were gone from her face and she looked at him more earnestly than she had ever done before. Her face was pale again. "I cannot marry you. I cannot be a wife. I cannot be a mother."

He searched her eyes but they gave nothing away. They never did. This woman hid very effectively behind her many masks, he realized suddenly. He did not know her at all, even though he had had thorough sexual knowledge of her body.

"Why not?" he asked.

"Because." She smiled the old smile. "Because, Mr. Downes. Because."

"And yet," he said, "you are to be a mother whether you wish it or not. The deed is done and cannot be undone."

She closed her eyes and looked as if she were about to sway on her feet. But she mastered herself and opened her eyes again. "I will deal with it," she said. "I cannot keep the child. I cannot marry you. I would destroy both of you. Believe me, Mr. Downes. I speak the truth."

He frowned, trying to read her eyes again. But there were no depths to them. They were quite unreadable. "Who hurt you?" he asked her. He remembered asking her the question before.

She laughed. "No one," she said. "Absolutely no one, sir."

"I am going to be your husband," he said. "I would hope to be your companion and even your friend as well. There may be many years of life ahead for us."

"You are not going to be talked out of this, are you?" she said. "You are not going to take no for an answer. Are you?"

He shook his head.

"Well, then." Her head went back and both her eyes and her lips mocked him. "Behold your Christmas bride, Mr. Downes. It is a Christmas and a bride that you will come to regret, but we all choose our own personal hells with our eyes wide open, I have found. And it will happen at Mobley. I would see the ecstasy in your father's eyes as we tie the eternal knot." There was harsh bitterness in her voice.

He inclined his head to her. "I do not believe I could ever regret doing the right thing, ma'am," he said. "And before you can tell me how bourgeois a sentiment that is, let me forestall you. I believe we bourgeoisie have a firmer, less cynical commitment to decency and honor than some of the gentry and aristocracy. Though I daresay that like all generalizations there are almost as many exceptions as there are adherents to the rule."

"I will not allow you to dominate me," she said.

"I would not wish to dominate a wife," he told her.

"Or to touch me."

"As you wish," he said.

"I will make you burn for me, Edgar," she said. "But will not let you touch me."

"Perhaps," he said.

Her lip curled. "I cannot make you quarrel, can I?" she said. "I would love to have a flaming row with you, Mr. Downes. It is your power over me, perhaps, that you will not allow it."

"Perhaps," he agreed.

"Do you realize how frustrating it is," she asked him, "to quarrel with someone who will not quarrel back?"

"Probably as frustrating," he said, "as it is going to be to burn for you when you refuse to burn for me."

She smiled slowly at him. "I believe," she said, "that if I did not resent and hate you so much, Mr. Downes, I might almost like you."

He did not hate her or particularly resent her. He did not like the situation in which he found himself, but in all fairness he could not foist the blame entirely on her. It took two to create a child, and neither of them had been reluctant to engage in the activity that had left her pregnant. He did not like her. She was bitter and sharp-tongued and did nothing to hide her contempt for his origins. But there was something about her that excited him. There was her sexual allure, of course. He had no doubt that his frustrations would be very real indeed if she meant what she said. But it was not just a sexual thing. There was something challenging, stimulating about her. She would not be easy to manage, but he was not sure he wanted to manage her. She would never be a comfortable companion, but then comfort in companionship could become tedious. Life with her would never be tedious.

"Have I silenced you at last?" she asked. "Are you wounded? Are you struggling not to humiliate yourself by confessing that you *love* me?"

"I do not love you," he said quietly. "But you are to be my wife and to bear my child. I will try to respect and like you, ma'am. I will try to feel an affection for you. It will not be impossible, perhaps. We are to share a child. I will certainly love our child, as will you. We will have that to bring us together."

"Why, Mr. Downes," she said, "I do believe there is a streak of the romantic in you after all."

The door opened behind them.

"Oh," Mrs. Cross said, startled. "Mr. Downes is here with you. I am so sorry, Helena. I assumed you were alone. I wondered why you were back so soon."

"You need not leave, Aunt," Lady Stapleton said, moving past Edgar to take Mrs. Cross by the arm. She was smiling when she turned back to him. "You must make your curtsy to Mr. Downes, who is now my affianced husband. We are to marry at Mobley Abbey before Christmas."

Mrs. Cross's face was the picture of astonishment. She almost gaped at Edgar. He bowed to her.

"I have offered for Lady Stapleton's hand, ma'am," he told her, "and she has done me the great honor of accepting me."

"Oh, come now, Mr. Downes." Lady Stapleton sounded amused. "This is my aunt you are talking to. The truth is, Letty, that I am two months with child. Edgar and I became too—*ardent* one night before your return from the country and having learned of the consequences of that night, he has rushed here to make amends. He is going to make an honest woman of me. Wish us joy."

Mrs. Cross appeared speechless for a few moments. "I do," she said finally. "Oh, I do indeed. Pardon me, Helena, Mr. Downes, but I do not know quite what to say. I do wish you joy."

"Of course you do," Lady Stapleton said. "You commented just this morning, did you not, that Mr. Downes had a soft spot for me." Her eyes mocked him even as her aunt flushed and looked mortified. "It appears you were right."

"Ma'am." Edgar addressed himself to Mrs. Cross, ignoring the bitter levity of his betrothed's tone. "We will be marrying by special license at Mobley Abbey, as Lady Stapleton mentioned. My father and my sister will be in attendance, as well as a number of our friends. I would be honored if you would be there, too, and would remain to spend Christmas with us. My father would be honored."

"How kind of you, sir." The lady was recovering some of her composure. "How very kind. I would, of course, like to be at Helena's wedding. And I have no other plans for the holiday."

Edgar looked at Lady Stapleton. "There will perhaps be time to invite other members of your family or other particular friends if you wish," he said. "Is there anyone?"

"No," she said. "This is no grand wedding celebration we are planning, Edgar. This is a marriage of necessity."

"Your stepson is at Brookhurst only thirty miles from Mobley, is he not?" he said. "Perhaps—"

Her face became a mask of some strong emotion— horror, terror, revulsion, he could not tell which.

"No!" she said icily. "I said no, Mr. Downes. No! I will have my aunt with me. She will be family enough. She is the only relative I wish to acknowledge. But, yes, you must come, Letty. I will not be able to do this without you. I do not wish to do it at all, but Mr. Downes has been his usual obnoxious, domineering self. I shall lead him a merry dance, as you said I would if I ever married him, but he has been warned and has remained obdurate. On his own head be it, then. But you must certainly come to Mobley with me."

"Have you offered Mr. Downes a cup of tea, Helena?" her aunt asked, looking about her at the empty tables.

"No, I have not," her niece said. "I have been trying to get rid of him since he set foot inside the door. He will not leave."

"Helena!" her aunt said, looking mortified again. "Mr. Downes, do let me send for some tea or coffee."

"Thank you, ma'am." He smiled. "But I have other business to attend to. I shall see you both in my sister's drawing room this evening? I shall have the announcement made there and put in tomorrow morning's papers. Good day to you, Mrs. Cross. And to you, Lady Stapleton." He bowed to each of them as he retrieved his greatcoat.

"I must remember," Lady Stapleton said, "to start offering you tea whenever I set eyes on you, Edgar. It seems the only sure way to be rid of you."

He smiled at her as he let himself out of the room, feeling unexpectedly amused. For a mere moment there seemed to be an answering gleam in her own eyes.

His betrothed. Soon to be his wife. The mother of his child. He shook his head as he descended the stairs in an effort to clear it of that dizziness again.

E dgar was glad to get out again during the afternoon. He had arrived home to find both Cora and Francis there, having just returned from their usual morning outing with their children.

"Edgar," Cora had said, smiling brightly, "have you concluded all your business? Are you going to be ready to leave for Mobley tomorrow after tonight's farewell party? We met Lady Grainger and Miss Grainger in the park, did we not, Francis? They are extremely gratified to have been invited to Mobley. I have written to Papa to tell him—"

Cora's monologues could sometimes continue for a considerable length of time. Edgar had cut her off.

"Lady Stapleton and Mrs. Cross will be coming, too," he had told her and Francis. Francis's eyebrows had gone up.

"Are they?" Cora had said. "Oh. How splendid. We will be a merry house party. Papa will—"

"I will be marrying Lady Stapleton at Mobley before Christmas," Edgar had announced.

For once Cora had been speechless—and inelegantly open-mouthed. Lord Francis's eyebrows had remained elevated.

There had been no point in mincing matters. It was rather too late for that. "She is two months with child," he had said. "With my child, that is. We will be marrying."

Francis had shaken his hand and congratulated him and said all that was proper. Cora had been first speechless and then garrulous. By the time Edgar escaped the house, she had talked herself into believing that she, that he, that Francis, that everyone concerned and unconcerned must be blissfully happy with the betrothal. Lady Stapleton would be *just* the bride for Edgar, Cora had declared. Lady Stapleton would not allow herself to be swept along by the power of his character, and he would be the happier for it. Cora had never been so pleased by anything in her life, and Papa would be deliriously happy. Francis was called upon to corroborate these chuckle-headed notions.

"I believe it might well turn into a good match, my love," he had said less effusively than she, but with apparent sincerity. "I cannot imagine Edgar being satisfied with anything less. And the lady certainly has character—and beauty."

But of course Cora had issued the reminder Edgar had not needed before he made his escape.

"Oh, Edgar!" Her eyes had grown as wide as saucers and her hand had flown to her mouth and collided with it with a painful-sounding slap. "Whatever are you going to do about Fanny Grainger? You have all but *offered* for her. And she is coming to *Mobley*."

Edgar had no idea what he was going to do about Fanny Grainger, apart from the fact that he was not going to marry her. He had not offered for her, but he had come uncomfortably close. And last evening he had even taken the all-but-final step of inviting her and her parents to spend Christmas at Mobley. Everyone of course took for granted that he had invited her there for only one reason.

He liked the girl, even though he had not wished to marry her. The last thing he wanted to do was to leave her publicly humiliated. But it seemed that that was what he was fated to do. Unless . . .

It was purely by chance—entirely, amazingly coincidental—that as he was walking along Oxford Street he caught a glimpse of the young man she had met on almost the exact same spot a few weeks ago when Edgar had come upon them. Jack Sperling was hurrying along, his head down, clearly intent on getting where he was going in as little time as possible. One could understand why. The wind cut down the street rather like a knife.

Edgar stepped to one side to impede his progress. Sperling looked up, startled. "I do beg your pardon," he said before frowning and looking distinctly unfriendly. "Oh, you," he added.

"Good afternoon." Edgar touched the brim of his beaver hat and did what it was not in his nature to do—he acted on the spur of the moment. "Mr. Sperling, is it not?"

"I am in a hurry," the young man said ungraciously.

"I wonder if I could persuade you not to be?" Edgar said.

Unfriendliness turned to open hostility. "Oh, you need not fear that your territory is going to be poached upon," he said. "She has sent me a letter this morning and has explained that it will be the last. *She* will not see me again, and *I* will not see her. We both have some sense of honor. Sir," he added, making the word sound like an insult.

"I really must persuade you not to be in a hurry," Edgar said. "I need to talk to you."

"I have nothing to say to you," Jack Sperling said. "Except this. If you once mistreat her and if I ever hear of it, then you had better learn to watch your back." His voice shook.

"It is dashed cold out here," Edgar said, shivering. "That coffee shop is bound to be a great deal warmer. I believe they serve good coffee. Let us go and have some."

"You may drop dead, sir," the young man said.

"I do hope not," Edgar said. "Let me say this. I am going to be married within the next week or so—but not to Miss Grainger. However, she is to be a guest at my father's home and I feel a certain sense of responsibility for her happiness, since I seem to have been at least partly responsible for her unhappiness. Perhaps you and I could discuss the matter in civil fashion together?"

Jack Sperling stared at him for a few moments, deep

suspicion in his face. Then he turned abruptly and strode in the direction of the coffee shop.

They emerged half an hour later and went their separate ways after bidding each other a civil good afternoon. His father was going to have far more than he bargained for this Christmas, Edgar thought, having added yet one more guest to the list.

Chapter Ten

———✻———

The marriage of Lady Stapleton and Edgar Downes was solemnized in the small church at the village of Mobley, two miles from the abbey, six days before Christmas. There was a respectable number of guests in attendance, all the invited house guests having already arrived for the holiday, with the exception of the Graingers and Jack Sperling. A few of Edgar's closer colleagues and some of the elder Mr. Downes's old friends had been invited to come out from Bristol.

Edgar's first intention, which was to marry quickly and quietly in London, had been set aside—partly by Lady Stapleton's choice. There was no point in undue stealth. The truth would soon be known whether they tried to stifle it or not. And neither one of them made any attempt to stifle it. She had announced the truth to her aunt; he had confessed it to his sister and brother-in-law. She had talked about it quite freely and unblushingly during the party at which the announcement of their betrothal was made—just as if there were nothing shameful in such an admission and nothing ungenteel about such a public topic of conversation.

But then Lady Stapleton had always been known for her outspoken ways—and for treading very close to the edge of respectability without ever stepping quite beyond.

Lady Stapleton and Mrs. Cross had shared a carriage to Mobley Abbey with Cora and her youngest child, Annabelle. Lord Francis had ridden with Edgar, one or other of the former's three sons as often as not up before them. The Duke and Duchess of Bridgwater with their infant son, the Earl and Countess of Thornhill, the Marquess and Marchioness of Carew, the Earl and Countess of Greenwald, all with three children apiece, had left London in a vast cavalcade of carriages a day later.

Before any of them had arrived, wedding preparations had been in full flight at Mobley—Cora had written again to her father. And the elder Mr. Downes had greeted his future daughter-in-law with hearty good humor, regardless of either her age or her condition.

For a few days there was no chance to think about Christmas. The wedding superseded it in importance and excitement value. Edgar had brought home a Christmas bride.

Helena armed herself with scorn—for herself and her own weakness in agreeing to this marriage, for Edgar's foolish sense of honor, for the whole hypocrisy of the joyful nuptials for which everyone seemed to be preparing.

She had prepared herself to find his father coarse and vulgar. She found instead a man who was loud and hearty and who bore an almost uncanny physical resemblance to his son—but who was not vulgar. He lacked Edgar's refinement of speech and manner—he had, of course, had his son educated in the best schools—but he was no less genteel than many gentlemen of her acquaintance. She had prepared herself to find Mobley Abbey a garish and distasteful display of wealth. A great deal of wealth had quite obviously been expended on its restoration so that its ecclesiastical origins were breathtakingly apparent; at the same time it was a cozy and comfortable private home. Every last detail gave evidence of impeccable taste.

It was disappointing, perhaps, to have little outside of herself on which to turn her scorn. But then she had never deceived herself about the main object of her bitterness and hatred. She had always been fair about that at least.

At first she decided to wear her bronze silk for her wedding. But she had an unaccustomed attack of conscience just the day before. None of these people—not even Edgar—had deserved such a show of vulgarity. She had an ensemble she had bought for a winter fête in Vienna and had worn only once—she had never found a suitable occasion on which to wear it again. She wore it for her wedding—a simple, expertly designed white wool dress with a round neck, straight long sleeves, and a straight skirt slightly flaring from its high waistline; a white pelisse and bonnet, both trimmed with white fur; and a white muff and half boots.

At least there was an element of irony in the simple, elegant, eminently respectable attire, she thought, surveying herself in the mirror before leaving for the church. It was a wonderfully virginal outfit.

She did not want to marry. Not Edgar. Anyone but him. But there was no choice, of course. She would not allow the twinge of panic she felt to grow into anything larger. She smiled mockingly at her image. She was a bride—again. She wondered if she would make as much a disaster of this marriage as she had of the first. Undoubtedly she would. But he had been warned. He could never say he had not been.

She had asked the Marquess of Carew if he would be so good as to give her away, though she imagined that that foolish formality might have been dispensed with if she had talked to the vicar. The idea of a thirty-six-year-old widow having to be given away to a new husband was rather absurd. She had asked Lord Carew because he was a mild-mannered, kindly gentleman. Sometimes he reminded her of—no! He did not. He walked with a limp and had even been thoughtful enough to ask her if it would embarrass her. She had assured him it would not. It rather fascinated her to observe that the marchioness, who was many times more beautiful than he was handsome, nevertheless seemed to worship the ground he trod on. But Helena had never denied the existence of romantic and marital love—only of it as a possibility in her own life.

Her bridegroom was dressed very elegantly and fashionably in a dark blue, form-fitting tailed coat, buff pantaloons, white linen, and highly polished Hessians. She looked at him dispassionately as she walked toward him along the aisle of the small old church, oblivious to the guests, who turned their heads to watch her approach, and oblivious to either the marquess's limp or the steadying hand he had laid over her own on her arm. Edgar Downes looked solid and handsome and very much in command of his own life. He looked magnificent.

She experienced a growingly familiar feeling as she stood beside him and the marquess gave her hand into his. The feeling of being small and frail and helpless—and safe and secure. All illusions. His eyes, she saw when she looked up, were steady on hers. She did not want to gaze back, but having once looked, she had no choice. She would not lower her eyes and play the part of the demure bride. She half smiled at him, hiding her fear behind her customary mask.

Fear? Yes, she admitted, turning the mockery inward, too. Fear.

She listened to him promise her the moon and the stars in a firm voice that must have carried to the back pew of the church. She heard herself, almost as if she listened to someone else, promise him her soul. She watched the shiny gold ring, bright symbol of ownership, come to rest on her finger. She heard the vicar declaring that they were man and wife. She lifted her face to her new husband, feeling a wave of the nausea that had been disappearing over the past week.

He looked into her eyes and then at her lips, which she had drawn into a smile again. And then he took her completely by surprise. He clasped both her hands in his, bowed over them, and raised them one at a time to his lips.

She could have howled with fury. Tears sprang to her eyes and she bit hard on her upper lip. With her eyes and her lips she might have mocked his kiss on the mouth. She might have reminded him silently of his promise never to touch her without her permission. She might have put him subtly in the wrong. His kiss on her hands was startling in the illusion it gave of reverence and tenderness. She had to fight a painful ache in her throat to keep the humiliating tears from spilling over. But he must have seen them swimming in her eyes—he looked into them as soon as he raised his head. How she hated him.

He was her husband. And already he was establishing mastery.

Before suspecting her pregnancy, he had not once thought of marrying her. He had been horrified by his suspicions and even more so by their confirmation. He had felt that he was being forced into something very much against his will. He had not wanted to marry her.

And yet once it had become fact, once he had persuaded her to accept him, once he had acquired the special license, once the wedding preparations had been set in motion, he had felt a curious elation, a strange sense of—rightness. He found it hard to believe that the obvious had been staring him in the face ever since his arrival in London and he had not opened up his eyes and seen.

She was the very woman for him.

She was a woman of character and experience, someone he would find an interesting and a stimulating companion. He knew that he had a strong tendency to dominate other people, to take charge, to insist on doing things the way he knew they must be done. It was a tendency that worked to his advantage in his professional life. It was a tendency that might well be disastrous in his marriage. He would make a timid mouse out of a young, inexperienced girl—Miss Grainger, for example—within a month of wedding her. He did not want a timid mouse. He wanted a companion.

Even one who had sworn that she would never allow him to touch her. Even one who had promised to lead him a merry dance. Even one who rarely looked at him without that mockery in her eyes and on her lips.

He had always intended to make a marriage with whomever he ended up wedding. He intended to make a marriage with Helena Stapleton. A real marriage. The challenge of overcoming such hostility was strangely exhilarating. And he would overcome it.

The woman herself was exciting, of course. She was extremely beautiful, the sort of woman who was probably lovelier now in her maturity than she had been as a young girl. Or perhaps it was just that he was a mature man who saw more beauty in a woman of his own age than in someone who was little more than a child.

By the time his wedding day arrived, Edgar had admitted to himself that he was in love with his bride. He would not go as far as believing that he loved her. He was not even sure he liked her. He did not know her well enough to know if the unpleasant side of her nature she delighted in showing to him was the product of a basically unpleasant disposition or if it was merely the outer symptom of a troubled, wounded soul. He rather suspected the latter, though she denied having ever been deeply hurt. He faced the challenge of getting to know her. He might well not like her when he did. And even if he did, he might never grow to love her as he had always dreamed of loving a wife.

But he was certainly *in* love with her. It was a secret which he intended to guard very carefully indeed, for a lifetime if necessary. The woman did not need any more weapons than she already possessed.

His wedding was like a dream to him. And as with many dreams, he determinedly imprinted every detail on his memory so that he would be able to relive it in the future. There was his father, hearty and proud—and afraid for the son whom he loved with unabashed tenderness. There was Cora, armed with half a dozen of Francis's large handkerchiefs because she always cried at weddings, she had explained, but was sure to cry *oceans* at her only brother's. And there was Francis beside her, looking faintly amused and also solicitous of the wife he adored. There were all the other guests, an illustrious gathering for the wedding of a man who could not even claim the title of gentleman for himself.

And then there was his bride—and once she appeared, nothing and no one else mattered until they were out on the church steps some time later. She usually wore vivid colors and dramatically daring styles and looked vibrantly beautiful. This morning, all in pure white from head to toe, she looked almost ethereal. It was an incongruous word to use of her of all people. Her beauty robbed him of breath and of coherent thought. He felt, he thought in some alarm as she came closer to the altar rail, almost like weeping. He did not do so.

He spoke his commitment to her and to their marriage in the guise of the words of the nuptial service. He ignored the slight tone of mockery with which she made her promises to him. She would live those promises and mean them eventually. She was going to be a challenge, but he had never yet failed in any of the challenges he had set himself. And success had never been as important to him as it was with this one.

She was his wife. He heard the vicar announce the fact and felt the shock of the reality of the words. She was his wife. It was the moment at which he was invited to kiss her, though the vicar did not say so in words. He felt the expectation in the gathered guests. She lifted her face to his— and he saw the mockery there and remembered the promise he had made her. This was ritual, of course, and hardly subject to that promise. But he would give her no weapon wittingly.

He kissed the backs of her hands instead of her lips and for that public moment made no secret of his feelings for his new wife. He felt a moment of exultation when he raised his head and saw the brightness of tears in her eyes. But he did not doubt she would make him pay for that moment of weakness.

Oh, he did not doubt it. He counted on it!

He led his bride from the dark unreality of the church

interior into the reality of a cold, bright December outdoors.

"You look remarkably beautiful this morning, Helena,"
he told her in the brief moment of privacy before their
guests came spilling out after them.

"Oh, and so do you, Edgar," she said carelessly. "Remarkably beautiful."

Touché!

Helena was feeling irritable by the time she was finally
alone in her own bedchamber for the night. The combination of a wedding and an imminent Christmas was
enough, it seemed, to transport everyone to great heights of
delirious joy. What she had done by coming here with Edgar and marrying him was land herself in the middle of
glorious domesticity.

It was the last thing she wanted.

Domesticity terrified her more than anything else in
life.

The elder Mr. Downes—her father-in-law, who had actually invited her today to call him *Papa*—seemed end-
lessly genial. The noise and activity by which he had been
surrounded all day—by which they had *all* been
surrounded—had been appalling to say the least. The
adults had been in high spirits. There was no word to describe in what the children had been—and there had been
hordes of children, none of whom had been confined to the
nursery. Helena had understood—she hoped fervently that
she had misunderstood—that they would not be, this side of
Christmas.

She had found it impossible to sort them all out, to work
out which children belonged to which adults, which names
belonged to which children. The smallest infant belonged
to the Bridgwaters, and she *thought* she knew which four
belonged to Cora and Francis. Gracious heaven, they were
her niece and nephews. But the others were unidentified
and unidentifiable. And yet her father-in-law knew them all

by name and they all knew him by name. He was Grand-papa to every last one of them—except to the one who could not yet talk and even he had bounced on the grand-parental knee, gurgling and chuckling with glee.

She would go mad if every day between now and Christmas was like today, Helena thought. Unalloyed exuberance and merriment. Families. Happy couples—were there no *un*happy couples in this family or among their friends? Except for Edgar and herself, of course. And children. Children made her decidedly nervous. She did not like being around them. She did not like them being around her. And yet she was to have one of her own.

She was poking at the fire, trying to coax the coals into a position in which they would burn for a long time, when the door opened abruptly behind her and Edgar walked in, wearing a dressing gown. She stood up and glared, the poker clutched in one hand.

"And what do you think you are doing here?" she asked him, preparing for battle, almost glad that there was to be someone on whom to vent her irritation. It might be their wedding night, but there were going to be no exceptions to the rule. If he wanted to know how loudly and how embarrassingly she could squawk, let him take one step farther into the room.

He took it. And then another.

"Going to bed here," he said. "Sleeping here. It is my room, Helena. Ours. I slept elsewhere until tonight for form's sake."

"Oh, no, it is not ours," she said. "It is yours or it is mine. If it is yours, I shall go somewhere else. You will not break your promise as easily as that, Edgar."

"I have no intention of breaking my promise." His voice and his whole demeanor were maddeningly cool. "The bed is wide enough to accommodate both of us without touching, and I have enough control over my instincts and emotions to keep my hands off you. We will both sleep here. In my family—in my world, I believe—husbands and wives sleep in the same bed. All night, every night."

"And you have not the courage to fight family tradition," she said, throwing into her voice all the contempt she could muster.

"I have not the inclination," he said, removing his dressing gown and tossing it over the back of a chair. She was relieved to see that he wore a decent nightshirt beneath. "You are quite safe from me, Helena. And you need to sleep. I would guess that you have not been doing enough of it lately."

"I am looking haggard, I suppose," she said testily.

"Pale and interesting." He smiled. "Come to bed. Even with that fire, the room is chilly."

There was no point in arguing with Edgar when he was cool and reasonable, she was finding. And he was always cool and reasonable. But one day she was going to goad him into a loud, undignified brawl, and then he would find that he had met his match.

She lay on her back, staring up at the canopy, her eyes gradually accustoming themselves to the darkness. He lay on his side facing away from her. He said nothing. He made no move to break his promise. She fumed. How could he expect her to *sleep*?

Was he sleeping? She listened for the sound of his breathing. She would surely hear it if he slept. Yet he was apparently relaxed. He was probably in the process, she thought, of having a good night's rest just as if he slept alone or with a bundle of rags beside him. How could he *sleep*? How could he humiliate her so?

"Damn you, Edgar," she said. One of these times she would think of something original to say, but at the moment she was not in the business of originality.

He turned over to face her and propped himself on one elbow. He rested the side of his head on his hand. "My only hope," he said, "is that you will not be standing beside St. Peter when I appear at the pearly gates."

"I am not in the mood for silly jokes," she said. "This is ridiculous. I am nothing better than a puppet, forced to move whenever you jerk on a string. I do not like the feeling."

"If you feel strings connecting you and me," he said, "they are of your own devising, Helena. I will not touch you—even with a string."

"Damn your damnable control," she told him. "I will have none of it. Make love to me. It is what we both wish to do. Let us do it, then." She surged onto her side and put herself against him. She was immediately engulfed by heat and hard muscles and masculinity—and a soaring desire. She rubbed her breasts against his chest and reached for his mouth with her own.

He kissed her back softly and without passion. She drew back her head, breathing hard.

"It is for mutual comfort, Helena," he said quietly, "and for the procreation of children. Sometimes it is for love. It is not for anger or punishment. We will not punish each other with angry passion. You need to sleep." He slipped an arm beneath her head and drew her more snugly against him. "Relax and let yourself sleep, then."

She thought she would want to die of humiliation if it had not been for one thing. He was fully aroused. She could feel the hardness of his erection against her abdomen. It was not that she had failed to make him want her, then. It was just that he wanted a submissive wife, who would give him comfort rather than passion. Never! She had only passion to give.

"Go to sleep," he murmured against her ear.

"I thought you were ruthless, Edgar," she said into his shoulder. "I expected an overbearing tyrant. I expected that you would take advantage of the smallest opportunity to get past that promise and master me. I should have known the truth when you would not quarrel with me. You think to master me in this way, do you not?"

"Go to sleep, Helena," he said, his voice sounding weary. "We are not engaged in battle but in a marriage. Go to sleep." He kissed her temple.

She closed her eyes and was quiet for a while. If he knew her as she really was, he would not wish to share a bed with her, she thought. Once he got to know her, he would leave her alone fast enough. She would be alone again. She was alone now. But he was seducing her senses with this holding and cuddling and these murmured words. He was giving her the illusion of comfort.

"Comfort," she said. "It is for comfort, you say. Do you think I do not need comfort, Edgar? Do you think it? Do you? Do you think I am made of iron?"

He sighed and dipped his head to take her mouth. His was open this time and warm and responsive. "No," he said. "I do not think that."

"Make love to me, then," she said. "Let us do it for comfort, Edgar." She was being abject. She was almost crying and her voice revealed the fact. But she would think of that later. She would despise herself—and hate him—later. At this moment she was desperate for comfort and she would not remember that there was no comfort. That there could not be any. Ever.

He lifted her nightgown and his nightshirt before turning her onto her back, coming on top of her with the whole of his weight, and pushing her legs wide apart with his knees. She would have expected to hate being immobilized by his weight. But it was deliriously arousing. There was no foreplay. She would have expected to wish for it, to need it. But she wanted only to be penetrated, to be stretched, to be filled, to be ridden hard and deep.

He was a man of such control, her husband. He was hot and damp with need. He was rigid with desire. But he worked her slowly, withdrawing almost completely before thrusting firmly and deeply inward again. If there had been foreplay, she would have been in a frenzy of passion by the time he entered her, clamping about him with inner muscles to draw him to climax and to reach desperately for her own fleeting moment of happiness.

But there had been no foreplay. Incredibly, she felt herself gradually relaxing, lying still and open beneath him, taking exquisite enjoyment from the rhythmic strokes with which he loved her. She had no idea how many minutes passed—but it seemed like a long, long time—before she heard herself moaning and realized that enjoyment had turned to a pleasurable ache and that he was going to take her over the edge to peace and happiness without any active participation on her part. For a moment she considered fighting such passivity, but the ache, the certainty that he was going to take her through it and past it to the other side was too seductive to be denied.

She sighed and shivered beneath him as he made it happen and then with dreamy lethargy observed while he completed his own journey toward comfort. It was a moment of happiness blissfully extended into several moments—a gift she accepted with quiet gratitude. The moments would pass, but for now they were hers to hold in her body and her soul. They were like the peace that was supposed to come with Christmas. And for these moments—they would pass—she loved him utterly. She adored him.

He moved off her and drew her against him again. They were both warm and sweaty. She breathed in the smell of him.

"Comforted?" he asked softly.

"Mmm," she said.

"Sleep now, then," he told her.

"Mmm." Had she been just a little wider awake, perhaps she would have fought him since the suggestion had been issued as a command. But she slid into instant obedience.

Chapter Eleven

Although it was the week before Christmas and life could not be said to be following any normal pattern, nevertheless Helena began to have some inkling of how her life had changed. Permanently changed.

No longer would she travel almost constantly. The realization did not upset her enormously. Traveling could be far more uncomfortable and tedious than those who only longed to do it could ever realize. More disturbing was the understanding of why she had traveled and why she had never arrived at any ultimate destination. She had traveled for escape. It was true that she had derived great pleasure from her experiences, but never as much as she had hoped for. She knew finally, as she supposed she had known all along, that she could never in this life—and perhaps beyond this life, too—leave behind the thing she most wished to escape. She could never escape from herself. Wherever she went, she took herself with her. Yes, she had known it before. She had known that she lived in her own particular hell.

She would live at Mobley Abbey much of the time from now on. Edgar explained to her that his ties with his father had always been close ones and would undoubtedly remain so. For the rest of the time she would live in Bristol, in a home she had not yet seen. It was a large home, Edgar had told her. From the sketchy descriptions he had given of it in answer to her questions, she guessed that it was also an elegant home.

She was Mrs. Downes. Her title had never meant a great deal to her. She would have shed it if she could after her first husband's death. It was a reminder of a part of her life she would forget if she could. But there had been a certain dash to being Lady Stapleton, wealthy, independent widow. She had carefully cultivated that image of herself. There was something very solidly respectable about being Mrs. Edgar Downes.

She was part of a family. Not just some cousins in Scotland and an aunt whom she treated as much as a friend as a relative, but a real family, who prided themselves on their familial closeness.

Cora had hugged her hard immediately after the wedding and cried over her and insisted that they be on a first-name basis now that they were sisters. And so must her husband and Helena be, she had commanded. They really had been given no choice in the matter. Lord Francis had laughed and Helena had thought how attractive laugh lines in the corners of a man's eyes could be.

"Shall we bow to tyranny?" he had asked her, bowing over her hand. "I say we should. I must be plain Francis to you from this moment on, if you please."

What choice had Helena had but to reply graciously in kind?

Her father-in-law, that genial older version of Edgar—genial, yes, but Helena had the strange feeling that she would not wish to be the person to cross his will in any matter of importance—was all that was paternal. One would almost have sworn that he was delighted by his son's choice of a bride. He rose from the table when she entered the breakfast parlor the morning after her wedding, mortifyingly late, and reached out both hands for hers. He had kept a chair empty beside him.

"Good morning, Daughter," he said, taking both her hands in his, wringing them painfully hard, and drawing her close enough to plant a hearty kiss on her cheek.

Again, what choice did she have? She could not reply to such a greeting with a mere curt good morning. She could not call him Mr. Downes.

"Good morning, Papa," she said and took the chair beside him. The combination of calling him that and of realizing that this was the morning after her wedding night and the eyes of all the family and house guests and of Edgar himself, seated farther down the table, were on her caused her to disgrace herself utterly. She blushed. Everyone in the room knew why she and Edgar had married—and yet on the morning after her wedding night she *blushed*. How terribly gauche!

She felt trapped. Trapped into something she could not escape simply by packing her bags and planning her itinerary to wherever her fancy led her. This was to be her life, perhaps forever. And last night she had given up the one illusion of freedom and power she had still possessed. She had lacked his control, and so she had given up the greater good for—for what? Not for passion. There had been surprisingly little of that. Not even for pleasure. There had been pleasure—quite intense pleasure, in fact—but it was not for that she had begged. She had begged for comfort. And he had comforted her.

The memory frightened her. It suggested that she had needed him. Worse, it suggested that he could satisfy her need. She had been so satisfied that she had slept the night through without once waking, even when he had left the bed. But she needed no one! She refused to need anyone. Least of all Edgar. She would be swallowed up whole by him. And then, because she did not enjoy the sensation of being swallowed whole, she would find ways to fight back, to fight free. And she would destroy him. He did not deserve the misery of a shrewish wife.

She conversed brightly at the breakfast table, telling her father-in-law and her aunt, who sat at his other side, about Christmases she had spent in Vienna and Paris and Rome. Soon her audience consisted of most of the people at the table.

"And this year," Mr. Downes said, patting her hand on the table, "you will enjoy a good old-fashioned English Christmas, Daughter. There is nothing to compare to it, I daresay, though I have never been to those other places to judge for myself. I have never had a hankering for foreign parts."

"There will be the greenery to gather for the house decorations," Cora said, "and the decorating itself. And the children's party on Christmas Day and the adult ball in the evening. There will be baskets to deliver and skating parties down at the lake—the ice will be firm enough in a day or two if the weather stays cold. There will be—oh, so much. I am so *glad* that Christmas is here this year. And Helena, *you* shall help with all the plans since you are more senior in this family now than I am. You are Edgar's wife." She looked quite unabashed at having been supplanted in the role of hostess.

"It would not surprise me if there were even snow for Christmas," Mrs. Cross said, looking toward the window and drawing general attention that way. The outdoor world did indeed look gray and chilly.

"Of course there will be snow, ma'am," Mr. Downes said. "I have decreed that this is to be a perfect Christmas."

"The children will be ecstatic," the Earl of Thornhill said.

"The children of *all* ages," his wife said with a smile. "No one is more exuberant on a sleigh than Gabriel."

"And no one makes more angelic snow angels than Jane," the Earl of Greenwald said.

"I may have to challenge you on that issue," the Marquess of Carew said with a grin, "and put forward the claims of my own wife. Samantha's snow angels come with haloes."

"I notice," Cora said, "that you are conspicuously silent, Francis."

"It is against my religion, my love," he said, "to fight duels at Christmastime. Now any other time . . ." He raised his eyebrows and winked at her.

"I believe, Corey," Edgar said, "there are in the hierarchy of heavenly beings warrior angels as well as cherubic ones."

Francis laughed. So did everyone else at the table, Cora loudest of all.

"What an abomination brothers are," she said. "You are welcome to him, Helena. Perhaps you can teach him some manners."

Helena smiled and met Edgar's eyes along the table—he looked despicably handsome and at ease—but she could not join in the lively banter. It was too—cozy. Too alluring. Too tempting. It continued without her participation.

Edgar must be put in his place this morning, she decided, before he could get any ideas about last night's having begun an era of domestic bliss. And so at the end of the meal, when he waited at the door to escort her from the room, she ignored his offered arm.

"Oh, you need not worry about me, Edgar," she said carelessly. "I have things to do. You may amuse yourself to your heart's content with the other gentlemen or with whatever it is you do when you are at Mobley."

"You will need boots and a warm cloak and bonnet," he told her. "Everyone has been so caught up in the events surrounding our wedding during the past few days that my father is feeling that he has been derelict in his duties as host. He is taking everyone on an exploratory walk about the park. Most of his guests, like you, are here for the first time, you see."

"Oh," she said. And so once again she had no choice. She had not been asked if she would like to trek about the park on a gray, cold day, in company with a number of other couples. She was half of a couple now and it was assumed that she would do what Edgar decided they should do. Besides, he was the heir to all this. Of course she must go. It would be ill-mannered to refuse. And she was finding it very hard here at Mobley to be bad mannered.

"Take my arm," he said. "I will come up with you."

Staying aloof would have to be a mental thing, then, she decided. And perhaps something of a physical thing, too. Tonight she would reestablish the rules. He would learn that though she had allowed him to touch her once, she had not issued a general invitation to conjugal relations at his pleasure.

"You are feeling well enough to walk?" he asked her as they entered their bedchamber.

It was the excuse she might have thought of for herself downstairs. It was the easy solution. But she would not use her condition as an excuse for anything. She would not hide behind female frailty.

"I am quite well, thank you," she said, slipping her arm from his and making her way to her dressing room. "Why would I not be? I am expecting a baby, Edgar. Thousands of women are doing it every day."

"But only one of them is my wife," he said. "And only one of them is expecting *my* baby."

She did not even try to interpret the tone of his voice. If he was trying to establish ownership, he might save his breath. He had done that quite effectively yesterday. She belonged to him body and soul. But she would not curl into the safety and comfort that fact offered her.

"I hope, Edgar," she called from inside her dressing room, making sure that there would be no mistaking the tone of her voice at least, "you are not going to start fussing over me. How tiresome that would be."

The bedchamber was empty when she came back into it. He had gone into his own dressing room. She was not sure whether he had heard her or not.

The walk was going to be far worse an ordeal than she had anticipated, she saw immediately on their return downstairs. The hall was teeming with not only adult humans but also hordes of infant humans, too. Every child had spilled from the nursery in order to enjoy the walk. The noise was well above comfort level. Helena grimaced and would have returned to her room if she decently could.

She, it soon became apparent, was to be favored by the personal escort of her father-in-law. He took her arm and directed Edgar to escort her aunt.

And so by association she became the focal point of all the frolicking children as they walked. Mr. Downes had four grandchildren of his own among the group and clearly he was one of their favorite humans. But there were ten other children—Helena finally counted them all—who had fully adopted him during the few days of their acquaintance with him. And so every discovery along their route, from a misshapen, cracked chestnut to a gray, bedraggled bird feather was excuse enough to dash up to "Grandpapa" so that he might scrutinize the treasure and exclaim on its uniqueness. And Helena was called upon to exclaim enthusiastically about everything, too.

The Bridgwater baby was too heavy for his mama and papa to carry by turns, Mr. Downes decided after they had walked through a landscaped grotto and about the base of a grassy hill, which the older children had to run over, whooshing down the far side with extended arms and loud shrieks like a flock of demented birds. And so he enticed the babe into his own arms and made it bounce and laugh as he tickled it and talked nonsense to it. And then he decided that he would pass along the privilege and the pleasure to his new daughter-in-law.

Helena found herself carrying the rosy-cheeked little boy, who gazed at her in the hope that this new playmate would prove as entertaining as the last. The innocence of babyhood shone out at her from his eyes and the total trust of a child who had not yet learned the treachery of the world or of those he most loved.

She was terrified. And fascinated. And very close to tears. She smiled and kissed him and made a play out of stealing the apples from his cheeks. He chuckled and bounced and invited a repetition of the game. He was soft and warm and surprisingly light. He had tiny white baby teeth.

Helena drew in a deep breath. She had a surprising memory of wanting children of her own during the early years of her first marriage, of her disappointment each month when she had discovered that she had not conceived. She had been so relieved later and ever since to be childless that she had forgotten that once upon a time she had craved the experience of motherhood. There was a child in her womb—now. This time next year, if all went well, she could be holding her own baby like this, though hers would be somewhat younger.

A surge of yearning hit her low in her womb, almost like a pain. And then an equivalent dose of panic made her want to drop the Bridgwater child and run as far and as fast as she could go. She was being seduced by domesticity.

"Let me take him from you, ma'am." The Duke of Bridgwater was a coldly handsome man, whom she would have considered austere if she had not occasionally glimpsed the warmth of his relations with his wife and son. "He entertains the erroneous belief that the arms of adults were made to be bounced in. Come along, rascal."

The child was perfectly happy to be back with his papa. He proceeded to bounce and gurgle.

"Ah, the memories, Daughter," Mr. Downes said. "Having my children small was the happiest time of my life. I would have had more if my dear Mrs. Downes had not died giving birth to Cora. After that, I did not have the heart to remarry and have children with another wife."

If Christian had lived, Helena thought, he would be older than her father-in-law was now. He would have been seventy-one. It was a fascinating thought. "Children like you," she said.

"It is because I like them," he said with a chuckle. "There is no child so naughty that I do not like him. And now I have grandchildren. I see Cora's children as often as I can. I will see yours more frequently. I will lure you from Bristol on every slight pretext. Be warned."

"I believe it will always be a pleasure to be at Mobley, sir," she said.

He looked at her with raised eyebrows.

"Papa," she added.

"I believe," he said as he turned onto a different path, leading the group downhill in the direction of what appeared to be extensive woods, "you will do very well for my son. He has waited perhaps overlong to choose a bride.

His character has become set over the years and has grown in strength, in proportion to his successes in life. I was successful, Daughter, as witness Mobley Abbey, which I purchased rather than inherited. My son is many more times successful than I. It will take a strong woman to give him the sort of marriage he needs."

"You think I am a strong woman?" Helena asked.

"You were a widow for many years," he said, "when you have the beauty and the rank and wealth to have made an advantageous match at any time. You have traveled and been independent. Edgar reported to me that he had the devil's own time persuading you to marry him, despite the fact that you are with child. Yes, I believe you are a strong woman."

How looks could deceive, she thought.

A lake had come into view through the trees. A lake that was iced over.

"This will be the scene of some of our Christmas frolics," her father-in-law said. "There will be skating, I do believe. And the greenery will be gathered among these trees. We will make a great ritual of that, Daughter. Christmas is important in this family. Love and giving and peace and the birth of a child. It is a good time to have a houseful of children and other guests."

"Yes," she said.

"And a good time to have a new marriage," he said. "There are worse things to be than a Christmas bride."

The children were whooping and heading either for the lake or for the nearest climbable trees.

It seemed that he was fated to have a very prickly wife, Edgar thought the morning after his wedding. He had had hopes after their wedding night that, if they could not exactly expect to find themselves embarking on a happily-ever-after, at least they would be able to enjoy a new rapport, a starting ground for the growth of understanding and affection. But as soon as she entered the breakfast parlor he had known that she had retreated once more behind her mask. She had looked beautiful and proud and aloof—and slightly mocking. He had known that she had no intention of allowing last night to soften their relations. Her rebuff as they left the breakfast room had not taken him at all by surprise.

He watched with interest as they walked outside and he made conversation with Mrs. Cross. He watched both his father and his wife. His father, he knew, though he had said nothing to his son, was deeply disturbed by his marriage and the manner in which it had been brought about. Yet he talked jovially with Helena and involved her with the children who kept running up to him for attention and approval.

Helena disliked children, a fact that Edgar had come to realize with cold dread. And yet he learned during the course of the walk that it was not strictly the truth. When his father first deposited the Duke of Bridgwater's young son in her arms, she looked alarmed as if she did not know quite what to do with him. What she proceeded to do was amuse the child—and herself. Edgar watched, fascinated, as all the aloof mask came away and left simply a lovely woman playing with a child. The mask came back on as soon as Bridgwater took the baby away from her.

And then they were at the lake and everyone dispersed on various courses—the children to find the likeliest playgrounds, the adults to supervise and keep them from breaking something essential, like a neck. Cora was testing the ice with a stout stick, his father with the toe of his boot. Francis was bellowing at his youngest son to get off the ice—*now*! One group of children proceeded to play hide-and-seek among the tree trunks. The more adventurous took to the branches. Helena stood alone, looking as if she would sneak off back home if she could. Mrs. Cross had first bent to listen to something Thornhill's daughter was saying to her and had then allowed herself to be led away.

Edgar was about to close the distance between himself and his wife, though she looked quite unapproachable. Why could she not simply relax like everyone else and enjoy the outing? Was she so determined *not* to enjoy it? He felt a certain annoyance. But then Cora's youngest son, who had escaped both the ice and his father's wrath, tugged on his greatcoat and demanded that Uncle Edgar do up a button that had come undone at his neck. Edgar removed his gloves, went down on his haunches, and wrestled with the stubborn buttonhole.

When he stood up again, he could not immediately see Helena. But then he did. She was helping one of the Earl of Greenwald's young sons climb a tree. Edgar had noticed the lad standing forlornly watching some larger, bolder children, but lacking the courage to climb himself. Helena had gone to help him. She did so for all of ten minutes, patiently helping him find his footing on the bark and then slide out along one of the lower branches, encouraging him, congratulating him, laughing at his pleasure, catching him when he jumped, coaxing him when he lost his courage, starting all over again when he scampered back to the starting point.

She was that woman unmasked again—the one who forgot to be the dignified, cynical Lady Stapleton, the one who had forgotten her surroundings, the one who clearly loved children with a patient, compassionate warmth.

Edgar stood with his shoulder against a tree, watching, fascinated.

And then the child jumped with a bold lunge and bowled her right off her feet in his descent so that they both went down on the ground, the child squealing first with fright and then with delight when he realized he was not hurt, Helena laughing with sheer amusement.

She turned her head and caught herself being watched.

She lifted the child to his feet, dusted him off with one hand, directed him to his father, and sent him scampering away. She dusted herself off, her face like marble, and turned to walk away into the trees, in a direction no one else had taken. She did not look at Edgar or anyone else.

He sighed and stood where he was for a moment. Should he go after her? Or should he leave her alone to sulk? But sulk about what? That he had watched her? There was nothing secret in what she had been doing. She had been amongst the crowd, playing with one of the children. But her awareness that he was watching her had made her self-conscious or angry for some reason. It was impossible to know what was wrong.

He knew his wife as little today, Edgar thought, as he had known her that first evening, when he had looked up from his conversation with the Graingers and had seen her standing in the doorway, dressed in scarlet. She was a mystery to him—a prickly mystery. Sometimes he wondered if the mystery was worth probing.

But she was his wife.

And he was in love with her, even if he did not love or even particularly like her.

He pushed his shoulder away from the tree and went after her.

Chapter Twelve

She had not wandered far. But she was half hidden behind the tree trunk against which she leaned. She was staring straight ahead and did not shift her gaze when Edgar came in sight. But he cut into it when he went to stand before her. He set one hand against the trunk beside her head and waited for her eyes to focus on his.

"Tired?" he asked.

"No."

"It has been a long walk for you," he said, "with the added strain of having to converse with a new father-in-law."

"Would you make a wilting violet of me, Edgar?" she asked, one corner of her mouth tilting upward. "It cannot be done. You should have married one of the young virgins."

"You are good with children," he said.

"Nonsense!" Her answer was surprisingly sharp. "I dislike them intensely."

"Greenwald's little boy had been abandoned by the older tree climbers," he said. "He would have been left in his loneliness if you had not noticed. You made him happy."

"Oh, how easy it is to make a child happy," she said impatiently, "and how tedious for the adult."

"You looked happy," he said.

"Edgar." She looked fully into his eyes. "You would possess me body and soul, would you not? It is in your nature to want total control over what is in your power. You possess my body and I suppose I will continue to allow you to do so, though I did resolve this morning to remind you of your promise and to force you on your honor to keep it. But there is that damnable detail of a shared bed, and I never could resist an available man. You will *not* possess my soul. You may prod and probe as much as you will, but you will not succeed. Be thankful that I will not allow you to do so."

He was hurt. Partly by her careless dismissal of him as merely an available man—but then such carelessness was characteristic of her. Mainly he was hurt to know that she was quite determined to keep him out of her life. He might possess her body but nothing else. More than ever she seemed like a stranger to him—a stranger who was not easy to like, but one he craved to know and longed to love.

"Is the reality of your soul so ugly, then?" he asked.

She smiled at him and lifted her gloved hands to rest on his chest. "You have no idea how appealing you look in this greatcoat with all its capes," she said, "and with that frown on your face. You look as if you could hold the world on your shoulders, Edgar, and solve all its problems while you did so."

"Perhaps," he said, "I could help solve your problems if you would share them with me, Helena."

She laughed. "Very well, then," she said. "Help me solve this one. How do I persuade a massive, masterly, frowning man to kiss me?"

He searched her eyes, frustrated and irritated.

She pulled a face and then favored him with her most mocking smile. "You like only more difficult problems, Edgar?" she asked him. "Or is it that you have no wish to kiss me? How dreadfully lowering."

He kissed her—hard and open-mouthed. Her hands came to his shoulders, her body came against his, and for a few moments hot passion flared between them. Then he set his hands at her waist, moved her back against the tree, and set some space between them. Irritation had turned to anger.

"I do not like to be played with like a toy, Helena," he said, "to be used for your pleasure at your pleasure, to be seduced as a convenient way of changing the subject. I do not like to be mocked."

"You are very foolish, Edgar," she said. "You have just handed me a marvelous weapon. Do you not like to be *mocked,* my dear? I am an expert at mockery. I cannot be expected to resist the challenge you have just set to me."

"Do you hate me so much then?" he asked her.

She smiled. "I lust after you, Edgar," she said. "Even with your child in my womb, I still lust after you. Is it not enough?"

"What have I done to make you hate me?" he asked. "Must I take sole blame for your condition?"

"What have you done?" She raised her eyebrows. "You have married me, Edgar. You have made me respectable and safe and secure and rich. You *are* very wealthy, are you not? Wealthier than your father even before you inherit what is his? You have made me part of an eminently respectable family. You have brought me to this—to Mobley Abbey at Christmastime and surrounded me with respectable families and children. *Children* wherever I turn. It is to be what your father calls a good old-fashioned Christmas. I do not doubt it, if today is any indication—yet today Christmas has not even started. And if all this is not bad enough, you have tried to take my soul into yourself. You have suffocated me. I cannot breathe. This is what you have done to me."

"My God." His hand was back on the tree trunk beside her head. He had moved closer to her though he did not touch her. "My God, Helena, who was he? What did he do to you? Who was it who hurt you so badly?"

"You are a fool, Edgar," she said coldly. "No one has hurt me. No one ever has. It is I who have done all the hurting. It is in my nature. I am an evil creation. You do not want to know me. Be content with my body. It is yours. You do not want to know *me.*"

He did not believe her. Oh, yes, she hurt people. He did not doubt that he was not the first man she had used and scorned. But he did not believe it was in her very nature to behave thus. There would not be the bitterness in her smile and behind her eyes if she were simply amoral. Nor that something more than bitterness that he sometimes almost glimpsed, almost grasped. What was that other something? Despair? Something or someone had started it all. Probably someone. Some man. She had been very badly hurt at some time in her past. So badly that she had been unable to function as her real self ever since.

But how was he to find out, to help her when she had shut herself off so entirely from help?

There was a glimmering of hope, perhaps. The things that suffocated her must also frighten her—her marriage to him, his family, his father's guests and their children, Christmas. Why would she fear such benevolent things? Because they threatened her bitterness, her masks? The masks had come off briefly already this morning—first with the Bridgwater baby and then with the Greenwald child. And perhaps even last night when she had allowed herself to be comforted.

"You were right about one thing," she said. "I *am* tired. Take me home, Edgar. Fuss over your pregnant wife."

He took her arm in his and led her back to the others so that he could signal to his father that he was taking Helena back to the house. His father smiled and nodded and then bent down to give his attention to Jonathan, the Thornhills' youngest son. Greenwald's little boy briefly danced up to Helena and told her that he was going skating as soon as the ice was thick enough.

"I am going to skate like the wind," he told her.

"Oh, goodness," she said, touching a hand lightly to his woolly cap. "That *is* fast. Perhaps all we will see is a streak of light and it will be Stephen skating by."

He chuckled happily and danced away.

Her voice had been warm and tender. She might believe that she disliked children, but in reality she loved them altogether too well.

They walked in silence through the woods and up the slope to the wider path. She leaned on him rather heavily.

He should not, he thought, have allowed her to make such a lengthy walk when only a week or so ago she had still been suffering from nausea and fatigue.

"Tell me about your first marriage," he said.

She laughed. "You will find nothing there," she said. "It lasted for seven years. He was older than your father. He treated me well. He adored me. That is not surprising, is it? I am reputed to have some beauty even now, but I was a pretty girl, Edgar. I turned heads wherever I went. I was his prize, his pet."

"You were never—with child?" he asked.

"No." She laughed again. "Never once, though not for lack of trying on his part. You can imagine my astonishment when you impregnated me, Edgar. Seven years of marriage and a million lovers since then had convinced me that I was safely barren."

Did she realize, he wondered, how her open and careless mention of those lovers cut into him? But he had no cause for complaint. He had never been deceived about her promiscuous past, of which he had been a part. She had never even tried to keep it a secret.

"His poor first wife suffered annual stillbirths and miscarriages for years and years," she said. "Was not I fortunate to be barren?"

"There was only one survivor?" he asked.

"Only Gerald, yes," she said. "Though why he survived when none of the others did was a mystery—or so Christian always said. He was neither tall nor robust nor handsome; he was shy and timid; he was not overly intelligent. He excelled at nothing he was supposed to excel at. He had only one talent—a girlish talent, according to his father. He played the pianoforte. I believe Christian would have been just as happy if none of his offspring had survived."

Her first husband did not sound to have been a pleasant man. Edgar could not imagine his own father being impatient with either him or Cora if they had been less than he had dreamed of their being. His father, for all his firm character and formidable abilities in his career, gave unconditional love to those nearest and dearest to him—and to their spouses, too. Had Sir Christian Stapleton treated Helena, as he appeared to have treated his only son, with such contempt that she had forever after treated herself that way? Could that account for her bitterness? Her despair?

"Your child will have his father's love," he told her. "Or hers. I do not care what its gender is or its looks or abilities or nature or talents or lack thereof. I do not care even if there are real handicaps. The child will be mine and will be deeply loved."

If he had thought to soften her, he was much mistaken.

"You think that now, Edgar," she said contemptuously. "But if it is a son and he has not your splendid physique or can look at two numbers and find himself unable to add them together or sneaks away to play the pianoforte when you are trying to train him to take over your business, then you will compare him to yourself and to his grandfather and you will find him wanting. And he will know himself despised and become a weak, fragile creature. But he may not come to me for comfort. I shall not give it. I shall turn my back on him. I will not have this pregnancy romanticized. I will not think in hazy terms of a cuddly baby and doting motherhood and strong, protective fatherhood. The stable at Bethlehem must have been drafty and uncomfortable and smelly and downright humiliating. How dare we make beatific images of it! It was nasty. That was the whole point. It was meant to be nasty just as the other end of that baby's life was. *This* is what I am prepared to do for you, that stable was meant to tell us. But instead of accepting reality and coping with it, we soften and sentimentalize everything. What did you *do* to inspire this impassioned and ridiculous monologue?"

"I dared to think of my child with love," he said, "though she or he is still in your womb."

"Oh, Edgar," she said wearily, "I did not realize you were such a decent man. One's first impression of you is of a large, masterful, ruthless man. Our first encounter merely confirmed me in that belief. I wish you were not so decent. I am terrified of decency."

"And I, ma'am," he admitted, "am totally baffled by you. You would have me believe that you are anything but decent. And yet you will help a lonely child climb a tree and touch his head with tenderness. And you will passionately defend a woman and child whose courage and suffering have been softened to nothing by the sweet sentiments that surround the Christmas story. And you keep me at arm's length so that I will not be drawn into your own unhappiness. That *is* the reason, is it not?"

She set the side of her head against his shoulder and sighed. "The walk out did not seem nearly this long," she said. "I am very weary, Edgar. Weary of being prodded and poked and invaded by your questions. Have done now. Come upstairs with me when we reach the house. Lie down with me. Hold me as you did last night. You did, did you not? All night? Your arm must have gone to sleep. Hold me again, then. And draw me farther into this terror of a marriage. Perhaps I will sleep and when I awake will have more energy with which to fight you. I will fight, you know. I hate you, you see."

Surprisingly he smiled and then actually chuckled aloud. She had spoken the words almost with tenderness.

Oh, yes, he would draw her farther into the terror—of their marriage, of her new family, of her proximity to children, of Christmas. She was right about one thing. He could be a ruthless man when his mind was set upon something. His mind was set upon something now. More than his mind—his heart was set upon it. He wanted a marriage with this woman.

A real marriage.

He had spotted her weakness now—she had handed him the knowledge on a platter. He was an expert—a ruthless expert—at finding out weaknesses and probing and worrying them until he had gained just what he wanted. He would have to say that Helena, Mrs. Edgar Downes, did not stand one chance in a million.

Except that she was quite irritatingly stubborn. A worthy opponent. He could not stand an opponent who cowered into submission at the first indication of the formidable nature of his foe. There was no challenge in such a fight. Helena was not such an opponent. She could still tell him she hated him, even while conceding a physical need for his arms to hold her.

"Shall I carry you the rest of the way?" he asked her, feeling her weariness.

"If you try it, Edgar," she said, "I shall bar the door of your bedchamber against you from this day forward and screech out most unladylike answers to anything you care to call through it. I shall shame you in front of your father and your sister and all these other nauseatingly respectable people. I am not a sack of potatoes to be lugged about merely because I have the despicable misfortune to be in a delicate condition and to be your property."

"A simple no, thank you would have sufficed," he said.

"I wish you were not so large," she said. "I wish you were small and puny. I *hate* your largeness."

"I believe," he said as they stepped inside the house, "I have understood your message. Come. I'll take you up and hold you while you sleep."

"Oh, go away," she said, dropping his arm, "and play billiards or drink port or do whatever it is you do to make another million pounds before Christmas. I have no need of you or of sleep either. I shall write some letters."

"After you have rested," he said firmly, taking her arm and drawing it through his again. "And if it is a real quarrel you are hankering for, Helena, I am almost in the mood to oblige you." He led her toward the stairs.

"Damn you," she said. "I am not. I am too weary."

He chuckled again.

Jack Sperling arrived at Mobley Abbey early in the afternoon, the Graingers just before teatime.

Jack was shown into the library on his arrival, and Edgar joined him there with his father.

"Sperling," he said, inclining his head to the young man,

who bowed to him. "I am pleased to see that you had a safe journey. This is the young gentleman I spoke of, Father."

"Mr. Sperling." The elder Mr. Downes frowned and looked him over from head to toe. "You are a very young gentleman."

"I am two-and-twenty, sir," the young man said, flushing.

"And I daresay that like most young gentlemen you like to spend money as fast as you can get your hands on it," Mr. Downes said. "Or faster."

The flush deepened. Jack squared his shoulders. "I have worked for my living for the past year, sir," he said. "Everything I earn, everything I can spare from feeding myself and setting a roof over my head is used to pay off debts that I did not incur."

"Yes, yes," Mr. Downes said, his frown suggestive of irritation. "You are foolish enough to beggar yourself for the sake of an extravagant father, I daresay. For the sake of that ridiculous notion of a gentleman's honor."

The young man's nostrils flared. "Sir," he said, "with all due respect I will not hear my father insulted. And a gentleman's honor is his most precious possession."

Mr. Downes waved a dismissive hand. "If you work for my son and me, young man," he said, "you may grow rich. But if you intend to spend your hard-earned pounds on paying a father's debts, you are not the man for us. You will need more expensive and more fashionable clothes than those you are wearing and more than a decent roof over your head. You will need a wife who can do you credit in the business world. I believe you have a lady in mind. You will need to think of yourself, not of creditors to whom you owe nothing if you but forget about a gentleman's honor. The opportunity is there. My son has already offered it and I am prepared to agree with him. But only if you are prepared to make yourself into a single-minded businessman. Are you?"

Jack had turned pale. He could work for these two powerful men, who knew how to be successful, how to grow rich. As a gentleman with a gentleman's education and experience as his father's steward and more lately as a London clerk, he could be trained by them, groomed by them for rapid promotion until he was in a position to make his own independent fortune. It was the chance of a lifetime, a dream situation. He would be able to offer for Fanny Grainger. All he had to do was swallow a few principles and say yes.

Edgar watched his face. This was not an approach he would have taken himself. His father had grown up in a harsher world.

"No, sir." Jack Sperling's face was parchment white. The words were almost whispered. But they were quite unmistakable. "No, thank you, sir. I shall return to town by stage. I thank you for your time. And for yours, sir." His eyes turned on Edgar.

"Why not?" Mr. Downes barked. "Because you are a *gentleman,* I suppose. Foolish puppy."

"Yes, sir," Jack said, very much on his dignity. "Because I am a gentleman and proud of it. I would rather starve as a gentleman, sir, than live as a rich man as a— As a—" He bowed abruptly. "Good day to you."

"Sit down, Mr. Sperling," Mr. Downes said, indicating a chair behind the young man. "My son judged you rightly, it seems. I might have known as much. We have business to discuss. Men who go into trade for the sole purpose of getting rich, even if it means turning their backs upon all their responsibilities and obligations and even if it means riding roughshod over the persons and livelihoods and feelings of everyone else—such men often do prosper. But they are not men I care to know or do business with. You are not such a man, it seems."

Jack looked from him to Edgar.

"It was a test," Edgar said, shrugging. "You have passed it."

"I would have appreciated your trust, sir," the young man said stiffly, "without the test. I am a gentleman."

"And I am not, Mr. Sperling," Mr. Downes said. "I am a businessman. Sit down. You are a fortunate young man. You know, I suppose, what gave my son the idea of taking you on as a bright prospect for our business."

"Mr. Downes was obliged to marry Lady Stapleton," Jack Sperling said, "and wished to reduce the humiliation to Miss Grainger, who expected his offer. Yes, I understand, sir."

"It is in our interest to make you an acceptable groom for the lady," Mr. Downes said, "who will be arriving here with her mama and papa before the day is out, I daresay." Jack Sperling flushed again. "But make no mistake, young man. There is no question of your being paid off. We demand work of our employees."

"I would not accept a single farthing that I had not earned, sir," Jack said. "Or accept a bride who had been bought for me."

"And about your father's property," Mr. Downes said. "Your *late* father?"

The young man inclined his head. "He died more than a year ago," he said.

"And the property?" Mr. Downes was drumming the fingers of one hand on the arm of his chair. "It has been sold?"

"Not yet," Jack said. "It is in a state of some dilapidation."

"I am willing to buy it," Mr. Downes said. "As an investment. As a business venture. When the time is right I will sell it again for a profit—or my son will if it is after my time. To you, Mr. Sperling. When you can afford to buy it. It will not come cheaply."

Edgar noted the whiteness of the young man's knuckles as his hands gripped the chair arms. "I would not expect it to, sir," he said. "Thank you, sir."

"We are good to our employees, Mr. Sperling," Mr. Downes said. "We also expect a great deal of them."

"Yes, sir."

"For the next week, we will expect you to enjoy Christmas at Mobley and to court that young lady with great care. Her father does not know you are to be here unless you have informed the lady and she has informed him. He will not take kindly to a suitor who is to be a clerk in my son's business until he has earned his first promotion—not when he expected my son himself."

"No, sir."

"He will perhaps be reconciled when he understands that you are a favored employee," Mr. Downes continued. "One who is expected to rise rapidly in the business world and eventually rival us in wealth and influence. Being a gentleman himself, he will doubtless be even further reconciled when he knows that our business is to invest in buying and improving your father's property with a view to preparing it as your country residence when you achieve stature in the company."

The young man's eyes closed tightly. "Yes, sir."

Mr. Downes looked at his son. "I believe we have said everything that needs to be said." He raised his eyebrows. "Have we forgotten anything?"

Edgar smiled. "I believe not," he said. "Except to thank Mr. Sperling for his willingness to help me out of a tight spot."

"You will go to Bristol when my son returns there after Christmas, then," Mr. Downes said. "He will put you to work. For a trial period, it is to be understood. Pull the bell rope, will you please, Edgar? My butler will show you to your room, Mr. Sperling, and explain to you how to find the drawing room. We will be pleased to see you there for tea at four o'clock."

"Thank you, sir." Jack got to his feet and bowed. He inclined his head to Edgar. He followed the butler from the room.

"I have never regretted my retirement," Mr. Downes said after the door had closed behind them. He chuckled. "But it feels damned good to come out of it once in a while. I believe you judged his character well, Edgar. I thought for one moment that he was going to challenge me to a duel."

"You were formidable." Edgar laughed, too. "Poor young man. One almost forgot that he is the one doing me a favor."

"One cannot afford to have weak employees merely as a

favor, Edgar," his father said. "That young man will do
very nicely indeed if I am any judge of character. You do
not regret the young lady?"

"I am married to Helena," Edgar said rather stiffly.

"The answer you would give, of course," his father said.
"Damn it, Edgar, we did not go around bedding respectable
women before marrying them in my day. I am disappointed
in you. But you have done the right thing and one can only
hope all will turn out for the best. She is a handsome
woman and a woman of character. Though one wonders
what she was about, allowing herself to be bedded and her
a lady."

"That is her concern, Father," Edgar said firmly, "and
mine."

"The right answer again." Mr. Downes rose to his feet.
"I have promised to show Mrs. Cross the conservatory. A
very ladylike person, Edgar. She reminds me of your
mother, or the way your mother would have been." He
sighed. "Sometimes I let a few days go by without thinking
about her. I must be getting old."

"You must be forgiving yourself at last," Edgar said quietly.

"Hmm." His father led the way from the room.

Chapter Thirteen

❈

The Graingers arrived at Mobley Abbey in time to join the family and the other guests in the drawing room for tea. Helena had at first been rather surprised to find that they still planned to come for Christmas, even after learning of Edgar's betrothal and imminent marriage to her. But it was not so very surprising after she had had time to think about it a little more.

The Graingers were not wealthy. It was very close to Christmas. If they admitted to their disappointment and returned to their own home, they would be compelled to go to the expense of celebrating the holiday there with all their expectations at an end. General opinion had it that Sir Webster would not be able to afford to take his daughter back to town for a Season. She would sink into spinsterhood and he would have the expense of her keep for the rest of his life.

They had lost the very wealthy Edgar Downes as a matrimonial prospect, but spending Christmas at Mobley Abbey would at least give them the chance of continuing in the company of several of the *ton*'s elite, of enjoying the hospitality of wealthy hosts, and of keeping their hopes alive for a little longer. In such a social setting, who knew what might turn up?

And so it was not so surprising after all that they had come, Helena thought, greeting them as they appeared in the drawing room. They were gracious in their congratulations to her. Miss Grainger was quite warm in hers.

"Mrs. Downes," she said. "I am very pleased for you. I am sure you will be happy. I like Mr. Downes," she added and blushed.

Helena guessed that the girl was sincere. She would have married Edgar without a murmur of protest, but she would have been overwhelmed by him.

"Thank you," she said and saw the girl almost at the same moment suddenly stare off to her right as if her eyes would pop from their sockets. She visibly paled.

"Oh," she murmured almost inaudibly.

Edgar had come up and was greeting the Graingers. Helena linked her arm through Fanny's. "Come and meet my father-in-law," she said. He was speaking with Helena's aunt and the young man who had arrived earlier. Helena had been introduced to him but had not had a chance to converse with him.

"Papa," she said, "this is Miss Grainger, just lately arrived from London with her mama and papa."

Fanny curtsied and focused the whole of her attention on Mr. Downes. It seemed to Helena that she was close to fainting.

"Ah," Mr. Downes said heartily. "As pretty as a picture. Welcome to my home, Miss Grainger. And—Sir Webster and Lady Grainger?" Edgar had brought them across the room. "Welcome. You met Mrs. Cross in London, I daresay. Allow me to present Mr. Sperling, a young gentleman my son recently discovered in London as a particularly bright prospect for our business. We need gentlemen of education and breeding and enterprise to fill the more challenging positions and to rise to heights of responsibility and authority and wealth. I daresay that in five or ten years Mr. Sperling may make me look like a pauper." He rubbed his hands together and laughed merrily.

Mr. Sperling bowed. Fanny curtsied deeply without once looking at him. Sir Webster cleared his throat.

"We are acquainted with Mr. Sperling," he said. "We are—or were—neighbors. How d'ye do, Sperling?" He had pokered up quite noticeably.

"Acquainted? Neighbors?" Mr. Downes was all astonishment. "Well now. Who says that coincidences never happen these days? Amazing, is it not, Edgar?"

"Astonishing," Edgar agreed. "You and Lady Grainger—and Miss Grainger, too—will be able to help us make Mr. Sperling feel more at home over Christmas, then, sir."

"Yes, certainly. My dear Mrs. Cross," Mr. Downes was saying, beaming with hearty good humor, "please do pour the tea, if you would be so good."

Helena caught him alone after he had escorted her aunt to the tea tray. The Carews, she noticed, those kindest of kind people, were taking a clearly uncomfortable Mr. Sperling and Fanny Grainger under their wing while Edgar had taken the Graingers to join Cora and Francis.

"Sit here, Daughter," Mr. Downes said, indicating a large wing chair beside the fire. "We have to be careful to look after you properly. It was thoughtless of me to take you so far from the house this morning."

"Nonsense," she said briskly. "What are you up to, Papa?"

"Up to?" He looked at her in astonishment. "I am protecting my daughter-in-law and my future grandchild. Both are important to me."

"Thank you." She smiled. "Who is Mr. Sperling? No." She held up a staying hand. "Not the story about Edgar's having discovered a prodigy quite by chance. The real story."

His eyes were shrewd and searching. "Edgar has not told you?" he asked.

"Let me guess." She perched on the edge of the chair he had indicated and looked up at him. "It does not take a great deal of ingenuity, you know. Mr. Sperling is a young and rather good-looking gentleman. He is a neighbor of the Graingers. Fanny Grainger, when she set eyes on him a few minutes ago, came very near to fainting—a little excessive for purely neighborly sentiment. His own face, when we came closer, turned parchment pale. Can he by any chance be the ineligible suitor? The man she is not allowed to marry?"

"I suppose," her father-in-law conceded, "since we have

just established that coincidences do happen, it might be possible, Daughter."

"And Edgar, feeling guilty that the necessity of marrying me forced him to let down the Graingers, whose hopes he had raised," Helena said, "devised this scheme of making Mr. Sperling more eligible and bringing the lovers together. And you are aiding and abetting him, Papa. A more unlikely pair of matchmakers it would be difficult to find."

"But make no mistake," Mr. Downes said. "Business interests always come first with Edgar, as with me. He would not have brought that young man to Mobley or offered him the sort of employment that will involve a great deal of trust on his part if he had not been convinced that Mr. Sperling was the man for the job. There is no sentiment in this, Daughter, but only business."

"Poppycock!" she said, startling him again. "Perhaps the two of you believe the myth that has grown up around you that you are ruthless, hard-nosed, heartless businessmen to whom the making of money is the be-all and end-all of existence. Like most myths, it has hardly a grain of truth to it. You are soft to the core of your foolish hearts. You, sir, are an impostor."

His eyes twinkled at her. "It is Christmas, Daughter," he said. "Even men like my son and me dream of happy endings at Christmas, especially those involving love and romance. Leave us to our dreams."

Edgar, Helena noticed, was laughing with the rest of his group and setting an arm loosely about Cora's shoulders in an unconscious gesture of brotherly affection. He looked relaxed and carefree. But dreams—they were the one thing she must never cultivate. When one dreamed, one began to hope. One began to have images of happiness and of peace. Peace on earth and goodwill to all men. How she hated Christmas.

Her father-in-law patted her shoulder even as her aunt brought them their tea. "Let me dream, Daughter," he said. And she knew somehow that he was no longer talking about Fanny Grainger and Mr. Sperling.

* * *

The next day saw the return of some of the wedding guests who had come out from Bristol for that occasion and now came to Mobley Abbey to spend Christmas. Some of Edgar's personal friends were among them and some of his father's. Almost without exception, they had sons and daughters of marriageable age.

He had invited them, Mr. Downes explained to his son, when it had become obvious to him that his home was to be filled with aristocratic guests. He had welcomed the connections—he had wanted both his son and his daughter to marry into their class, after all—but he would not turn his back on his own. He was a man who aimed always to expand the horizons of his life, not one who allowed the old horizons to fade behind him as he aggressively pursued the new.

"But more than that, Edgar," he explained, "I realized the great gap there would be between the older, married guests and the children, with only Miss Grainger between. This was when it appeared that you would be celebrating your betrothal to her over Christmas. It seemed important that she have company of her own age. Under the changed circumstances, it seems even more important. And I like young people. They liven up a man's old age."

"The old man being you, I suppose," Edgar said with a grin. "You have more energy than any two of the rest of us put together, Papa."

His father chuckled.

But Edgar was pleased with the addition of more young people and of his own friends. He was more relaxed. He was able to see Fanny Grainger and Jack Sperling relax more.

The house guests had all arrived safely—and only just in time. The following night, the night before the planned excursion to gather greenery for decorating the house, brought a huge fall of snow, one that blanketed the ground and cut them off at least for a day or two from anywhere that could not be reached by foot.

"Look," Edgar said, leaning against the windowsill of his bedchamber just after he had got out of bed. He turned his head to glance at Helena, who was still lying there, awake. "Come and look."

"It is too cold," she complained.

"Nonsense," he said, "the fire has already been lit." But he went to fetch her a warm dressing gown and set it about her as she got out of bed, grumbling. "Come and look."

He kept an arm about her shoulders as she looked out at the snow and the lowering clouds which threatened more. Indeed more was already sifting down in soft, dancing flakes. She said nothing, but he saw wonder in her eyes for a moment—the eternal wonder that children from one to ninety always feel at the first fall of snow.

"Snow for Christmas," she said at last, her voice cool. "How very timely. Everyone will be delighted."

"My first snowball will be targeted for the back of your neck," he said. "I will treat you to that delicious feeling of snow melting in slow trickles down your back."

"How childish you are, Edgar," she said. "But why the back of the neck? My first one will splatter right in your face."

"Is this a declaration of war?" he asked.

"It is merely the natural reaction to a threat," she said. "Will the gathering of greenery have to be canceled? That snow must be several inches deep."

"Canceled?" he said. "Quite the contrary. What could be better designed to arouse the spirit of Christmas than the gathering of greenery in the snow? There will be so many distractions that the task will take at least twice as long as usual. But distractions can be enormous fun."

"Yes," she said with a sigh.

It struck him suddenly that he was happy. He was at Mobley Abbey with his family and friends, and Christmas was just a few days away. There was enough snow outside that it could not possibly all melt before Christmas. And he was standing in the window of his almost warm bedchamber with his arm about his pregnant wife. It was strange how happiness could creep up on a man and reveal itself in such unspectacular details.

He dipped his head and kissed her. She did not resist. They had made love each night of their marriage and though there had been little passion in the encounters, there had been the warmth of enjoyment—for both of them. He turned her against him, opened her mouth with his own, and reached his tongue inside. One of her arms came about his neck and her fingers twined themselves in his hair.

He would enjoy making love with her in the morning, he thought, with the snow outside and all the excitement of that fact and the Christmas preparations awaiting them. There could surely be no better way to start a day. It felt good to be a married man.

She drew back her head. "Don't, Edgar," she said.

He released her immediately. How foolish to have forgotten that it was Helena with all her prickliness to whom he was married. "I beg your pardon," he said. "I thought I had been given permission to have conjugal relations with you."

"Don't be deceived by snow and Christmas," she said. "Don't imagine tenderness where there is none, Edgar— either in yourself or in me. We married because I seduced you and we enjoyed a night of lust and conceived a child. It can be a workable marriage. I like your father and your sister and your friends. And I am reconciled to living in one place—even Bristol, heaven help me—and doing all the domestic things like running your home and being your hostess. I am even resigned to being a mother and will search out the best nurse for the child. But we must not begin to imagine that there is tenderness. There is none."

If he had fully believed her, he would have been chilled to the bone. As it was, he felt as if someone had thrown a pail of snow through the window and doused him with it.

"There must at least be an attempt at affection," he said.

"I cannot feel affection," she said. "Don't try to tempt me into it, Edgar. You are a handsome man and I am strongly attracted to you. I will not try to deny that what we do together on that bed is intensely pleasurable to me. But it is a thing of the body, not of the emotions. I respect you as a man. I do believe sometimes I even like you. Do the same for me if you must. But do not waste emotion on me."

"You are my *wife*," he said.

"I hurt badly what I am fond of," she said. "I hurt badly and forever. I do not *want* to be fond of you, Edgar. And I am not trying to be cruel. You are a decent man—I do wish you were not, but you are. Don't make me fond of you."

Did she realize what she was saying? She was *fond* of him and desperately fighting the feeling. But what had she done? He had been very deaf, he realized. She had insisted every time he had asked that no one had ever hurt her, that she had done the hurting. He had not listened. Someone must have hurt her, he had thought, and he had asked his questions accordingly. He had asked the wrong questions. Whom had she hurt? *I hurt badly and forever.* The words might have sounded theatrical coming from anyone else. But Helena meant them. And he had felt the bitterness in her, the despair, the refusal to be drawn free of her masks, the refusal to love or be loved.

"Very well, then," he said and smiled at her. "We will enjoy a relationship of respect and perhaps even liking and of unbridled lust. It sounds good to me, especially the last part."

He drew one of her rare amused smiles from her. "Damn you," she said without any conviction at all.

"We had better dress and go downstairs," he said, "before all the snow melts."

"I would hate that snowball to miss its destiny and never collide with your face," she said.

They were back down by the lake, spread along one of its banks, searching for holly and mistletoe and well-shaped evergreen boughs of the right size. The lake itself was like a vast flat empty field of snow on which some of the children—and three or four of the young people, too—had made long slides while whooping with delight. The snow would have to be swept off before anyone could skate, though the ice had been pronounced by the head gardener to be thick enough to bear any human weight. But the skating would have to wait until tomorrow, they had all been told. Today was strictly for the gathering of greenery and the decorating of the house.

Of course it had turned out not to be strictly for any such thing, just as Edgar had predicted. There had been a great deal of horseplay and noise ever since the first one of them had set foot outside the house. A vicious snowball fight had been waged and won and lost before any of them had succeeded in getting even twenty yards from the house. Edgar's first snowball had been safely deflected by Helena's shoulder—she had seen it coming. Her own had landed squarely in the middle of his laughing face.

"If you think to win any war against me, Edgar," she had told him while he shook his head like a wet dog and wiped his face with his snowy gloves, "let that be a warning to you."

"You win," he had said, smiling ruefully and setting a hand at the back of her neck. When he had picked up a palmful of snow she did not know. But every drop of it, she would swear, had found its way down inside her cloak and dress.

Samantha, Marchioness of Carew, and Jane, Countess of Greenwald, had shown all the little girls and some of the older ones, too, how to make snow angels and soon there was a heavenly host of them spread out on what was usually a lawn.

By slow degrees they had all made their way to the lake and the woods and been divided into work parties. Both her father-in-law and her husband had tried to persuade Helena to return to the house instead of going all the way. She wished they had not. She might have gone back if she had been left to herself. But once challenged, she had had no choice but to go. Not that she felt too weak or fatigued. She just did not want any more merriment.

In the event she soon became involved in it. It really was irresistible. There were children to be helped and children to be played with and young people and people of her own generation to be laughed with. She had forgotten how warm and wonderful family life could be. She had forgotten how exhilarating a good old-fashioned English Christmas could be. She had forgotten how sheerly pleasurable it was to relax and interact with other people of all ages, talking and teasing and laughing.

It was so easy to be seduced by Christmas. The thought was conscious in her mind more than once, but she could not seem to fight against it. Stephen, the little Greenwald boy, appeared to have adopted her as a favored aunt and had persuaded a few of the other children of similar age to do likewise. When she should have been directing them in the carrying of a largish pile of holly to the central cache close to the lake, she found herself instead dancing in a ring with the children, chanting "Ring around the rosy" and actually tossing herself into the snow with them when everyone's favorite line had been chanted—"We all fall down." And laughing as merrily as any of them as she staggered back to her feet and dusted herself off.

She had known it would happen. She had fought weakly against it and allowed Christmas and the snow to win—for now. Perhaps even in the afterlife, she thought, there were brief vacations from hell. Perhaps only so that it would appear even worse afterward. She tried not to watch Edgar climbing trees for mistletoe, lifting nephews and a niece and other children on his broad shoulders by turns so that they could reach the desired holly branches—why did the best ones always seem to be above the reach of an outstretched arm? Why were the best of all things just beyond one's grasp?

A surprise awaited everyone when the greenery was finally gathered and piled neatly in one place ready to be hauled back to the house. A group of warmly clad gardeners and house servants had built a large bonfire and were busy warming chocolate and roasting chestnuts over it.

They all suddenly realized how cold they were and how tired and thirsty—and hungry. There was a great deal of foot stamping and glove slapping and talking and laughing.

And someone—Helena thought it was probably one of the Bristol guests—started singing, a bold gamble when he might have ended up singing an embarrassed solo. But of course he did not. Soon they were all singing one carol after another and being very merry and very sentimental and only marginally musical. Helena shivered and found a log on which to sit, her gloved hands warming about her chocolate cup.

"I suppose," Edgar said, seating himself beside her, "I will have my head bitten off when I ask if you are over-tired?"

"Yes," she said, "I suppose you will."

He had been offering affection this morning. It was some-thing Edgar would do, of course. A perfectionist in all things, he would not be satisfied with a forced marriage to a woman whose behavior in London must have disgusted as well as excited him. He would try to create a marriage of affection out of what they had. And she had rebuffed him.

Would it be possible? she wondered, and was frightened by the question that expressed itself quite verbally in her mind. The answer was very clear to her. Of course it would be possible. One could not respect a man and like him and admire him and find him attractive and enjoy intimacies with him without there being the possibility of affection for him. Indeed, if she let down all her inner guard, she might even admit to herself . . . No!

Dared she allow the element of affection to creep into their relationship? Perhaps after all there was an end to punishment and self-loathing. Perhaps Edgar was strong enough . . . Certainly he was stronger than . . . No!

Her cup was empty and had lost its comforting warmth. She set it down on the ground at her feet. When Edgar took her hand in his, she curled her fingers about it. He was singing with everyone else. He had a good tenor voice. She had not heard him sing before. He was her husband. Their lives were linked together for all time. It was his child she carried. They were to be parents together—perhaps more than once. That was a new thought. Perhaps they would have more than one child. There would be other occasions like this down the years.

Did she dare to let go and simply enjoy? When someone else, because of her, would suffer for the rest of a lifetime?

She turned her head to look at her husband. Decent, strong, honorable Edgar. Who deserved far better. But who would never have it unless she dared give more in her marriage than she had been prepared to give. And who might forever be sorry if she did.

He looked back at her and stopped singing. He smiled and lowered his head to kiss her briefly on the lips. A small token of—affection. Was he going to pay her warning no heed, then?

"Such a bleak look, Helena," he said. "Yet you have been looking so happy."

"Let us not start this again," she said.

But his next words had her jumping to her feet in terror and panic.

"Tell me about your stepson," he said. "Tell me about Sir Gerald Stapleton."

She turned and stumbled off in the direction of the house. She tried to shake off his arm when he caught up to her and took her in his grasp.

"I was right, then," he said. "I picked on the right person. Steady, Helena. You cannot run all the way home. We will walk. You cannot run from yourself either. Have you not realized that yet? And you will not run from me. But we will take it slowly—both the walk and the other. Slow your steps."

A chaplain praying over a condemned man must speak in just that quiet, soothing voice, she thought.

"Damn you, Edgar!" she cried. "Damn you, damn you, damn you!"

"Calm yourself," he said. "Walk slowly. There is no hurry."

"I hate you," she said. "Oh, how I hate you. You are loathsome and I hate you. Damn you," she added for good measure.

Chapter Fourteen

———✦———

Incredibly, nothing more was said on the subject of Helena's stepson. They walked home in silence and Edgar took her straight to their bedchamber, where she slumped wearily onto the bed, taking the time only to remove her boots and outdoor garments before she did so. He went to stand at the window until he looked over his shoulder and noticed that she had not covered herself, though the room was rather chilly. He wrapped the top quilt carefully about her to the chin. She was already asleep.

She slept deeply for two hours while Edgar first watched her, then returned to his place at the window, and finally went downstairs when he saw that everyone else was coming back to the house, loaded with greenery. He helped to carry armfuls inside while their original bearers stamped snow-packed boots on the steps and slapped at snowy clothing. He took the Bridgwater baby from the duke's arms and had unwound him from his many layers of warm clothing before a few of the nurses came hurrying downstairs to whisk him and most of the other children back up to the nursery with them. They were to be tidied and warmed and fed and put down for an obligatory rest before the excitement was to resume with the decoration of the house.

Edgar told several people who asked that his wife had merely felt herself tiring and was now having a sleep.

"I warned her that it would be too much for her," Mr.

Downes said. "You should have taken a firmer hand with her yourself, Edgar. You must not allow her to risk her health."

"I believe Helena is not one to take orders meekly, Papa," Edgar said.

"Oh, dear, no," Mrs. Cross agreed. "There was never anyone more stubborn than Helena, Mr. Downes. But she was exceedingly happy this morning. She still has a way with children, just as she always used to have. Children warm quickly to her, perhaps because she warms quickly to them. Yes, thank you, sir. You are most kind." Mr. Downes was taking her cloak and bonnet from her and looking around in vain for a footman who might be standing about doing nothing.

"Let me take you to the drawing room, ma'am," Edgar said, offering his arm, "where there will be a warm fire and probably some warm drinks too before nuncheon."

"Thank you," she said. "I must admit to feeling chilly. But I do not know when I have enjoyed myself as much as I have this morning, Mr. Downes. You cannot know what it means to me to be part of such a happy family Christmas."

"You always will be from now on, ma'am," he said, "if my wife and I have anything to say in the matter. Did you ever visit Helena during her first marriage?"

"Oh, yes, indeed," she said, "two or three times. She had a gift for happiness in those days. I suppose the marriage was not entirely to her liking—Sir Christian Stapleton was so much older than she, you know. But she made the best of it. She had that vibrancy and those smiles." She smiled herself. "Perhaps they will come back now. I am confident they will. This is a far better match for her."

"Thank you," he said. "I hope you are right. Did you know Sir Christian's son?"

"Poor boy," she said. "He was very lonely and timid and not much loved by his father, I believe. But Helena was good to him. She set herself to mothering him and shielding him from his father's impatience—she could always wheedle him with her sunny ways. They both worshiped her. But you do not want to be hearing this, Mr. Downes. That was a long time ago. I am very glad Helena has a chance at last to have a child of her own—and a husband of her own age. I was shocked at first and was perhaps not as kind to you as I ought to have been. I do apologize for that. You are a fine young man, I believe."

"You were all that was gracious, ma'am," he said. "Take this chair while I fetch you a drink. You should be warm again in a moment."

By the time Helena woke up nuncheon was over—Edgar had a tray sent up to her—and the drawing room, the dining room, the ballroom, and the hall were being cleared, ready for the decorating. The older children had already come downstairs and the younger ones were being brought just as she came down herself. There was much to do and many people to do it. It was certainly not the time for a serious talk.

Edgar had been appointed to direct most of the men and some of the bigger children in the decoration of the ballroom. It involved much climbing of ladders and leaning out precariously into space. Cora shrieked when she saw her eldest son, ten rungs up one of the ladders, intent on handing his father a hammer. She showed every intention of climbing up herself to rescue him, though she was terrified of heights, and was banished to the drawing room.

Stephanie, Duchess of Bridgwater, and Fanny Grainger, self-proclaimed experts in the making of kissing boughs, were constructing the main one for the drawing room with the help of some of the other ladies. Helena, self-proclaimed nonexpert, was making another with the help of far too many children for any degree of efficiency. She had thrown herself into the task, Edgar noticed, with bright-faced enthusiasm. Of course the sleep had done her good, she had assured his father and a few other people who had thought to ask. All her energy was restored and redoubled. She smiled dazzlingly. She ignored her husband as if he did not exist.

She could not continue to do so indefinitely, of course. Finally all was done and they were summoned to the drawing room for hot punch—hot lemonade for the children—and for the first annual ceremony of the raising of the kissing bough, Mr. Downes announced when they were all assembled. Adults chuckled and children squealed with laughter.

It was finally in place at the very center of the room below the chandelier. They all gazed at it admiringly. The Marquess of Carew began a round of applause and Fanny blushed while the duchess laughed.

"It would seem appropriate to me," Mr. Downes said, "for the bough to be put to the test by the new bride and groom. We have to be sure that it works."

There was renewed applause. There were renewed shrieks from the children. The Earl of Thornhill whistled.

"Pucker up, Edgar, old chap," Lord Francis said.

Well, Edgar thought, stepping forward and reaching for his wife's hand, he had not kissed her at their wedding. He supposed he owed everyone this.

"Now, let me see." He played to the audience, setting his hands on Helena's shoulders and looking upward with a frown of concentration. "Ah, yes, there. Dead center. That should work." He grinned at her. She gazed back, the afternoon's bright gaiety still in her face. "Happy Christmas, Mrs. Downes."

They lingered over the kiss, entirely for the benefit of their cheering audience. It was not exactly his idea of an erotic experience, Edgar thought, to indulge in public kissing. But he was surprised by the tide of warmth that flooded over him. Not physical warmth—or at least not *sexual* warmth. Just the warmth of love, he and his wife literally surrounded by family and friends at Christmas.

He smiled down at her when they were finished. "It works exceedingly well," he said. "But we do not expect anyone to believe it merely because we have said so. Do we, my love? You are all welcome to try for yourselves."

Rosamond, young daughter of the Carews, pulled the marquess out beneath the bough, and he bent over her, smiling, and kissed her to the accompaniment of much laughter. No one, it seemed, was prepared to take Edgar at his word or that of anyone who came after him and confirmed his opinion. Hardly anyone went unkissed, and those who did—those children of middle years who were both too old and too young to kiss and pulled gargoyle faces at the very thought—did so entirely from choice.

Jack Sperling and Fanny Grainger were almost the last. Edgar had watched them grow progressively more self-conscious and uncomfortable until finally Jack got up his courage, strode toward her, and led her onto the recently vacated space beneath the bough with all the firm determination any self-respecting man of business could possibly want in an employee. Their lips clung together with very obvious yearning—for perhaps the duration of one whole second. And then she scurried away, scarlet to the tips of her ears, her eyes avoiding those of her suitor—and those of her barely smiling parents.

The elder Mr. Downes was last.

"Well, Mrs. Cross," he said heartily, "I am not sure I believe all these young folk. There is something sorry seeming about that bough, pretty as it is and loaded down with mistletoe as it is. I believe you and I should see what all the fuss is about."

Mrs. Cross did not argue or even blush, Edgar was interested to note. She stepped quietly under the bough and lifted her face. "I believe we should, sir," she said.

It felt strange watching his father kissing a woman, even if it was just a public Christmas kiss beneath mistletoe. One tended not to think of one's own father in such terms. It was not the sort of smacking kiss his father often bestowed on Cora and his grandchildren. Brief and decorous though it was, it was definitely the sort of kiss a man exchanges with a woman.

"Well, what do you say, ma'am?" His father was frowning ferociously and acting to the audience of shrieking, bouncing children, who had lost some interest in the proceeding until Grandpapa had decided to take a turn.

"I think I would have to say it really is a kissing bough, sir," Mrs. Cross said calmly and seriously. "I would have to say it works very nicely indeed."

"My sentiments entirely," he said. "Now I am not so sure about the monstrous concoction of ribbons and bows that is hanging in the hall. The children's creation with the help of my daughter-in-law, I believe. *That* is no kissing bough." He still had his hands on Mrs. Cross's waist, Edgar noticed, while grimacing from the noise of children screeching in indignation.

"*What?*" his father said, looking about him in some amazement. "It *is*?"

The children responded like a Greek chorus.

And so nothing would do but Mr. Downes had to tuck Mrs. Cross's arm beneath his and lead them all in an unruly procession down the stairs to the hall, where Helena's grotesque and ragged creation hung in all its tasteless glory. He kissed Mrs. Cross again, with a resounding smack of the lips this time, and pronounced the children's kissing bough even more effective than the one in the drawing room.

The children burst into mass hysteria.

It had been a thoroughly enjoyable afternoon for all. But parents were only human, after all. The children were gradually herded in the direction of the nursery, where it fell to the lot of their poor nurses to calm their high spirits. Something resembling quiet descended on the house. The conservatory would be the quietest place of all, Edgar thought. He would take his wife there. They could not suspend indefinitely the talk that this morning's revelation had made inevitable.

He had to find out about Gerald Stapleton.

But Cora had other ideas. She reached Helena's side before he did. "The children's party on Christmas Day needs to be planned, Helena," she said, "as well as the ball in the evening. Papa has had all the invitations sent out, of course, and the cook has all the food plans well in hand. But there is much else to be organized. Shall we spend an hour on it now?"

"Of course," Helena said. "Just you and I, Cora?"

"Stephanie was a governess before she was a duchess," Cora said. "Did you know that? She is wonderful with children."

"Then we will ask her if she wishes to help us plan games," Helena said.

They went away to some destination unknown, taking the duchess with them as well as the wife and daughter of one of Edgar's Bristol friends. After they returned, it was time to change for dinner. And dinner, with so many guests, and with so many Christmas decorations to be exclaimed over and so many Christmas plans to be divulged and discussed, lasted a great long while. So did coffee in the drawing room afterward, with several of the young people entertaining the company informally with pianoforte recitals and singing.

But it could not be postponed until bedtime, Edgar decided. And certainly not until tomorrow. He had started this. He had thought methodically through all he knew of Helena, and all she had told him, and not told him, and had concluded that her first husband was not the key figure in her present unhappiness and bitterness. It was far more likely to have been the son. Her reaction to his question this morning had left him in no doubt whatsoever. She had been so shocked and so distressed that she had not even tried to deceive him with impassivity.

They must talk. She must tell him everything. Both for her own sake and for the sake of their marriage. Perhaps forcing her to confront her past in his hearing was entirely the wrong thing to do. The bitterness that was always at the back of her eyes and just behind her smiles might burst through and destroy the fragile control she had imposed on her own life. The baring of her soul, which she had repeatedly told him she would never do, might well destroy their marriage almost before it had begun. She might loathe him with a very real intensity for the rest of their lives.

But their marriage stood no real chance if she kept her secrets. They might live together as man and wife in some amity and harmony for many years. But they would be amicable strangers who just happened to share a name, a home, a bed, and a child or two. He wanted more than that. He could not be satisfied with so little. He was willing to risk—he *had* to risk—the little they had in the hope that he would get everything in return and with the very real risk that he would lose everything.

But then his life was constantly lived on a series of carefully calculated risks. Of course, as an experienced and successful businessman, he never risked all or even nearly all on one venture. No single failure had ever ruined him, just as no single success had ever made him. This time it was different. This time he risked everything—everything he had, everything he was.

He had realized in the course of the day that he was not only in love with her. He loved her.

He might well be headed toward self-destruction. But he had no choice.

She was conversing with a group of his friends. She was being her most vibrant, fascinating self, and they were all charmed by her, he could see. He touched her on the arm, smiled, and joined in the conversation for a few minutes before addressing himself just to her.

"It is a wonderfully clear night," he said. "The sky will look lovely from the conservatory. Come and see it there with me?"

She smiled and he caught a brief glimpse of desperation behind her eyes.

"That is the most blatantly contrived invitation a man ever offered his new bride, Edgar," one of his friends said. "We have all done it in our time. 'Come and see the stars, my love.'"

The laughter that greeted his words was entirely good-natured.

"Take no notice, Edgar," one of the wives told him. "Horace is merely envious because he did not think of it first."

"I will come and see the stars," Helena said in her lowest, most velvet voice, leaving with their friends the impression that she expected not to see a single one of them.

Which was, in a sense, true.

He stood at one of the wide windows of the conservatory, his hands clasped at his back, his feet slightly apart. He was looking outward, upward at the stars. He looked comfortable, relaxed. She knew it was a false impression.

She liked the conservatory, though she had not had the chance to spend much time here. There were numerous plants and the warmth of a summer garden. Yet the outdoors was fully visible through the many windows. The contrast with the snowy outdoors this evening was quite marked. The sky was indeed clear.

"The stars are bright," she said. "But you must not expect to see the Bethlehem star yet, Edgar. It is two nights too early."

"Yes," he said.

She had not approached the windows herself. She had seated herself on a wrought-iron seat beneath a giant palm. She felt curiously calm, resigned. She supposed that from the moment she had set eyes on Edgar Downes and had felt that overpowering need to do more than merely flirt with him this moment had become inevitable. She had become a firm believer in fate. Why had she returned to London at very much an off-season for polite society? Why had he chosen such an inopportune time to go to London to choose a bride?

It was because they had been fated to meet. Because *this* had been fated.

"He was fourteen when I married his father," she said. "He was just a child. When you are nineteen, Edgar, a fourteen-year-old seems like a child. He was small and thin and timid and unappealing. He did not have much promise." Because she had been unhappy herself and a little bewildered, she had felt instant sympathy for the boy, more than if he had been handsome and robust and confident.

"But you liked him," Edgar said.

"He had had a sad life," she said. "His mother abandoned him when he was eight years old to go and live with her two sisters. He had adored her and had felt adored in return. Christian tried to soften the blow by telling him that she was dead. But when she really did die five years later, Gerald suddenly found himself thrust into mourning for her and knew that she had loved him so little. Or so it seemed. One cannot really know the truth about that woman, I suppose. Everything about him irritated Christian. Poor Gerald! He could do nothing right."

"And so you became a new mother to him?" he asked.

"More like an elder sister perhaps," she said. "I talked to him and listened to him. I helped him with his lessons, especially with arithmetic, which made no sense at all to him. When Christian was from home I listened to him play the pianoforte and sometimes sang to his accompaniment. He had real talent, Edgar, but he was ashamed of it because his father saw it as unmanly. I helped him get over his terrible conviction that he was unlovable and worthless and stupid. He was none of the three. He was sweet. It is a weak word to use of a boy, but it is the right word to use of Gerald. There was such sweetness in him." He had filled such a void in her life.

"I suppose," Edgar said, breaking the silence she had been unaware of, "he fell in love with you."

"No," she said. "He grew up. At eighteen he was pleasing to look at and very sweet natured. He was—he was youthful."

Edgar had braced his arms wide on the windowsill and hung his head. "You seduced him," he said. He was breathing heavily. "Your husband's son."

She set her head back against the palm and closed her eyes. "I loved him," she said. "As a *person* I loved him. He was sweet and trusting and far more intelligent and talented than he realized. And he was vulnerable. His sense of his own worth was so very fragile. I knew it and feared for him. And I—I wanted him. I was horrified. I hated myself—*hated* myself. You could not know how much. No one could hate me as I hated myself. I tried to fight it but I was very weak. I was sitting one day on a bridge, one of the most picturesque spots in the park at Brookhurst, and he was coming toward me, looking bright and eager about something—I can no longer remember what. I took his hands and . . . Well, I frightened him and he ran away. Of all the shame I have felt since, I do not believe I have ever known any of greater intensity than I felt after he had gone. And yet it happened twice more before he persuaded Christian to send him away to university."

She had thought of killing herself, she remembered. She had even wondered how she might best do it. She had not had enough courage even for that.

"Now tell me that you are glad I have told you, Edgar," she said after a while. "Tell me you are proud to have such a wife."

There was another lengthy silence. "You were young," he said, "and found yourself in an arranged marriage with a much older man. There were only five years between you and your stepson. You were lonely."

"Is it for me you try to make excuses, Edgar?" she asked. "Or for yourself? Are you trying to convince yourself that you have not made such a disastrous marriage after all? There are no excuses. What I did was unforgivable."

"Did you beg his pardon later?" he asked. "Did he refuse to grant it?"

"I saw him only once after he left for university," she said. "It was at his father's funeral three years later. We did not speak. There are certain things for which one cannot ask for pardon, Edgar, because there is no pardon."

He turned to look at her at last. "You have been too hard on yourself," he said. "It was an ugly thing, what you did, but nothing is beyond pardon. And it was a long time ago. You have changed."

"I seduced you a little over two months ago," she said.

"I am your equal in age and experience, Helena," he said, "as I suppose all your lovers have been. You have had to convince yourself that you are promiscuous, have you not? You have had to punish yourself, to convince yourself that you are evil. It is time you put the past behind you."

"The past is always with me, Edgar," she said. "The past had consequences. I destroyed him."

"That is doubtless an exaggeration," he said. "He would not dally with his father's wife and went away. Good for him. He showed some strength of character. Perhaps in some way the experience was even the making of him. You have been too hard on yourself."

"It is what I hoped would happen," she said. "I went to Scotland after Christian's death and waited and waited for word that Gerald was somehow settled in life. Then I went traveling and waited again. I finally heard news of him last year in the late summer. Doubtless you would have, too, Edgar, if you moved in *ton*nish circles. Doubtless Cora and Francis heard. He married."

"Well, then." He had come to stand in front of her. He was frowning down at her. "He has married. He has found peace and contentment. He has doubtless forgotten what has so obsessed you."

"Fool!" she said. "I finally confirmed him in what all the experiences of his life had pointed to—that he was unlovable and worthless. He married a whore, Edgar."

"A whore?" he said. "Those are strong words."

"From a woman who has admitted to having had many lovers?" she said. "Perhaps. But she worked in a brothel. Half the male population of London paid for her services, I daresay. I suppose that is where Gerald met her. He took her and made her his mistress and then married her. Is that the action of a man with any sense of self-worth?"

"I do not know," he said. "I do not know the two people or the circumstances."

She laughed without any humor whatsoever. "I do know Gerald," she said. "It is just what he would do and just the sort of thing that for years I dreaded to hear. He thought himself worthy of nothing better in a wife than a whore."

"How old was he last year?" Edgar asked. "Twenty-nine? Thirty?"

"No," she said, "you will not use that argument with me, Edgar. I will not allow you to talk me out of my belief in my own responsibility for what has become of him. I will not let you forgive me. You do not have the power. No one does."

He went down on his haunches and reached out his hands to her.

"Touch me now," she said, "and I will never forgive you. A hug will not solve it, Edgar. I am not the one who needs the hug. And you cannot comfort me. There is no comfort. There is no forgiveness. And do not pretend you do not feel disgust—for what I did, for what I trapped you into, for the fact that I am bearing your child."

He drew breath and sighed audibly. "How long ago did this happen, Helena?" he asked. "Ten years? Twelve?"

"Thirteen," she said.

"Thirteen." He gazed at her. "You have lived in a self-made hell for thirteen years. My dear, it will not do. It just will not do."

"I am tired." She got to her feet, careful not to touch him. "I am going to bed. I am sorry you have to share it with me, Edgar. If you wish to make other arrangements—"

He grabbed her then and drew her against him and she felt the full force of his strength. Although she fought him, she could not free herself. After a few moments she did not even try. She sagged against him, soaking up his warmth and his strength, breathing in the smell of him. Feeling the lure of a nonexistent peace.

"Hate me if you will," he said, "but I will touch you and hold you. When we go to bed I will make love to you. You are my wife. And if you are so unworthy to be forgiven and to be loved, Helena, why is it that I can forgive you? Why is it that I love you?"

She breathed in slowly and deeply. "I am so tired, Edgar," she said. So tired. Always tired. Not just from her pregnancy, surely. She was soul-weary. "Please. I am so tired." Was that abject voice hers?

"We will go to bed, then," he said. "But I want you to see something first." He led her to the window, one arm firmly about her waist. "You see?" He pointed upward to one star that was brighter than all the others. "It is there, Helena. Not only on the night of Christmas Eve. Always if we just look for it. There is always hope."

"Dreamer," she said, her voice shaky. "Sentimentalist. Edgar, you are supposed to be a man of reason and cold good sense."

"I am also a man who loves," he said. "I always have, from childhood on. And I am what you are stuck with. For life, I am afraid. I'll never let you forget that star is always there."

There was such a mingling of despair and hope in her that her chest felt tight and her throat sore. She buried her face against his shoulder and said nothing. After a few minutes of silence he took her up to bed.

Chapter Fifteen

Edgar was up before dawn the next morning, a little earlier than usual. The fire had not yet been made up. He shivered as he stretched his arms above his head and looked out through the window. As last night's clear sky had suggested, there had been no more snow.

He was tired. Nevertheless he was glad to be up. He had slept only in fits and starts through the night, and he had felt Helena's sleeplessness, though they had not spoken and had lain turned away from each other for most of the night after he had made love to her.

Her story had been ugly enough. What she had done had been truly shameful. She had been a married woman, however little say she had had in the choice of her husband. She had known and understood the boy's vulnerability—and he had been her husband's son. She had been old enough to know better, and of course she *had* known better. The attraction, the desire had been understandable—the son had been far closer to her own age than the father. That she had given in to temptation was blameworthy. She had been morally weak.

Her conscience had not been correspondingly weak. She had punished herself ever since. She had refused either to ask forgiveness or to forgive herself simply because she thought her sin unforgivable. She had never allowed herself to be happy or to love—or be loved. He guessed that her extensive travels had been her way of trying to escape from

herself. It might be said that true repentance should have
made her celibate. But Edgar believed he had been right in
what he had said to her the night before. She had punished
herself with promiscuity, with the conviction that she was
truly depraved.

Their marriage stood not one chance in a million of
bringing either of them contentment. Unless . . .

It would be an enormous risk. He had known that all
through the night. She was quite convinced that she had
destroyed her stepson, that her betrayal had been the final
straw in an unhappy life of abuse. And she had been quite
certain of her facts when describing the man's marriage. He
had married a prostitute taken from a London brothel.

It seemed very probable that she was right. And if she
was, there would never be any peace for her. He might argue until kingdom come that Sir Gerald Stapleton had been
abused by both his father and mother, far more important
people in his life than she had ever been, and that he had
not used his individual freedom when he was old enough to
fight back against his image of himself as a victim. Helena
would forever blame herself.

And so he must do today the only thing he could do. It
was the only hope left, however slim it might be. He must
remember what he had told his wife last night about the
star. It was always there, the Christmas star perhaps, constant symbol of hope. There must always be hope. The only
thing left when there was no hope was despair. Helena had
lived too long with despair.

Her stillness and quietness did not deceive him. She was
awake, as she had been most of the night. He crossed to the
bed and set a hand on her shoulder.

"I am going to Bristol," he said. "There is some business
that must be taken care of before the holiday. I will stay at
the house tonight and return tomorrow."

He expected questions. What business could possibly
have arisen so suddenly two days before Christmas when
there had not even been any post yesterday?

"Yes," she said. "All right."

He squeezed her shoulder. "Get some rest," he said.
"Yes."

The dusk of dawn had still not given place to the full light of day when Edgar led his horse from the stables, set it to a cautious pace to allow it to become accustomed to the snowy roads, and set his course for Brookhurst, thirty miles away.

It was an enormous relief to have Edgar gone for the day. It would have been difficult to face him in the morning after the night before. Helena was annoyed with herself for giving in to his constant needling and pestering. She should never have told him the truth. She had done so as a self-indulgence. It had felt surprisingly cathartic sitting there in the quiet, darkened conservatory, reliving those memories for someone else's ears. She almost envied papists their confessionals.

But it had not just been self-indulgence. She had owed him the truth. He was her husband. And therein lay the true problem. She was unaccustomed to thinking sympathetically about another person, caring about his feelings. It was something she had not done in years. And something she ought not to do now. What good could ever come of her sympathy, of her compassion?

She cared about him. He was a decent man, and he had been good to her. But she must not care *for* him or allow herself to be comforted *by* his care. She remembered what he had said the night before—*why is it that I love you?* She shook her head to rid her mind of the sound of his voice saying those words.

She was glad he had gone. There was no business in Bristol, of course. His friends had looked surprised and his father astonished when she had given that as an explanation for his absence. He had gone there so that he could be away from her for a day, so that he could think and plan. There would be a greater distance between them by the time he returned, once he had had the chance to digest fully what she had told him. And a greater distance on her part, too—she must return to the aloofness, the air of mockery that had become second nature to her for a number of years but that had been deserting her since their marriage. She was glad she had not told him the one, final truth.

She was glad he had gone.

She spent a busy day. She walked into the village during the morning with Cora and Jane, Countess of Greenwald, to purchase some prizes for the children's games at the Christmas party. The children, the young people, and most of the men had gone out to the hill to ride the sleds down its snowy slopes. After nuncheon she was banished to her room by her father-in-law for a rest and was surprised to find that she slept soundly for a whole hour. And then she went outside when it became obvious that the duke and duchess, who were going to build a snowman for their little boy, had acquired a sizable train of other small children determined to go along to see and to help.

"You are remarkably good with children, Mrs. Downes," the Duke of Bridgwater told her when three snowmen of varying sizes and artistic merit were standing in a row. "So is Stephanie. I might have stayed inside the house and toasted my toes at the fire."

It was surprising in a way that he had not done so. Helena had been acquainted with him for several years and had always known him as an austere, correct, rather toplofty aristocrat. He still gave that impression when one did not see him in company with his wife or his son. Their company was obviously preferable to toasted toes this afternoon, despite his words.

For a moment Helena felt a pang of emptiness. She favored the duke with her mocking smile. "It must be incipient maternity that is causing me to behave so much out of character, your grace," she said. "I have never before been accused of anything as shudderingly awful as being good with children."

"I do beg your pardon, ma'am," he said with a gleam in his eye. "I experienced much the same horror less than a

month ago when my butler observed me to be galloping—
galloping, ma'am—along an upper corridor of my home
with my son on my shoulders. Why I confess to this next
detail I do not know—I was *whinnying*." He grimaced.

Helena laughed.

The evening was spent in the drawing room. Family and
guests passed the time with music and cards and conversation and a vigorous game of charades, suggested by the
young son and daughter of one of Mr. Downes's friends and
participated in with great enthusiasm by all the young people and a few of the older ones, too.

A definite romance was developing between Fanny
Grainger and Mr. Sperling, Helena noticed. They were being very careful and very discreet and were watched almost
every moment by Sir Webster and Lady Grainger, who
dared not appear too disapproving, but who were far from
being enthusiastic. But matters had been helped along by
her father-in-law's apparently careless remark at tea that Edgar's business was to buy and renovate Mr. Sperling's country estate as a future home for the young man when he
should have risen high enough in the company's ranks to
need it as a sign of status.

Edgar either felt very guilty about Miss Grainger, Helena
concluded, or he had a great soft heart, inherited with far
tougher attributes from his father. She strongly favored the
soft heart theory.

It felt good to be alone again, Helena thought, to be free
of him for one day at least. She wondered if he had got
safely to Bristol. She wondered if he had dressed warmly
enough for the journey or if he had caught a chill. She wondered what he was doing this evening. Was he sitting at
home, brooding? Or enjoying his solitude? Was he out visiting friends or otherwise amusing himself? She wondered
if he kept mistresses. She supposed he must have over the
years. He was six-and-thirty after all and had never before
been married. Besides, he was an experienced and skilled
lover. But she could not somehow imagine the very respectable, very bourgeois Edgar Downes keeping a mistress now

that he had a wife. Not that she would mind. But she had a
sudden image of Edgar doing with another woman what he
did with her in their bed upstairs and felt decidedly
irritable—and even murderous.

She did not care what he was doing tonight in Bristol.
She was just happy to be able to converse and laugh and
even join in the charades without feeling his eyes on her.

Was he thinking about her?

She hoped he was not wasting time and energy doing
any such thing, since she was certainly not thinking
about him.

Sir Gerald Stapleton's butler would see if he was at home,
he told Edgar with a stiff bow when the latter presented
himself and his card at the main doors of Brookhurst late
in the afternoon. He showed Edgar into a salon leading off
the hall.

At least, Edgar thought, the long journey had not been
quite in vain. Stapleton might refuse to see him, but clearly
he had not gone away for Christmas. The butler would have
known very well then that he was not at home. He stood at
the window. There was as much snow here as at Mobley. It
was an elegant house. The park was large and attractive,
even with its snow cover.

He turned when the door opened again. The man who
stepped inside did not surprise him, except perhaps in one
detail. He was not particularly tall or broad or handsome. He
was well dressed though with no extravagance of taste. There
was something quite ordinary and unremarkable about his
appearance. Except for his pleasant, open countenance—
that was the surprise. Though a man might look that way
merely out of politeness when he had a visitor, of course.

"Mr. Downes?" he said, looking at the card in his hand.

Edgar inclined his head. "From Bristol, as you see on
the card," he said. "My father owns Mobley Abbey thirty
miles from here."

"Ah, yes," Sir Gerald Stapleton said. "That is why the

name seemed familiar to me. The snow must make for slow travel. You are on your way to Mobley for Christmas? I am glad you found Brookhurst on your way and decided to break your journey here. I will send for refreshments."

"I came from Mobley Abbey today," Edgar said, "specifically to see and to speak with you. I am recently married. My wife was Lady Stapleton, your father's widow."

Sir Gerald's expression became instantly more guarded. "I see," he said. "My felicitations to you."

"Thank you," Edgar said. It was very difficult to know how to proceed. "And to my wife?" he asked.

Sir Gerald looked down at the card and placed it absently into a pocket. He was clearly considering his reply. "I mean you no offense, sir," he said at last. "I have no kind feelings for Mrs. Downes."

Ah. It was not simply a case then of something Helena had blown quite out of proportion with reality. Sir Gerald Stapleton had neither forgotten nor forgiven.

"Then you mean me offense," Edgar said quietly.

Sir Gerald half smiled. "I would offer you the hospitality of my home," he said, "but we would both be more comfortable, I believe, if you stayed at the village inn. It is a posting inn and quite respectable. I thank you for informing me."

"She believes she destroyed you," Edgar said.

Sir Gerald pursed his lips for a moment. "She did not do that," he said. "You may inform her so, if you wish."

"She believes she betrayed your trust at a time in your life when you were particularly vulnerable," Edgar said. "She believes you have never recovered from her selfish cruelty. And so she has never forgiven herself or stopped punishing herself."

"Helena?" Sir Gerald said, walking toward the fireplace and staring down at the fire burning there. "She was so much in command of herself. So confident. So without conscience. I remember her at my father's funeral, cold and proud—and newly wealthy. I beg your pardon, sir. I speak of your wife and do not expect you to remain quiet while you hear her maligned. You may assure her that she has had no lasting effect on my life. You may even say, if you will, that I wish her well in her new marriage. That is all I have to say on the subject. If we can find some other topic of mutual interest, I will order hot refreshment to warm you before you return to the cold. I would like to hear about Mobley Abbey. I hear that it has been restored to some of its earlier splendor."

There was no avoiding it. "My wife believes that your marriage was an outcome of your lasting unhappiness," Edgar said, wondering if he was going to find himself fighting a duel before the day was out—or at dawn the next day.

"My marriage." Sir Gerald's face had lost all traces of good humor. "Have a care what you say about my marriage, sir. It is not open for discussion. I believe it would be best for both of us if we bade each other a civil good afternoon while we still may."

"Sir Gerald," Edgar said, "I love my wife."

Sir Gerald closed his eyes and drew breath audibly. "You can love such a woman," he said, "and yet you believe that I cannot? You believe that I must have married out of contempt for my wife and contempt for myself?"

"It is what my wife believes," Edgar said.

Sir Gerald stood in silence with his back to the fire for a long while. Finally he strode toward the door and Edgar prepared to see him leave and to know that he must return to Mobley with nothing more comforting for Helena than an assurance from her stepson that she had had no permanent effect on his life. But Sir Gerald stood in the doorway, calling instructions to his butler.

"Ask Lady Stapleton if she would be so good as to step down here," he said.

He returned to his position before the fire without looking at Edgar or exchanging another word with him. A few minutes passed before the door opened again.

She was a complete surprise. She was small, slender, dark-haired, decently dressed, and very pretty in an entirely wholesome way. She had a bright, intelligent face.

She glanced at Edgar and then looked at her husband in inquiry.

"Priss?" Sir Gerald held out one arm to her, his expression softened to what was unmistakably a deep affection. "Come here, my love. This is Mr. Edgar Downes of Bristol. He has recently married Helena. My wife, Lady Stapleton, sir."

She looked first into her husband's face with obvious concern and deep fondness as she moved toward him until he could circle her waist with his arm and draw her protectively to his side. Then she turned to Edgar. Her eyes were calm and candid. "Mr. Downes," she said, "I wish you happy."

"You sent Peter back to the nursery?" Sir Gerald asked her.

"Yes." She smiled at him and then turned back to Edgar. "Has my husband offered you refreshments, Mr. Downes? It is a chilly day."

She spoke with refined accents and with a graciousness that appeared to come naturally to her.

"Priss." Sir Gerald took one of her hands in both of his. "Mr. Downes says that Helena has never forgotten what happened and has never forgiven herself."

"I told you she probably had not, Gerald," she said.

"She believes she destroyed me," he said.

She tipped her head to one side and looked at him with such tenderness that Edgar found himself almost holding his breath. "She was very nearly right," she said.

Sir Gerald closed his eyes briefly. "She considers our marriage as evidence that she succeeded," he said.

"It is understandable that she should think that," she said gently.

"She wants my forgiveness." He looked up. "I suppose that *is* why you came, Mr. Downes? I cannot give it. But you may describe my wife to her, if you wish, and tell her that Lady Stapleton is the woman I honor above all other women and love more than my own life. Will it suffice? If it will not, I have nothing more to offer, I am afraid."

Edgar found himself locking eyes with Lady Stapleton and feeling shock at the sympathy that passed between them.

"If Mrs. Downes has not forgotten the pain of that time in her life, sir," she said, "neither has my husband. It is a wound very easily rubbed raw. I have tried to convince Gerald that in reality there are very few people who are monsters without conscience. I have told him that Helena has probably always regretted what happened. She is very unhappy?"

"Very, ma'am," he said.

"And you are fond of her." It was a statement, not a question. Her intelligent eyes searched his face.

"Yes, ma'am."

"Gerald." She turned to him and looked earnestly at him. "Here is your chance for final peace. If you forgive her, you may finally forget."

Edgar tried to picture her performing her tricks at a London brothel. It was impossible.

"You are soft-hearted and sweet-natured, Priss," her husband said. "I cannot forgive her. You know I cannot."

"And yet," she said softly, flushing, "you forgave me."

"There was nothing to forgive," he said hotly. "Good God, Priss, there was *nothing to forgive*."

"Only because you knew me from the inside," she said. "Only because you knew of my suffering and my yearning to rise above my suffering. There are few deeds in this life beyond forgiveness, Gerald. For our own sakes we must forgive, as much as for the sake of the person we forgive. I find it hard to forgive Helena. She made you so desperately unsure of yourself. But without her, dear, I would never have met you. I would still be where you found me. And so I can forgive her. She is unhappy and has been for all these years, I daresay."

Sir Gerald stood with bowed head and closed eyes. "You are too good, my love," he said after a while.

"Suffering teaches one compassion, Gerald," she said. "You know that. You can feel compassion for everyone except Helena, I believe. Mr. Downes, there is a bigger and warmer fire burning in the drawing room. Will you come up there? You still have had no refreshments. And it is dusk outside already. Will you stay here for tonight? You cannot possibly drive all the way home, and inns are dreary places at which to put up. Stay with us?"

Edgar looked at Sir Gerald, who had raised his head.

"Please accept our hospitality," he said. "Ride back to Mobley Abbey tomorrow and inform Mrs. Downes that she has my full and free forgiveness." His voice was stiff, his face set and pale. But the words were spoken quite firmly.

"Thank you," Edgar said. "I will stay."

Lady Stapleton smiled. "Come upstairs, then," she said. "I hope you like children, Mr. Downes. Our son Peter was very cross to be taken back to the nursery so early. I will have him brought back down if I may. He is a little over a year old and terrorizes his mama and papa." She crossed the room and linked her arm through Edgar's.

"I like children," he said. "My wife and I are expecting one of our own next summer."

"Oh?" she said. "Oh, splendid. And Gerald and I, too, Mr. Downes."

The drawing room was cozy and looked lived-in. Its surfaces were strewn with books and needlework, but not with breakables. The reason was evident as soon as Peter Stapleton arrived in the room. He toddled about, exploring everything with energetic curiosity, before climbing onto his father's lap and playing with his watch chain and fob.

The room was decorated for Christmas. A warm fire burned in the hearth. Sir Gerald sat in his chair by the fire, looking at ease with his child on his lap. Lady Stapleton bent her head over her embroidery after pouring the tea and handing around the cups and a plate of cakes.

It was a warm family circle, into which Edgar had been drawn by the courtesy of his hostess, who soon had him talking about his life in Bristol and about Mobley Abbey.

But it was Christmas and there was no sign of other guests and no sign that they were preparing to go elsewhere for the holiday. They were to spend it alone? He asked the question.

"Yes." Lady Stapleton smiled. "The Earl of Severn, Gerald's friend, invited us to Severn Park, but his mother and all his family are to be there and we would not intrude on a family party."

Sir Gerald's eyes watched his wife gravely.

"We are happy here together," he said.

They were not. Contented, perhaps. They were a couple who very clearly shared an unusually deep love for each other. But perhaps circumstances had deepened it. Lady Stapleton had been a whore. She would now be a pariah in society.

"I wish," Edgar said, taking himself as much by surprise as he took them, "you would return to Mobley Abbey with me tomorrow and spend Christmas there."

They both looked at him, quite startled. "To Mobley?" Lady Stapleton said.

"Impossible!" her husband said at the same moment.

"I would like you and my wife to meet each other again," Edgar said to Sir Gerald. "To see each other as people again. To recapture, perhaps, some of the sympathy and friendship you once shared. Christmas would seem the ideal time."

"You push too hard, sir," Sir Gerald said stiffly.

"There is a large house party there," Edgar said, turning to Lady Stapleton. "My father and I have friends and their families there, all members of the merchant class. My sister—she is Lady Francis Kneller—has several of her friends there with their families. They are aristocrats and include the Duke and Duchess of Bridgwater and the Marquess and Marchioness of Carew. It would be pleasant to add three more people to our number."

She was a woman of dignity and courage, he saw. She did not look away from him as she spoke. "I believe you are fully aware, sir," she said, "of what I once was and always will be in the eyes of respectable society. I am not ashamed of my past, Mr. Downes, because it was a means of survival and I survived, but I am well aware of the restrictions it imposes upon the rest of my life. I have accepted them. So has Gerald. I thank you for your invitation, but we must decline."

"I believe," he said, not at all sure he was right, "that you might well find your fears ill-founded, ma'am. I went into polite society myself a few months ago when I was in London. I am what is contemptuously called a cit, yet I was treated with unfailing courtesy wherever I went. I know our situations are not comparable, but I know too that my father and my sister will receive with courtesy and warmth anyone I introduce to them as my friend. Lord Francis Kneller and his friends are people of true gentility. And my wife needs absolution," he added.

"Mr. Downes." She had tears in her large, intelligent eyes. "It is impossible, sir."

"I will not take my wife into a situation that might pain her," Sir Gerald said. "I will not have her treated with contempt or worse by people who are by far her inferior."

Edgar's eyes focused on the little boy, who had wriggled off his father's lap and was into his mother's silk threads, undetected.

"There are children of all ages at Mobley," he said. "I counted fourteen, but there may well be three or four more than that. Children have an annoying tendency not to stand and be counted. Your child would have other children to play with for Christmas, ma'am."

She bit her lower lip and he saw her eyes before she turned them on her husband. They were filled with yearning. Her child was her weakness, then. And she expected another. How she must fear for their future, isolated from other children of their class.

"Gerald—" she said.

"Priss." There were both pain and tenderness in Sir Gerald's voice.

If he had calculated wrongly, Edgar thought, he had several people headed in the direction of disaster. He felt a moment's panic. But it was the sort of exhilarated panic with which he was familiar in his business life. It was a calculated risk he took. Forgiveness was not enough. Helena needed to know that she had not permanently blighted the life of her stepson. Contented as the Stapletons clearly were together, they were equally clearly not living entirely happy lives. And those lives would grow progressively less happy as the years went on and their children began to grow up.

"Please come," he said. "I will promise you the happiest Christmas you have ever known."

Lady Stapleton smiled at him, her moment of weakness already being pushed aside in favor of her usual serenity. "You can do no such thing, Mr. Downes," she said. "We would not put such responsibility on your shoulders. It is just as likely to be the most uncomfortable Christmas of our lives. But I think we should go. Gerald, I think we should."

"Priss." He frowned. "I could not bear it. . . ."

"And I cannot bear to hide here for the rest of my life," she said. "I cannot bear to keep you hiding here. And Peter adores other children. You can see that at church each week. Besides, I want to meet Helena. I want you to see her again. I want—oh, Gerald, I want freedom even if it must come at the expense of some contentment. I want freedom— for both of us and for Peter and the new baby."

"Then we will go," he said. "Mr. Downes, I hope you know what you are doing. But that is unfair. As my wife says, you cannot be held fully responsible for what we decide to do. Let us bring everything into the open, then. I will see Helena, and Priss will be taken into society. And Peter will be given other children with whom to play. We will leave in the morning? Christmas Eve? You are quite sure, Priss?"

"Quite sure, dear." She smiled at him with a calm she could not possibly be feeling.

But then Edgar, too, sat outwardly calm while inwardly he quaked at the enormity of what he had just set in motion.

Sir Gerald and his wife pounced simultaneously in the direction of their son, who was absorbed in making an impossible tangle of bright threads.

Chapter Sixteen

❖

Christmas Eve. It had been a relatively quiet day for Helena. Although several of the adults had made visits to the village for last-minute purchases, and the young people had gone outside for a walk and come back again with enough snow on their persons to suggest that they had also engaged in a snowball fight, and several individual couples had taken their children outside for various forms of exercise—despite these things, there had been a general air of laziness and waiting about the day. Everyone conserved energy for Christmas itself, which would start in the evening.

Dinner was to be an hour earlier than usual. The carolers would come during the evening, and Mr. Downes and all his guests would greet them in the hall and ply them with hot wassail and mince pies after they had sung their carols. Then there would be church in the village, which it seemed everyone except the younger children was planning to attend. And afterward a gathering in the drawing room to provide warm beverages after the chilly walk and to usher in the new day.

Christmas Day itself, of course, would be frantically busy, what with the usual feasting and gift-giving with which the day was always associated and the children's party in the afternoon and the ball in the evening.

Her father-in-law had not insisted today that Helena rest after nuncheon, though he did ask her if she felt quite well.

He and everyone else, of course, wondered why Edgar had gone to Bristol just two days before Christmas and why he was still not back on the afternoon of Christmas Eve. She could feel the worry and strain behind Mr. Downes's smile and Cora's. She decided of her own accord an hour before tea to retire to her room for a rest.

She did not sleep. She was not really tired. That first phase of pregnancy was over, she realized. She had come for escape more than rest. There was such an air of eager anticipation in the house and of domestic contentment. One would have thought that in such a sizable house party there would be some quarreling and bickering, some jealousies or simple dislikes. There were virtually none, apart from a few minor squabbles among the children.

It was just too good to be true. It was cloying.

She felt lonely. As she had always felt—almost all her life. It seemed to her that she had always been on the outside looking in. Yet when she had tried to get in, to be a participant in a warm love relationship, she had done a terrible thing, trying to add a dimension to that love that just did not belong to it. And so she had destroyed everything—everything! If she had only remained patient and true to Christian, she realized now—and it would not have been very difficult, as he had always been good to her—she might have mourned his death for a year and still been young enough to find someone else with whom to be happy.

But then she would never have met Edgar, or if she had, she would have been married to someone else. Would that have made a difference? If she had been married this autumn and had met him in the Greenwald's drawing room, would she have recognized him in that single long glance across the room as that one person who could make her life complete? As the one love of her life?

She lay on her bed, gazing upward, swallowing several times in an attempt to rid herself of the gurgle in her throat.

Would she? Would she have fallen as headlong, as irrevocably in love with him no matter what the circumstances of her life? Had they been made for each other? It was a ridiculous question to ask herself. She did not believe in such sentimental rot. Made for each other!

But had they been?

She wished they had not met at all.

If they had not met, she would be in Italy now. She would be celebrating the sort of Christmas she was accustomed to. There would be no warm domestic bliss within a mile of her. She would not have been happy, of course. She could never be happy. But she would have been on familiar ground, in familiar company. She would have been in control of her life and her destiny. She would have kept her heart safely cocooned in ice.

Would he come home today? she wondered. Would he come for Christmas at all? But surely he would. He would come for his father's sake. Surely he would.

What if he did not? What if he never came?

She had never been so awash in self-pity, she thought. She hated feeling so abject. She hated him. Yes, she did. She hated him.

And then the door of her bedchamber opened and she turned her head to look. He stood in the open doorway for a few moments, looking back at her, before stepping inside and closing the door behind him.

She closed her eyes.

All day Edgar had been almost sick with worry. He was taking an enormous risk with several people's lives. If things went awry, he might have made life immeasurably worse for both Sir Gerald and Lady Stapleton as well as for Helena. He might have destroyed his marriage. He might have exposed his father to censure for behavior unbecoming a man with pretensions to gentility.

But events had been set in motion and all he could do now was try to direct them and control them as best he could.

The Stapletons had not changed their minds overnight. And so they set off early for Mobley Abbey on Christmas

Eve on roads that were still covered with snow and still had to be traveled with care. Sir Gerald, Edgar noticed, was very tense. His wife was calm and outwardly serene. Each of them, Edgar had learned during his short acquaintance with them, felt a deep and protective love for the other. Without a doubt they had found comfort and peace and harmony together. Equally without a doubt, they were two wounded people whose wounds had filmed over quite nicely during a little more than a year of marriage—their marriage, he guessed, must have coincided almost exactly with the birth of their son. But were the wounds healed? If they were not, this journey to Mobley might rip them open again and make them harder than ever to heal.

They arrived at Mobley Abbey in the middle of the afternoon, having made good time. Edgar, who had ridden, set down the steps of the carriage himself, though it was Sir Gerald who handed his wife and sleeping child out onto the terrace. The child's nurse came hurrying from the accompanying carriage and took the baby, and Edgar directed a footman to escort them to the nursery and summon the housekeeper. He took Sir Gerald and Lady Stapleton to the library, which he was thankful to find empty, ordered refreshments brought for them, and excused himself.

He went first to the drawing room. Helena was not there. His father was, together with a number of his guests.

"Edgar!" Cora came hurrying toward him and took his arm. "You wretch! How dare you absent yourself for almost two full days so close to Christmas? Helena has been quite disconsolate and I have scarce removed my eyes from the sky for fear lest another snowstorm prevent your coming back. It is to be hoped that you went to Bristol to purchase a suitably extravagant Christmas present for your wife. Some *almost* priceless jewel, perhaps?"

"Edgar," his father said, rising from the sofa on which he had been sitting and conversing with Mrs. Cross, "it is good to see you home before dark. Whatever did take you to Bristol?"

"I did not go to Bristol," Edgar said. "I told Helena I was

going there because I wished to keep my real destination a secret. We are all surrounded by family and friends while Helena has only one aunt here." He bowed in Mrs. Cross's direction. "I went to see her stepson, Sir Gerald Stapleton, at Brookhurst and persuade him to come back with me to spend Christmas."

"Splendid!" Mr. Downes rubbed his hands together. "The more the merrier. My daughter-in-law's stepson, you say, Edgar?"

"What a very kind thought Mr. Downes," Mrs. Cross said.

"Sir Gerald Stapleton?" Cora's voice had risen almost to a squeak. "And he has come, Edgar? *Alone?*"

Cora had always been as transparent as newly polished crystal. The questions she had asked only very thinly veiled the one she had not asked. Edgar looked steadily at her and at his brother-in-law beyond her.

"It is Christmas," he said. "I have brought Lady Stapleton, too, of course, and their son. If you will excuse me, Papa. I must find Helena and take her to meet them in the library. Do you know where she is?"

"She is upstairs resting," Mr. Downes said. "This will do her the world of good, Edgar. She has been somewhat low in spirits, I fancy. But then your absence would account for that." The statement seemed more like a question. But Edgar did not stay to pursue it. He left the room and, almost sick with apprehension, went up to his bedchamber.

She was lying on the bed, though she was not asleep. Their eyes met and held for a few moments and he knew with dreadful clarity that the future of her life and his, the future of their marriage, rested upon the events of the next hour. He stepped inside the room and shut the door. She closed her eyes, calmly shutting him out. She looked quite unmoved by the sight of him. Perhaps she had not missed him at all. Perhaps she had hoped he would not return for Christmas.

He sat down on the edge of the bed and touched the backs of his fingers to her cheek. She still did not open her eyes. He leaned down and kissed her softly on the lips. He felt a strong urge to avoid the moment, to keep the Stapletons waiting indefinitely in the library.

"Your father will be happy you have returned, Edgar," she said without opening her eyes. "So will Cora. Go and have tea with them. As you will observe, I am trying to rest."

"I have brought other guests," he said. "They are in the library. I want you to meet them."

She opened her eyes then. "More friends?" she said. "How pleasant for you. I will meet them later."

She was in one of her prickly moods. It did not bode well.

"Now," he said. "I wish you to meet them now."

"Oh, well, Edgar," she said, "when you play lord and master, you know, you are quite irresistible. If you would care to stop looming so menacingly over me, I will get up and jump to your command."

Very prickly. He went to stand at the window while she got up and straightened her dress and made sure at the mirror that her hair was tidy.

"I am ready," she said. "Give me your arm and lead me to the library. I shall be the gracious hostess, Edgar, never fear. You need not glower so."

He had not been glowering. He was merely terrified. Was he going about this the right way? Should he warn her? But if he did that, the chances were good that she would flatly refuse to accompany him to the library. And then what would he do?

He nodded to a footman when they reached the hall, and the man opened the library doors. Edgar drew a slow, deep breath.

"Sir Gerald and Lady Stapleton." Cora whirled around and looked at her husband, her eyes wide with dismay.

"My new daughter's stepson," Mr. Downes said, beaming at Mrs. Cross and resuming his seat beside her. "And his wife and son. More family. When was there ever such a happy Christmas, ma'am?"

"I am sure I have never known a happier, sir," Mrs. Cross said placidly.

"Tell me what you know of Sir Gerald Stapleton," Mr. Downes directed her. "I daresay Edgar will bring them to tea soon."

"Yes, my love," Lord Francis said, going to Cora's side.

"Oh, dear," Cora said. "Whatever can Edgar have been thinking of? Perhaps he does not even know." She looked suddenly belligerent and glared beyond her husband to the group of their friends, who were regarding her in silence. She lifted her chin. "Well, *I* will be civil to her. She is Helena's relative by marriage, even if it is only a *step* relationship. And she is Edgar's and Papa's guest. No one need expect me to be uncivil."

"I would be vastly disappointed in you if you were, Cora," her husband said mildly.

"And why would anyone even think of treating a lady, the wife of a baronet, a fellow guest in this home, with incivility?" the Earl of Thornhill asked, eyebrows raised.

"You do not remember who she is, Gabriel?" his wife asked. "Though I do hope you will repeat your words, even when you do."

"The lady did something indiscreet, Jennifer?" he asked, though it was obvious to all his listeners that he knew the answer very well and had done so from the start. "Everyone has done something indiscreet. I remember a time when you and I were seen kissing by a whole ballroomful of dancers—while you were betrothed to another man."

"Oh, bravo, Gabe," Lord Francis said as the countess blushed rosily. "The rest of us have been tactfully forgetting that incident ever since. Though something very similar happened to Cora and me. Not that we were kissing. We were laughing and holding each other up. But it looked for all the world as if we were engaged in a deep embrace—and it caused a delicious scandal."

"The *ton* is so foolish," Cora said.

"Sir Gerald and Lady Stapleton are guests in this home,"

the Duke of Bridgwater said. "As are Stephanie and I, Cora. I shall not peruse them through my quizzing glass or along the length of my nose. You may set your mind at ease."

"Of course," the duchess said, "Alistair does both those things to perfection, but he reserves them for pretentious people. I can remember a time when I was reduced to near-destitution, Cora. I can remember the fear. I was fortunate. Alistair came along to rescue me."

"There are all too many ladies who are not so fortunate," the Marquess of Carew said gently. "The instinct to survive is a strong one. I honor those who, reduced to desperation, contrive a way of surviving that does not involve robbery or murder or harm to anyone else except the person herself. Lady Stapleton is, I believe, a lady who has survived."

"Oh, Hartley," his wife said, patting his hand, "you would find goodness in a murderer about to be hanged, I do declare."

"I would certainly try, love," he said, smiling at her.

"I know the Countess of Severn," Jane, Countess of Greenwald, said. "She and the earl have befriended the Stapletons. They would not have done so if Lady Stapleton was impossibly vulgar, would they?"

"There, my love," Lord Francis said, setting an arm about Cora's waist. "You might have had more faith in your friends and in me."

"Yes," she said. "Thank you. Now I wonder how poor Helena will be feeling about all this. Edgar and his surprises! One is reminded of the saying about bulls charging at gates."

"I believe both Edgar and Helena may be trusted," Lord Francis said. "I do believe those two, by hook or by crook, are going to end up quite devoted to each other."

"I hope you are right," Cora said with a loud sigh.

"What was that, Francis?" Mr. Downes called across the room. "Edgar and my daughter-in–law? Of course they are devoted to each other. He went off to bring her this secret present and she has been moping at his absence. I have great hopes. Not even hopes. Certainties. What say you, ma'am?" He turned to Mrs. Cross.

"I will say this, sir," she said. "If any man can tame my niece, Mr. Edgar Downes is that man. And if any man deserves Helena's devotion, he is Mr. Edgar Downes."

"Precisely, ma'am." He patted her hand. "Precisely. Now where is that son of mine with our new guests? It is almost teatime."

Helena looked first at the woman, who was standing to one side of the fireplace. A very genteel-looking young lady, she thought, slim and pretty, with intelligent eyes. She smiled and turned her eyes on the man. Pleasant looking, not very comfortable. Decidedly uncomfortable, in fact.

And then she recognized him.

Panic was like a hard ball inside her, fast swelling to explosion. She turned blindly, intent on getting out of the room as fast as she could. She found herself clawing at a very broad, very solid chest.

"Helena." His voice was impossibly steady. "Calm yourself."

She looked up wildly, recognized him, and was past that first moment and on to the next nightmare one. "I'll never forgive you for this," she whispered fiercely. "Let me past. I'll never forgive you."

"We have guests, my dear." His voice—and his face—was as hard as flint. "Turn and greet them."

Fury welled up in wake of the panic. She gazed into his face, her nostrils flaring, and then turned. "And *you,* Gerald," she said, looking directly at him. "What do *you* want here?"

"Hello, Helena," he said.

He looked as quiet, as gentle, as peaceful as he had always appeared. She could not believe that she had looked at him for a whole second without recognizing him. He had scarcely changed. Probably not at all. That outward appearance had always hidden his sense of rejection, insecurity, self-doubt.

"I have the honor of presenting my wife to you," he said. "Priscilla, Lady Stapleton. Helena, Mrs. Edgar Downes, my dear."

Helena's eyes stayed on him. "I have nothing to say to you, Gerald," she said, "and you can have nothing to say to me. I have no right to ask you to leave. You are my husband's guest. Excuse me, please."

She turned to find herself confronted by that same broad, solid chest.

"How foolish you are, Edgar," she said bitterly. "You think it is enough to bring us together in the same room? You think we will kiss and make up and proceed to live happily ever after? We certainly will not *kiss*. You foolish, interfering man. Let me past."

"Helena," he said, his voice arctic, "someone has been presented to you and you have not acknowledged the introduction. Is that the behavior of a lady?"

She gazed at him in utter incredulity. He dared instruct her on ladylike behavior? And to reprove her in the hearing of other people? She turned and looked at the woman. And walked toward her.

"Lady Stapleton. Priscilla," she said quietly, bitter mockery in her face, "I do beg your pardon. How pleased I am to make your acquaintance."

"I understand," the woman said, looking quite calmly into Helena's eyes. Her voice was as refined as her appearance. "I had as little wish for your acquaintance when it was first suggested to me, Helena, as you have for mine. I have had little enough reason to think kindly of you."

How dared she!

"Then I must think it remarkably kind of you to have overcome your scruples," Helena said sharply.

"I have done so for Gerald's sake," Lady Stapleton said. "And for the sake of Mr. Downes, who is a true gentleman, and who cares for you."

The woman spoke with *dignity*. There was neither

arrogance nor subservience in her and certainly no vulgarity—
only dignity.

"I could live quite happily without his care," Helena
said.

"Helena." It was Gerald this time. She turned to look at
him and saw the boy she had loved so dearly grown into a
man. "I never wanted to see you again. I never wanted to
hear your name. I certainly never wanted to forgive you.
Your husband is a persuasive man."

She closed her eyes. She could not imagine a worse
nightmare than this if she had the devising of it. "I cannot
blame you, Gerald," she said, feeling all the fight draining
out of her. "I would have begged your pardon, perhaps, before your father died, at his funeral, during any of the years
since, if I had felt the offense pardonable. But I did not feel
it was. And so I have not begged pardon and will not do so
now. I will take the offense to the grave with me. I have
done enough permanent damage to your life without seeking shallow comfort for myself."

"I must correct you in one misapprehension," he said,
his voice shaking and breathless. "I can see that you mis-
apprehend. Forgive me, Priss? I met my wife under circumstances I am sure you are aware of, Helena. She had been
forced into those circumstances, but even in the midst of
them she remained cheerful and modest and kind and dignified. She has always been far my superior. If anyone is to
be pitied in this marriage, it is she."

"Gerald—" Lady Stapleton began, but he held up a staying hand.

"She is not to be pitied," he said. "Neither am I. Priss is
the love of my heart and I am by now confident in the conviction that I am the love of hers. I am not in the habit of
airing such very private feelings in public, but I have seen
from your manner and have heard from your husband that
you have bitterly blamed yourself for what happened between us and have steadfastly refused to forgive yourself or
allow yourself any sort of happiness. I thought I was still
bitter. I thought I would never forgive you. But I have found

during the past day that those are outmoded, petty feelings. You were young and unhappy—heaven knows *I* was never happy with my father either. And while youth and unhappiness do not excuse bad behavior, they do explain it. To hold a grudge for thirteen years and even beyond is in itself unpardonable. If it is my forgiveness you want, then, Helena, you have it—freely and sincerely given."

No. It could not possibly be as easy as that. The burden of years could not be lifted with a single short speech spoken in that gentle, well-remembered voice.

"No," she said stiffly. "It is not what I want, Gerald. It is not in your power."

"You will send him away still burdened, then?" Priscilla asked. "It is hard to offer forgiveness and be rejected. It makes one feel strangely guilty."

"It is Christmas." Edgar stepped forward. He had been a silent spectator of the proceedings until now. Helena deeply resented him. "We are all going to spend it here at Mobley Abbey. Together. And it is teatime. Time to go up to the drawing room. I wish to introduce you to my father and our other guests, Stapleton, Lady Stapleton."

They had not been introduced? *Lady Stapleton* had not yet been introduced to the Duke and Duchess of Bridgwater, the Marquess and Marchioness of Carew, the Earl and Countess of Thornhill, and everyone else? She would be *cut*. And she must know it. She must have known it before she came. Why had she come, then? For Gerald's sake? Did she love him so much? Would she risk such humiliation for his sake? So that he, too, might find a measure of peace? But Gerald had done nothing to regret. Except that she had refused to accept his forgiveness.

"Take my arm, Priss." Gerald's voice was tense with protective fear.

"No." Helena stepped forward and took the woman's arm herself. Gerald's wife was smaller than she, daintier. "We will go up together, Priscilla. I will present you to my father-in-law and my sister-in-law and my aunt. And to all our friends."

"Thank you, Helena," Priscilla said quietly. If she was afraid, she did not show it.

"I must show everyone what a delightful gift my husband has brought me on Christmas Eve," Helena said. "He has brought my stepson and his wife to spend Christmas with me."

"And our son," Priscilla said. "Peter. Thank you, Helena. Gerald has told me what a warm and charming woman you were. I can see that he was right. And you will see in the next day or two what a secure, contented man he is and you will forgive yourself and allow him to forgive you. I have seen enough suffering in my time to know all about the masks behind which it hides itself. It is time we all stopped suffering."

And this just before they stepped inside the drawing room to what was probably one of the worst ordeals of Priscilla's life?

"I can certainly admire courage," Helena said. "I will take you to my father-in-law first. You will like him and he will certainly like you."

"Thank you." Priscilla smiled. But her face was very pale for all that.

Chapter Seventeen

❖

Edgar gazed upward through the window of his bed-chamber. By some miracle the sky was clear again. But then it was Christmas. One somehow believed in miracles at Christmas.

"Come here," he said without turning. He knew she was still sitting on the side of the bed brushing her hair, though her maid had already brushed it smooth and shining.

"I suppose," she said, "the Christmas star is shining as it was when we walked home from church a couple of hours ago. I suppose you want me to gaze on it with you and believe in the whole myth of Christmas."

"Yes," he said.

"Edgar." He heard her sigh. "You are such a romantic, such a sentimentalist. I would not have thought it of you."

"Come." He turned and stretched out one arm to her. She shrugged her shoulders and came. "There." He pointed upward unnecessarily. "Wait a moment." He left her side in order to blow out the candles and then joined her at the window again and set one arm about her waist. "There. Now there is nothing to compete with it. Tell me if you can that you do not believe in Christmas, even down to the last detail of that sordid stable."

She nestled her head on his shoulder and sighed. "I should be in Italy now," she said, "cocooned by cynicism. Why did I go to London this autumn, Edgar? Why did you? Why did we both go to the Greenwalds' drawing room that

evening? Why did we look at each other and not look away
again? Why did I conceive the very first time I lay with you
when I have never done so before?"

"Perhaps we have our answer in Christmas," he said.

"Miracles?" The old mockery was back in her voice.

"Or something that was meant to be," he said. "I used not
to believe in such things. I used to believe that I, like everyone else, was master of my own fate. But as one gets older,
one can look back and realize that there has been a pattern
to one's life—a pattern one did not devise or control."

"A series of coincidences?" she said.

"Yes," he said. "Something like that."

"The pattern of each of our lives merged during the autumn, then?" she said. "Poor Edgar. You have not deserved
me. You are such a very decent man. I could have killed
you this afternoon. Literally."

"Yes," he said, "I know."

She turned her head on his shoulder and closed her eyes.
"She is very courageous," she said. "I could never do what
she did today. She did it for him, Edgar. For Gerald."

"Yes," he said, "and for their son and their unborn child.
And for herself. For them. You were wonderful. I was very
proud of you."

She had taken Priscilla Stapleton about in the drawing
room at teatime, introducing her to everyone as her stepson's wife, her own manner confident, charming, even regal. She had scarcely left the woman's side for the rest of
the day. They had walked to and from church with Sir Gerald and his wife and shared a pew with them.

"But I did nothing," she said. "Everyone greeted her
with courtesy and even warmth. It was as if they did not
know, though I have no doubt whatsoever that they all did.
She—Edgar, there is nothing vulgar in her at all."

"She is a lady," he said.

"Gerald is happy with her." Her eyes, he saw, had
clenched more tightly shut. "He *is* happy. Is he, Edgar? Is
he?" She looked up at him then, searching his eyes.

"I believe," he said, "the pattern of his life merged with

the pattern of hers in a most unlikely place, Helena. Of course they are happy. I will not say they are in love, though I am sure they are. They *love* deeply. Yes, he is happy."

"And whole and at peace," she said. "I did not destroy him permanently."

"No, love," he said. "Not permanently."

She shivered.

"Cold?" he asked.

"But I might have," she said, "if he had not met Priscilla."

"And if she had not met him," he said. "They were both in the process of surviving, Helena. We do not know how well they would have done if they had not met each other. Perhaps they were both strong people who would have found their peace somehow alone. We do not know. Neither do they. I do believe, though, that they could not be so happy together if they merely used each other as emotional props. But they did meet, and so they are as we see them today."

She withdrew from him and rested her palms on the windowsill as she looked out. "I will not use you as an emotional prop either, Edgar," she said. "It would be easy to do. You organize and fix things, do you not? It comes naturally to you. You have seen that my life is all in pieces and you have sought to mend it, to put the pieces back together again, to make all right for me. You took a terrible risk today and won—as you almost always do, I suspect. It would be easy to lean into you as I was just doing, to allow you to manage my life. You can do it so much better than I, it seems. But it is my life. I must live it myself."

He felt chilled. But he had said it himself of her stepson and his wife—they could not be happy together if they depended too much upon each other. And he had spoken the truth. He could not be happy as the totally dominant partner in a marriage—even though by his nature he would always try to dominate, thinking he was merely protecting and cherishing his wife.

"Then you will do so," he said, "without my further interference. I am not sorry for what I did yesterday and today. I would do it again given the choice—because you are my wife and because I love you. But you must proceed from here, Helena—or not proceed. The choice is yours. I am going to bed. It is late and I am cold."

But she turned from the window to look at him, the old mocking smile on her lips—though he had the feeling that it was turned inward on herself rather than outward on him.

"I was not quarreling with you, Edgar," she said. "You do not need to pout like a boy. I want to make love. But not as we have done it since our marriage. I have allowed you your will because it has been so very enjoyable to do so. You are a superlative lover, unadventurous as are your methods."

He raised his eyebrows. Unadventurous?

"I want to be on top," she said. "I want to lead the way. I want you to lie still as I usually do and let me set the pace and choose the key moments. I want to make love to you."

He had never done it like that. It sounded vaguely wrong, vaguely sinful. He felt his breath quicken and his groin tighten. She was still smiling at him—and though she was dressed in a pale dressing gown with her hair in long waves down her back, she looked again in the faint light of the moon and stars like the scarlet lady of the Greenwalds' drawing room.

"Then what are we waiting for?" he asked.

He stripped off his nightshirt and lay on his back on the bed. He was thankful that a fire still burned in the grate, though the air felt chill enough—for the space of perhaps one minute. She kneeled, naked, beside him and began to make love to him with delicate, skilled hands and warm seeking mouth. The minx—of course she was skilled. He did not wish to discover where she had acquired those skills—though he really did not care. He had acquired his own with other women, but they no longer mattered. Just as the other men would no longer matter to her. He would see to it that they did not.

It was difficult to keep his hands resting on the bed, to submit to the sweet torture of a lovemaking that proceeded altogether too slowly for his comfort. It was hard to be passive, to allow himself to be led and controlled, to give up all his own initiative.

She came astride him when he thought the pain must surely soon get beyond him, positioned herself carefully, her knees wide, and slid firmly down onto him. His hands came to her hips with some urgency, but he remembered in time and gentled them, letting them rest idly there.

"Ah," she said, "you feel so good. So deep. You have not done this before, have you?"

"No."

"I will show you how good it feels to be mastered," she said, leaning over him and kissing him open-mouthed. "It does feel good, Edgar, provided it is only play. And this is play—intimate, wonderful play, which we all need in our lives. I do not wish to master you outside of this play—or you to master me. Only here. Now."

He gritted his teeth when she began to move, riding him with a leisurely rocking of her hips while she braced her hands on his shoulders and tipped back her head, her eyes closed. Fortunately the contracting of inner muscles told him that she was at an advanced stage of arousal herself. It was not long before she spoke again.

"Yes," she whispered fiercely. "Yes. Now, Edgar. *Now!*"

His hands tightened on her hips and he drove into her over and over again until they reached climax together.

"Ah, my love," she said in that throaty, velvet voice that most belonged here, in their bed. "Ah, my love." Her head was still tipped back, her eyes still closed.

He would perhaps not have heard the words if they had not sounded so strange and so new to his ears. He doubted that she heard them herself.

She did not lift herself away. She lowered herself onto him and straightened her legs so that they lay on either side of his. She snuggled her head into the hollow between his shoulder and neck and sighed.

"Do I weigh a ton?" she asked as he contrived somehow to pull the covers up over them.

"Only half," he told her.

"You are no gentleman, sir," she said. "You were supposed to reply that I feel like a mere feather."

"Two feathers," he said.

"Good night, Edgar. I did enjoy that."

"Good night, love." He kissed the side of her face. "And I enjoyed being mastered."

She laughed that throaty laugh of hers and was almost instantly asleep.

They were still coupled.

It was going to be an interesting marriage, he thought. It would never be a comfortable one. It might never be a particularly happy one. But strangely, he felt more inclined to favor an interesting marriage over a comfortable one. And as for happiness—well, at this particular moment he felt thoroughly happy. And life was made up of moments. It was a shame that this one must be cut short by sleep, but there would be other moments—tomorrow or the next day or the next.

He slept.

Christmas Day was one of those magical days that Helena had studiously avoided for ten years. It was everything that she had always most dreaded—a day lived on emotion rather than on any sane rationality. And the emotions, of course, were gaiety and love and happiness. The Downes family, she concluded—her father-in-law, her husband, her sister-in-law—used love and generosity and kindness and openness as the guiding principles of their own family lives, and they passed on those feelings to everyone around them. It seemed almost impossible that anyone *not* have a perfectly happy Christmas in their home.

And it seemed that everyone did.

The morning was spent in gift-giving within each family group. For Helena there was a great deal more to do than that. There were the servants to entertain for an hour while Mr. Downes gave them generous gifts, and there were baskets to be delivered to some of the poorer families in their country cottages and in the village. Cora and Francis delivered half of them, while Helena and Edgar delivered the others.

It felt so very good—Helena was beginning to accept the feeling, to open herself to it—to be a part of a family. To recognize love around her, to accept that much of it was directed her way—not for anything she had ever done or not done, but simply because she was a member of the family. To realize that she was beginning to love again, cautiously, fearfully, but without resistance.

She had decided to enjoy Christmas—this good old-fashioned English Christmas of her father-in-law's description. Tomorrow she would think things through, decide if she could allow her life to take a new course. But today she would not think. Today she would feel.

The young people had contrived to find time during the morning to walk out to the lake to skate. They were arriving back, rosy cheeked, high spirited, as Helena and Edgar were returning from their errands. Fanny Grainger and Jack Sperling were together, something they had been careful to avoid during the past few days.

Fanny smiled her sweet, shy smile. Jack inclined his head to them and spoke to Edgar.

"Might I have a word with you, sir?" he asked.

"Certainly," Edgar said, indicating the library. "Is it too private for my wife's ears?"

"No." Jack smiled at Helena and she adjusted her opinion of his looks. He was more than just mildly good looking. He was almost handsome. He offered his arm to Fanny and led her toward the library.

"Well." Edgar looked from one to the other of them when they were all inside the room. "The hot cider I asked for should be here soon. What shall we toast?"

"Nothing and everything." Jack laughed, but Helena noticed that his arm had crept about Fanny's waist and she was looking up at him with bright, eager eyes.

"It sounds like a reasonably good toast to me." Edgar

smiled at Helena and indicated two chairs close to the fire. "Do sit down, Miss Grainger, and warm yourself. Now, of what does this nothing and this everything consist?"

"I have been granted permission by Sir Webster Grainger," Jack said, "to court Miss Grainger. There is to be no formal betrothal until I can prove that I am able to support her in the manner of life to which she is accustomed and no marriage until I am in a fair way to offering her a home worthy of a baronet's daughter. That may be years in the future. But F— Miss Grainger is young and I am but two-and-twenty. Waiting seems heaven when just a few weeks ago we thought even that an impossibility."

Helena hugged Fanny. She was not in the habit of hugging people—had not been for a long while. But she was genuinely happy for the girl and her young man. And she was happy for Edgar, who must have felt guilty about the expectations he had raised in the Graingers.

"Well." Edgar was smiling. "The long wait can perhaps be eased a little. Since you have become a close friend of my family, Miss Grainger, and you are to be a favored employee, Sperling—provided you prove yourself worthy of such a position, of course—I daresay the two of you might meet here or at my home in Bristol with fair frequency."

Fanny bit her lip, her eyes shining with tears.

"I thank you, sir," Jack Sperling said. "For everything. We both do, don't we, Fan?"

She nodded and turned her eyes on Helena. There was such happiness in them that Helena was dazzled. The girl had a long wait for her marriage—perhaps years. But happiness lay in hope. Perhaps in hope more than in any other single factor. The moment might be happy, but unless one could feel confident in the hope that there would be other such moments the happiness was worth little.

"I will be new to Bristol," Helena said. "And though I will have Edgar and have already met here some of his friends, I will still feel lonely for a while. Perhaps we can arrange for you to stay with me for a month or two in the spring, Fanny. I believe you have an aunt in Bristol? I would be pleased to make her acquaintance."

Two of the tears spilled over onto Fanny's cheeks. "Thank you," she murmured.

The hot cider had arrived. They were all still chilled from the outdoors. They toasted one another's happiness and Christmas itself and sipped on the welcome warmth of their drinks.

Edgar did not plan to attend the children's party in the ballroom during the afternoon. They could be dizzyingly noisy and active, even the fourteen who were house guests—fifteen now that the young and very exuberant Peter Stapleton had been added to their number. With several neighborhood children added, the resulting noise was deafening. He intended only to poke his head inside the door to make sure that the ballroom was not being taken to pieces a bit at a time.

In the event he stayed. Cora's four descended upon him just as if he had a giant child magnet pinned to his chest. Then Cora herself called to him and asked if he would head one of the four race teams with Gabriel, Hartley, and Francis. Then he spotted Priscilla Stapleton and his wife playing a game in a circle with the younger children. And finally he noticed that the person seated at the pianoforte ready to play the music for the game was Sir Gerald Stapleton.

It was his wife who kept him lingering in the ballroom even after he had served his sentence as race-team leader. Children always seemed the key to breaking through all her masks to the warm, vibrant, fun-loving woman she so obviously was. Perhaps she did not know it yet and perhaps she would resist it even when she did—but she was going to be a perfectly wonderful mother. Her resistance was understandable, of course. She had convinced herself that her stepson was a child when she had tried to corrupt him. And so she feared her effect on children. But her effect was quite benevolent. The Greenwalds' Stephen adored her—

she came third in his affections, behind only his mama and papa.

Edgar had decided to enjoy Christmas, to relax and let go of all his worries. He had decided not to try to control events or people any longer—not in his personal life, anyway. He had married Helena and he loved her. He had discovered her darkest secrets and had made an effort to give her the chance to put right what had happened in the past. She had not entirely spurned his efforts—she had been remarkably kind to Priscilla and to the child. She had been civil to Gerald. But she had not reacted quite as Edgar had hoped she would.

He could do no more. Or rather, he *would* do no more. The rest was up to her. If she chose to live in the hell of her own making she had inhabited for thirteen years, then so be it. He must allow it. He must allow her the freedom she craved and the freedom he knew was necessary in any relationship in which he engaged.

He was going to enjoy Christmas. It was certainly not difficult to do. Apart from the basic joyfulness of the day and its activities, there had been the happy—or potentially happy—outcome of his scheme to bring Fanny Grainger and Jack Sperling together. And there was more. His father had made several appearances at the children's party and had been mobbed each time. On his final appearance, just as the party was coming to an end, he invited Edgar and Helena, Cora and Francis to his private sitting room.

"After all," he said as they made their way there, "a man is entitled to snatch a half hour of Christmas Day to spend just with his very nearest and dearest."

But there was someone else in the sitting room when they arrived there. Edgar suppressed a smile. They would have to have been blind and foolish during the past week not to have guessed that some such thing was in the works.

Mrs. Cross smiled at them, but she looked a little less placid than her usual self. She looked very slightly anxious.

Mr. Downes cleared his throat after tea had been poured and they had all made bright, self-conscious conversation for a few minutes. "Edgar, Cora," he began, "you are my children and of course will inherit my fortune after my time. Edgar will inherit Mobley, but I have seen to it that Cora will receive almost as much since it seems unfair to me that my daughter should be treated with less favor than my son. You are wealthy in your own right, Edgar, as you are in yours, Francis. It would seem to me, therefore, that perhaps neither of my children would be too upset to find that they will receive a little less than they have always expected."

"Papa," Cora said, "I have never *seen* you so embarrassed. Why do you not simply say what you brought us here to say?"

"My love," Francis said, "you cannot know how difficult it is for a man to say such a thing. You ladies have no idea."

Helena was smiling at her aunt, who was attempting to remove a particularly stubborn—and invisible—speck of lint from her skirt.

"Neither Cora nor I covet your property or your wealth, Papa," Edgar said. "We love *you*. We would rather have you with us forever. Certainly while we do have you, we want nothing more than your happiness. Do we, Corey?"

"How foolish," she said, "that I am even called upon to answer that. Papa! Could you ever have doubted it?"

"No." Their father actually look sheepish. "I loved your mother dearly. I want all here present to know that and not to doubt it for a moment."

There was a chorus of protests.

"Your children never have, Joseph," Mrs. Cross said, looking up at last. "Of course, they never have. Neither have I. You loved Mrs. Downes just as I loved Mr. Cross."

Mr. Downes cleared his throat again. "This may come as a great surprise—" he began, but he was halted by another cry—of hilarity this time. He frowned. "Mrs. Letitia Cross has done me the great honor of accepting my hand in marriage," he said with an admirable attempt at dignity.

There was a great clamor then, just as if they really had all been taken by surprise. Cora was crying and demanding a handkerchief of Francis, who was busy shaking his father-in-law's hand. Helena was hugging her aunt tightly and shedding a tear or two of her own. Edgar waited his turn, wondering that it had never happened before. His father, with a huge heart and a universe of love to give, had mourned his wife for almost thirty years and lavished all his love on his children. But they were both wed now and paternal love was not enough to satisfy a man's heart for a left-over lifetime.

Mrs. Cross was a fortunate lady. But then, Edgar thought, his father was probably a fortunate man, too.

His father turned to him, damp-eyed—and frowning ferociously. Edgar caught him in a bear hug.

Chapter Eighteen

———— ✦ ————

Helena had worn her scarlet gown to the Christmas ball. It was perhaps a little daring for an entertainment in a country home, especially when she was a matron of six-and-thirty. More especially when she was fast losing her waistline. But it was not indecent—and the soft folds of the high-waisted skirt hid the slight bulge of her pregnancy—and it suited her mood. She felt brightly festive.

And desperately unwilling for the day to be over. It almost was. It was already late in the evening, after supper.

Tomorrow Christmas would linger, but in all essentials it would be over. Just as it always was. The great myth lifted one's spirits only to dash them afterward even lower than they had been before. She had feared it this year and sworn to resist it, but she had given in to it. Christmas!

But having given in, she would take from the celebrations all she could. And give, too. That was an essential part of it, the giving. And it was that she had shunned as much as the taking—more. She was terrified of giving. Once upon a time she believed she had had a generous spirit. Despite the disappointment of a lost love at the age of nineteen, she had put a great deal into her marriage with Christian. She might have settled into unhappiness and bitterness and revulsion, but she had not done so. She had set out to make him happy and had succeeded, God help her. But she had focused the largest measure of her generosity and the sympathy of her loving heart on Gerald. She had tried to help him overcome the setbacks of his mother's desertion and his father's dislike. She had tried to help him gain confidence in himself, to realize that he was a boy worthy of respect and love.

And then she had destroyed him.

But not forever. She had perhaps overestimated her own importance. She had harmed him. She had made him suffer, perhaps for a long time. But he had recovered. And she dared to believe that he was now happy. He was still gentle, quiet Gerald, but he was at peace with himself. She did not know all the circumstances surrounding his strange marriage, but there was no doubt of the fact that he and Priscilla were devoted to each other and suited each other perfectly. And their son, little Peter, was a darling. Today there was an extra glow of happiness about all three of them. Peter must have been starved for the company of other children. He had steadfastly made up for lost time. Priscilla had been accepted at Mobley just as if she had never been anything but a lady. Helena guessed that her happiness was as much for Gerald's sake as her own. He would no longer feel that he must absent himself from society for her sake. And Gerald's happiness doubtless had a similar unselfish cause. His wife need no longer hide away from the company of her peers.

Helena watched them dance a cotillion as she danced with her father-in-law. Though they were not the only ones she watched. There were Edgar and her aunt—dear Letty. She was quietly contented. She would have a home of her own again at last and a husband who was clearly very fond indeed of her—as she was of him. And never again would she find herself in the position of being dependent upon relatives.

If she had not married Edgar, Helena thought, her aunt would not have met Mr. Downes and would never have found this new happiness. Neither would he. If she had not married Edgar, Fanny Grainger would not now be dancing with Jack Sperling and looking as glowingly happy as if she expected her nuptials within the month. She would instead be dancing with Edgar and wearing forced smiles. If Helena had not married Edgar, Gerald and Priscilla would be at Brookhurst, alone with their son, trying to convince themselves that they were utterly happy.

Really, when she thought about it, very cautiously, so that she would not jump to the wrong conclusions, nothing very disastrous had happened lately for which she could blame herself. Except that she had forced Edgar into marrying her—though he was the one who had done the actual forcing. He did not seem wildly unhappy. He claimed to love her. He had said so several times. She had refused to hear, refused to react.

She had been afraid to believe it. She had been afraid it was true.

It was as if a door had been held wide for her for several days now, a door beyond which were bright sunlight and birdsong and the perfumes of a thousand flowers. All she had to do was step outside and the door would close forever on the darkness from which she had emerged. But she had been afraid to take that single step. If she did, perhaps she would find storm clouds blocking out the sunlight and silencing the singing and stifling the perfumes. Perhaps she would spoil it all.

But she had not spoiled anything yet this Christmas. Perhaps she should dare. Perhaps she could take that step. If all turned to disaster, then she could only find herself back where she expected to be anyway. What was there to lose?

It seemed suddenly that there was a great deal to lose. The cotillion had ended and her father-in-law was kissing her hand and Edgar was smiling and bending his head to hear something Letty was saying to him. Cora was laughing loudly over something with one of Edgar's friends, and Francis was smiling in some amusement at the sound. The Duke of Bridgwater was joining Gerald and Priscilla—and addressing himself to Priscilla. He must be asking her for the next set. The smell of the pine boughs and the holly with which the ballroom was festooned outdid the smells of the various perfumes worn by the guests. There was a very strong feeling of Christmas.

Oh, yes, there was a great deal to lose. But the sunlight and the birdsong and the flowers beckoned. Edgar was coming toward her. The next set was to be a waltz. She longed to dance it with him. But not this one, she decided suddenly. Not yet. Later she would waltz with him if there was another before the ball ended. She turned and hurried away without looking at him, so that he would think she had not seen him.

"The next is to be a waltz," she said unnecessarily as she joined the duke and Gerald and Priscilla.

"Yes, indeed," his grace said. "Lady Stapleton has agreed to dance it with me."

It seemed strange to hear another woman called that, to realize that the name was no longer hers. She was not sorry, Helena thought. *Mrs. Downes* sounded a great deal more prosaic than *Lady Stapleton*, but the name seemed somehow to give her a new identity, a new chance.

"Splendid," she said. "Then you must dance it with me, Gerald. It would never do for you to be a wallflower."

He looked at her in some surprise, but she linked her arm through his and smiled dazzlingly at him. They had not avoided each other since that first meeting in the library the day before, but they had not sought each other out either.

"It would be my pleasure, Helena," he said.

And so they waltzed together, smiling and silent for a few minutes.

"I am glad we came," he said stiffly after a while. "Mr. Downes and your husband have been extraordinarily kind to Priss and to me. So has everyone else. And Peter is ecstatic."

"I am glad," she said. She was aware that she wore her mocking smile. It was something to which she clung almost in terror. But it was something that must go. She stopped smiling. "I really am glad, Gerald. She is charming and delightful. You have made a wonderful match."

"Yes," he said. "And I might say the same of you, Helena. He is a man of character."

"Yes." She smiled at him and this time it was a real smile. He smiled back.

"Gerald." She was alarmed to find her vision blurring. She blinked her eyes firmly. "Gerald, I am so very sorry. I have never been able to say it because I thought my sin unforgivable. I thought its effects permanent and irreversible. I was wrong. I was, was I not? It is not a meaningless indulgence to say I am sorry?"

"It never was," he said. "It never is, Helena. There is nothing beyond forgiveness—even when the effects are irreversible. We all do terrible things. All of us. For a long time before our marriage I treated Priss as if the label of her profession was the sum total of her character. If that is not an apparently unforgivable sin, I do not know what is. I had to lose her before I realized what a precious jewel had been within my grasp. You do not have a monopoly on dastardly deeds."

"If I had asked forgiveness at your father's funeral," she asked him, "would you have forgiven me, Gerald?" Had she been responsible, too, for all the wasted years?

He did not answer for a while. He took her into an intricate twirl about one corner of the dance floor. "I do not know," he said at last. "Perhaps not. I felt terribly betrayed, the more so because I had loved you more than I had loved anyone else in my life since my mother. But in time I believe it would have helped to know that at least you had a conscience, that you regretted what had happened. Until a few days ago I assumed that you felt no guilt at all—though Priss has always maintained that you must. Priss has the gift of putting herself into other people's souls and understanding what must be going on deep within them even when the outer person shows no sign of it. And she did not even know you."

"I am hoping," she said, "that I can have the honor of a close friendship with my stepdaughter-in-law. If you can say again what you said yesterday, Gerald, and mean it. Can you forgive me? Will you?"

He smiled at her, all the warm affection and trust she had used to see in his face there again. "Priss was right," he said. "She so often is. The one flaw to my peace of mind has been my enduring resentment of you. I have accepted my father for what he was and am no longer hurt by the memory of his dislike. I like the person I am, even though I am not the person he would have had me be. And I have the memory of my mother back. She did not desert me, Helena. She was banished—by my father—and forbidden to see me or communicate with me in any way. I visited my aunts and found out the truth from them."

"Oh, Gerald—" Helena said, feeling all the old pain for his brokenness.

"Sometime," he said, "perhaps I could tell you the whole story. It brought pain. It also brought ultimate peace. She loved me. And you loved me. I have thought about it during the past few days and have realized that it is true. You were very good to me—and not for ulterior motives as I have thought since. You did not plot. You were merely—young and lonely. But even if all my worst fears had been correct, Helena—about my mother, about you—they would not be an excuse for the failed, miserable life to which you thought you had doomed me. I am an individual with a mind and a will of my own. We all have to live life with the cards that have been dealt us. We all—most of us—have the chance to make of life what we will. You would not have been responsible for my failed life—I would have been."

"You are generous," she said.

"No." He shook his head. "Just reaching the age of maturity, I hope. Have you really denied yourself happiness for thirteen years, Helena?"

"I did not deserve it," she said.

"You deserve it now." He twirled her again. "And happiness is yours for the taking, is it not? I believe he is fond of you, Helena. I do not wish to divulge any secrets, but you must know anyway. He told Priss and me when he came to

Brookhurst that he loves you. We have both seen since coming here that it is true. He is the man for you, you know. He is strong and assertive and yet sensitive and loving. It is quite a combination. You must be happy to be having a child. I remember how you used to share your disappointments with me when you were first married—because you felt you could not talk to my father on such a topic, you said. How you longed for a child! And how good you were with the children you encountered—myself included."

"I have been afraid of being a mother," she told him.

"Do not be." Their roles had been reversed, she realized suddenly. He was the comforter, the reassurer, the one to convince her that she was capable of love and worthy of love. "All the little children here adore you, Helena, including Peter, who is shy of almost all adults except Priss and me. He fought with the rest of the children this afternoon to be the one to hold your hand in their circle games. You will be a wonderful mother."

"I am so old," she said, pulling a face.

"God—or nature if you will—does not make mistakes," he said. "If you are able to be a mother at your age, then you are not too old to be a mother. Enjoy it. Parenthood is wonderful, Helena. Exhausting and terrifying and wonderful. Like life."

"Gerald," she said. But there was nothing more to say. Some feelings were quite beyond words. And hers at this particular moment ran far too deep even for tears. "Oh, Gerald."

He smiled.

"You want to do *what*?"

Edgar bent his head closer to his wife's, though he had heard her perfectly clearly. The ball was over, the guests who were not staying at the house had all left, the house guests had begun to drift away to bed, the servants had been instructed to leave the clearing away until morning. And he was eager to get to bed. Helena had glowed all evening—especially after the waltz which he had wanted, but which she had danced with her stepson. She looked more beautiful even than usual. Edgar was feeling decidedly amorous.

"I want to go skating," she told him again.

"Skating," he said. "At one o'clock in the morning. After a dizzyingly busy day. With a mile to walk to the lake and a mile back. In arctically cold weather. When you are pregnant. Are you mad?"

"Edgar," she said, "don't be tiresome. It is so bourgeois to feel that one must go to bed merely because it is late and one has had a busy day and it is cold outside."

"Bourgeois," he said. "I would substitute the word *sane.*"

But she whirled about and with a single clap of the hands and a raising of arms she had everyone's attention.

"It is Christmas," she said, "and a beautiful night. The ball is over but the night is not. And Christmas is not. Edgar and I are going skating. Who else wants to come?"

Everyone looked as stunned as Edgar had felt when she first mentioned such madness. But within moments he could see the attraction of the idea take hold just as it was doing with him. The young people were almost instantly enthusiastic, and then a few of the older couples looked at each other doubtfully, sheepishly, inquiringly.

"That is one of the best ideas I have heard today, Daughter," Mr. Downes said, rubbing his hands together. "Letitia, my dear, how do you fancy the thought of a walk to the lake?"

"I fancy it very well, Joseph," Mrs. Cross replied placidly. "But I hope not just a walk. I have not skated in years. I have an inclination to do so again."

And that was that. They were going, a large party of them, with only a few older couples wise enough to resist the prevailing madness. At one o'clock in the morning they were going skating!

"You see, Edgar?" his wife said. "Everyone is not as tiresome and as staid as you."

"Or as bourgeois," he said. "I should not allow you to

skate, Helena, or to exert yourself any more today. You are with child. Can you even skate?"

"Darling," she said, "I have spent winters in Vienna. What do you think I did for entertainment? Of course, I skate. Do you want me to teach you?"

Darling?

"I shall escort you upstairs," he said, offering his arm. "You will change into something *warm*. We will walk to the lake at a sedate pace and you will skate *for a short while* with my support. You are not to put your health at greater risk than that. Do you understand me, Helena? I must be mad, too, to give in to such a whim."

"I said I would lead you a merry dance, Edgar," she said, smiling brightly at him. "The word *merry* was the key one." She slipped her arm through his. "I will not risk the safety of your heir, never fear. He—or she—is more important to me than almost anything else in my life. But I am not yet willing to let go of Christmas. Perhaps I never will. I will carry Christmas about with me every day for the rest of my life, a sprig of holly behind one ear, mistletoe behind the other."

She was in a strange mood. He was not sure what to make of it. The only thing he could do for the time being was go along with it. And there *was* something strangely alluring about the prospect of going skating on a lake one mile distant at something after one o'clock of a December morning.

"The holly would be decidedly uncomfortable," he said.

"You are such a realist, darling," she said. "But you could kiss me beneath the other ear whenever you wished without fear that I might protest."

He chuckled. *Darling* again? Yes, life with Helena really was going to be interesting. Not that there was just the future tense involved. It *was* interesting.

She had married a tyrant, Helena thought cheerfully—she had told him so, too. The surface of the ice was, of course, marred by an overall powdering of snow which had blown across it since it had last been skated upon. And in a few places there were thicker finger drifts. It took several of the men ten minutes to sweep it clean again while everyone else cheered them on and kept as warm as it was possible to keep at almost two o'clock on a winter's night.

Edgar had flatly refused to allow Helena to wield one of the brooms. He had even threatened, in the hearing of his father and everyone else present, to sling her over his shoulder and carry her back to the house if she cared to continue arguing with him. She had smiled sweetly and called him a tyrant—in the hearing of his father and everyone else.

And then, as if that were not bad enough, he had taken her arm firmly through his when they took to the ice, and skated with her about the perimeter of the cleared ice just as if they were a sedate middle-aged couple. That they were precisely that made no difference at all to her accusation of tyranny.

"I suppose," he said when she protested, "that you wish to execute some dizzying twirls and death-defying leaps for our edification."

"Well, I did wish to *skate*, Edgar," she told him.

"You may do so next year," he told her, "when the babe is warm in his cot at home and safe from his mother's recklessness."

"Or hers," she said.

"Or hers."

"Edgar," she asked him, "is it horridly vulgar to be increasing at my age?"

"Horridly," he said.

"I am going to be embarrassingly large within the next few months," she said. "I have already misplaced my waist somewhere."

"I had noticed," he said.

"And doubtless think I look like a pudding," she said.

"Actually," he said, "I think you look rather beautiful and will look more so the larger you grow."

"I do not normally look beautiful, then?" she asked.

"Helena." He drew her to a stop, and four couples imme-

diately zoomed past them. "If you are trying to quarrel with
me again, desist. One of these days I shall oblige you. I
promise. It is inevitable that we have a few corkers of quarrels down the years. But not today. Not tonight."

"Hmm." She sighed. "Damn you, Edgar. How tiresome
you are."

"Guilty," he said. "And bourgeois and tyrannical. And
in love with you."

This time she heard and paid attention. This time she
dared to consider that perhaps it was true. And that perhaps
it was time to respond in kind. But she could not say it just
like that. It was something that had to be approached with
tortuous care, something to be crept up on and leapt on
unawares so that the words would come out almost of their
own volition. Besides, she was terrified. Her legs felt like
jelly and she was breathless. It was not the walk or the
skating that had done it. She was not that unfit.

"If we are not to skate even at a snail's pace, Edgar," she
said, "perhaps we should retire from the ice altogether."

"I'll take you home," he said. "You must be tired."

"I do not want to go home," she said, looking up to see
that the stars were no longer visible. Clouds had moved
over. "We are going to have fresh snow. Tomorrow we will
probably be housebound. Let us find a tree behind which
we can be somewhat private. I want to kiss you. Quite
wickedly."

He laughed. "Why waste a lascivious kiss against a
tree," he asked, "when we would be only *somewhat* private? Why not go back home where we can make use of a
perfectly comfortable and entirely private bed—and do
more than just kiss?"

"Because I want to be kissed *now*," she said, wrestling
her arm free of his grip and taking him by the hand. She
began to skate across the center of the ice's surface in the
direction of the bank. "And because I may lose my courage
during the walk back to the house."

"Courage?" he said.

But she would say no more. They narrowly missed col-

liding with Letty and her father-in-law. They removed their
skates on the bank. They almost chose a tree that was already occupied—by Fanny Grainger and Jack Sperling.
They finally found one with a lovely broad trunk against
which she could lean. She set her arms about him and lifted
her face to his.

"You are quite mad," he told her.

"Are you glad?" she whispered, her lips brushing his.
"Tell me you are glad."

"I am glad," he said.

"Edgar," she said, "he has forgiven me."

"Yes, love," he said, "I know."

"I have loved during this Christmas season and have
been loved," she said, "and I have brought disaster on no
one."

"No," he said, and she could see the flash of his teeth in
the near darkness as he smiled. "Not unless everyone
comes down with a chill tomorrow."

"What a horrid threat," she said. "It is just what I might
expect of you."

He kissed her—hard and long. And then more softly and
long, his tongue stroking into her mouth and creating a
definite heat to combat the chill of the night.

"You have brought happiness to a large number of people," he said at last. "You are genuinely loved. Especially
by me. I do not want to burden you with the knowledge,
Helena, and you need never worry about feeling less
strongly yourself, but I love you more than I thought it possible to love any woman. I do not regret what happened. I
do not regret marrying you. I do not care if you lead me a
merry dance, though I hope it will always be as merry as
this particular one. I only care that you are mine, that I am
the man honored to be your husband for as long as we both
live. There. I will not say it again. You must not be distressed."

"Damn you, Edgar," she said. "If you maintain a stoic
silence on the subject for even one week I shall lead you the
unmerriest dance you could ever imagine."

He kissed her softly again.

"Edgar." She kept her eyes closed when the kiss ended. "I have lied to you."

He sighed and set his forehead against hers for a moment. "I thought we came here to kiss wickedly," he said.

"Apart from Christian," she said, "I have never been with any man but you."

"What?" His voice was puzzled. She did not open her eyes to see his expression.

"But I could not *tell* you that," she said. "You would have thought you were *special* to me. You would have thought me—*vulnerable*."

"Helena," he said softly.

"You were," she said. "I was. You are. I am. Damn you, Edgar," she said crossly, "I thought it was *men* who were supposed to find this difficult to say."

"Say what?" She could see when she dared to peep that he was smiling again—grinning actually. He knew very well what she could not say and the knowledge was making him cocky.

"I-love-you." She said it fast, her eyes closed. There. It had not been so difficult to say after all. And then she heard a loud, inelegant sob and realized with some horror that it had come from her.

"I love you," she wailed as his arms came about her like iron bands and she collided full length with his massive body. "I love you. Damn you, Edgar. I love you."

"Yes, love," he said soothingly against one of her ears. "Yes, love."

"I love you."

"Yes, love."

"What a tedious conversation."

"Yes, love."

She was snickering and snorting against his shoulder then, and he was chuckling enough to shake as he held her.

"Well, I do," she accused him.

"I know."

"And you have nothing better to say than that?"

"Nothing *better*," he said, putting a little distance between them from the waist up. "Except a tentative, tiresome, bourgeois suggestion that perhaps it is time to retire to our bed."

"Tiresome and bourgeois suddenly sound like very desirable things," she said.

They smiled slowly at each other and could seem to find nothing better or more satisfying to do for the space of a whole minute or so.

"What are we waiting for?" she asked eventually.

"For you to lead the way," he said. "You will start damning me or otherwise insulting me if I decide to play lord and master."

"Oh, Edgar," she said, taking his arm. "Let us go *together*, shall we? To the house and to bed? Let us make love together—to each other. Whose silly idea was it to come out here anyway?"

"I would not touch that question with a thirty-foot pole," he said.

"Wise man, darling." She nestled her head against his shoulder as they walked.

Epilogue

✦

Cora had come hurtling down to the drawing room of the Bristol house, in her usual undignified manner. But she had said only that all was well and that Edgar must go up immediately. When Francis had raised his eyebrows in expectation of more information and Mr. Downes had openly asked for it, she had smiled dazzlingly and asked her brother if he was about to faint.

He had stridden from the room without further ado and taken the stairs to the bedchamber two at a time—even though there *was* a strange buzzing in his head and the air in his nostrils felt cold.

All is well, Cora had said.

His father's new wife came bustling toward him when he opened the bedchamber door, the doctor at her heels, bag in hand. Letty beamed at him and stood on her toes to kiss his cheek; the doctor bowed and made his exit with her.

Edgar was left alone. Though not quite alone. Helena was lying on the bed, pale and silent, her eyes closed. Beyond her was a small bundle that had him swallowing convulsively. It was moving and making soft fussing noises. But it was not his main concern. She looked too still and too pale for all to be well—and she had labored for all of fourteen hours. He took a few fearful steps toward the bed. Was it possible that she was . . .

"Damn you, Edgar," she said without opening her eyes. Her voice sounded strangely normal. "If I had known—

though I might have guessed, of course—that you would beget such large children, I would not in a million years have seduced you."

He could feel no amusement. Only relief—and guilt. It had been unbearably hard to pace downstairs, his father and Francis in tow, for fourteen hours. What must it have been like . . .

"You had a hard time," he told her just as if she did not know it for herself. "I am so sorry, Helena. I wish I could have suffered the pain for you."

She opened her eyes and looked up at him. "He well nigh tore me apart," she told him.

He winced even as one of her words caught him like a blow low in his stomach. *He?* He swallowed again. "We have a son, Helena?" Not that the gender mattered. He had rather hoped for a daughter. What he really meant was—*we have a child, Helena*? Fruit of his body and hers? Product of their love? Their very own baby? The miracle of it all left him feeling paralyzed.

"Are you pleased that I have done my duty like a good wife?" she asked him. "I have presented you with an heir for the Downes fortune."

"To hell with the Downes fortune," he said, forgetting himself in the emotion of the moment. "We have a child, my love. A baby."

She smiled fleetingly. He could see that she was desperate with weariness.

"Meet your son," she said, and she turned to draw back the blanket from the moving bundle. A red, wrinkled, ugly little face, its eyes gazing vacantly about it, was revealed to his view—for a moment. Then he lost sight of it.

"Foolish Edgar," his wife said. "How bourgeois to weep at sight of your newborn child. You are supposed to look closely for a moment to assure yourself that he has the requisite number of eyes, noses, and mouths, all in the appropriate places, and then you are supposed to return to your brandy and your dogs and your hunting."

"Am I?" She was lifting the bundle and then holding it

up to him. He did not dare. He would drop it. How could a human life be so small? "But I am bourgeois, Helena, and so I will cry at the sight of my son." He took the bundle gingerly into his own arms. It was warm and soft and alive.

"Is he not the most beautiful child ever born?" Her voice had lost its mocking tone.

"Yes." He lifted the bundle and set his lips lightly to the soft, warm cheek of his son. "At *least* the most beautiful. Thank you, my love." He reached over her to set the child back on the bed before he could drop it in his clumsiness. He smiled at her. "You must rest now."

"Oh, damn you," she said, lifting one hand to dash across her cheeks. "Now you have started me weeping. It is because I am tired after all that damnable *work*. I would not do it otherwise."

But she grabbed for him as he would have straightened up and moved away. She wrapped her arms tightly about his neck and hid her face against his neckcloth. "Edgar," she said fiercely, "we have a *child*. At the age of seven-and-thirty!"

"Yes." He kissed the top of her head. "And Priscilla and Gerald have a new daughter. A letter came just this morning. All is well, my love."

She said nothing, but she sighed aloud against him and relaxed. She had forgiven herself for the past, he knew, and had set up a close relationship with her former stepson and his wife. But a part of her would always yearn to know that they were eternally happy, that what she had done no longer had any negative effect on their lives.

"All is well," he whispered again.

And all *was* well, he thought as he kissed her, got up from the bed, and crossed quietly to the door. Their marriage, begun under such inauspicious circumstances, was bringing them more joy than they could possibly have expected; his father and Letty were contentedly married; Gerald and Priscilla were being accepted by society; the business was prospering; and he was a father.

He was a father!

"I love you, Edgar Downes," she said as his hand closed around the knob of the door. Her eyes were closed again, he saw. But there was a smile on her pale face. "And if I had everything to do over, I would seduce you again. I swear I would."

He grinned at her even though she did not open her eyes. "It *was* a night to remember," he said, "in more ways than one. But it can be repeated and will be. Not now. Not soon. But it will happen—with me as seducer. I owe it to you—and to myself. You have been given fair warning."

He could hear her chuckling softly as he let himself out of the room and shut the door behind him before going back downstairs to rejoice with his family.

He and Helena were parents. They had a child.

He took the stairs down two at a time.

A FAMILY
CHRISTMAS

"**W**ell?" Lady Templar watched impatiently as her daughter folded her letter and set it down beside her plate on the breakfast table.

"Mr. Chambers will be coming for Christmas," Elizabeth replied, rearranging the napkin across her lap.

"*Here?* To Wyldwood Hall?" Her mother looked aghast. "How dreadfully inconvenient."

"It *is* his home, Mama," Elizabeth reminded her.

"His father purchased it as a trophy," Lady Templar said disdainfully, as if that fact made it less a possession. "He thought it would elevate him into the ranks of the beau monde and erase the vulgar smell of commerce from his person. He thought to make doubly sure by purchasing a well-bred bride for his son. Well, the son may have both the home and the bride, but he is as much a cit as his father, Lizzie. He is an embarrassment. I wish in my heart now that we had not invited the whole family to spend Christmas here. But it is too late to change our plans. Tomorrow everyone will be arriving. How very provoking, to be sure, that Mr. Chambers will be here too."

We? Elizabeth thought. *Our plans?* It was her mother who had invited everyone to Wyldwood. She had written the invitations and sent them on their way before Elizabeth had even known about her plan for a family Christmas.

Elizabeth folded her napkin again, set it neatly beside

her plate, and rose to her feet. She had not eaten, but she had lost her appetite. Mr. Chambers was coming home.

"Will you excuse me?" she asked. "There are a thousand and one tasks I must attend to."

"All of which you will leave to me, Lizzie," her mother said firmly. "You know I am far more experienced than you in managing servants and organizing large house parties."

Elizabeth smiled at her but did not sit down again. She left the room and made her way straight up to the nursery. It was not time to feed Jeremy yet. There would have been time first to complete several of the tasks she had spoken of. But she needed to compose herself. The letter had upset her. So had her mother's open contempt for Mr. Chambers. Lord and Lady Templar had come to Wyldwood in August to be close to their daughter during her confinement in September, and they still had not returned home. Lady Templar had taken over the running of the household, and it had run smoothly ever since.

Elizabeth could not dispute the truth of what her mother had just said about her superior competence. But oh, how she longed to have her home back to herself again, even if she *was* less experienced at running a large house. But how could she say anything to hurt her mother? She had never been an assertive person.

Now all of her aunts and uncles and cousins, as well as her brother and his wife and son, were coming for Christmas—and so was Mr. Chambers. She really had not expected that he would come. She had not even written to inform him of the family Christmas that her mother had planned and to which she had acquiesced after the fact because it was always easier to let Lady Templar have her way than try to fight her.

The baby's nurse was sitting close to the window, sewing. Elizabeth indicated with one raised hand that she was not to get up. Jeremy was awake in the crib, making little baby noises, though he was not crying. She bent over him, smiling and cooing to him, and lifted him out. She could never resist holding him; he was so soft and cuddly, even though her mother had warned her during the month after his birth that she would spoil him if she gave him too much attention. If love could spoil a person, then so be it.

It was her one little rebellion against her mother.

Mr. Chambers was coming home. *Edwin.* She formed his name with her lips, though she did not speak it aloud. She never had said it aloud—except during their nuptial service.

Her mother had just spoken with the utmost disdain of Mr. Chambers's father, who had attempted to buy his way into the upper classes by purchasing a viscount's daughter for his son. But Mama had been quite as eager for the marriage, Elizabeth thought with some bitterness, and Papa had voiced no complaint. The marriage settlement had enabled them to pay off all the considerable family debts, the result of years of gaming and extravagant living. It had not seemed to matter then that Mr. Chambers's father was a city merchant without birth or connections and spoke with a hearty Cockney accent. The only important consideration had been that he was as wealthy as a nabob. Privately, of course, they had considered it lowering to have to marry their only daughter to his son, but sacrifices had to be made if they were to maintain the style of living to which their consequence entitled them.

Elizabeth had been the sacrifice. She had been married off to Mr. Edwin Chambers a little over a year ago, early in December, two weeks before the elder Mr. Chambers died of a heart seizure. During those two weeks Jeremy had been conceived. After the funeral of his father, the younger Mr. Chambers had settled his wife on the grand estate his father had purchased less than a year before, and returned to London to manage the family business. She had seen him on only one occasion since. He had come to Wyldwood after the birth of their son in September. He had visited her in her bedchamber for ten minutes each day, but even during those brief sessions her mother had always been present and had dominated the conversation, choosing topics—deliberately, it had seemed to Elizabeth—designed to exclude her son-in-law or demand only one-word answers from him. He had returned to London after less than a week, with only a few brief words of good-bye to Elizabeth—in her mother's company.

He was a stiff, proud, humorless, morose man. As handsome as sin, it was true, with his blond hair and regular features and trim, elegant figure, but with no character or personality or human warmth with which to attract even the mildest affection. He had been a dreadful disappointment to Elizabeth. Nevertheless, he was her husband, and it hurt to hear her mother belittle him.

When the nurse went downstairs to fetch more mending, Elizabeth sat down. She set the baby on her lap, his head nestled between her knees. She held him by the ankles and lifted his legs one at a time to kiss the soft soles of his feet.

"And he is your papa, my precious," she said aloud. "He is coming home for Christmas."

Jeremy blew a bubble.

Perhaps, she thought, if he stayed for a week or two he could leave her with child again. It was not an entirely unwelcome prospect. Jeremy gave meaning to her lonely life. Another child could only enliven her existence even more. It was only the process she dreaded. He had not treated her roughly during the two weeks following their wedding— not by any means. He had done only what her mother had warned her he would do. It had not even been painful, except a little the first time. But she had been chilled and humiliated by the impersonality of it all.

"But I will say this," Elizabeth told her son, taking his little hands in hers and clapping them while he cooed at her. "You were worth every minute of it. And your brother or sister would be worth as many minutes more."

It was strange how sometimes she ached for what she had found so terribly disappointing.

Sometimes Edwin thought that perhaps he had been too fond of his father, who had loved him with every beat of his great, generous heart. His father had worked for years longer than necessary in order to make sure that his son would live the life of a gentleman. Edwin had had an expensive tutor and had later gone to one of the best schools in England and then to Cambridge. He had been given, in fact, every social and educational advantage that money could buy, as well as oceans of love. Wyldwood Hall had been bought for him. So had his bride, with the idea that she would provide him with an entrée to the highest ranks of the society into which he had not been born but for which he had been raised and educated. If it was possible to die happy, the elder Mr. Chambers had done it.

His son had made him happy by allowing himself to be formed into the sort of person he would rather not have been and placed in the sort of world he would rather not live in with a wife not of his own choosing. He had loved his father—perhaps too much.

It was a gray, blustery, raw day, two days before Christmas, when Edwin Chambers rode up the long driveway toward Wyldwood Hall. He looked ahead to the imposing stone mansion with a sinking heart. It was his, but it did not feel like home. It never had. He would rather be going almost anywhere else on earth to spend Christmas, he thought—except that his wife was here. And his child. And when all was said and done, he was sufficiently his father's son that he could not simply turn from what was his or shirk his responsibilities altogether.

His father had never understood that all Edwin had ever wanted was to be proudly his son, to allow him into the family business, to speak with a Cockney accent if he so wished, to marry a woman of his own choosing from his own world and bring up sons and daughters to be proud of their heritage. But it was not his father's fault that he had never understood. Edwin had never told him, had never been willing to dash the dearest dream of his father's life. In addition, he had known for a number of years that his father was dying of a heart disease.

Perhaps it was wrong to allow one's life to be manipulated, even when the motive was nothing more heinous than love. But he had done it, and he must live with the consequences.

Lord and Lady Templar would still be here, he did not doubt. They had come for a month or so and stayed for almost five. They would continue to live here, he supposed, for the rest of their lives. Their own home was shabby and in dire need of all sorts of repairs, none of which they could afford. And so Christmas must be spent, not only with his wife and son, but with his mother-and-father-in-law, who had never made any secret of the disdain they felt for their daughter's husband. They had driven him away in September. He had been unwilling to assert his will against them—most particularly his mother-in-law—while his wife was still so weak after giving birth to Jeremy. They would not drive him away this time until he was ready to leave. But the thought of the inevitable conflict was a dreary one.

He swung down from the saddle outside the great double front doors and handed the reins to a groom, who had materialized from the stables without having to be summoned. He wondered if his approach had been noted from the house too, if it had been watched for with as much reluctance as he felt. Even as he wondered, the front doors swung open from within, and the butler was bowing regally to him and welcoming him home.

Edwin nodded affably and bade the butler a good afternoon.

"Is Mrs. Chambers at home?" he asked.

But she was coming through the stairway arch even as he spoke, and he was struck again, as he had been thirteen months or so ago, when he had set eyes on her for the first time, by her breathtaking beauty. She was on the tall side, slender and yet shapely. She bore herself with an aristocratic grace that was bred into her very bones. She had dark golden hair, large blue eyes, and perfect features.

She was like an icicle, he had thought from the start—and nothing had happened since to cause him to change that initial impression—ethereally lovely, but icy cold, frigid to the heart. Everything about her bearing and manner proclaimed her contempt for the man who had allowed his father to purchase her as a trophy for his son.

She curtsied. "Mr. Chambers," she said. "I trust you had a pleasant journey?"

He inclined his head to her as he handed a footman his hat and greatcoat and gloves. She had never called him by his given name, though he had invited her to do so when he had called upon her to go through the farce of proposing marriage to her. He had deliberately called her by hers after their nuptials, though she had never invited him to do so. Her greeting chilled and irritated him. The married couples from his world did not address each another with such impersonal formality.

"Yes, thank you, Elizabeth," he said. "You are well? You have recovered your health?"

"Yes, thank you," she said.

"And my son?"

The tightening of her lips was almost imperceptible, but it suggested unexpressed annoyance. He wished he could recall his words and speak them again to refer to Jeremy as *their* son. But he was accustomed to boasting to his friends about his golden-haired boy—*my* son—whom he had last seen when the child was ten days old.

"He is well, thank you," she said.

If, he thought ruefully, he had married a woman from his own world, she would perhaps have greeted him each evening of the past year on his return home from work with a smile and a kiss and warm, open arms and an eagerness to share her day with him and to hear about his. He would naturally have thought of their child as *ours*. He would have seen their son every day of the child's life.

But he had only himself to blame that things were not so. His father had not forced him into this marriage. Indeed, he would have been horrified if he had realized that Edwin did not really want it.

"Would you like to go to your room to freshen up?" she asked, her eyes moving over him and making him intensely

aware of the less than pristine state of the clothes in which
he had been riding for the better part of the day. "I have
guests in the drawing room."

"Lord and Lady Templar?" he said. "I trust they are well?"

"Yes, thank you," she said. Her chin rose a notch, and
she suddenly looked arrogant as well as cold. "We decided
to have a family Christmas here. All the members of my
family arrived yesterday."

What? Good Lord! Without any consultation with him?
Was he even to have been informed? How disastrous his
own decision to come home at such short notice must have
seemed to his wife and her family. How disastrous it
seemed to him! If he could, he would have turned and left
the house without further ado and ridden away back to London. *All* her family? He had never even met most of them.
Their wedding had been a fair-sized affair, but apart from
Lord and Lady Templar and their son and daughter-in-law,
all the guests had been his family and his friends and his
father's. He could not leave now, though.

He *would* not leave. This was, after all *his* home.

"I will meet and welcome them to Wyldwood later," he
said. "But first I would like to go to the nursery. Will you
come there with me?"

"Of course." She turned to accompany him through the
arch to the staircase. She clasped her hands gracefully in
front of her, discouraging him from offering his arm.

"How many guests?" he asked as they ascended the
stairs. He could hear the chill in his own voice. He had
never been able to inject warmth into it when speaking with
his wife. How could one hold a warm conversation with an
icicle?

"Thirty-two adults altogether," she said. "Thirty-three
now."

He winced inwardly. Under different circumstances he
might have felt some amusement over the realization that
he had made the numbers odd. Doubtless his wife and his
mother-in-law had planned meticulously in order to ensure
even numbers. He would even be willing to wager that of

the other thirty-two adults sixteen were gentlemen and six-teen ladies, even though normally one would not expect a family to fall into such a neat pattern.

He was surprised when he opened the nursery door and stood to one side to allow his wife to precede him inside. He had expected a hush appropriate for a sleeping baby. Instead there was a noisy, cheerful hubbub. But of course—there must be children as well as adults in her family. There was a vast number of the former, it seemed, all rushing about at play, all talking—or, rather, yelling—at once. A few nurses were supervising, but by no means subduing them.

Several of the children stopped what they were doing to see who was coming in. A few of them came closer, and a copper-haired, freckled little boy demanded to know who Edwin was.

"You must remember to mind your manners, Charles," Elizabeth said, nevertheless showing a human touch by ruf-fling the hair of the offender. "This is your . . . uncle. Charles is Bertie's eldest," she explained, naming her brother. She identified the other children in the group, all of them cousins or the children of cousins.

"What is *your* name?" Charles asked.

"Charles!" Elizabeth exclaimed, sounding embarrassed.

But Edwin held up a hand. "Have you noticed," he asked, winking at the boy, "that when a lad does not know some-thing he ought to know, adults invariably tell him he should have asked? Yet when he does ask, he is treated as if he had been impertinent?"

"Ye-e-es!" The children were all in loud agreement, and Edwin grinned at them all.

"He is Uncle . . . Edwin," Elizabeth explained.

There was a chorus of requests that Uncle Edwin come and play with them. He held up a staying hand again, chuckling as he did so. Almost all his closest friends had young families, who for some inexplicable reason always saw him as a potential playmate. His friends claimed that it happened because he was still a child at heart. He liked children.

"Tomorrow," he promised. "We will play so hard that you will not have to be told to go to bed in the evening. In fact, you will beg your nurses to let you go there."

There was a swell of derisive denials. Charles, who was obviously something of a leader, snorted.

"It is a promise," Edwin told them. "But today I have come to see a certain baby by the name of Jeremy, who is mine. Has anyone seen him running around here, by any chance?" He looked around him with a frown of concentration.

"Nah," a plump little boy told him, the utmost contempt in his voice. "He's just a *baby*."

"I wanted to play with him," a little girl added, "but he had to go to sleep. Is he yours? He is Aunt Lizzie's too."

Elizabeth led the way to a room beyond the nursery.

"You ought not to have said that about tomorrow," she said with quiet reproach. "They will be disappointed when you do not keep your promise. Children do not forget, you know."

He did not answer. The room was quiet and in semidarkness with the curtains drawn across the window. But the baby was not asleep. Edwin could hear him cooing and could see him waving his fists in the air as he lay on his back in his crib. His eyes focused on his father when Edwin stepped closer. Edwin swallowed hard and was glad that his wife was standing well behind him. He had ached for this moment for almost three months.

Being separated from his child was the most bitter experience of his life. He had considered a number of schemes for bringing him closer, including buying a second house in London for Elizabeth to live in. But there would be too many awkward questions if he and his wife both lived in London but not together. Yet it seemed somehow impossible to set his family up in his own London home, formerly his father's, even though it was large and tastefully decorated and furnished and well staffed and situated in a fashionable part of town. It was, nevertheless, well-known as the home of a prosperous merchant.

"He has grown," Edwin said.

"Of course. You have not seen him for almost three months."

Was it an accusation?

"He has lost much of his hair," he said.

"That is natural," she told him. "It will grow back."

"Do you still . . . nurse him?" He could remember his surprise when her mother and the doctor had been united in their protest against her decision not to hire a wet nurse. It was one issue on which she had held out against her mother's will.

"Yes."

She made no move to pick up the child, who admittedly seemed happy enough where he was. Edwin longed to do so himself, but he was afraid even to touch him.

"He looks healthy enough," he said.

Why was it that with Elizabeth words never came naturally to him, and that the ones he chose to speak were stiff and banal? They had never had a conversation. They had been bedfellows for two weeks he would prefer to forget— she had been a cold, unresponsive, sacrificial lamb beneath him on the bed each night—but they had remained awkward, near-silent strangers.

"You will wish to go to your room," she informed him. "Will you join us for tea later?"

"I believe I will forgo the pleasure of meeting our guests until dinnertime," he told her.

She nodded. Even through the cold impassivity of her face he thought he could detect her relief. He gestured to the door so that she would precede him. He did not offer his arm.

It had been a mistake to come—and that was a colossal understatement. He should have stayed in London, where he had had numerous invitations to spend the holiday with friends whose company he found congenial and in whose presence he could relax and be himself. But he had remembered his father and imagined how sad he would be if he could see his son apart from his wife and child at Christmas, just one year after the wedding that had brought all the elderly man's dreams to happy fulfillment.

Elizabeth, dressed with greater care than usual in an evening gown of pale blue, a color she knew became her well, went down early to the drawing room before dinner. Even so, Mr. Chambers was there before her, standing before the marble fireplace, his hands clasped behind his back, looking like the master of the house. She was relieved to see that he was clothed severely but immaculately in black and white. Had she expected otherwise? She had never seen him look slovenly or heard him speak in anything other than refined accents. He bowed formally to her and she curtsied. It seemed strange to realize that he had been her husband for longer than a year—and that this was his home.

They had no chance for conversation. The door opened again to admit Lord and Lady Templar and Elizabeth's Aunt Martha and Uncle Randolph.

"Ma'am. Sir," Mr. Chambers said in greeting to his parents-in-law, bowing courteously. "How do you do?"

"Mr. Chambers," Lady Templar said with distant hauteur, her hair plumes nodding as she inclined her head. "I trust you are well?"

Elizabeth introduced her aunt and uncle, and Mr. Chambers greeted them with a bow.

"Welcome to Wyldwood," he said to them. "I am delighted you were able to join Elizabeth and me here for Christmas."

It was a sentiment he repeated over and over again during the next half hour as the rest of the family came down for dinner. Elizabeth stood beside him, making the introductions and feeling enormous relief. She had feared that he would allow himself to be dominated by her mother, that he would allow her to treat him as a guest—an inferior, uninvited guest. How humiliating that would have been.

He was to be put to a further test, though.

When the butler came to announce that dinner was served, Lord and Lady Templar were close to the door and proceeded to the dining room without delay. Everyone else held back until Mr. Chambers had offered his arm to Aunt Martha and followed them. Elizabeth, on Uncle Randolph's arm, cringed at the discourtesy of her parents preceding a man in his own home, and hoped there was to be no unpleasant scene.

"Perhaps, sir," Mr. Chambers said with quiet deference when they entered the dining room, addressing his father-in-law, "you would care to take the place at Elizabeth's right hand at the foot of the table. Ma'am," he added, addressing Elizabeth's mother, "will you honor me by sitting to my right at the head of the table?"

With the rest of the family crowding into the room behind them, Elizabeth looked fearfully at her mother, whose bosom was swelling with outrage.

"Lizzie," she said, ignoring Mr. Chambers, "your papa is the gentleman of highest rank here, and he is head of our family."

But not of Mr. Chambers's family, Elizabeth might have pointed out, and perhaps would have if her father had not saved her by exerting his authority—a rare occurrence.

"Take a damper, Gertrude," he said, and moved off toward the foot of the table.

Lady Templar had no choice then but to proceed in the opposite direction, from which vantage point she displayed her displeasure by ignoring her son-in-law all through dinner and conversing with gracious warmth with Uncle Oswald on her other side. Mr. Chambers conversed with Aunt Martha and Bertie beyond her and looked perfectly composed and agreeable, as if entertaining a tableful of members of the *ton* were something he did every evening of his life.

Had she expected him to be gauche? Certainly she had feared that he might.

He also looked gloriously handsome. Elizabeth, playing the unaccustomed role of hostess in her own home, was nevertheless distracted by the sight of her husband and by the disturbing memories of their two weeks together last year, and wished he had not come to spoil her Christmas and everyone else's—including his own, she did not doubt. At the same time, she regretted the sudden death of his father, whom she had liked. Had he lived, she and Mr. Chambers would very likely not have lived separately for the past year. Perhaps they would have made something workable out of their marriage. She had been quite prepared to make it work. Indeed, she had been eager to move away from her mother's often burdensome influence in order to become mistress of her own home.

And she had fallen in love with Mr. Chambers on sight.

Lady Templar was still bristling with indignation when the ladies withdrew to the drawing room after dinner, leaving the gentlemen to their port.

"Well!" she exclaimed. "Of all the impertinence! I must say I am surprised, Lizzie, that you would stand by and watch your father humiliated by a man very far beneath our touch without uttering one word of protest."

"Shhh, Mama," Elizabeth said, mortified, since the words had been overheard by her sister-in-law and by all her cousins and aunts. "This *is* Mr. Chambers's own home." And the man very far beneath their touch was her husband.

"Lizzie!" Her mother's voice quavered with indignation. "Never did I think to live to see the day when you would tell your own mother to hush. And *did* you see what happened, Martha? Did you, Beatrice? When I would have stood, as was perfectly proper given my rank and position in this family, to lead the ladies from the dining room, that man had the effrontery to set four fingers on my arm and nod at *Lizzie* to give the signal."

Elizabeth was both mortified and distressed. She had never been able to stand up to her mother—not even when informed that she was to be sacrificed in matrimony to a wealthy cit in order to recoup the family fortunes. But Mr. Chambers was her *husband,* and she owed him loyalty more than she did anyone else—including her mother.

"Mr. Chambers has a right to expect me to be hostess in his own home, Mama," she said. "I am his wife. It is what all men expect."

"Well!" There were two spots of color high on her mother's cheekbones. "You are the most ungrateful of daughters, Lizzie! I am very vexed with you. Besides, how can you expect to be hostess of such a large house party when you have no experience? And when you have Jeremy to attend to? I have given you almost half a year of my time and this is the thanks I receive?"

"I do appreciate all your help, Mama," Elizabeth said. "You know I do."

But her sister-in-law set a hand on her arm and smiled at her. "Come and join the group about the pianoforte with me, Lizzie," she said. She had had her own conflicts with her mother-in-law during the eight years of her marriage.

Elizabeth, grateful for the excuse to avoid further conversation with her mother, nevertheless felt guilty as Annabelle linked an arm through hers and led her away. She had lied to her mother. She was not grateful. It was with dismay that she had watched September turn into October and October into November without any sign that her parents intended to return home and leave her mistress of Wyldwood again. Despite loneliness and depression over her apparently failed marriage, she had liked being mistress of her own home for a few months.

It was later in the evening, after they were all assembled in the drawing room, that trouble struck again. There were two tables set up for cards. Another group was gathered about the fireplace, conversing. A crowd of younger people was clustered about the pianoforte, listening to young Harriet perform. Elizabeth was on her feet watching the card games and reflecting on the fact that Christmas was already shaping up to be its usual predictable, tedious self. With what high hopes she had embarked upon a totally different life last year. She really had been happy about her arranged marriage, especially after meeting the jolly Mr. Chambers and then receiving his son. But nothing had come of her bright hopes after all, except that she had Jeremy.

Mr. Chambers was moving away from the fireside group and stopped beside her.

"We will be decorating the house tomorrow?" he asked.

"Decorating?" She looked blankly at him.

"For Christmas." He raised his eyebrows. "With holly and ivy and pine branches and mistletoe and all that."

"Oh," she said.

"And a kissing bough."

Harriet had just finished playing. At the same moment a lull had fallen on the conversation by the fire. His words were generally audible.

"A *what*?" Lady Templar asked, looking up from her cards.

"A kissing bough, ma'am," Mr. Chambers repeated. "And other decorations to make the house festive for the season. Have you made no plans, Elizabeth?"

"We have never used Christmas decorations," she said. She had sometimes wished they had. The assembly rooms in the village at home had been decorated one year for a Christmas ball. They had looked gloriously festive, and they had smelled richly of pine.

"Then we will this year," he announced.

There was an audible stirring of interest from the direction of the pianoforte.

"A *kissing* bough," young Sukie said, and there was a titter of self-conscious male laughter and the higher trill of girlish giggles.

"I always did like a few tasteful Christmas decorations in a house," Aunt Martha said with an apologetic glance at Lady Templar. "We had some one year when we remained at home for the holiday. Do you remember, Randolph? But never a kissing bough, I must admit. I believe that might be vulgar."

"There will certainly never be one in *this* house," Lady Templar said in the voice her family recognized as useless to argue with. "Such bourgeois vulgarity would not be tolerated in *this* family. I will direct the servants tomorrow, Lizzie, to bring in some greenery, if it is Mr. Chambers's wish, but I will give strict instructions about what is suitable."

"Oh, it *is* my wish, ma'am," Mr. Chambers assured her. "But the servants need not be burdened with the extra task when I daresay they are already far busier than usual. Half the fun of Christmas decorating is doing it all oneself. I will go out and gather the greenery tomorrow morning. There should be more than enough in the west woods. Would anyone care to join me?"

A number of the young people spoke up with cautious enthusiasm, and a few others stole self-conscious glances at their parents and Lady Templar and would have spoken up if they had dared, Elizabeth thought. She stared silently at her husband, marveling that he would defy her mother yet again. He had seemed so quietly obedient to his father's will last year that she had concluded he was a man easily dominated.

"I must ask the gardeners," he said, "if there is mistletoe anywhere in the park. It would not be Christmas without mistletoe."

The young people tittered and giggled again.

"The children must come too," he said. "I promised to play with them tomorrow. I also promised to exhaust them. Gathering greenery and then decorating the house will serve both functions."

"The offspring of *this* family," Lady Templar said with awful civility, "will remain in the nursery with their nurses, where they belong, Mr. Chambers. Children may be allowed to romp about the houses you are accustomed to frequent, but such is not the case in genteel society."

Elizabeth bit her lip. She dared not look at her husband.

"Well," he replied amiably, "we must allow their parents to decide, ma'am. Now, we will need to be up and out early." He held up a staying hand when there was a collective groan from the direction of the pianoforte. "Tomorrow is Christmas Eve. There will be all the decorating to do afterward, and it must be done well. It is going to be a busy day."

Uncle Oswald cleared his throat and set down his hand of cards. "I do some whittling now and then," he said, looking embarrassed. "I daresay I could put together some sort of Nativity scene if you wish, Chambers. It seems to me that I did it a few times at Christmas when the children were young."

"Yes, you did, Papa," Sukie said. "Please, please may I go out gathering greenery with Cousin Edwin? May I, Mama?"

"I used to help you, Papa," young Peregrine added. "I would help again this year, except that I don't want to miss the outing."

"You can do both," Mr. Chambers assured him. "You can help your father in the afternoon while the rest of us hang up the greenery."

"Martha and I were planning to take a drive into the village tomorrow morning," Aunt Beatrice said. "I daresay we will find some satin ribbon in the shop there if we look. Will we, Lizzie? It will be needed to make the decorations pretty," she added without looking at Lady Templar.

"I doubt you will be able to take the carriage anywhere tomorrow, Beatrice," that lady said, a note of triumph in her voice. "Neither will anyone be able to set foot beyond the door to gather greenery. It is almost certain to snow before morning, and we will all be housebound."

"But I am counting upon its snowing, ma'am," Mr. Chambers assured her. "All work and no play would make for a thoroughly dull Christmas Eve. A snowball fight would be just the thing to lift our spirits, get the blood moving in our veins, and yet not slow us down fatally. We will definitely need to make an early start, though."

There was a swell of unabashed excitement from the younger people at the mention of snow.

Lady Templar got to her feet and surveyed the gathering with haughty disdain. "I, for one, will not stand for such vulgar nonsense," she declared. "And if Lizzie will not assert herself as mistress of this house, then I—"

"Mama!" Elizabeth cut her off sharply. "If Mr. Chambers says that our home is to be decorated for Christmas, then it will be decorated. Even with a kissing bough."

"Lizzie!" Her mother's bosom swelled with outrage.

"Stow it, Gertrude," Elizabeth's papa advised from the other card table, exerting his authority briefly for the second time in one evening, without raising his eyes from his cards.

Elizabeth met her husband's gaze but then looked sharply away. Her heart was beating a wild tattoo in her bosom. She had just openly defied her mother! But how could she not have done so?

"Excuse me," she said abruptly. "I must go up to Jeremy." He would be ready for his night feeding. She just hoped her milk had not been soured.

She had never seen Mr. Chambers smile before today, she thought as she hurried up the stairs. But he had smiled at the children this afternoon, and he had done more than that to all her young cousins in the drawing room—he had actually grinned at their enthusiasm over his plans for tomorrow. And he had suggested something that sounded so much like fun that her heart ached with longing.

Fighting in the snow.

Gathering greenery in the woods.

Decorating the house.

Making a kissing bough.

She had never been kissed—a ridiculous truth in light of the fact that she was a wife and mother. But he had never kissed her. And she had never had a beau before him.

They were going to decorate the house for Christmas—*they,* not the servants. They were going to have a kissing bough. She hurried lightly along the corridor to the nursery.

They were going to have *fun.*

At least, she thought, amending the idea as her footsteps slowed, the children and young people were going to have fun. But she was not in her dotage, she reminded herself. She was not even twenty yet. It just seemed that somehow, somewhere, she had misplaced her youth.

She was a matron with a child. She would be expected to remain at the house.

L ady Templar's prediction had proved quite correct. Yesterday's gray, raw day had been transformed into today's magical white world. A few inches of snow blanketed the outdoors, and more was falling. They were to enjoy that rare phenomenon, Edwin realized early—a white Christmas.

All the parents of young children not only had given permission for them to join the expedition to gather greenery but also had decided to go outside themselves. Only two babies, Edwin's own included, stayed in the nursery. The remaining children, their parents, and most of the younger cousins gathered in the hall soon after breakfast, bundled up warmly, chattering and laughing and in exuberant high spirits.

Most of the parents and young people were there, Edwin saw. One was conspicuously absent. Had he expected her to come? She had surprised him the evening before by defending him against her mother, but she had done so with a cool dignity that had proclaimed only wifely obedience. There had been no indication that she was enthusiastic about his plans or that she intended to participate in them in any way. It would be as well to take no notice of her absence. She was still the ice maiden he had married, even though she was a maiden no longer. Her cool demeanor had kept him from going to her bed last night, though he had wondered before he arrived at Wyldwood if he would. They were not officially estranged, after all.

But despite himself he hesitated, even as the crowd in the hall looked to him for direction.

"I have forgotten something," he said. "Give me five minutes."

He hurried through the arch and ascended the stairs two at a time, imagining with a certain feeling of amusement what Lady Templar's reaction would be if she should happen to see him. She had ignored him with haughty dignity at breakfast.

Elizabeth was not in her room. She might be anywhere, but he took a chance on finding her in the nursery. He was not mistaken. She was standing at the window of Jeremy's room looking downward, as if she expected the outdoor party to emerge from the door below at any moment. The baby was asleep in his crib.

"We are about to leave," he said.

"Are you?" She turned toward him, straight-backed and regal and unsmiling.

He had wasted his time coming up here to talk to her, he thought. He had probably ruined her Christmas, in fact.

"Does the baby need you?"

"He has just been fed," she told him. "Your eagerness to see him has certainly diminished since yesterday." She spoke softly, but the rebuke was unmistakable.

"I came up here early," he said, feeling a stirring of anger against her. Why had she married him if she despised him so? But the answer to that question was obvious, at least. It had certainly not been from personal choice. "His nurse was changing his nappy, and he was as cross as blazes, though she assured me that he could not possibly be hungry. I held him for half an hour." He had held his tiny son against his shoulder with an intense ache of tenderness. "He almost deafened my right ear for a few minutes, but he finally found amusement in chewing on the brocade collar of his papa's dressing robe."

Not for the first time he wondered how his son would grow up. Would he, too, despise his father and be embarrassed by his origins?

"I did not know that," his wife said. "Nurse did not tell me."

"I suppose," he said, "you do not want to come outside with us?"

"Gathering greenery?" she said. "And engaging in a snowball fight?" She sounded shocked.

"No." He nodded briskly and turned back to the door. "I did not think so. We will probably be back late for luncheon. You may wish to have the meal set back an hour." If her mother would permit such a disruption of the household routine, that was.

He was at the door of the outer nursery—deserted this morning—when her voice stopped him. She had stepped out of Jeremy's bedchamber and was closing the door behind her.

"Mr. Chambers," she called, her formal words of address increasing his irritation, though he turned politely toward her, "do you *want* me to come?"

She looked different somehow, less serene, less sure of herself. There was an expression almost of longing in her eyes. She looked suddenly youthful, and he remembered that indeed she was little more than a girl. She had been eighteen when they married, five years younger than he.

He swallowed his first impulse, which was to tell her that she might please herself.

"Yes," he said abruptly. And it was true. He was as irrationally head-over-ears in love with her as he had been when he first set eyes on her. If she still despised him for his origins and his willingness to have his father purchase her for her birth and rank, well, so be it. But he had come here to see if something could be made of his marriage before their separation had continued for so long that it would be virtually irreversible.

"Very well," she said, her cool, reserved self again. "I will go and change. You need not wait for me."

Had he imagined that look of longing? Was she coming merely because he had asked? Merely because she owed him obedience? Would she be miserable outside in the snow and the cold? Would she spoil the outing for everyone else?

"We will wait outside for you," he said.

I t was still snowing. Thick white flakes fluttered down from a heavy gray sky. The steps outside the front doors had been swept recently, but there was a thin film of snow on them again. Elizabeth stepped out onto the top step and felt as if she were walking into an alien, enchanted world.

Snow had always meant being housebound. Snow was something one could slip and break a leg on. Worse, snow was something that had to be waded through with an accompanying loss of dignity, especially if one skidded inelegantly. Walking out into the snow, making slides of it, sledding over it, building snowmen with it, clearing it from a frozen pond or lake in order to make a skating surface, were all activities designed for the lower classes, who had no dignity to lose. Fighting with snowballs was simply beyond imagination, even for children.

There were times when she was a child that Elizabeth had guiltily wished she had been born into the lower classes.

They were out there on the great white expanse that was the south lawn—all the children, most of the cousins who were in Elizabeth's own age group, her brother Bertie, Annabelle, and Mr. Chambers. The children were dashing about and screeching as they chased one another. The ladies were laughing; the men were whooping as they tried sliding on snow that was too deep, and kept coming to grief. They were all very obviously enjoying themselves.

Even Aunt Amelia and Uncle Horace were outside, standing in the snow on the terrace, watching the activities and laughing.

It was a scene so alien to Elizabeth's experience, so full of wild, uninhibited joy that she felt overwhelmed by it. Could she ever give herself up to such sheer fun? She had been brought up to think that having fun and lacking ladylike dignity were synonymous terms. She almost turned and hurried back inside before anyone saw her. But Mr. Chambers must have been watching for her. He came wading toward her, his eyes bright with animation, his face already flushed from the cold and exertion. He looked incredibly virile and handsome.

"Take my hand," he said when he reached the bottom step.

She set her hand in his outstretched one and remembered with almost painful intensity her first enchanted sight of him when he had come to offer her marriage. He would be her escape, she had thought naively then, from her dull, restricted life into a world where warmth and love and laughter would transform her. She had already met his father and had liked him immensely, despite—or perhaps because of—those qualities her mother had despised as vulgar. Absurdly, she had wanted him as *her* father. The son was so very handsome, and younger than she had expected. It had not taken her long, though, to realize that his very correct, unsmiling demeanor hid scorn for her for allowing herself to be bought. But this morning she would not think of that. He had chosen to come to Wyldwood for Christmas, and he had come to the nursery this morning with the express purpose of inviting her out here.

He released her hand as soon as she was safely down the steps, set two fingers to his lips, and let out a piercing whistle. Elizabeth looked at him in astonishment, as did everyone else.

It was easy to believe over the next couple of minutes that he was a successful businessman, accustomed to organizing and commanding. He announced that the snowball fight was about to begin and soon had everyone divided into two teams of roughly equal numbers and firepower. Elizabeth would gladly have stood watching with her aunt and uncle, but she was given no choice. She was named to a team and waded gingerly out onto the lawn to join her teammates. Annabelle caught her by the hand and squeezed it.

"Lizzie," she said, "I am so glad you have come to enjoy the snow. But however did you escape from Mama-in-law?" She laughed and slapped one mittened hand over her mouth. "Forget I said that. Oh, goodness, I have to face both Bertie and Charles on the other team."

The snow was soft beneath Elizabeth's feet and not as slippery as she had expected it to be. It reached almost to the top of her boots.

"It sparkles," she said, "even though the sun is not shining, as if someone has sprinkled the surface with thousands of miniature sequins. How beautiful it is."

But she was not given long to admire her first real experience of snow. The two teams were facing each other across a neutral expanse of it, and Mr. Chambers whistled again, the signal for the snowball fight to begin. Most of the players, it soon became obvious to Elizabeth, had armed themselves in advance. Snowballs zoomed through the air, and squeals and shouts and laughter revealed that many of them had found their mark.

Elizabeth shied away from all the vigorous action, uncertain what to do herself. She felt the beginnings of misery in the midst of such bubbling animation. She had never been allowed to play and enjoy herself—she did not know how. She was a lady.

And then a snowball collided with her chin and dripped down inside the collar of her cloak before she could brush it away. Another struck her on the shoulder. She could think only of her discomfort, of getting back indoors, where it was warm and quiet and dry and sane and all was familiar to her.

"The best defense is invariably offense," her husband advised from close beside her, and he struck Peregrine, her chief tormentor, on the nose with a large, wet snowball.

Elizabeth laughed and felt suddenly, unexpectedly exhilarated. She stooped to gather a handful of snow, formed it into a ball, and hurled it, also at Peregrine, who was still sputtering and trying to clean off his face. It struck him in the chest, and Elizabeth laughed with delight, even as another snowball from an unidentified assailant shattered against her shoulder.

After that she forgot about discomfort and cold and dignity and hurled snowballs as fast as she could mold them at any foe within her range. Soon, without even realizing it, she was helpless with laughter. She was also liberally caked with snow from head to foot. But several minutes passed before she spared a moment to slap ineffectually at her cloak with snow-clogged mittens.

By that time the fight was losing momentum, the children having discovered an even more amusing activity. They had captured Mr. Chambers, two of them hanging off each arm, one off each leg, while a few others pushed and shoved. With a ferocious roar he went down on his back.

"Bury Uncle Edwin!" Charles shrieked over and over again, and the other children took up the cry until it became a chant.

They proceeded to heap snow over him until only his shoulders and head were visible—and his hat, which had tipped to a rakish angle.

"Poor Mr. Chambers," Aunt Amelia remarked.

"He is a jolly good sport, I must say," Uncle Horace commented. "You would not catch me letting them do that to me."

Elizabeth stood and watched while the other adults and young people slapped themselves and one another relatively free of snow and recovered their breath. Mr. Chambers was laughing good-naturedly and putting up only enough of a struggle to amuse the children. She felt as if she were gazing at a stranger. Where was the cold, humorless, dour man she had married? By some instinct, the children had picked out the very adult who would indulge them and play with them and allow himself to be played with. How had they known?

For the first time Elizabeth could see her husband as the son of that hearty, jolly man who had arranged the marriage with her own parents and insisted upon having a private word with her in order to assure himself that she was not being coerced into anything against her will. Her husband, it seemed, possessed the same generous, fun-loving nature, though he had never displayed it for her benefit.

She felt plunged into sudden depression again. He had not wanted to marry her, of course. He disliked her. He very probably despised her.

Five minutes later the play portion of the morning was over and they were all trudging off in relatively good order toward the west woods. Mr. Chambers had accomplished the transition without any apparent effort, Elizabeth noticed. And indeed, there was no feeling among them that they were now off to dull work. It was as if they were merely heading off toward some new game.

Mr. Chambers had divided them into four groups, two to cut down pine boughs, one to gather holly, and a group of four to search for the mistletoe the gardeners had assured Mr. Chambers was to be found growing on the older oaks. He was himself a part of the last group, as was Elizabeth. The other two were Cousin Miranda and Sir Anthony Wilkins, her betrothed.

Elizabeth could not quite believe she was doing this. The snow was deep and heavy underfoot, her fingers inside her gloves were tingling from the cold, her cheeks and nose were almost numb and must be unbecomingly red, and yet at this point in the morning she would not go back to the house for all the inducement in the world. She knew suddenly that she had never enjoyed herself even half as much as she was enjoying herself today. And there would be *only* today, and perhaps tomorrow, though Christmas Day had always been one of her least favorite days of the year. After that Mr. Chambers would surely return to London, and it might be a long time before she saw him again. She might never see him quite like this ever again.

"Perhaps you can lead us to where the oaks are," he said to Elizabeth.

But although she was familiar with the park, she had never ventured deep into the woods. They searched for many minutes before finding what they had come for. Fortunately the snow was not as deep here, as the canopy of branches overhead acted as a sort of roof.

"As I suspected," Mr. Chambers said when they were all standing beneath a particularly stout, ancient oak. "It is rather far from the ground."

It was the mistletoe he was talking about. Elizabeth tipped back her head and saw it an impossible distance overhead. Surely he was not intending . . .

"Are you willing to risk your neck?" he asked, looking at Sir Anthony.

Anthony was in love with Miranda, as everyone knew, and was eager to impress her. And so the two men swung up into the branches of the tree while Miranda gasped nervously and Elizabeth pressed one gloved hand to her mouth. They would kill themselves!

"Don't slip," Miranda admonished her betrothed. She lowered her voice. "Oh, Lizzie, I *do* so admire Mr. Chambers. He is not at all stuffy, is he? Yet he is not vulgar either. I am very happy for you. Mama said last year that it was a great shame you were forced to marry a cit only because Aunt and Uncle were improvident, but this year I do not doubt she will declare that you were fortunate. He is such fun."

Yes, he was. With other people. Not with her, though. He did not like her.

"Oh, Edwin, do be careful!" She clapped a hand to her mouth again. His foot had slipped, but he recovered his balance almost immediately and grinned down at her.

Her knees turned weak. Because he had almost fallen? Or because he had smiled at her? And she had, she realized in some embarrassment, called him by his given name.

Anthony was the first down. He held a clump of mistletoe triumphantly in one hand.

"Now, then," he said while Miranda laughed again, "the victor claims his prize." And he raised his hand aloft, dangled it over her head while he caught her by the waist with his free hand, and kissed her with smacking relish on the lips.

"Tony!" she scolded. "Mama would have a fit of the vapors."

"But we have Mrs. Chambers to act as chaperon," he said.

"Lizzie is *younger* than I," she told him.

He turned to look at Elizabeth in some surprise. She was feeling so embarrassed that she would have been blushing rosily if her cheeks had not already been bright red from the cold. She had never before seen two adults kiss. Mr. Chambers had just reached the ground and was looking down ruefully at a deep scuff mark along the inside of one boot. Elizabeth hoped he had not seen the kiss.

"In that case," Anthony said, grinning, "*you* must chaperon Mrs. Chambers, Miranda."

"Absurd!" she said, laughing too. "Lizzie is *married* to Mr. Chambers. He may kiss her whenever he pleases."

Elizabeth scarcely knew where to look. She had not stepped away from the tree as the gentlemen descended, with the result that she was suddenly almost toe-to-toe with Mr. Chambers, and he was looking into her face, a question in his own. He was holding mistletoe. Did he think she had held her ground deliberately? Did he think . . . ? She stared back at him. She was having trouble with her breathing.

"A man really ought to be rewarded," he murmured, "for risking both his life and his boots."

He intended to *kiss* her?

She had shared the intimacy of the marriage bed with him on fourteen successive nights. She had taken his seed into her womb and borne his child. Yet she felt suddenly as if they had never touched at all. Certainly he had never kissed her.

"Oh, how foolish!" she said in what she hoped was a light tone, turning sharply away. "All the magic will be gone from the mistletoe even before we take it back to the house."

"Well, there is something in that," her husband said from behind her, his tone matching her own. "But I reserve the right to be the first to test it there after the kissing bough has been made and hung—with the lady of my choice."

Miranda and Anthony laughed. Elizabeth forced herself to turn her head back toward her husband and join in their laughter. Had he really *wanted* to kiss her? He was looking at her with narrowed eyes, an unreadable expression in them.

Had she ruined the morning?

But he strode up beside her, and they led the way out of the deeper woods. Soon they could hear other voices and see the other groups busy about their tasks. Indeed, when they reached their starting point, they found an impressive mound of greenery waiting to be hauled to the house.

"How are we going to get it there?" Cousin Alex asked, lifting his beaver hat in order to scratch his head through unruly chestnut curls.

"Carry it?" Peregrine suggested.

But Mr. Chambers, as they might have expected, had organized everything in advance. Gardeners were to bring carts drawn by teams of horses, he explained. Indeed, they came into sight, raising clouds of snow, almost before he had finished explaining.

And so they all trudged empty-handed back to the house, having to wade through snow that was considerably deeper than it had been when they set out. Elizabeth did not know who it was who began singing "The Holly and the Ivy," but soon they were all singing lustily and not particularly musically and following it with other Christmas carols. Mr. Chambers, who was walking beside her, four-year-old Louisa perched on one of his shoulders, had a good tenor voice, she discovered.

Elizabeth felt awkward and shy with him. Why had she avoided his kiss? She had wanted it. But had he laid claim to kissing her later beneath the kissing bough? *With the lady of my choice.* Surely that must be what he had meant. He was not angry with her, then?

She would not think of his being angry. She would not think of her own lost opportunity. There was much to look forward to for the rest of the day. At this particular moment she was chilly, untidy, weary, heavy with milk—and suddenly so filled to the brim with happiness that somehow it seemed more painful than pleasurable.

The children were shooed off to the nursery as soon as they returned to the house. They ate luncheon up there, and some of the younger ones, despite loud protests, were put to bed for a sleep afterward. But all were promised by

Edwin, who stayed with them while Elizabeth was feeding Jeremy, that they could come down and help afterward.

"Children have never been allowed out of the nursery during our family gatherings," his wife told him as they made their way downstairs later.

He did not know if she was rebuking him for the promise he had made the children or for suggesting that they bring Jeremy downstairs with them now since he had not gone back to sleep after his feeding. He was tucked into the crook of one of Edwin's arms.

"I was brought up with the idea that children are to be enjoyed as an integral part of a family," he said. "Am I spoiling your Christmas, Elizabeth?"

"No." She spoke quickly, though he was not convinced that she meant it.

And yet he could have sworn that she had enjoyed the morning outdoors after the first few minutes, when he had expected her to return to the house at any moment. She had looked startlingly, vividly lovely while engaging in the snowball fight and laughing helplessly. He had found himself aching with longing to have all that animation and joy focused on him.

"What are your family Christmases usually like?" he asked.

She walked down half a flight of stairs before answering. "There is a great deal of eating," she said. "And drinking. And card playing and billiards. And sleeping."

"Do you enjoy them?"

"I have always *hated* Christmas," she said with quiet vehemence.

There was no chance for further conversation. They were entering the dining room, where everyone else was already gathered. There was a minor sensation, as Edwin had expected, over the appearance of Jeremy. Predictably, Lady Templar, completely ignoring her son-in-law, ordered Elizabeth to summon his nurse to take him back to the nursery.

"It is Mr. Chambers's wish that Jeremy stay with us until he becomes cross or tired, Mama," his wife explained with her usual quiet dignity.

"That child will be ruined," her mother said tartly.

"By spending time with his papa?" Elizabeth said. "Surely not."

"Well, do not say I did not warn you," her mother told her.

Edwin realized suddenly in just how awkward a situation he had placed his wife, who had always obeyed her mother without question, he guessed, and yet who must also have been brought up to believe that she must give the same unquestioned obedience to her husband after she married. Now he was forcing her into making a difficult choice. So far it seemed that she was putting duty to her husband ahead of compliance with her mother's will.

What *her* will was, he did not know. Had she ever exercised it? Had she ever been given a chance? If he had a daughter, he thought, he would want to raise her to think and act for herself, to have opinions, to balance personal identity against duty.

If he had a daughter . . .

He wished suddenly that he could go back and deal differently with his marriage after his father's death last year. He wished he had persevered more to make something workable of what had begun so inauspiciously.

He sat at the table, Jeremy nestled in the crook of one arm, and proceeded to eat his luncheon one-handed. Only for a short while, though. The baby went from hand to hand about the table during the meal, to the delight of most of the lady guests and the silent, haughty disapproval of Lady Templar.

When it came time to decorate the house later, Lady Templar and a few of the other older relatives retreated to the morning room. Elizabeth's uncle Oswald removed to the library with his son, Peregrine, and a couple of the children to work on the carving of the Nativity scene.

It would be as well, Edwin thought with an inward chuckle when he peeped in there once, if his mother-in-law did not stray in that direction. There were wood shavings, tools, and unrecognizable wooden objects strewn everywhere.

The drawing room was a hive of industry. A few ladies were tying lavish bows out of the satin ribbon from the village shop and attaching the little brass bells that had been found there too. A few of the more intrepid young people were risking making pincushions out of their fingers as they fashioned wreaths and sprays out of the holly and then attached a bow to each. A large group was earnestly engaged in designing a kissing bough, using all available materials and weaving in the all-important mistletoe. Three young girls, too old for the schoolroom set but not quite old enough to be accepted as adults, took turns holding Jeremy and the other baby, who had also been brought down. A few children darted happily about doing nothing in particular and getting under everyone's feet. A couple of men were balanced on chairs, pinning decorations to wall sconces and pictures and door frames while their womenfolk tilted their heads from one side to another and advised raising the decoration half an inch to the right and then one and a half inches to the left. In the dining room much the same thing was going on. On the grand staircase two footmen and a parlor maid, who had jumped eagerly into the spirit of things, were twining ivy about the banister.

Elizabeth was moving from group to group, helping, advising, encouraging. In the absence of her mother, she had come naturally into her own as hostess, and glowed with what appeared to be pure pleasure.

Edwin did his share of climbing and precarious leaning. But he also recognized the yearning of some of the children to feel useful. He took several of them astride his shoulders while they reached high to balance a pine bough along the top of a picture frame or to spread holly along the top of the mantel. He could do the job at least twice as fast without their "help," of course, but there was no hurry. This was what Christmas was all about.

They were almost finished when Lord and Lady Templar and the others who had retired from the chaos entered the drawing room with the announcement that the tea tray had been sent for. But the kissing bough group had just declared that it was ready for hanging.

"Do let us put it up before the tray arrives," Elizabeth said, looking flushed and animated and quite incredibly beautiful. "In the center of the ceiling between the two chandeliers, I believe. Does everyone agree?"

There was a buzz of acquiescence, a smattering of applause, and a few stray giggles. The family had livened up considerably since the day before, Edwin thought.

"If you believe, Lizzie, that I am going—" Lady Templar began.

"Cut line, Gertrude," Lord Templar said.

Edwin smiled at his wife. "The lady of the house must be humored," he said. "The center of the ceiling it will be, and now, before tea. We will need the ladder. Is it still in the dining room? Jonathan, would you fetch it, please? With Charles to help you?"

Five minutes later, he was perched in his shirtsleeves at the top of the high ladder beneath the coved ceiling, securing the gaily decorated kissing bough in its place while a chorus of conflicting advice came from below. Elizabeth stood at the foot of the ladder, her face upturned, Jeremy asleep openmouthed against her shoulder.

"Oh, that is perfect," she said before he descended carefully.

"Now," he remarked when he was safely down, "kissing boughs are not merely pretty decorations, you know. They have a practical function. And there is an obscure law, I believe, that the master of the house must be first to put it to use."

Elizabeth turned that look of beauty on him. She also blushed and looked the nineteen-year-old she was, even though she was holding the baby. Her lips parted. She did not, as she had done in the woods during the morning, turn abruptly away or try to avoid what was coming.

She closed her eyes just before his lips touched hers. Her lips were trembling. They were also soft and still slightly parted, warm and moist. It was strange that after his wedding to an aristocratic iceberg he had performed his duty in the marriage bed but had never found the courage to kiss her. He had wanted to quite desperately.

But she was not an iceberg after all, he realized— perhaps he had been realizing it all day. Perhaps she did not like him, perhaps she resented his coming here with such little notice, but she was not frigid.

The kiss, very public and therefore very chaste, lasted for perhaps ten seconds.

Then it was over.

Their first kiss.

He slid one arm about Elizabeth's waist, the baby nestled between them, and smiled into her eyes while several members of her family laughed or whistled or clapped their hands. Was it just Christmas that was putting this flush in her cheeks, this glow in her eyes, this warmth in his heart? he wondered.

But this was not the time to muse on the answer.

"I would have to say," he said, looking about him and grinning, "that the kissing bough works very well indeed. I invite any skeptics to try it for themselves."

Bertie drew a laughing Annabelle beneath the bough, and Lady Templar haughtily demanded her husband's arm to lead her to a chair by the fire.

Edwin organized the removal of the ladder and other clearing-up tasks, and the tea trays were carried in while cousins and fiancés and a few older spouses merrily jostled for position beneath the kissing bough. Elizabeth disappeared upstairs, the baby having woken up at the increased noise to the discovery that he was very hungry indeed.

This family, Edwin thought, was really not very unlike any other of his acquaintances once the repressive influence of Lady Templar was challenged and busy activities were offered. There was beginning to be both the look and the feel of Christmas about Wyldwood.

* * *

By dinnertime, Elizabeth was feeling quite weary from the unaccustomed activity and excitement, but she also knew that she did not want this day to come to an end. It was by far the happiest of her life. It was also the day during which she had really fallen in love with her husband. Oh, it was true that she had been dazzled by him the first time she saw him, only to be disappointed and disillusioned soon after. But she had been wrong about him for a whole year. He was not humorless or without character or personality. Quite the contrary. He was far more like his father than she had realized.

She wondered if he understood just how totally he had transformed their usual Christmas.

She wondered if he realized how very affected she had been by her first kiss, public and brief as it had been. She had relived it over and over again while feeding Jeremy afterward, her cheeks hot with pleasure. But it was not only the kiss she had recalled, startlingly intimate and wonderful as it had been. She had also remembered his smile, warm, almost tender, and directed fully at her, while his arm had circled her waist and their child had been safely nestled between them.

It was the sort of memory on which she would feed during the lonely times ahead.

But the happy novelty of this Christmas was still not over, as she discovered after dinner, even before she rose to lead the ladies to the drawing room so that the gentlemen might be left to their port. Uncle Oswald cleared his throat and spoke up for everyone at the table to hear.

"The Nativity scene is completed," he announced, "and will be set up in the drawing room after dinner with the help of the children. I have been up to the nursery to arrange it. They will all come down, with your permission, Lizzie."

"Definitely not again today, Oswald," Lady Templar said. "It is far too close to their bedtime. I daresay that even in the homes of the middle classes children are not allowed into the drawing room during the evening."

But Elizabeth had spoken up at the same moment. "Oh, yes, certainly," she said, clasping her hands to her bosom. "What a lovely surprise!"

"It is Christmas Eve," Uncle Oswald continued, "and the story of the Nativity must be told. Edwin has agreed to do it."

So Mr. Chambers had been a part of these secret plans too, had he? He smiled at Elizabeth along the length of the table, and she felt her heart turn over. Was it possible that he liked her a little better today than he had before? But he was speaking to her.

"For such an important family celebration," he asked, "shall we have Jeremy brought down too, Elizabeth?"

"Yes," she said quickly before her mother could finish drawing breath to answer for her. "Having our children about us must be a part of all future family gatherings at Wyldwood. Especially Christmas. Christmas is about children—about a child."

"Oh, I *do* agree with you, Lizzie," Annabelle said fervently. "Don't you, Bertie?"

"You know I do, Bella," he said, though he cast a swift, self-conscious glance at his mother as he spoke.

Half an hour later all the adults and children, except those involved in the unveiling of the Nativity scene, were seated expectantly in the drawing room, one large family group, sharing together the warm anticipation of the approaching holy day.

Finally the door opened and Mr. Chambers came inside. He stepped to one side and opened the great leather-bound Bible he carried, while a hush fell on the gathering.

"'And it came to pass in those days that there went out a decree from Caesar Augustus, that all the world should be taxed,'" he read in a rich, clear voice.

As he read Saint Luke's account of the arrival of Mary and Joseph in Bethlehem, two of the children came through the door, one carrying a folded piece of sacking, which he proceeded to spread out on the floor beneath the center window, and the other a roughly carved manger filled with straw, which she set down on the sacking.

" 'And she brought forth her firstborn son, and wrapped him in swaddling clothes, and laid him in a manger; because there was no room for them in the inn.' "

Three more children entered, one carrying Joseph, another Mary, and the third the baby Jesus, wrapped tightly in a piece of white cloth. He was laid carefully on the straw, and his parents were set down on either side of the manger.

A group of shepherds, all carved together out of one piece of wood, came next.

" 'And lo, the angel of the Lord came upon them, and the glory of the Lord shone 'round about them; and they were sore afraid.' "

Two children entered, bearing a paper angel and a paper star, which they pinned to the curtain above the stable.

" 'Mary kept all these things, and pondered them in her heart.' " Mr. Chambers closed the book as Uncle Oswald stepped quietly into the room.

There was no applause. It was perhaps the best compliment to the skill of Uncle Oswald, whose figures were large and rudely carved and yet evocative of the ageless wonder of the Christmas story.

There was a moment of silence, during which Elizabeth, holding Jeremy, fought tears and failed to stop one from trickling down each cheek.

"Thank you," she said. She swallowed and spoke more firmly. "Oh, thank you so very much, Uncle Oswald, children, and M . . . and Edwin. This is the crowning moment of a truly wonderful day."

There was a chorus of voices then—the adults complimenting the performers and the carver, the children explaining loudly to anyone who would listen how they had been told to walk *slowly* and had almost forgotten but had remembered at the last moment and then could not remember whether Mary went at the right side of the manger or the left or whether the angel went above or below the star.

Someone wanted to know why there were no Wise Men, and Uncle Oswald explained that they appeared only in Saint Matthew's gospel, and he had had no time to carve them anyway.

Aunt Maria got to her feet and seated herself on the pianoforte bench. She did not have to call for silence. Somehow it fell of its own accord as she played the opening bars of "Lully, Lulla, Thou Little Tiny Child."

They all sang. And they all surely felt the wonder and warmth and healing power of love in the form of the baby, invisible inside his swaddling clothes, and of Christmas itself. Oh, surely they all felt it, Elizabeth thought. She could not be the only one.

She was aware as Aunt Maria proceeded to a second Christmas carol that Mr. Chambers was standing beside her chair. His hand came to rest on her shoulder as he sang with everyone else, and then, when Jeremy began to fuss, he leaned over her and picked up the baby, as if it were the most natural thing in the world to do.

Elizabeth swallowed against the lump in her throat. How would she ever be able to face her life when Christmas was over and everyone had left except her mother and father? But she would not think of that yet. Not tonight.

They sang for half an hour before the tea tray was brought in.

"There is a service in the village church at nine o'clock in the morning, I have been told," Edwin said after the children had all been sent off to bed, yawning and protesting.

Everyone looked at him rather as if he had sprouted a second head. They were not much of a churchgoing family. But several people had an opinion.

"Much too early," Michael said.

"The carriages could not be taken out in all this snow."

"We could walk, silly. It is less than two miles."

"Go to *church*? On *Christmas Day*?"

"Peregrine, you will not call your sister silly."

"That is the whole point, my dear."

"I'll come," Elizabeth said, smiling at Mr. Chambers,

and remembering how unexpectedly pleasant it had been to speak his given name a few minutes ago.

The chorus of comments continued.

"It *would* be fitting, after all we have done today."

"We could have another snowball fight on the way home."

"The service could not come even close to being as affecting as this little ceremony here this evening, though, could it?"

"And build an appetite for the goose and the plum pudding."

"Does the vicar give long sermons, Lizzie?"

"*You* never lack for appetite, exercise or no."

"Oh, yes, let's go to church," Annabelle said. "Let's walk there through the snow. Together, as a family. What a perfectly delightful Christmas this is turning out to be. The best ever. Thanks to Lizzie and Edwin, that is. You can invite us here every year, you two."

There was a burst of hearty laughter and even a smattering of applause.

"Consider the invitation extended," Mr. Chambers said with a twinkle in his eye. "And after we have feasted and stuffed ourselves tomorrow, we will go down to the lake and make a slide. Unfortunately we have no skates, though I promise there will be some next year. But a slide we will have—and a contest to see who can skid the farthest without coming to grief."

They drank their tea and finally dispersed for the night with warm, cheerful good-nights. Mr. Chambers was talking with a group of uncles and aunts when Elizabeth slipped away to the nursery to give Jeremy his night feeding. Her mother caught up with her on the stairs.

"It is to be hoped, Lizzie," she said, "that tomorrow you will exert more control over your own home than you did today. I cannot tell you how shocked I have been—and all this family has been—over the indiscretion of allowing the children out of the nursery to mingle with the adults when their nurses are being paid to keep them under control in

the nursery. And the vulgarity of all those decorations, including the embarrassingly amateurish efforts of Oswald to
produce a Nativity scene. And the *kissing bough.* I never
thought to live to see such a day in any home occupied by
the members of my own family. It comes, of course, of the
unfortunate circumstance of your having to marry a cit.
Tomorrow you must look to me for guidance. *I* will not be
overpowered by such a domineering man."

Elizabeth stopped outside the door of the nursery. She
had been hoping to avoid her mother tonight. Mama had
been looking sour and outraged all day. Elizabeth still did
not know when she drew breath to speak if she would have
the courage to say what she wanted to say, what she had
been longing to say for the past month or two, in fact.

She had *never* been able to stand up to her mother.

"Mama," she said, "will you and Papa be returning
home after Christmas? You have been kind enough to stay
with me here far longer than you originally intended, but
you must be longing to be at home again."

"Leave you?" Lady Templar said. "When you do not
have any idea how to be mistress of your own home, Lizzie,
or how to be a good mother to your son? I would not dream
of being so selfish. You must not fear that I will desert you
when you have such need of me."

"But Mama," Elizabeth said, her heart thumping loudly
in her chest and her throat and ears, "I do not. I have much
to learn before I can run a household as efficiently as you,
but Wyldwood ran smoothly enough before you came here
and will do so after you leave. You trained me well when I
was a girl. And truth to tell, I look forward to the challenge
of managing on my own again. I have been very grateful
indeed for your help when I needed it, but I do not need it
any longer. And I believe I am a good mother."

"Lizzie!" Lady Templar's bosom swelled, and her face
was blotched with red patches. "Never did I think to hear
such words of ingratitude from you of all people. It is the
influence of that dreadful man, I expect. You were always
an impressionable girl."

"I *am* grateful to you," Elizabeth said again. "But I would not keep on expecting you and Papa to sacrifice your own comfort for me, Mama. It would be selfish of me. And against my inclinations," she added lest she weaken.

"You will allow him to make you as vulgar as he is," her mother said disdainfully.

"I do hope so, Mama," Elizabeth said quietly. "A wife ought to allow herself to be influenced by her husband, especially when he was chosen for her by her own parents. Just as I hope Mr. Chambers will allow himself to be influenced by me."

She did not know if her marriage stood any chance of becoming a real one. But she would prefer the aloneness of being a neglected, half-abandoned wife, she had realized today, than the oppression of living under her mother's thumb, as she had all her life except for the few brief months between Christmas last year and her confinement.

Her mother turned and walked away without another word, her back stiff and bristling with righteous indignation. Elizabeth fought the wave of guilt that swept over her. She had been polite. She had been grateful. But she had said what she had wanted and needed to say for a long time. She wanted her home to herself again, to herself and Jeremy and Mr. Chambers whenever he chose to visit them.

Separation from him after Christmas this year was going to be very much more painful than it had been last year, she thought as she let herself quietly into the nursery. Last year she had been upset, but she had also been disillusioned too. Part of her had been relieved to find herself alone. This year, though, she had seen another, warmer, more charming, more fun-loving side to her husband's personality. This year he had kissed her beneath the kissing bough and smiled at her. The house was going to seem empty indeed when he left.

Her life was going to seem empty indeed.

But she had been firm with her mother. She had asserted herself as mistress of Wyldwood. She had made progress. She was proud of herself.

Jeremy was waiting for her with noisy impatience, she heard even before she entered his room. She smiled. For longer than three months he had been her world, her life. He would continue to be after Christmas. How could she even think of emptiness when there was a baby to nurture and love?

Edwin Chambers's baby and hers.

Elizabeth was sitting by the window of Jeremy's room in the dim light of one flickering candle, the baby at her breast. She looked up when Edwin opened the door from the nursery quietly and stepped inside, and pulled hastily at Jeremy's blanket in order to cover herself.

"I beg your pardon." He moved a few steps closer to her. "I did not intend to embarrass you."

But he was not going to go away either—not unless she directly asked him to. They had circled about each other for too long, he and his wife. He wanted to be a part of their son's life. Oh, yes, and of hers too.

She gazed at him tensely for a few moments before lowering her eyes and relaxing back into the chair. She smoothed her free hand over the soft golden down of the baby's hair, just visible above the blanket.

Edwin clasped his hands behind his back and watched.

They did not talk. The only sound that broke the silence was the hungry sucking of their child.

If only this moment could be immortalized, carried with him forever, Edwin thought. He felt absurdly close to tears. But he wondered which Elizabeth would leave the nursery with him when she had finished feeding the baby. The cold, dignified aristocrat he had known her as until today? Or the warm, smiling, quietly assertive woman she had been for much of today?

Was it just Christmas that had effected the change in her? Would she be herself again once Christmas was over? Even tomorrow, perhaps? But who *was* her real self? He really did not know her, did he? He had met her twice before their wedding, there had been the two weeks after it, and he had spent a few days here after Jeremy's birth, always with her mother in attendance. They were essentially strangers.

He had never been particularly shy with women. He had not known many sexually, but he was acquainted with many as friends and had looked forward to making a marriage for companionship and affection as well as for physical gratification. He still had female friends. But Elizabeth was different. It was not so much that he was shy with her as that he was a little in awe of her—though he was not in awe of her mother. Elizabeth seemed the perfect lady to him, someone far above him in some indefinable way. The feeling annoyed him. He had never been awed by social rank.

The sucking noises gradually slowed and then stopped altogether. Edwin stepped forward and lifted the sleeping baby from his wife's arms as she set the bodice of her dress to rights. He turned and set the child down gently in his crib after kissing his soft, warm cheek and breathing in the baby smell of him.

It was Christmas Eve, he thought. He did not want to end it.

He held the door open for Elizabeth to precede him into the nursery and then the door into the corridor beyond. He closed it behind them.

She turned to say good night to him. He could read her intent as she drew breath.

"Elizabeth," he said quickly, before he could be caught again in the grip of his eternal awkwardness with her, "may I come to you tonight?"

He knew even as he asked that she would not refuse. She had always been the perfectly obedient wife—he must grant her that. But he desperately wanted to see the light of something more than duty in her eyes.

"Yes, of course," she said with her customary quiet dignity.

He offered his arm and she took it, her hand exerting very little pressure on his sleeve. They did not speak a word as he led her to her room, opened the door for her, and bowed. She stepped inside, and he closed the door from the outside.

What had happened to the warmly happy woman he had seen a few times in the course of the day? he wondered. She seemed to have disappeared. Was this to be an ordeal to her? And why would he want it when the two weeks following their wedding had brought him no pleasure at all?

But he was mortally tired of wondering and guessing. He wanted her. It was up to him, he supposed, to bed her in such a way that at least it would not be a repulsive experience for her. But damn it, that was exactly the attitude with which he had approached her bed during those two ghastly weeks. It was up to him to see to it that their coupling was a pleasurable experience for her.

He turned in the direction of his own room, next to his wife's.

E lizabeth stood looking out through the window. The snow had stopped falling, but the sky must still be cloudy. There was not a star in sight. The snow made the landscape unnaturally bright, though. It was Christmas Eve, soon to be Christmas Day

She shivered. Not that she was really cold. There was a fire burning in the hearth, and she was wearing a long-sleeved, high-necked nightgown—the lace-trimmed one she had worn on her wedding night last year. Indeed, she felt almost too warm.

With what high expectations she had awaited him on that night just a little over a year ago. She had fully expected a happily-ever-after. How disappointed she had been.

And this year? Did she have expectations now? She knew what it would feel like, not unpleasant but . . . disappointing. She longed for it anyway, for that touch of intimacy, that illusion of closeness.

And what were her expectations of the future? *Was* there a future? It was best not to think of it. After all, there never was a future, only an eternal present moment, all too often lost because human nature had a tendency to yearn toward the nonexistent future. What did it matter that he might leave the day after tomorrow and not return for months or even a year? Tonight he was here, and he was coming to her bed.

There was a light tap on the door of her bedchamber even as she thought it, and it opened before she could either cross the room or call out.

He was wearing a long dressing robe of green brocade with slippers. His blond hair had been brushed until it shone. He was freshly shaved.

It was like their wedding night all over again. Elizabeth could hear her heartbeat thudding in her ears. She clasped her hands loosely before her and concentrated upon relaxing, or at least upon not showing any of the turmoil of her feelings.

"You told me you have always hated Christmas," he said, coming closer to her. "Are you hating this one too, Elizabeth?"

"No, of course not," she said.

He stopped a foot or so away from her.

"Because I am the one asking you, and it would not be at all the thing to say yes?" he asked her, tipping his head a little to one side and looking closely at her.

She frowned slightly before smoothing out her expression again. What did he mean? She did not know how to reply.

"I am enjoying it more than I expected when I arrived," he said.

"I am glad," she told him.

"Are you?" He reached out one hand and took one lock of her hair between his fingers—she had had her maid leave it loose.

It was one of their usual conversations, saying nothing and leading nowhere. She had always felt more awkward with him than with any other man of her acquaintance.

He bent his head then and kissed her.

She was taken totally by surprise. *This* was different from their wedding night.

He did not immediately draw back. Instead he parted his lips and settled them more comfortably over her own. She tasted heat and moisture and wine. At the same time he settled his hands on either side of her waist and drew her against him. She lifted her hands and set them on his shoulders—broad, solidly muscled shoulders. He was solid everywhere, she noticed as if for the first time. He seemed terribly male.

She had never really touched him before, she realized. Not with her hands—she had kept them flat on the bed during all their encounters last year. And not really with her body—she had felt his weight and his penetration, that was all.

She felt his tongue prodding against the seam of her lips and jerked back her head—and then wished she had not done so. He stared into her eyes, his hold still firm on her waist, his expression unreadable.

"Is this just duty to you, then, Elizabeth?" he asked her. "Is this what the whole of today has been about for you?"

What did he expect her to say? What did he want her to say? Last year had been easy in a way. He had spoken scarcely a word to her in her bedchamber—or out of it, for that matter.

"I have tried to do my duty," she said. "Have I not pleased you? I am sorry about . . . about just now. I was not . . . expecting it. I am sorry."

He took a half step back from her, though he still kept his hands where they were.

"If this is duty and nothing else, Elizabeth," he said, "say so now and send me on my way."

It was not just duty. She would not have dreamed of saying no to him anyway, of course, but it was not just duty. She had wanted him to come. She wanted him in her bed again even though she knew now from experience that the encounter would not measure up to her dreams. It did not matter. She wanted him inside her again. She wanted to feel like his wife.

She had taken too long in answering. He dropped his hands abruptly, turned, and strode toward the door.

"Mr. Chambers," she said sharply.

"For God's sake, Elizabeth." He stopped and turned back to her, anger in his face. "Call me Edwin or nothing at all."

"I am sorry." She tried not to show her distress. He was angry with her. He had spoken sharply to her. He had said *for God's sake* in her hearing.

"Don't be." He lifted one hand and ran the fingers through his hair. "There is no need to be eternally sorry. You owe me nothing. You married me in obedience to your parents' will, you lay with me in the weeks following our marriage, and you presented me with a son in due course. Your life is essentially your own now. You are not my slave. I have never believed in slavery, especially the marital kind."

"I owe you obedience," she said.

"You owe me *nothing*." For a moment his eyes blazed. Then he shook his head slightly, and his anger faded. "I would far rather hear you consign me to the devil than tell me you owe me obedience. But no matter. It is late and we are both tired. Good night, Elizabeth."

All the joy of the day had been drained away, leaving only an intense pain behind it. His hand was on the doorknob. In another moment he would be gone—and they would be forever estranged. She would not be able to bear it.

"Mr. Chambers," she said. She lifted one hand to her mouth even as he paused without turning. "Edwin. Please don't leave."

He turned his head to look at her.

"Please don't," she whispered.

He did not move and so she did. She crossed the room to the bed, removed her slippers, and lay down on her back, all without looking at him. He stood there at the door for a few moments longer before walking to the mantel and blowing out the candles. There was still plenty of light from the fire and the window to illumine his way to the bed.

And enough light for Elizabeth to see when he removed his dressing robe that he wore nothing beneath it. At first she was shocked, but she did not look away. She had never thought of any man as beautiful. Handsome, yes, but not beautiful. Edwin was beautiful—all well-muscled, perfectly proportioned male beauty.

He lay down beside her and turned to her. He raised himself on one elbow, leaned over her, and kissed her again, his hand cupping her cheek, his fingers pushing into her hair. This time when he parted his lips and touched hers with his tongue, she did not flinch—though she did feel a raw and unfamiliar sensation in her mouth, in her breasts, in her womb, down between her thighs. She parted her lips and opened her mouth, and he pressed his tongue deep inside.

For a few moments she hardly noticed that his hand had moved down to fondle her breasts. She did notice, though, when the hand moved to the ribbons that held her night-gown closed to the waist and pulled them loose one by one. His hand slid along bare flesh to cup her breast. He ran his thumb lightly over her nipple.

She thought she would surely die of pleasure. She heard herself make a sound deep in her throat.

"Touch me," he whispered against her lips.

She set one hand tentatively against his chest—it was hard and dusted with hair. The other arm she set about his waist. She had always wanted to touch him, she realized, but she had never laid claim to him as her own. Hers had always been the passive role of obedient wife. Was it possible for a woman to claim a man? Was it right? Was it seemly?

He was not simply going to lift her nightgown tonight, bring himself down on top of her, and penetrate her. That was already clear. She was enormously thankful. It had always been over so very quickly, long before she could even begin to draw any secret pleasure from it.

She was not prepared, though, for all the things he did before the inevitable moment came. He touched her everywhere, with his hands, with his mouth, even with his teeth, first through her nightgown, then beneath it. Finally he slid both hands beneath the gown and lifted it up her body and over her head and along her lifted arms.

And they were both naked.

She should have been horribly shocked, especially as there was so much light in the room and the bedcovers had been pushed back. But her body was humming with pleasure, and his hands and his mouth and his eyes made her feel beautiful. She was having a hard time containing the sensations that were pulsing with her blood into every nerve ending in her body. She throbbed between her thighs and up inside, longing for his penetration, not wanting it too soon, knowing that all would be over within moments once it did happen.

She touched him lightly with her hands—above the waist—and said nothing.

When his hand slid between her legs and explored and caressed the soft secret folds, she knew that she was wet and hot—his fingers felt contrastingly cool. He slid a finger up inside her. She kept her eyes closed and tried to concentrate upon her breathing.

And then he moved over her and lowered his weight on her and spread her legs wide with his own. Familiarity returned as he slid his hands beneath her buttocks and she spread her arms across the bed and pressed her palms into the mattress and drew a slow, deep breath.

He came inside slowly, sliding into wetness, stretching her, filling her. He felt gloriously hard. She fought the urge to tighten inner muscles about him, and lay still.

It lasted far longer than she remembered. He worked her with a slow, deep, firm rhythm for a long time, filling her with himself, filling her, too, with a longing so intense that she wondered if indeed there was any difference between pain and pleasure. By the time he quickened and deepened the rhythm, she was digging into the mattress with her fingers and biting hard on her upper lip in an effort to control herself—though what it was she controlled or stopped from happening she did not know.

He made a guttural sound of satisfaction against the side of her face, and she felt the remembered heat at her core. She was taking his seed into herself again. Despite the slight, unidentified dissatisfaction she felt as all his weight relaxed down onto her and he fell still, Elizabeth smiled and felt happiness well inside to replace the raw discomfort of physical desire not quite allowed to complete itself.

They were not estranged.

Perhaps there would be another child.

When he came for an occasional visit to Wyldwood— and surely he would come for Jeremy's sake—they would perhaps share a bed for a few minutes each night and she would be able to feel this pleasure again.

She tried not to feel dejection when he drew free of her and moved off her. He would return to his room now, and she would feel the remembered emptiness of being alone once more. But differently from all those other times, she would have pleasant memories with which to warm herself until she slept. And perhaps he would come back tomorrow night.

He lay beside her for a while, turned toward her. Then he rested a hand on her stomach and made light circles with it. He sighed audibly.

"For a while," he said, "I thought it was perhaps more than duty."

She turned her head sharply to look at him. He was half smiling.

"It was not duty," she said.

"You just do not like me very much, do you?" he said. "Or is it sex you do not like? Or both?"

Joy went crashing out of her again, and she felt her eyes fill with tears.

"I am sorry," she said. "I did not satisfy you. I did my best. I am sorry."

"Damn," he said so softly that she was not even sure he had uttered such a shocking word.

He turned sharply away and sat up on the side of the bed, his elbows on his knees, the fingers of both hands pushing through his hair. Elizabeth felt two tears spill over, one to pool against her nose, the other to plop off onto her pillow.

"I am sorry," she said again. "What did I do wrong? Tell me, and I will do better next time."

"What has she done to you?" he said. "This is all her doing, is it not?"

"Whose?" she asked, bewildered.

"Your mother's," he said. "You are not naturally frigid, are you? I thought so until today, but I have seen you laughing and flushed and happy. You are warmly maternal with Jeremy. Do you hate me so much? Or are you merely a product of your mother's rigid ideas of what a lady should be?"

But she had heard only one thing. She stared at his back in horror.

"I am not frigid," she protested. "I am *not*. I feel things as deeply as anyone else. How could you say such a cruel thing? I am sorry if I do not satisfy you, but I am *not frigid*."

She turned over onto her side, spread her hands over her face, and tried—unsuccessfully—to muffle the sobs she could not control.

"Elizabeth—"

"Go away," she wailed. "Go away. You are horrid, and I hate you. I am not *fr-frigid* I wish you would . . . I wish you would go to the devil." She had never, ever said such a thing aloud, or even thought it, until now.

For a few moments she did not know what he was doing. She waited for the sound of the door opening and closing. But then the bed beside her depressed. He had come around it and sat down. He was wearing his dressing robe. He set the backs of his knuckles against her hot, wet cheek and rubbed them back and forth lightly.

"Forgive me," he said. "Please forgive me."

She turned her face into the mattress, shrugging his hand away.

"No," she said. "How could you say such a thing after . . . after what happened. I thought it was wonderful.

Obviously I know nothing. It was not wonderful at all, was it? Go away, then. Go away and never come back. Jeremy and I have lived without you for three months. We can live without you for the rest of our lives."

"Elizabeth," he said, and she had the satisfaction of hearing distress in his voice. "My dearest, I had no intention of hurting you. Curse me for a fool that I ever said such a thing. I do not believe it. We did everything wrong from the start, did we not? We allowed this marriage to be arranged for us. There was nothing too wrong in that—it happens all the time. But we made no attempt to make it our own marriage. We allowed awkwardness and perhaps some resentment to keep us almost silent with each other. And then my father died and everything fell to pieces. It was all my fault. I should have persevered. I should have been more patient, gentler with you. I should have tried to talk with you."

Again, she had heard only one thing, her face still buried in her pillow. *My dearest.* He had called her *my dearest.* No one, in her whole life, had ever called her by any endearment, except the shortened form of her name—Lizzie.

"Is it too late for us?" he asked her. "Is there any chance of making a workable marriage of this one we are in together?"

She shrugged her shoulders but said nothing. She did not trust her voice yet.

"How have you thought of me all year?" he asked her. "I have thought of you as a beautiful, unattainable, aristocratic icicle. You cannot have thought of me in any more flattering terms."

"Morose," she said into her pillow. "Dour, humorless. Wondrously handsome."

"Am I still all those things?" he asked after a short pause.

"You are still wondrously handsome," she said.

"I have assumed," he said, "that you despise me for marrying social position."

She turned her face out of the pillow, though she did not look at him.

"I have assumed," she said, "that you despise me for marrying money."

"Lord God," he said after another pause, "you would think that two reasonably intelligent adults who happen to be married to each other would have found a moment in which to talk to each other in a whole year, would you not?"

"Yes," she said.

He sat there looking down at her for a while. She lay still and did not look directly at him. She felt that a great deal had already been said. But what, really, had changed?

He got to his feet suddenly and turned to slap her lightly on one buttock.

"Get up," he said, his voice brisk and cheerful. "Get dressed."

"Pass me my nightgown, then," she said. He had dropped it over the other side of the bed.

"Dressed," he said with more emphasis. "Put on your warmest clothes."

"Why?"

"We are going out," he said.

"Out?" She stared at him with wide eyes. "Why?"

"Who knows why?" He looked down at her and grinned— her stomach turned a complete somersault inside her, she would swear. "We are going to talk. Perhaps we will build a snowman. Or make snow angels. That would be appropriate for the occasion, would it not?"

"The doors are all bolted," she said foolishly. "It is almost midnight."

He said nothing. He merely continued to look down at her and grin at her.

He was mad. Wondrously, gloriously mad.

Elizabeth laughed.

"You are mad," she said.

"You see?" He pointed a finger at her. "That is something you have not known about me all year. There is a great deal more. And I have not known that you could possibly laugh at the prospect of being dragged outside on a cold, snowy night in order to make snow angels. I daresay there is a great deal I do not know of you. I am going out. Are you coming with me or are you not?"

"I am coming," she said, and laughed again.

"I'll be back here in five minutes," he told her, and he strode to the door and left the room without a backward glance.

Elizabeth gazed after him and laughed again.

And jumped out of bed.

Five minutes! Never let it be said that she had kept him waiting.

"You lie down on your back," he explained, "and spread out your arms and legs and swish them carefully back and forth. Like this." He demonstrated while she watched and then got to his feet again and looked down at the snow angel he had made. "Rather a large one."

"The angel Gabriel," she said softly.

She was wearing a pale, fur-lined cloak with the hood drawn over her head. She looked ethereally lovely in the reflected light from the snow. She also looked very much on her dignity. But she lay down carefully on the snow beside his own angel and made one of her own with slow precision and downcast eyes.

He was so much in love with her that he wanted to howl at the moon. He was also afraid, uncertain. Was this his dutiful wife he had with him? Or was she the repressed daughter of a humorless tyrant, ready to break free, like a butterfly from the cocoon? But would she simply fly past him when she discovered her wings?

"Ah," he said after she had got back to her feet again, "a dainty angel. A guardian angel, I believe. Jeremy's, perhaps. Mine, perhaps."

She looked at him and smiled—and then her eyes went beyond him to the sky.

"Oh, look," she said, "the clouds are moving off. Look at the miracle."

The moon was almost at the full, and suddenly, it

seemed, the sky was studded with stars. They looked un-usually bright tonight, perhaps because he was in the coun-try rather than in London, as he usually was. One in particular drew his eyes. He stepped a little closer to her and pointed, so that she could look along the length of his arm to that particular star.

"I believe the Wise Men are on their way after all," he said.

"Edwin," she said softly, "have you ever known a more perfect Christmas?"

The sound of his name on her lips warmed him. No, he never had—he had never known a more perfect Christmas or a more perfect moment. If he held his breath, could he hold on to it forever?

"I have not," he told her.

He was about to set one arm about her waist, to draw her to him, to begin, perhaps—one year late but surely not *too* late—to speak the words of the heart, so difficult for a man who spent his days speaking the practical words of busi-ness and commerce. But she spun around to face him be-fore he could lift his arm, and in the semidarkness he could see that her body was tense and her expression agitated.

"Take us back with you," she said. "When you go home to London, take us with you."

The words were so stunningly unexpected, so exactly what he wanted to hear that he stared stupidly at her for several moments without speaking.

"Why?"

She stared back at him, still tense, before closing her eyes and turning away from him.

"Jeremy needs you," she said.

Again there was a long pause, during which he dared not ask the question whose answer might shatter his newfound, fragile dream. How foolishly hesitant he was with his wife—so different from the way he was in all other aspects of his life. But she answered the question before he could ask it.

"*I* need you."

"Do you?" His heart felt as if it might burst.

"Edwin," she said in a rush, her voice breathless, her face still turned away, "I should have said no. Even though Mama and Papa were in desperate financial straits, I should not have agreed to buy their reprieve at the cost of your freedom and happiness. But I had met your father and liked him enormously, and I knew that he really wanted me for you. And so I persuaded myself that perhaps you wanted me too. But it was purely selfish of me. I thought I could leave behind the cold, loveless world in which I had grown up and become part of your father's warm, joy-filled world. Instead I killed any joy you might have had. I am so sorry. But let us go home with you, and I will try . . ."

His hand closed tightly about one of her arms, and she stopped talking as he turned her to him and gazed down into her face, bathed in the light of the moon and the Christmas star.

"Elizabeth," he said, "I am the one who destroyed *your* happiness, taking you away from your own world only because I knew my father was dying and I could not say no to him. I despised myself for agreeing to that bargain when you must have dreamed of making a dazzling match with a titled gentleman of the *ton*, someone who was your social equal. All I could think to do after my father died was to bring you here, to a home that at least would be familiar to you in size and grandeur, and to give you a measure of freedom from me and my world. Yet now you want to come back to me?"

She bit her lip. "You did not despise me?"

"*Despise* you?" He took both her arms in his hands and drew her closer. "Elizabeth, I fell head over ears in love with you the moment I set eyes on you. I tried to . . . treat you with restraint and respect. I thought that perhaps after you had grown accustomed . . . But you seemed to turn to stone. And then my father died."

When she lifted one gloved hand to cup his cheek, he could see that it was trembling. He could also see stars reflected in her eyes.

"Edwin," she whispered, "I thought you despised me. I wanted that marriage so very, very much—with you, with your father's son. You were to be my escape from a life I had never enjoyed, and I was so very enchanted when I first saw you. But when you said nothing after our marriage about love or even affection, but were so . . . *respectful*, I thought you despised me."

"We have been such idiots," he said, raising her hand to his cheek and holding it there. He grinned at her. "I thought it was just me, but it was you too. I know so little about pleasing a woman, Elizabeth, especially the woman I love."

Her eyes looked even brighter suddenly, and he knew they were filled with tears.

"You do know," she said. "Today has been the happiest of my life—to see you smile and laugh, to see you hold Jeremy, to have you kiss me beneath the kissing bough, to—" She stopped abruptly and bit her lip again.

He turned his head and kissed her gloved palm.

"I will teach you to enjoy what happens in our marriage bed, Elizabeth," he said. "I promise. Just give me time. I have to learn how to please you."

"You pleased me." She snatched her hand away from his cheek to set it, with her other hand, on his shoulders. She gazed earnestly into his face. "You pleased me, Edwin. I thought I would die of pleasure. But I did not show it, did I? Perhaps I ought to have done so. Mama told me—before our nuptials—that I must always lie still and pray for it to be soon over. But tonight I did not want it to be over. I prayed for it never to end. You pleased me, Edwin. Oh, you did!"

He chuckled and then wrapped his arms about her and held her tight. He laughed aloud, and she joined him.

"I must tell you," she said, "that I have told Mama that she and Papa must leave Wyldwood after Christmas. Even if I must stay here alone with Jeremy, I will be happier without Mama's influence. I want to be your *wife*, even if I am to see you only once or twice a year."

He caught her to him even more tightly.

"My dearest," he said. "Oh, my love. I will not let you out of my sight again for longer than a day at a time—and even that will be too long."

She drew back her head and smiled at him. He smiled back before lowering his head and kissing her. This time there was no audience, as there had been in the drawing room before tea, and this time there was no anxiety or uncertainty, as there had been in their bedchamber earlier. This time there was all of love to be shared openly and joyfully. And the knowledge that a future together stretched ahead of them even after Christmas had passed into a new year and a new spring and a new hope.

When he lifted his head, they smiled at each other again. The house—their house, the house his father had purchased for him, really a rather lovely house—was behind her at the top of the snow-clad lawn. In fancy he could almost see the rudely carved Nativity scene behind the dark drawing room windows. He knew exactly which window Jeremy slept behind, warm and safe in his crib. Their son.

Above them, the sky was moonlit and starlit, the Christmas star beaming softly down on their heads—or so it seemed.

"It must be after midnight," he said, his arms still about her waist, hers about his neck. "Happy Christmas, my dearest."

"Happy Christmas, Edwin," she said.

"I do not know about you," he said, grinning down at her, "but I am frozen out here. Whose idea was this, anyway?"

She smiled back at him, a radiant smile that lit her with beauty.

"It was the most wonderful idea in the world," she said. "I have seen Christmas angels and the Christmas star, and I have taken all the love and joy of Christmas into my heart and my life. But I *am* chilly," she admitted.

"We had better go back to bed, then," he said, "and see if we can warm each other up."

Even in the moonlight he knew that she blushed. But she did not stop smiling or gazing into his eyes.

"Yes," she said. "Oh, yes, Edwin. Let's do that."

The Christmas star shed its radiant light onto Wyldwood long after they had gone inside and warmed each other and loved each other and fallen asleep, twined together beneath the rumpled bedcovers.

THE STAR OF
BETHLEHEM

"I've lost the Star of Bethlehem," she told him bluntly when he came to her room at her maid's bidding. There was some sullenness in her tone, some stubbornness, and something else in addition to both, perhaps.

He stood just inside the door of her bedchamber, his feet apart, his hands clasped behind him, staring at her, showing little emotion.

"You have lost the Star of Bethlehem," he repeated. "Where, Estelle? You were wearing it last night."

"I still have the ring," she said with a nonchalance that was at variance with her fidgeting hands. She noticed the latter, and deliberately and casually brushed at the folds of her morning wrap in order to give her hands something to do. "But the diamond is gone."

"Was it missing last night when we came home?" he asked, his eyes narrowing on her. Having assured herself that her wrap fell in becoming folds, she was now retying the satin bow at her throat. She looked as if she cared not one whit about her loss.

"I would have mentioned it if I had noticed, would I not?" she said disdainfully. "I really don't know, Allan. All I do know is that it is missing now." She shrugged.

"It probably came loose when you hurled the ring at my head last night," he said coolly. "Did you look at it when you picked it up again?"

She regarded him with raised chin and eyes that matched

his tone. Only the heightened color of her cheeks suggested the existence of some emotion. "Yes, I did," she said. "This morning. The star was gone. And there is no point in looking about you as if you expect it to pop up at you. Annie and I have been on our knees for half an hour looking for it. It simply is not here. It must have fallen out before we came home."

"I was standing at the foot of the bed when you threw it," he said. "You missed me, of course. The ring passed to the left of me, I believe."

"To the right," she said. "I found it at the far side of the bed."

"To the right, then," he said irritably. "If I were to say that you threw it up into the air, you would probably say that you threw it under the floorboards."

"Don't be ridiculous!" she said coldly.

"The diamond probably landed on the bed," he said.

"What a brilliant suggestion!" She looked at him with something bordering on contempt. "Both Annie and I had similar inspiration. We have had all the bedclothes off the bed. It is not there. It is not in this room, Allan."

She reached into the pocket of her wrap and withdrew a ring, which she handed to him, rather unnecessarily. There was certainly no doubt of the fact that the diamond was missing.

The Earl of Lisle took it in the palm of his hand and looked down at it—a wide gold band with a circlet of dark sapphires and an empty hole in the middle where the diamond had nestled. The Star of Bethlehem, she had called it—her eyes glowing like sister stars, her cheeks flushed, her lips parted—when he had given her the ring two years before, on the occasion of their betrothal.

"Look, my lord," she had said—she had not called him by his given name until he had asked her to on their wedding night a few minutes after he had finished consummating their marriage. "Look, my lord, it is a bright star in a dark sky. And this is Christmas. The birthday of Christ. The beginning of all that is wonderful. The beginning for us. How auspicious that you have given me the Star of Bethlehem for our betrothal."

He had smiled at her—beautiful, dark-haired, dark-eyed, vivacious Estelle, the bride his parents had picked out for him, though his father had died a year before and unwittingly caused a delay in the betrothal. And holding her hand, the ring on her finger, he had allowed himself to fall all the way in love with her, though he had thought that at the age of thirty there was no room in his life for such deep sentiment. He had agreed to marry her because marriage was the thing to do at his age and in his position, and because marrying Estelle made him the envy of numerous gentlemen—married and single alike—in London. She would be a dazzling ornament for his home and his life.

It would have been better if he had kept it so, if he had not done anything as foolish as falling in love with her. Perhaps they would have had a workable relationship if he had not done that. Perhaps after almost two years of marriage they would have grown comfortable together.

"Well," he said, looking down at the ring in his hand and carefully keeping both his face and voice expressionless, "it is no great loss, is it, Estelle? It was merely a diamond. Merely money, of which I have an abundance." He tossed the ring up, caught it, and closed his hand around it. "A mere bauble. Put it away." He held it out to her again.

Her chin lifted an inch as she took it from him. "I am sorry to have taken your time," she said, "but I thought you should know. I would not have had you find out at some future time and think that I had been afraid to tell you."

His lips formed into something of a sneer. "We both know that you could not possibly fear my ill opinion, don't we?" he said. "I am merely the man who pays the bills and makes all respectable in your life. Perhaps the diamond fell into the pocket or the neckcloth of Martindale last evening. You spent enough time in his company. You must ask him next time you see him. Later today, perhaps?"

She ignored his last words. "Or about the person of Lord Peterson or Mr. Hayward or Sir Caspar Rhodes," she said.

"I danced with them all last evening, and enticed them all into anterooms for secret dalliances." Her chin was high, her voice heavy with sarcasm.

"I believe we said—or rather yelled—all that needs to be expressed about your behavior at the Eastman ball—or your lack of behavior—last night," he said. "I choose not to reopen the quarrel, Estelle. But I have thought further about what I said heatedly then. And I repeat it now when my temper is down. When Christmas is over and your parents return to the country, I believe it will be as well for you to return with them for a visit."

"Banishment?" she said. "Is that not a little gothic, Allan?"

"We need some time apart," he said. "Although for the past few months we have seen each other only when necessary, we have still contrived to quarrel with tedious frequency. We need a month or two in which to rethink our relationship."

"How about a lifetime or two?" she said.

"If necessary." He looked at her steadily from cold blue eyes. Beautiful, headstrong Estelle. Incurably flirtatious. Not caring the snap of a finger for him beyond the fact that he had had it in his power to make her the Countess of Lisle and to finance her whims for the rest of a pampered life, despite the occasional flaring of hot passion that always had him wondering when it was all over and she lay sleeping in his arms if she had ever gifted other men with such favors. And always hating himself for such unfounded suspicions.

She shivered suddenly. "It is so cold in here," she said petulantly. "How can we be without fires in December? It is quite unreasonable."

"You are the one being unreasonable," he said. "You might be in the morning room now or in the library, where there are fires. You might have slept in a bedchamber where there was a fire. Chimneys have to be swept occasionally if they are not to catch fire. Half the house yesterday; the other half today. It is not such a great inconvenience, is it?"

"It should be done in the summertime," she said.

"During the summer you said it could wait until the winter, when we would be going into the country," he reminded her. "And then you had this whim about having Christmas here this year with both our families. Well, I have given you your way about that, Estelle—as usual. But the chimneys have been smoking. They must be cleaned before our guests arrive next week. By tomorrow all will be set to rights again."

"I hate it when you talk to me in that voice," she said, "as if I were a little child of defective understanding."

"You hate it when I talk to you in any voice," he said. "And sometimes you behave like a child of defective understanding."

"Thank you," she said, opening her hand and looking down at the ring. "I wish to get dressed, Allan, and go in search of a room with a warm fire. I am grateful that you have seen fit not to beat me over the loss of the diamond."

"Estelle!" All his carefully suppressed anger boiled to the surface and exploded in the one word.

She tossed her head up and glared across at him with dark and hostile eyes. He strode from the room without another word.

Estelle returned her gaze to the ring in the palm of her hand. The back of her nose and throat all the way down to her chest were a raw ache. The diamond was gone. It was all ruined. All of it. Two years was not such a very long time, but it seemed like another Estelle who had watched as he slid the ring onto her finger and rested her hand on his so that she could see it.

It had been Christmas, and she had been caught up in the usual euphoric feelings of love and goodwill, and the unrealistic conviction that every day could be Christmas if everyone would just try hard enough. She had looked at the diamond and the sapphires, and they had seemed like a bright symbol of hope. Hope that the arranged marriage she had agreed to because Mama and Papa had thought it such a splendid opportunity for her would be a happy marriage. Hope that the tall, golden-haired, unsmiling, rather austere figure of her betrothed would turn out to be a man she could like and be comfortable with—perhaps even love.

The ring had been the Star of Bethlehem to her from the start and without any effort of thought. And he had smiled one of his rare smiles when she had looked up at him and named the ring that. Looking into his blue eyes at that moment, she had thought that perhaps he would grow fond of her. She had thought that perhaps he would kiss her. He had not, though he had raised her hand to his lips and kissed both it and the ring.

He had not kissed her mouth at all before their marriage. But he had kissed her afterward on their wedding night in their marriage bed. And he had made a tender and beautiful and almost painless experience out of what she had anticipated with some fright.

She had thought . . . She had hoped . . .

But it did not matter. The only really tender and passionate moments of their marriage had happened in her bed. Always actions of the body. Never words.

They had not really grown close. He never revealed much of himself to her. And she shared only trivialities with him. They never really talked.

They were lovers only in fits and starts. Sometimes wild passion for three or four nights in a row. And then perhaps weeks of nothing in between.

She had never conceived. Not, at least . . . But she was not at all sure.

The only thing consistent in their relationship was the quarrels. Almost always over her behavior toward other gentlemen. His accusations had been unjust at first. It was in her nature to be smiling and friendly, flirtatious even. She had meant nothing by it. All her loyalty had been given to her new husband. She had been hurt and bewildered by his disapproval. But in the last year, she had begun to flirt quite deliberately. Never enough to deceive the gentlemen concerned. No one except Allan had ever been offered her lips or any other part of her body except her hand. And never even one small corner of her heart. But she had taken an almost fiendish glee in noting her husband's expression across a crowded drawing room or ballroom, and anticipating the wild rages they would both let loose when they came home.

Sometimes after the quarrels he would retire to his room, slamming the door that connected their dressing rooms behind him. Sometimes they would end up together in her bed, the heat of anger turned to the heat of sexual passion.

The night before had not been one of those latter occasions. She had dragged the Star of Bethlehem from her finger and hurled it at his head and screeched something to the effect that since the ring had become meaningless, he might have it back and welcome to it. And he had yelled something about its being less likely to scratch the cheeks of her lovers if she were not wearing it. And he had stalked out, leaving the door vibrating on its hinges.

And now she really was without the ring. No, worse. She had the shell of it left, just as the shell of her marriage still remained. The star was gone—from the ring and from her marriage.

She was taken by surprise when a loud and painful hiccup of a sob broke the silence of the room, and even more surprised when she realized that the sound had come from her. But it was a wonderful balm to her self-pity, she found. She allowed herself the rare indulgence of an extended and noisy cry.

It was all his fault. Nasty, unfeeling, sneering, cold, jealous monster! She hated him. She did not care that the ring was ruined. What did she care for his ring? Or for him? Or for their marriage? She would be delighted to go home with Mama and Papa when Christmas was over. She would stay with them, surrounded by all the peace and familiarity of her childhood home. She would forget about the turmoil and nightmare of the past two years. She would forget about Allan.

"Allan."

The name was spoken on a wail. She looked down at the ring and sniffed wetly and noisily.

"Allan."

She drew back her arm suddenly and hurled the ring with all her strength across the room. She heard it tinkle as it hit something, but she did not go in pursuit of it. She rushed into her dressing room and slammed the door firmly behind her.

Two minutes passed after the slamming of the door before there came a rustling from the direction of the cold chimney followed by a quiet plop and the appearance of a tiny, ragged, soot-smeared figure among the ashes. After looking cautiously around and stooping for a moment to grub about among the ashes, it stepped gingerly out into the room and revealed itself as a child.

The chimney sweep's boy looked briefly down at the diamond in his hand, a jewel he had mistaken for a shard of glass until he had overheard the conversation of the man and woman. His eyes darted about the room, taking in the door through which the woman had disappeared, and close to which she must have been standing while she was crying and when he had heard the tinkling sound.

She must have thrown the ring they had been talking about. It was just the sort of thing women did when they were in a temper.

His mind tried to narrow the search by guessing in which direction she would have thrown the ring from that particular door. But his wits really did not need sharpening, he saw as soon as he turned his eyes in the direction that seemed most likely. It was lying on the carpet in the open, the light from the window sparkling off the gold band.

What queer coves these rich people were, giving up the search for the diamond after only half an hour, if the woman was to be believed—and the man had not even searched at all. And throwing a gold band set full of precious stones across a room and leaving it lying there on the floor for anyone to take.

The child darted across the room, scooped up the ring, and pulled a dirty rag from somewhere about his person. He stopped when he had one foot back among the ashes, and tied his two treasures securely inside the rag. He must get back to old Thomas. The sweep would be hopping mad by now, and the old excuse of getting lost among the maze of chimneys had been used only three days before.

However, the child thought with a philosophy born of necessity, today's haul would probably be worth every stinging stroke of old Thomas's hand. As long as he did not use his belt. Even the costliest jewel did not seem quite consolation enough for the strappings he sometimes got from the sweep's belt.

The boy had both feet in the grate and was about to pull himself up into the darkness and soot of the chimney when the door through which the lady had disappeared opened abruptly again. He started to cry pitifully.

Estelle, now clad in a morning dress of fine white wool, even though her hair was still about her shoulders in a dark cloud, stopped in amazement.

The child wailed and scrubbed his clenched fists at his eyes.

"What is it?" she said, hurrying across the room to the fireplace and stooping down to have a better look at the apparition standing there. "You must be the chimney sweep's boy. Oh, you poor child."

The last words were spoken after she had had a good look at the grimy, skeletal frame of the child and the indescribable filth of his person and of his rags. Hair of indeterminate color stood up from his head in stiff and matted spikes. Two muddy tracks flowed from his eyes to his chin. He looked as if he were no older than five or six.

"It's dark up there," he wailed. "I can't breathe."

"You shouldn't be climbing chimneys," she said. "You are just a baby."

The child sniffed wetly and breathed out on a shuddering sob. "I got lost," he said. "It's dark up there."

"Oh, you poor child." Estelle reached out a hand to touch him, hesitated, and took hold of one thin arm. "Step out here. The ashes will cut your poor feet."

The boy started to cry in noisy earnest again. "He'll . . . thrash . . . me," he got out on three separate sobs. "I got lost."

"He will not thrash you," Estelle said indignantly, taking hold of the child's other arm with her free hand and helping him step out onto the carpet. He was skin and bones, she thought in some horror. He was just a frightened, half-starved little baby. "He will certainly not thrash you. I shall see to that. What is your name?"

"N-Nicky, missus," the boy said, and he hung his head and wrapped one skinny leg about the other and sniffed loudly.

"Nicky," she said, and she reached out and tried to smooth down the hair on top of his head. But it was stiff with dirt. "Nicky, when did you last eat?"

The child began to wail.

"Have you eaten today?" she asked.

He shuffled his shoulders back and forth and swayed on one leg. He muttered something.

"What?" she said gently. She was down on her knees looking into his face. "Have you eaten?"

"I don't know, missus," he said, his chin buried on his thin chest. And he rubbed the back of his hand over his wet nose.

"Did your master not give you anything to eat this morning?" she asked.

"I ain't to get fat," he said, and the wails grew to a new crescendo. "I'm so hungry."

"Oh, you poor, poor child." There were tears in Estelle's eyes. "Does your mama know that you are kept half-starved? Have you told her?"

"I ain't got no maw." His sobs occupied the child for several seconds. "I got took from the orphinige, missus."

"Oh, Nicky." Estelle laid one gentle hand against his cheek, only half noticing how dirty her hand was already.

"He'll belt me for sure." The child scratched the back of one leg with the heel of the other foot and scrubbed at his eyes again with his fists. "I got lost. It's dark and I can't get me breath up there."

"He will not hurt you. You have my word on it." Estelle straightened up and crossed the room to the bellpull to summon her maid. "Sit down on the floor, Nicky. I shall see that you have some food inside you, if nothing else. Does he beat you often?"

The child heaved one leftover sob as he sat down cross-legged on the carpet. "No more nor three or four times a day when I'm good," he said. "But I keep getting lost."

"Three or four times a day!" she said, and turned to instruct her maid to sit with the child for a few minutes. "I will be back, Nicky, and you shall have some food. I promise."

Annie looked at the apparition in some disbelief as her mistress disappeared from the room. She sat on the edge of the bed a good twenty feet away from him, and gathered her skirts close about her as if she were afraid that they would brush against a mote of soot floating about in his vicinity.

Estelle swept down the marble stairway to the hall below, her chin high, her jaw set in a firm line. At one glance from her eyes, a footman scurried across the tiles and threw open the doors of his lordship's study without even knocking first. His mistress swept past him and glared at her husband's man of business, who had the misfortune to be closeted with the earl at that particular moment.

"Can I be of service to you, my dear?" his lordship asked, as both men jumped to their feet.

"I wish to speak with you," she said, continuing her progress across the room until she stood at the window, gazing out at the gray, wintry street beyond. She did not even listen to the hurried leave-taking that the visitor took.

"Was that necessary, Estelle?" her husband's quiet voice asked as the doors of the study closed. "Porter is a busy man and has taken the time to come halfway across town at my request this morning. Such men have to work for a living. They ought not to be subject to the whims of the aristocracy."

She turned from the window. She ignored his cold reproof. "Allan," she said, "there is a child in my bedchamber. A thin, dirty, frightened, and hungry child."

He frowned. "The sweep's climbing boy?" he said. "But what is he doing there? He has no business being in any room where his master or one of our servants is not. I am sorry. I shall see to it. It will not happen again."

"He is frightened," she said. "The chimneys are dark and he cannot breathe. He gets lost up there. And then he is whipped when he gets back to the sweep."

He took a few steps toward her, his hands clasped behind his back. "They do not have an enviable lot," he said. "Poor little urchins."

"He is like a scarecrow," she said. "He cannot remember if he has eaten today. But he is not allowed to eat too much for fear he will get fat."

"They get stuck in the chimneys if they are too fat," he said, "or too big."

"He gets beaten three or four times a day, Allan," she said. "He does not have a mother or father to protect him. He comes from an orphanage."

He looked at her, his brows drawn together in a frown. "You ought not to be subjected to such painful realities," he said. "I shall have a word with Stebbins, Estelle. It will not happen again. And I shall see to it that the child is not chastised this time. I'm sorry. You are upset." He crossed the room to stand a couple of feet in front of her.

She looked up at him. "He is a baby, Allan," she said. "A frightened, starving little baby."

He lifted a hand to rest his fingertips against her cheek. "I will have a word with the sweep myself," he said. "Something will be done, I promise."

She caught at his hand and nestled her cheek against his palm. "You will do something?" she asked, her dark eyes pleading with him. "You will? You promise? Allan"—her voice became thin and high-pitched—"he is just a little baby."

"Is he still in your room?" he asked.

"Yes," she said. "I have promised him food."

"Have some taken to him, then," he said. "And keep him there for a while. I will come to you there."

"You will?" Her eyes were bright with tears, and she turned her head in order to kiss his wrist. "Thank you, Allan. Oh, thank you."

He held the door of the study open for her, his face as stern and impassive as usual, and summoned a footman with the lift of an eyebrow. He sent the man running in search of the butler and the chimney sweep.

A little more than half an hour later the Earl of Lisle was standing in his wife's bedchamber, his hands clasped behind his back, looking down at a tiny bundle of rags and bones huddled over a plate that held nothing except two perfectly clean chicken bones and a few crumbs of bread. The bundle looked up at him with wide and wary eyes. The countess's eyes were also wide, and questioning.

"You are Nicholas?" his lordship asked.

"Nicky, guv'nor," the child said in a high, piping voice.

"Well, Nicky," the earl said, looking steadily down at him. "And how would you like to stay here and not have to climb chimneys ever again?"

The boy stared, openmouthed. The countess clasped her hands to her bosom and continued to stare silently at her husband.

"I have talked with Mr. Thomas," the earl said, "and made arrangements with him. And I have instructed Mrs. Ainsford, the housekeeper, to find employment for you belowstairs. You will live here and be adequately fed and clothed. And you will continue to have employment with me for as long as you wish, provided you do the work assigned to you. You will never be whipped."

He paused and looked down at the boy, who continued to stare up at him openmouthed.

"Do you have anything to say?" he asked.

"No more chimbleys?" the child asked.

"No more chimneys."

Nicky's jaw dropped again.

"Does this please you?" the earl asked. "Would you like to be a part of this household?"

"Cor blimey, guv'nor," the boy said.

Which words the earl interpreted as cautious assent. He assigned his new servant to the tender care of the house-keeper, who was waiting outside the door and who considered that her position in the household was an exalted enough one that she could permit herself a cluck of the tongue and a look tossed at the ceiling before she took the little ragamuffin by the hand and marched him down the back stairs to the kitchen and the large tin bathtub that two maids had been instructed to fill with steaming water.

Estelle smiled dazzlingly at her husband and hurried after them. Her white dress, he noticed, as he stood and watched her go, his hands still clasped behind his back, was smudged with dirt in several places.

She looked more beautiful even than usual.

Estelle was lying in her husband's arms, feeling relaxed and drowsy, but not wanting to give in to sleep. It had been a happy and exciting day and she was reluctant to let it go.

The best part of it was that Allan had come to her after she had gone to bed, for the first time in two weeks. He had said nothing—he almost never did on such occasions—but he had made slow love to her, his hands and his mouth gentle and arousing, his body coaxing her response and waiting for it. They were good in bed together. They always had been, right back to that first time, when she had been nervous and quite ignorant of what she was to do. Even when there was anger between them, there was always passion too. But too often there was anger, and it always left a bitterness when the body's cravings had been satiated.

It was best of all when there was no anger. And when he

held her afterward and did not immediately return to his own room. She liked to fall asleep in his arms, the warmth and the smell of him lulling her.

Except that she did not want to fall asleep tonight. Not yet.

"Allan," she whispered hesitantly. They almost never talked when they were in bed. And very rarely when they were out of it, except when they were yelling at each other.

"Yes?" His voice sounded almost tense.

"Thank you," she said. "Thank you for what you did for Nicky. I think he will be happy here, don't you? You have taken him out of hell and brought him into heaven."

"Our home, heaven?" he said quietly, jarring her mood slightly. "But he will be safe here, Estelle, and warm and well fed. It is all we can do."

"He has a new home in time for Christmas," she said. "Poor little orphan child. He must be so very happy, Allan, and grateful to you."

"He has merely exchanged one servitude for another," he said. "But at least he will not be mistreated here."

"What did you say to the sweep?" she asked. "Did you threaten him with jail?"

"He was doing nothing that every other sweep in the country is not doing," he said. "The problem does not end with the rescue of the boy, Estelle. I merely bought him for twice his apprenticeship fee. The man made a handsome profit."

"Oh, Allan!" Her hand spread across his chest over the fabric of his nightshirt. "The poor little boys."

She felt him swallow. "Some members of the House are concerned over the matter," he said, "and over the whole question of child labor. I shall speak with them, find out more, perhaps even speak in the House myself."

"Will you?" She burrowed her head more deeply into the warmth of his shoulder. She wanted to find his mouth in the darkness. But she only ever had the courage to do that when he had aroused passion in her.

"In the meantime," he said, "you can console yourself

with the thought that at least your little Nicky has a warm and soft bed for the night and a full stomach."

And then a wonderful thing happened. Something that had never happened before in almost two years of marriage. He turned his head and kissed her, long minutes after their lovemaking was over, and turned onto his side and stroked the hair back from her face with gentle fingers. And before another minute had passed, she knew that he was going to come to her again.

She fell asleep almost immediately after it was over. It was not until later in the night, when she had awoken and nestled closer to the sleeping form of her husband, who was still beside her, that reality took away some of the magic of the previous day. He had done a wonderful thing for Nicky, she thought. They would be able to watch him grow into a healthy and carefree childhood, long after this particular Christmas was past.

They would be able to watch him? *He* would, perhaps. Allan would. But would she? She was to be banished to Papa's home after Christmas for a stay that would surely extend itself beyond weeks into months. Perhaps even years. Perhaps forever. Perhaps she would only ever see Allan again on brief visits, for form's sake.

He was sending her away. So that they might rethink their relationship, he had said. So that he might end their marriage to all intents and purposes. He didn't want her anymore. He did not want their marriage to continue. And even if he were forced to continue their marriage to some degree, even if her suspicion and hardly admitted hope proved right, it would be an empty thing, only a third person holding them together.

And there was that other thing. That thing that she had not allowed to come between her and her joy the previous day. The missing ring. Not just the diamond, but the whole ring. She had hunted for it until she had felt almost sick enough to vomit. But she had not found it. Or told Allan about its disappearance. She had repressed her panic and the terrible sense of loss that had threatened to overwhelm her.

Where could it have gone? Had it been swept up by the maids? She had even thought briefly of Nicky, but had shaken the thought off immediately. It had just disappeared, as the diamond had.

Christmas was coming, and there would be no Star of Bethlehem for her. No joy or love or hope.

But she would not think such depressing and self-pitying thoughts. She settled her cheek more comfortably against her husband's broad shoulder and rested a hand on his warm arm. And she deliberately thought back on the brighter part of the previous day. She smiled.

Nicky not wanting to be parted from his filthy rags and bursting into pitiful wailings when Mrs. Ainsford snatched away the rag of a handkerchief he clutched even after he had relinquished all else. He had a curl of his mother's hair in the little bundle, he had claimed, and a seashell that someone had given him at the orphanage. All his worldly possessions. Mrs. Ainsford had given the rag back to him and another clean one to use instead. But the child had not unpacked his treasures to their interested gaze.

Estelle smiled again, listened for a few moments to the deep and even breathing of the man beside her, and turned her head to kiss his shoulder before allowing herself to slip back into sleep.

The earl had not slept for a while after making love to his wife for the second time. He ought not to have come. Relations between them had been strained enough for several months, and the bitter quarrel of the night before had brought matters to a crisis. He had made the decision that they should live apart, at least for a time. They must keep up the charade over Christmas, of course, for the sake of her family and his own. But the pretense did not at least have to extend to the bedchamber.

There was no harmony between them—none—except in what passed between them in silence between the sheets of her bed. He had often wanted to try to extend that harmony into other aspects of their life by talking to her in the aftermath of passion, when they would perhaps feel more kindly disposed to each other than at any other time.

But he had never done so. He was no good at talking. He had always been afraid to talk to Estelle, afraid that he would not be able to convey his inner self to her. He had chosen to keep himself closed to her rather than try to communicate and know himself a failure. He had always been mortally afraid of having his love thrown back in his face. Better that she did not know. And so he had contented himself with giving his love only the one outlet. Only the physical.

But he should not have come tonight. The events of the day had created the illusion of closeness between them. And so he had come to her, and she had received him with something more than the usual passion, which he knew himself capable of arousing. There had been an eagerness in her, a tenderness almost. A gratitude for what he had done for her little climbing boy.

He should not have come. How would he do without her after she had left with her parents after Christmas?

How would he live without her?

What would he give her as a Christmas gift? It must be something very special, something that would perhaps tell her, as he could never do, that despite everything he cared.

Some jewels perhaps? Something to dazzle her?

He smiled bitterly into the darkness as Estelle made low noises in her sleep and burrowed more closely into his warmth. Something to remind her that she had a wealthy husband. More baubles for her to lose or to cast aside with that look of disdain that she was so expert at when he was angry with her for some reason.

Like that ring. He stared upward at the dark canopy over his head. The Star of Bethlehem. The ring that had told him as soon as he slid it onto her finger two years before that she was the jewel of his life, the star of his life. It was not a bauble. Not merely a symbol of wealth.

It was a symbol of his love, of his great hope for what their marriage might have been.

If he could replace the diamond . . .

Where had she put the ring? It had probably been tossed into a drawer somewhere. It should not be hard to find. He could probably find it with ease if he waited for her to go out and then searched her rooms.

He would have the diamond replaced for her. She had been careless about its loss. It had not really mattered to her. She had told him about it merely to avoid a scolding if he had discovered it for himself at a later date.

But surely if he could put it on her finger again this Christmas, whole again, the Star of Bethlehem new again, as Christmas was always new even more than eighteen hundred years after the first one, then it would mean something to her.

Perhaps she would be pleased. And perhaps in the months to come, when she had not seen him for a while, when the bitterness of their quarrels had faded, she would look at it and realize that he had put more than his money into the gift.

He turned his head and kissed his sleeping wife with warm tenderness just above her ear. There was an excitement in him that would surely make it difficult to get to sleep.

Estelle had been happy about Nicky. He remembered the look she had given him as she left this very room after Mrs. Ainsford and the child—a bright and sparkling look all focused on him. The sort of look he had dreamed of inspiring before he married her. Before he knew himself quite incapable of drawing to himself those looks that she bestowed so willingly on other men. Before he realized that he would find himself quite incapable of communicating with her.

He would bask in the memory. And the child had been saved from a brutal life. That poor little skeletal baby, who was probably sleeping peacefully at that very moment in another part of the house, as babies ought.

* * *

At that precise moment the former climbing boy, whom his new master thought to be peacefully asleep, was sitting cross-legged on the floor of a room in quite another part of London—a dingy, dirty attic room that was sparsely furnished and strewn with rags and stale remnants of food and empty jugs.

"I tell you, Mags," he was saying in his piping voice, which nevertheless did not sound as pathetic as it had sounded in the countess's bedchamber the previous day, "I took me life in me 'ands comin' 'ere in these togs." He indicated the white shirt and breeches, obviously of an expensive cut and equally obviously part of a suit of livery belonging to some grand house. "But there weren't nothin' else. They burned all me other things."

The Mags referred to shook with silent laughter. "I scarce knew you, young Nick," he said. "I always thought you 'ad black hair."

The child touched his soft fair hair. "Such a scrubbin' you never did 'ear tell of," he said in some disgust. "I thought she'd rub me skin away for sure."

"So yer can't be up to the old lark no more," Mags said, the laughter passing as silently as it had come.

"Naw." Nicky scratched his head from old habit. "Thought she was bein' a blessed angel, she did, that woman. And 'im standin' there arskin' me if I wanted to stay at their 'ouse. Exceptin' I couldn't say no. I would've given an 'ole farthin' to 'ave seen old Thomas's face." He giggled, sounding for a moment very much like the baby the Earl and Countess of Lisle had taken him for. He was in reality almost eleven years old.

"This might be better," Mags said, rubbing his hands together thoughtfully. "You can go 'round the 'ouse at leisure, young Nick, and lift a fork 'ere and a jeweled pin there. P'raps they'll take you to other 'ouses, and yer can 'ave a snoop around them too."

"It'll be almost too easy," Nicky said, rubbing the side

of his nose with one finger. His voice was contemptuous. "They're a soft touch if ever I seen one, Mags."

"Got anythin' for me tonight?" Mags asked.

The child shifted position and scratched his rump. "Naw," he said after a few moments' consideration. "Nothin' tonight, Mags. Next time."

"It weren't hardly worth comin', then, were it?" the older man said, his narrowed eyes on the child.

"Just wanted yer to know that me fairy godmother come," the child said, leaping lightly to his feet. "Did yer give the money to me maw for that thimble I brought you last week?"

"'Tweren't worth much," Mags said quickly. "But yes. Yer maw got her food money." He laughed silently again. "And yer sister got 'er vittles to grow on. Another two or three years, young Nick, and yer maw'll be rich with the two of yer."

"I got to go," the child said. And he climbed down the stairs from the attic and went out into the street, where for the first time in his life he had something to fear. His appearance made him fair game for attack. Only the filthy stream of curses he had been quite capable of producing had discouraged one pair of tough-looking urchins when he had been on his way to Mags's attic.

And unexpectedly he still had something to protect on his way back home. He still had the ring and the diamond pressed between the band of his breeches and his skin, although the main reason for his night's outing had been to deliver them to Mags for payment. One of his better hauls. But he had not given them up. That woman, whom he had been told he must call "your ladyship," had bawled like a baby after the man had left her, and flung the ring across the room.

And she had had food brought to him, and had sat and watched him eat it, and smiled at him. And she was the one who had told the big, sour-faced, big-bosomed woman to give him back his bundle—the bundle that held her ring and diamond, and who had stooped down and kissed him

on the cheek before he got dumped in that hot water up to
the neck and scrubbed raw.

She was pretty. Silly of course, and not a brain in her
brainbox—calling him a baby, indeed, and believing his
story about the orphanage and about his mother's lock of
hair! But very pretty. Well, he would keep her ring for a day
or two and sell it to Mags the next time he came. He would
have more things by then, though not much. The reason he
had never been caught was probably that he had never been
greedy. He had learned his lesson well from Mags. He had
never taken more than one thing from each house, and
never anything that he had thought would be sorely missed.

Nicky darted in his bare feet along a dark street in the
shadows of the buildings and cursed his clean hair and
skin, which would make him more noticeable, and his
clothes, which would·be like a red flag to a bull if the
wrong people were to spot him on these particular streets.

The bed was empty beside Estelle when she woke up the
following morning. She felt only a fleeting disappointment. After all, he never had stayed until morning. And if
he had been there, there would have been an awkwardness
between them. What would they say to each other, how
would they look at each other if they awoke in bed together
in the daylight? And remembered the hot passion they had
shared before they had fallen asleep.

When she met him downstairs—in the breakfast room
perhaps, or later in some other part of the house—he would
be, as always, his immaculate, taciturn, rather severe self
again. It would be easy to look at him then. He would seem
like a different man from the one whose hands and mouth
and body had created their magic on her during the darkness of the night.

It was a good thing that he was not there this morning.
The night had had its double dose of lovemaking and silent
tenderness. At least she could imagine it was tenderness

until she saw him again and knew him incapable of such a very human emotion.

Estelle threw back the bedclothes even though Annie had not yet arrived and even though the fire was all but extinguished in the fireplace. She shivered and stood very still, wondering if she really felt nausea or if she were merely willing the feeling on herself. She shrugged, and resumed the futile search for her ring. She had combed through every inch of the room the day before, more than once. It was not to be found.

What she should do was repeat what she had done the day before. She should send for Allan before she had time to think, and tell him the truth. If he ripped up at her, if he yelled at her, or—worse—if he turned cold and looked at her with frozen blue eyes and thinned lips, then she would think of some suitably cutting retort. And she need not fear him. He had never beaten her, and she did not think she could ever do anything bad enough that he would.

And what could he do that he had not already done? He had already decided to banish her. There was nothing he could do worse than that. Nothing.

"Oh, my lady," Annie said a few minutes later, coming into the room with her morning chocolate and finding her standing in the corner of the room where she had thrown the ring, "you will catch your death."

Estelle glanced down at herself and realized that she had not even put on a wrap over her nightgown. She shivered. And looked at her maid and opened her mouth to tell the girl to go summon his lordship.

"It is rather cold in here," she said instead. "Will you have some coals sent up, Annie?"

The girl curtsied and disappeared from the room.

And Estelle knew immediately that the moment had been lost. In the second that had elapsed between the opening of her mouth and the speaking of the words about coal being brought for the fire, she had turned coward.

It had been easy the morning before to have Allan called

and to tell him about the missing diamond. She had still been smarting from the accusations he had hurled at her the night before, and the sentence he had passed on her. She had derived a perverse sort of pleasure from telling him of the ruin of his first gift to her.

This morning it was different. This morning she could remember his kindness to a little child. And his gentle tenderness to her the night before. And she could hope that perhaps it would be repeated that night if nothing happened during the day to arouse the hostility that always lurked just below the surface of their relationship—except when it boiled up above the surface, that was.

This morning she was a coward. This morning she could not tell him.

She had arranged to go shopping with her friend Isabella Lawrence. There were all sorts of Christmas gifts to be purchased before their houseguests began to arrive to take up all her time. There was Allan's gift to be chosen, and she did not know what she would get him. She did have one gift for him already, of course. She had persuaded Lord Humber, that elderly miser, to part with a silver snuffbox Allan had admired months before, and she had kept it as a Christmas gift. But that had been a long time ago. And Lord Humber had refused to take anything but a token payment. Besides, she had given him a snuffbox the year before too. She wanted something else, something very special. But what did one buy for a man who had everything? Still, she would enjoy the morning despite the problem. Isabella could always cheer her up with her bright chatter and incessant gossiping.

She ate her breakfast in a lone state, her husband having already removed to his study, Stebbins told her. She did not know whether to be glad or sorry.

But there was one thing she had to do before going out. She had Annie bring Nicky to her dressing room.

She smiled at him when he stood inside the door, his chin tucked against his chest, one leg wrapping itself around the other. He was clean and dressed smartly in the livery of the house. But he was still, of course, pathetically thin and endearingly small.

"Good morning, Nicky," she said.

He muttered something into the front of his coat.

She crossed the room in a rush, stooped down in front of him, and set her hands on his thin shoulders. "Did you have a good breakfast?" she asked. "And did you sleep well?"

"Yes, missus," he said. "I mean . . ."

"That is all right," she said, lifting a hand to smooth back his hair. "You do look splendid. Such shiny blond hair. Are you happy, Nicky, now that you have a real home of your own?"

"Yes, missus," he said, sniffing and drawing his cuff across his nose.

"Nicky," she said, "I lost a ring yesterday. In my bed-chamber. You did not see it there when you came down the chimney, I suppose?"

The child returned his foot to the floor and scratched the back of his leg with his other heel.

"No, of course you did not," she said, putting her arms about his thin little body and hugging him warmly. "Oh, Nicky, his lordship gave me the ring when we were be-trothed. And now I have lost it. It was without question my most precious possession. Like the lock of your mama's hair is to you. And the seashell." She sighed. "But no mat-ter. Something else very precious came into my life yester-day. Even more precious perhaps because it is living." She smiled at his bowed head and kissed his cheek. "You came into my life, dear. I want you to be happy here. I want you to grow up happy and healthy. There will never be any more chimneys, I promise you. His lordship would not al-low it."

Nicky rubbed his chin back and forth on his chest and rocked dangerously on one leg.

"Annie is waiting outside for you," Estelle said. "She will take you back to the kitchen, and Mrs. Ainsford will find you jobs to do. But nothing too hard, I assure you. Run along now. I shall buy you a present for Christmas while I am out. And I will not add 'if you are good.' I shall give you a gift even if you are not good. Everyone should have a Christmas gift whether he deserves it or not."

Nicky looked up at her for the first time, with eyes that seemed far too large for his pale, thin face. Then his hand found the doorknob and opened the door. He darted out to join the waiting maid.

Estelle tied the strings of her bonnet beneath her chin and knew what she was going to buy for her husband for Christmas. It was not really a gift for him, she supposed. But it would do. It would be the best she could do, and perhaps after she had gone away into her banishment he would understand why she had chosen to give him such a strange gift. Perhaps—oh, just perhaps—her exile would not last a lifetime.

T he Earl of Lisle felt very guilty. He had often accused his wife of flirting, on the basis of very hard evidence he had seen with his own eyes. He had a few times accused her of doing more than flirting. She had always hotly denied the charges, though she had usually ended the arguments with a toss of the head and that look of disdain and the comment that he might believe what he pleased. And who, apart from him, would blame her anyway for taking a lover, when she was tied for the rest of a lifetime to such a husband?

He had never looked for evidence. And it was not because he was afraid of what he might discover. Rather it was out of a deep conviction that even though he was her husband, he did not own her. Although in the eyes of the law she was his possession, he would never look on her as such. She was Estelle. His wife. The woman he had secretly loved since before his marriage to her. And if she chose to flirt with other men, if she chose to be unfaithful to him with one or more of those men, then he would rant and rave and perhaps put her away from him forever. But he would never spy on her, never publicly accuse her, never publicly disown her.

He would endure if he must, as dozens of wives were expected to endure when their husbands chose to take mistresses.

It was with the greatest of unease, then, that he searched his wife's rooms after she had left on her shopping trip with Isabella Lawrence. He was looking for the ring. He was terrified of finding something else. Something that he did not want to find. Something that would incriminate her and destroy him.

He found nothing. Nothing to confirm some of his worst suspicions. And not the ring either. Wherever she had put it, it certainly was not in either her bedchamber or her dressing room.

It seemed to him, as he wandered through into his own dressing room, that he must now abandon the plan that had so delighted him the night before. But not necessarily so, he thought after a while. The diamond would have been new anyway. Why not the whole ring? Why not have the whole thing copied for her? A wholly new gift.

A wholly new love offering.

The trouble was, of course, that he would have to describe the ring very exactly to a jeweler in order that it could be duplicated. He had bought the ring for her two years before. He had put it on her hand. He had looked at it there, with mingled pride and love and despair, a thousand times and more. And yet he found that he could not be clear in his mind whether there had been eight sapphires or nine. And exactly how wide had the gold band been?

He tried sketching the ring, but he had never been much of an artist.

He would have to do the best he could. After all, it was not as if he were going to try to pretend to her that it was the original ring.

The idea of the gift excited him again. Perhaps he would even be able to explain to her when he gave it. Explain why he had done it, what the ring meant to him. What she meant to him.

Perhaps. Perhaps if he did so she would look at him in incomprehension. Or with that look of disdain.

Or perhaps—just perhaps—with a look similar to the
one she had given him the day before, after he had told the
little climbing boy that he would be staying with them.

He would go immediately, he decided. The ring would
have to be made specially. And there were less than two
weeks left before Christmas. He must go without delay.

He decided on eight sapphires when the moment came
to give directions to the jeweler he had chosen. And he
picked out a diamond that looked to him almost identical to
the Star of Bethlehem. And left the shop on Oxford Street
feeling pleased with the morning's work and filled with a
cautious hope for the future. Christmas was coming. Who
would not feel hopeful at such a season of the year?

But his mood was short-lived. As he walked past the
bow windows of a confectioner's shop, he turned his head
absently to look inside and saw his wife sitting at a table
there with Lady Lawrence. And with Lord Martindale and
Sir Cyril Porchester. Estelle's face was flushed and animated. She was laughing, as were they all.

She did not see him. He walked on past.

Estelle, inside the confectioner's shop, stopped laughing
and shook her head at the plate of cakes that Sir Cyril
offered to her. "What a perfectly horrid thing to say," she
said to Lord Martindale, her eyes still dancing with merriment. "As if I would buy Allan an expensive gift and have
the bill sent to him."

"There are plenty of wives who do just that, my dear
Lady Lisle," he said.

"I save my money for Christmas," she said, "so that I
can buy whatever I want without having to run to Allan."

"But you still refuse to tell us what you are going to buy
him, the lucky man?" Sir Cyril asked.

"Absolutely," she said, bright-eyed and smiling. "I have
not even told Isabella. It is to be a surprise. For Allan
alone."

Lord Martindale helped himself to another cake. "One

would like to know what Lisle had done to deserve such devotion, would one not, Porchester?"

Estelle patted him lightly on the arm. "He married me," she said, and looked at Lady Lawrence and laughed gaily.

"Oh, unfair, ma'am," Lord Martindale said. "Since he has already done so, you see, the rest of us poor mortals are unable to compete."

"We could find some excuse to slap a glove in his face and shoot him," Sir Cyril said.

They all laughed.

"But I should not like that at all," Estelle said. "I would be an inconsolable widow for the rest of my life, I warn you."

"In that case," Sir Cyril said with a mock sigh, getting to his feet and circling the table in order to pull out Lady Lawrence's chair, "I suppose we might as well allow Lisle to live. Lucky devil!"

When they were all outside the shop, the gentlemen bowed and took their leave, and Estelle promised to meet Lady Lawrence at the library as soon as she had completed her errand. She did not want her friend to come into the jeweler's shop with her—a different jeweler from the one her husband had visited half an hour before.

She was very excited. Surely he would understand when he saw it, even though strictly speaking it would not seem like a gift for him.

She had the advantage over the earl. She remembered quite clearly that there had been nine sapphires. And she was able to tell the jeweler exactly how wide the gold band was to be made. She took a long time picking out a diamond, and did so eventually only because she must do so unless the whole idea was to be abandoned, for none of them looked quite like the Star of Bethlehem.

But it did not matter. She was not going to try to deceive Allan. There was no question of trying to pass off this new ring as the lost one. She would give it to him only because she wanted him to know that the betrothal ring had been important enough to her that she would spend almost all she had on replacing it. She wanted him to know that there was still the hope in her that she had worn on her finger for two years.

The hope that one day he would come to love her as she loved him.

She was going to ask him to keep the ring until she came home to stay. Perhaps he would understand that she wanted that day to come.

Perhaps.

But she would want him to have it anyway.

She hurried along the street in the direction of the library a short while later, her cheeks still flushed, her eyes still bright. Everyone around her seemed to be loaded down with parcels. Everyone looked happy and smiled back at her.

What a wonderful time of year Christmas was. If only every day could be Christmas!

The Earl of Lisle was sitting in one corner of his darkened town carriage, his wife in the other. Heavy velvet curtains were drawn across the windows, it being late at night. Estelle's gaze was necessarily confined within the carriage, then. But she did not need to see out. Her gaze was fixed on an imaginary scene of some magnificence.

"'For unto us a child is born,'" she sang quietly to herself. "'Unto us a son is given; unto us a son is given.'" She looked across to her husband's darkened face. "Or is it 'a child is born' twice and 'a son is given' once?" she asked. "But no matter. Mr. Handel's *Messiah* must be the most glorious music ever composed. Don't you agree, Allan?"

"Very splendid," he agreed. "But I am surprised you heard any of it, Estelle. You did so much talking." He had meant the words to be teasing, but he never found it easy to lighten the tone of his voice.

"But only before the music began and during the interval," she said. "Oh, come now, Allan, you must admit it is true. I did not chatter through the music. How could I have done so when I was so enthralled? And how could I have sat silent between times when we were in company with friends? They would have thought I was sickening for something."

Her eyes fixed on the upholstery of the seat opposite her, and soon she was singing softly again. " 'There were shepherds abiding in the field, keeping watch over their flocks by night.' " She hummed the orchestra's part.

The earl watched her broodingly. He could not see her clearly in the darkness, but he would wager that her cheeks still glowed and that her eyes still shone. As they had done through dinner at the Mayfields', through the performance of Handel's *Messiah* they had attended in company with six friends, and through late-evening tea and cards at the Bellamys'.

She was so looking forward to Christmas, she had told everyone who had been willing to listen—and everyone was always willing to listen to Estelle, it seemed. The first that she and her husband had spent at their own home. And her mama and papa were coming, and her married brother with his wife and two children, and her unmarried brother. And her husband's mother and his two sisters with their families. And two aunts and a few cousins. One more week and they would begin to arrive.

She had been pleased when he had agreed a couple of months before to stay in London and host the family Christmas that year. But she had not bubbled over so with high spirits to him. He could not seem to inspire such brightness in her.

"I spent a fortune this morning, Allan," she said to him now, turning her head in his direction. And he could tell from her voice that she was still bubbling, though she had only him for audience. "I bought so many presents that Jasper looked dubious when I staggered along to the coach. I think he wondered how we were to get all the parcels inside." She laughed.

"Did you enjoy yourself?" he asked.

"I love Christmas," she said. "I live like the world's

worst miser from summer on just so that I can be extravagant at Christmas. I think I enjoy choosing gifts more than
I like receiving them. I bought Nicky a little silver watch
for his pocket. Such a dear little child's thing. You should
just see it." She giggled. "I suppose he cannot tell time. I
will have to teach him."

"Did you buy such lavish gifts for the other servants?"
he asked.

"Oh, of course not." She laughed again. "I would have
to live like a beggar for five years. But I did buy them all
something, Allan. And they will not mind my giving Nicky
something special, will they? He is just a child, and has
doubtless never had a gift in his life. Except for his seashell,
of course."

"Did you meet anyone you knew?" he asked.

"I was with Isabella," she said. "We nodded to a few
acquaintances." There was the smallest of hesitations. "No
one special."

"Martindale is not special?" he asked quietly. "Or
Porchester?"

There was a small pause again. "Someone told you," she
said. "We met them on Oxford Street and they invited us
for tea and cakes. I was glad to sit down for half an hour.
My feet were sore."

"Were they?" he said. "You did not look as if you were
in pain."

She looked sharply at him. "You saw us," she said. "You
were there, Allan. Why did you not come inside?"

"And break up the party?" he said. "And make odd numbers? I am more of a sport than that, Estelle."

"Oh," she cried, "you are cross. You think that I was
doing something I ought not to have been doing. It is quite
unexceptionable for two married ladies to take tea with two
gentlemen friends at a public confectioner's. It is too bad of
you to imply that it was some clandestine meeting."

His voice was cold. "One wonders why you decided not
to tell me about it if it was so unexceptionable," he said.

"Oh!" she said, exasperated. "For just this reason, Allan.

For just this reason. I knew you would read into it something that just was not there. It was easier not to tell you at all. And now I have put myself in the wrong. But if you will spy on me, then I suppose you must expect sometimes to be disappointed. Though when I think about that last statement, I don't suppose you were disappointed. Unless it was over the fact that it was not just me and one of the gentlemen. That would have suited you better, would it not?"

"One is hardly spying on one's wife by walking along Oxford Street in the middle of the day," he said.

"Then why did you ask me those questions?" she said. "In the hope that I would lie or suppress the truth? Why did you not simply remark that you had seen me with Isabella and Lord Martindale and Sir Cyril?"

"I should not have had to either ask or make the comment," he said. "If it was all so innocent, Estelle, you would have come home and told me about the afternoon and your encounters. You find it very easy to talk to all our friends and acquaintances, it seems. You never stop talking when we are out. Yet you have very little to say to me. How can I escape the conclusion sometimes that you have something to hide?"

"What nonsense you speak!" she said. "I have been talking to you tonight, have I not? I talked to you about the concert and you remarked that I had chattered too much. I told you about my Christmas gifts and you suggested that I had spent too much on Nicky. Do you think I enjoy such conversation? Do you think I enjoy always being at fault? I don't think I am capable of any goodness in your eyes."

"There is no need to yell," he said. "We are in a small space and I am not deaf."

"I am not yelling!" she said. "Oh, yes, I am, and I yell because I choose to do so. And if you were not so odious and so determined to put me in the wrong, you would yell too. I know you have lost your temper. You speak quietly only so that I will lose mine more."

"You are a child!" he said coldly. "You have never grown up, Estelle. That is your trouble."

"Oh!" she said. And then with a loudly indrawn breath, "I would rather be a child than a marble statue. At least a child has feelings. You have none, do you? Except a fanatical attachment to propriety. You would like a little mouse of a wife to mince along at your side, quiet and obedient and adding to your consequence. You have no human feelings whatsoever. You are incapable of having any."

"We had best be quiet," he said. "We neither of us have anything to say except what will most surely wound the other. Be quiet, Estelle."

"Oh, yes, lord and master," she said, her voice suddenly matching his in both volume and temperature. "Certainly, sir. Beg pardon for being alive to disturb you, my lord. Console yourself that you will have to put up with me for only another few weeks. Then I will be gone with Mama and Papa."

"Something to be looked forward to with eager anticipation," he said.

"Yes," she said.

They sat side by side for the remainder of the journey home in frigid silence.

Estelle had to keep swallowing against the lump in her throat. It had been another lovely day, though she had seen very little of her husband until the evening, when they had been in company. She had so hoped that they could get to the end of the day without trouble. She had hoped that he would come back to her that night so they might recapture the tenderness of the night before. And they had come so close.

She took his hand as he helped her from the carriage, and tilted her chin up at such an angle that he would know her unappeased. His jaw was set hard and his eyes were cold, she saw in one disdainful glance up at him.

He unlocked the door and stood aside to allow her to precede him into the hallway. Although the coachman had been necessarily kept up very late indeed, all the other servants were in bed. The Earl of Lisle refused to keep them up after midnight when he was perfectly capable of turning a key in a lock. He had explained his strange theories to his butler three years before, on his acquisition of the title and the town house.

Estelle waited in cold silence while he took her cloak and laid it on a hall stand, and picked up a branch of lit candles. But before she could reach out a hand to place on his sleeve so that he might escort her to her room, he set a warning hand on her arm and stood very still, in a listening attitude.

Estelle looked at him questioningly. He handed her the candlestick slowly and without a word, his eyes on a marble statue that stood to one side of the staircase, between the library and his study. A hand gesture told her that she was to stay exactly where she was. He moved silently toward the statue.

A child's treble wailing broke the silence before the earl reached his destination. The sounds of a child whose heart was breaking.

"What are you doing here?" the earl asked, stopping beside the statue and looking down. His voice was not ungentle.

Estelle hurried across the tiles to his side. Nicky was standing between the statue and the wall, his fists pressed to his eyes, one bare foot scratching the other leg through his breeches.

"I was thirsty," he said through his sobs. "I got lost."

The earl stooped down on his haunches. "You wanted a drink of water?" he asked. "Did you not go down the back stairs to the kitchen? How do you come to be here?"

The sobs sounded as if they were tearing the child's chest in two. "I got lost," he said eventually.

"Nicky." The earl reached out a hand and pushed back the boy's hair from his forehead. "Why did you hide?"

"I got scared," the boy said. "Are you goin' ter beat me?" His fists were still pressed to his eyes.

"I told you yesterday that you would not be beaten here, did I not?" the earl said.

Estelle went down on her knees and set the candlestick

on the tiled floor. "You are in a strange house and you are frightened," she said. "Poor little Nicky. But you are quite safe, you know, and we are not cross with you." She took the thin, huddled shoulders in her hands and drew the child against her. She patted his back gently while his sobs gradually subsided. She glanced across at her husband. He was still stooped down beside her.

The sobs were succeeded by a noisy and prolonged yawn. The earl and his countess found themselves smiling with some amusement into each other's eyes.

"Come on," Estelle said, "we will take you back to your bed, and you shall have your drink."

"I'll take him, Estelle," the earl said, and he stood up, scooping the small child into his arms as he did so. Nicky yawned again.

She picked up the candlestick and preceded them down the stone stairs to the kitchen for a cup of water and up the back stairs to the servants' quarters and the little room that she had been to once the day before. She helped a yawning Nicky off with his shirt and on with his nightshirt while her husband removed the child's breeches.

She smoothed back his hair when he was lying in his bed, looking sleepily up at her. "Sleep now, Nicky," she said softly. "You are quite safe here and must not be afraid of his lordship and me or of anyone else in the house. Good night." She stooped down and kissed him on the cheek.

"Bring a cup to bed with you at nights," the earl said, glancing to the washstand and its full jug of water. "And no more wanderings, Nicky. Go to sleep now. And there must be no more fear of beatings either." He touched the backs of two fingers to the child's cheek, and his lips twitched when a loud yawn was his only answer.

The yawning stopped abruptly when his door closed softly behind his new master and mistress. Nicky clasped his hands behind his head and stared rather glumly at the ceiling. Mags would kill him if he didn't show up with something within the next few days. More to the point, there would be no money for his mother.

But he was, after all, only ten years old. And the hour was something after two in the morning. Sleep overtook him. She smelled like a garden, he thought as he drifted off. Or as he imagined a garden would smell. A really soft touch, of course, as was the governor, for all his stern looks. But she smelled like a garden for all that.

The Earl of Lisle had taken the candlestick from his wife's hand. He held it high to light their way back to the main part of the house and their own rooms.

Estelle turned to face him when they entered her dressing room. Her eyes were soft and luminous, he saw. They had lost their cold disdain.

"Oh, Allan," she said, "how my heart goes out to that child. Poor little orphan, with no one to love him and hug him and tuck him into his bed at night."

"You were doing quite well a few minutes ago," he said.

There were tears in her eyes. "He is so thin," she said. "And he was so frightened. Thank you for being gentle with him, Allan. He did not expect you to be."

"I would not imagine he knows a great deal about gentleness or kindness," he said.

"He should not be working," she said. "He should be playing. He should be carefree."

He smiled. "Children cannot play all the time," he said. "Even children of our class have their lessons to do. Mrs. Ainsford will not overwork him. If you fear it, you must have a word with her tomorrow."

"Yes," she said. "I will. How old do you think he is, Allan? He did not know when I asked him."

"I think a little older than he looks," he said. "I will see what I can do, Estelle. I need to make a few inquiries."

Her face brightened. She smiled up at him. "For Nicky?" she said. "You will do something for him? Will you, Allan?"

He nodded and touched her cheek lightly with his knuckles as he had touched the child's a few minutes before. "Good night," he said softly, before taking one of the candles and going into his own dressing room. He shut the door quietly behind him.

Estelle looked at the closed door before beginning to undress herself rather than summon her maid from sleep. She wished fleetingly that she had apologized for calling him a marble statue. He was not. He did have feelings. They had shown in his dealings with Nicky. But what was the point of apologizing? If she could not call him that in all truth, there were a hundred other nasty things she would call him when next he angered her. And his own words and suspicions were unpardonable.

She climbed into bed ten minutes later and tried not to think of the night before. Soon enough she would have to accustom herself to doing without altogether. She needed to sleep anyway. It was very late.

But even before she had found a totally comfortable position in which to lie and quieted her mind for sleep, the door of her dressing room opened and closed and she knew that after all she was not to be alone. Not for a while anyway.

And as soon as he climbed into the bed beside her and touched her face with one hand so that his mouth could find hers in the darkness, she knew that he had not come to her in anger. She put one arm about his strongly muscled chest and opened her mouth to his seeking tongue.

During the week before their guests began to arrive and the Christmas celebrations could begin in earnest, Estelle kept herself happily busy with preparations. Not that there was a great deal for her to do beyond a little extra shopping. She was not the one who cleaned the house from top to bottom or warmed the extra bedrooms and changed their bed linen and generally readied them for the reception of their temporary occupants. She was not the one who would cook and bake all the mounds of extra food.

But she did confer with Mrs. Ainsford about the allocation of rooms and with the cook on the organization of meals. And she insisted, the day before her parents were to arrive, and her husband's mother, and a few of the other relatives, on decorating the drawing room herself with mounds of holly and crepe streamers and bows and a bunch of mistletoe.

The earl was called in to help, and it was generally he who was having to risk having all his fingers pricked to the bone, he complained, handling the holly and placing it and re-placing it while Estelle stood in the middle of the room, one finger to her chin, directing its exact placement.

But there was not a great deal of rancor in his complaints. There had been no more quarrels since the night of the concert. And Estelle seemed to be happy to be at home, aglow with the anticipation of Christmas. She smiled at him frequently. And he basked in her smiles, pretending to himself that it was he and not the festive season that had aroused them.

"Oh, poor Allan," she said with a laugh after one particularly loud exclamation of protest as he pricked his finger on a holly leaf. "Do you think you will survive? I will kiss it better if you come over here."

"I am being a martyr in a good cause," he said, not looking over his shoulder to note her blush as she realized what she had said.

The mistletoe had to be moved three times before it was in a place that satisfied her. Not over the doorway, she decided on second thought, or everyone would get mortally tired of kissing everyone else, and Allan's cousin Alma, who was seventeen, with all the giddiness of her age, would be forever in and out of the room. And not over the pianoforte, or only the musical people would ever be kissed.

"This is just right," she said, standing beneath its final resting place to one side of the fireplace. "Perfect." She smiled at her husband, and he half smiled back, his hands clasped behind his back. But he did not kiss her.

She made some excuse to see Nicky every day. Mrs. Ainsford would despair of ever training him to be a proper servant, the earl warned her at breakfast one morning when the child had come into the room to bring him his paper, if she persisted in putting her arm about his shoulders whenever he appeared, whispering into his ear, and kissing him on the cheek. And the poor housekeeper would doubtless have an apoplexy if she knew that her mistress was taking a cup of chocolate to the child's room each night after he was in bed.

But he did not forbid her to do either of those things. For entirely selfish reasons, he admitted to himself. Estelle was happy with the child in the house, and somehow her happiness extended to him, as if he were solely responsible for saving the little climbing boy from a life of drudgery. She smiled at him; her eyes shone at him; she gave him tenderness as well as passion at night.

The Earl of Lisle was not entirely idle as far as his new servant was concerned, though. He had learned during his interview with the chimney sweep, of course, that Nicky was no orphan, but that there was a mother at least and perhaps a father, and probably also some brothers and sisters somewhere in the slums of London. The mother had paid to have the boy apprenticed. The sweep had shrugged when questioned on that point. Someone had probably given her the money. He did not know who, and why should he care?

The mother had not come to protest the ending of the apprenticeship. Neither had anyone else. His lordship had not tried to penetrate the mystery further. He had decided not to question the child, not to confront him with his lie. Not that first lie, anyway. But the second? Had Estelle really believed that the boy had been in search of a drink and had got lost? Yes, doubtless she had. She had seen only a thin and weeping orphan, alone in the dark.

The earl had still not done anything about the matter five days after the incident. But on the fifth day he entered his study in the middle of the morning to find Nicky close to his desk, his eyes wide and startled.

"Good morning, Nicky," he said, closing the door behind him.

"I brought the post," the boy said in his piping voice, indicating the small pile on the desk and making his way to the door.

Lord Lisle did not stand aside. His eyes scanned the desk-top. His hands were behind his back. "Where is it, Nicky?" he asked eventually.

"What?" The eyes looked innocently back into his.

"The top of the inkwell," the earl said. "The *silver* top." He held out one hand palm-up.

The child looked at the hand and up into the steady eyes of his master. He lifted one closed fist slowly and set the missing top in the earl's outstretched hand. "I was just lookin' at it," he said.

"And clutched it in your hand when I came in?"

"I was scared," the child said, and dropped his head on his chest. He began to cry.

Lord Lisle strolled over to his desk, and sat in the chair behind it. "Come here, Nicky," he said.

The boy came and stood before the desk. His sobs were painful to hear.

"Here," the earl directed. "Come and stand in front of me."

The child came.

The earl held out a handkerchief. "Dry your eyes and blow your nose," he said. "And no more crying. Do you understand me? Men do not cry—except under very exceptional circumstances."

The boy obeyed.

"Now," the earl said, taking the crumpled handkerchief and laying it on one corner of the desk, "look at me, Nicky." The boy lifted his eyes to his master's chin. "I want you to tell me the truth. It must be the truth, if you please. You meant to take the inkwell top?"

"I didn't think you'd miss it," the boy said after a pause.

"Have you taken anything else since you have been here?"

"No." Nicky lifted his eyes imploringly to the earl's and shook his head. "I ain't took nothin' else."

"But you meant to a few nights ago when we found you outside this door?"

His lordship's eyes advised the truth. Nicky hung his head. "Nothin' big," he said. "Nothin' you'd miss."

"What do you do with what you steal, Nicky?" the earl asked.

"I ain't never stole nothin' before," the child whispered.

A firm hand came beneath his chin and lifted it.

"What do you do with what you steal, Nicky?"

The boy swallowed against the strong hand. "Sell it," he said.

"You must have a lot of money hidden away somewhere then," the earl said. "In that little bundle of yours, perhaps?"

Nicky shook his head. "I ain't got no money," he said.

The earl looked into the frightened eyes and frowned. "The man you sell to," he said, "is he the same man who apprenticed you to the sweep?"

The eyes grew rounder. The child nodded.

"Who gets the money?" the earl asked.

There was no answer for a while. "Someone," the boy whispered eventually.

"Your mother, Nicky?"

"Maw's dead," the boy said quickly. "I was in the orphinige."

The earl's tone was persistent, though not ungentle. "Your mother, Nicky?" he asked again.

The eyes, which were too old for the face, looked back into his. "Paw left," the child said. "Maw 'ad me an' Elsie to feed. 'E said we would all 'ave plenty if I done it."

The earl removed his hand from the child's chin at last. He leaned back in his chair and steepled his fingers against his mouth. The boy stood before him, his head hanging low, one foot scuffing rhythmically against the carpet.

"Nicky," Lord Lisle said at last, "I will need to know this man's name and where he may be found."

The boy shook his head slowly.

The earl sighed. "Your mother's direction, then," he said. "She will perhaps be worried about you. I will need to communicate with her. You will tell me where she may be found. Not now. A little later, perhaps. I want to ask you something. Will you look at me?"

Nicky did so at last.

"Do you like her ladyship?" the earl asked.

The child nodded. And since some words seemed to be required of him in response, he said, "She's pretty." And when his master still did not say anything, "She smells pretty."

"Would you want her to know that I found you with the silver top in your hand?" the earl asked.

The child shook his head.

"Neither would I," the earl said. "We are in entire agreement on that. What do you think she would do if she knew?"

Nicky swallowed. "She would cry," he said.

"Yes, she would," the earl agreed gently. "Very hard and very bitterly. She will not be told about this, Nicky. But if it happens again, perhaps she would have to know. Perhaps she would be the one to discover you. I don't want that to happen. Her ladyship is more important to me that anyone or anything else in this life. Do you know what a promise is?"

The child nodded.

"Do you keep your promises?"

Another nod.

"Are you able to look me in the eye and promise me that you will never steal again, no matter how small the object and no matter how little it will be missed?" Lord Lisle looked gravely and steadily back into the child's eyes when he looked up.

Another nod.

"In words, Nicky, if you please."

"Yes, guv'nor," he whispered.

"Good man. You may leave now." But before the child could turn to go, the earl set a hand on his head and shook it slightly. "I am not angry with you," he said. "And you must remember that we are now in a conspiracy together to make her ladyship happy."

He removed his hand, and the child whisked himself from the room without further ado. Lord Lisle stared at the door for a long while.

E stelle was not entirely pleased with the ring when she returned to the jeweler's to fetch it. It was very beautiful, of course, but she did not think she would have called it the Star of Bethlehem if this had been the one Allan had put on her finger. The diamond no longer looked like a star in a night sky. She did not know why. It was surely no larger or no smaller than the other had been, and yet it looked more prominent. It did not nestle among the sapphires.

But no matter. She had not expected it to look the same, anyway. There could be no real substitute for the original ring. This one would serve its purpose—perhaps. She took it home and packed it away with the rest of her gifts.

The following day the guests would begin to arrive. She would see her parents for the first time in six months. She had missed them. And everyone else would be coming, too, either on the same day or within the few days following. And Christmas would begin.

She was going to enjoy it more than any other Christmas in her life. It might be her last with Allan. The last during which they would be truly husband and wife, anyway. And though panic grabbed at her stomach when she thought of what must happen when the holiday was over and Mama and Papa began to talk about returning home, she would not think of that. She wanted a Christmas to remember.

The Earl of Lisle was no better pleased with his ring. He knew as soon as he saw it that the original must have had nine sapphires. The arrangement of eight just did not look right. They did not look like a night sky with a single star shining from it.

But it did not matter. Nothing could look quite like the Star of Bethlehem, and this ring was lovely. Perhaps she would know that it was not meant to be a substitute, but something wholly new. Perhaps. He wrapped the little velvet box and carried it about with him wherever he went.

Nicky, in the meanwhile, was feeling somewhat uncomfortable, for several reasons. There was the whole question, for example, of what Mags would do with him if he could get his hands about his throat. And what his new master would do with him if he caught him thieving again. Nicky had the uncomfortable feeling that it would not be a whipping, which would be easy to bear. The governor would force him to look into his eyes for a start, and that would be worse than a beating. He was proving to be not such a soft touch after all.

Then, of course, there was his mother. And Elsie. Were they starving? Was Mags bothering them? He knew what Mags did to help girls to a living. But Elsie was not old enough yet. Nicky did not know what he would do, short of abandoning his family to their fate. Nothing had been said about any money in this new position of his. Plenty of clothes and food, yes, and very light work. But no money.

There was, of course, the shiny shilling the lady had given him the first night she came to him with a cup of chocolate. Nicky had never seen so much money all at once. But he couldn't give that to his mother. He needed it for something else.

And that brought him to the nastiest problem of all. That ring and that diamond almost burned a hole in his stomach every day, pressed between the band of his breeches and his skin as they always were. He couldn't sell them to Mags now. It would seem like breaking his promise, though the things were already stolen when he had been forced to look into his master's eyes and make the promise, and though he had never thought of keeping a promise before.

And he couldn't put them back in the lady's room, though he had thought of doing so. Because she would tell the governor and he would know the truth. He was a real sharper, he was. And he would not whip or even scold. He would look with those eyes. He might even put a hand on his head again and make him squirm with guilt.

There was only one thing he could think of doing. And that would mean leaving his room again during the night, and the house, after the lady had brought him his chocolate and kissed him and allowed him to breathe in the scent of her. And the governor might catch him and look at him. And the stupid clothes he would be forced to wear would draw ruffians like bees to a honey pot. And Ned Chandler might refuse to help him at the end of it all and might not believe where he had got the things and what he meant to do with them.

Nicky sighed. Sometimes life was very hard. Sometimes he wished he were all grown up already so that he would know without any difficulty at all what was what. And he was getting used to a warm and comfortable bed and to a full night's sleep. He did not particularly want to be prancing about the meaner streets of London at an hour when no one would ever hear of him again if he were nabbed.

Ned Chandler had been a jeweler of sorts at one time. He still had the tools of his trade and still mended trinkets for anyone who came to ask and dropped a few coins his way. Nicky, as a very small child, had often crept into the man's hovel and sat cross-legged and openmouthed on the floor watching him when he was busy.

It was doubtful that Chandler had ever held in his hands a gold ring of such quality set with nine sapphires of such dark luster, and a diamond that must be worth a fortune in itself.

"Where did you get these 'ere, lad?" he asked in the middle of one particular night, not at all pleased at having been dragged from his slumbers and his two serviceable blankets. He held the ring in one hand, the diamond in the other.

"It belongs to my guv'nor's missus," the child said. "I'm 'avin' it mended for 'er. She sent me. She sent me a shillin'."

"A shillin'?" The former jeweler frowned. "And sent yer in the middle of the night, did she?"

Nicky nodded.

"Did you steal these 'ere?" Chandler asked grimly. "I'll whip the skin off yer backside if you did."

Nicky began to cry. His tears were perhaps somewhat more genuine than was usual with him. "She's pretty," he said, "an' she smells like a garden, an' she brings me choc'lut when I'm in bed. An' I'm 'avin' it mended for 'er."

"But she didn't send yer, lad." It was a statement, not a question.

Nicky shook his head. "It's to be a surprise," he said. "Honest, Mr. Chandler. She lost the di'mond, an' she cried, an' I found it. I'm 'avin' it mended for 'er. I'll give you a shillin'."

"I'll do it," Ned Chandler said with a sudden decision, looking ferociously down at the tiny child from beneath bushy eyebrows with a gaze that reminded Nicky uncomfortably of the earl. "But if I 'ear tell of a lady wot 'ad a ring stole, Nick, lad, I'll find yer and whip yer backside. Understood?"

"Yes." Nicky watched in silent concentration as the jeweler's tools were unwrapped from an old rag and the diamond replaced in the ring.

"You can keep yer shillin'," the man said, tousling the boy's hair when the mended ring had been carefully restored to its hiding place. "And you make sure to give that ring back, lad. Don't you be tempted to keep it, or I'll be after yer, mind."

"Take the money," the boy said, holding out his treasure, "or it won't be my present. Please?"

The man chuckled suddenly. "Well," he said. "I'll take it, 'cos it shows me yer must be honest. Off with yer then, lad. Be careful on your way back."

Nicky grinned cheekily at him and was gone.

Christmas Eve. It had always been Estelle's favorite day of the season. It was on Christmas Day, of course, that the gifts were opened and that one feasted and sat around all day enjoying the company of one's family. But there had always been something magical about Christmas Eve.

On Christmas Eve there was all the anticipation of Christmas.

And this year was to be no exception. There was all the hustle and bustle of the servants and all the tantalizing smells coming from the kitchen, that of the mince pies being the most predominant. And there was Alma pretending to forget a dozen times during the day that the mistletoe was hanging in that particular spot, and standing beneath it. Especially when Estelle's unmarried brother, Rodney, happened to be in the room.

And there was Papa working everyone's excitement to fever pitch, as he did every year, with hints dropped about the presents, hints that stopped just short of telling one exactly what the gift was. And Mama sitting with her needlepoint having a comfortable coze with Allan's mother. And the children rushing about getting under everyone's feet, and their parents threatening halfheartedly to banish them to the nursery even if it was Christmas.

And the men playing billiards. And the girls whispering and giggling. And Papa tickling any child who was unwise enough to come within arm's length of him. And Allan relaxed and smiling, playing the genial host. And Nicky following the tea tray into the drawing room with a plate of cakes and pastries, looking fit enough to eat himself, and the pleased way he puffed out his chest when Estelle caught his eye and smiled and winked at him.

And the group of carolers who came to the door before the family went to church and were invited inside the hall and stood there and sang, their cheeks rosy from the cold outside, their lanterns still lit and in their hands. And the noisy and cheerful exchange of season's greetings before they left again.

And the quiet splendor of the church service after the hectic day. And the Christmas music. And the Bible readings. And Bethlehem. And the star. And the birth of the baby, the birth of Christ.

And suddenly the meaning of it all, the quiet and breathless moment in the middle of all the noisy festivities surrounding it.

The birth of Christ.

Estelle was seated beside her husband, their arms almost touching. She looked at him, and he looked back. And they smiled at each other.

The drawing room was noisy again when they went back home, even though the children had been put to bed before they went to church. But finally the adults too began to yawn and make their way upstairs. After all, someone said, it would be a terrible tragedy if they were too tired to enjoy the goose the next day.

Estelle smiled rather regretfully at her husband when they were alone together. "It's going so quickly," she said. "One more day and it will all be over."

"But there are always more Christmases," he said.

"Yes." Her smile did not brighten.

"Are you tired, Estelle?" he asked.

She shrugged. "Mm," she said. "But I don't want the day to end. It has been lovely, Allan, hasn't it?"

"Come and sit down," he said, seating himself on a love seat. "I want to tell you about Nicky."

"About Nicky?" She frowned. And Allan wanted to talk to her?

One of his arms was draped along the back of the love seat, though he did not touch her when she sat down beside him. "I have been making some plans for him," he said. "I spoke with him in my study this morning. He seemed quite agreeable."

"Plans?" Estelle looked wary. "You are not going to send him away, Allan? Not another apprenticeship? Oh, please, no. He is too young."

"He is going to live with his mother and his sister," he said.

She looked her incomprehension.

"I am glad to say the orphanage was a fabrication," he said. "To win your sympathy, I do believe."

"He lied to me?" she said. "He has a family?"

"I am afraid he became the victim of a villainous character," he told her gently. "Someone who was willing to set him up in life, buy his apprenticeship to a chimney sweep in exchange for stolen items from the houses that a climbing boy would have access to."

Estelle's eyes were wide with horror. She did not even notice her husband take one of her hands in his.

"I told him I would not tell you," he said. "But I have decided to do so, knowing that you will not blame Nicky or think the worst of him. I caught him at it a week ago, Estelle, though I already had my suspicions."

She bit her upper lip. There were tears in her eyes.

"The money from his stolen goods—or some fraction of it—was going to the upkeep of his mother and sister," he said. "It seems the father took himself off sometime ago."

"Oh, the poor baby," she whispered.

"I have spoken with the mother." He was massaging her hand, which had turned cold, in both of his. "I had her brought here yesterday. I had from her the name of the villain who has been exploiting the child in this way and have passed it on with some pertinent information to the appropriate authorities. Enough of that. To cut a long story short, the mother has agreed that she would consider life in a country cottage as washerwoman to our house as little short of heaven. Nicky confessed this morning to a lifelong ambition to own a horse. I have suggested that he may enjoy working in our stables—when he is not at school, of course. Somehow he was not nearly so enthusiastic about the idea of school."

"So he is to live on your estate with his mother?" she asked.

"Yes." He raised her hand to his lips, and this time she did notice as she saw it there and felt his lips warm against her fingers. "Do you think it a good solution, Estelle? Are you pleased?" He looked almost anxious.

"And you did all this without a word to me?" she asked in some wonder. "You did it to save me some pain, Allan? Did you do it for me?"

His smile was a little twisted. "I must confess to a certain fondness for the little imp," he said. "But yes, Estelle. I thought it might make you happy. Does it?"

"Yes." She leaped to her feet in some agitation and stood quite unwittingly beneath the mistletoe.

He said nothing for a few moments, but he got to his feet eventually and came to stand behind her. He set his hands on her shoulders. "Now this is an invitation impossible to resist," he said, lowering his head and kissing the back of her neck.

She turned quickly and stared at him in some amazement. He had never—ever—held her or kissed her outside her bed. She had not even quite realized that he was so tall and that he would feel thus against her—strong and warm and very safe.

He lowered his head, and his mouth came down open on hers.

And how could a kiss when one was standing and fully clothed and in a public room that might possibly be entered by someone else at any moment seem every bit as erotic as any of the kisses they had shared in bed, when his hands were beneath her nightgown against her naked flesh and when his body was in intimate embrace with hers?

But it was so. She felt an aching weakness spiral downward from her throat to her knees.

When he removed his mouth from hers, it was only to set his forehead against her own and gaze downward at her lips.

"I want to give you your gift tonight," he said. "Now. I want to do it privately. No one else would understand. May I?"

Her senses were swimming, but she smiled at him. "I feel the same way about mine to you," she said. "Yes, now, tonight, Allan. Just the two of us." She ran across the room to where they had all piled their gifts and came back to him with a small parcel in her hands. He had removed his from a pocket.

"Open mine first," he said, and he watched her face as she did so. They were both still standing very close together, underneath the mistletoe. "It is not the original," he said quickly as she opened the velvet box. "It is not nearly as lovely. There were nine sapphires, were there not? I could not remember, but these do not look right. But I want you to have it anyway. Will you, Estelle? Will you wear it?" He took it from the box and slid it onto her nerveless finger.

"Allan!" she whispered. "But why?"

He was not sure he could explain. He had never been good with words. Especially with her. "You called it the Star of Bethlehem," he said. "I always loved that name, because it suggested Christmas and love and peace and hope. All the things I have ever wanted for you. And with you. I felt I could only tell you with the ring. Never in words. Until now."

He laughed softly. "It must be the mistletoe. I am not the man for you, Estelle. You are so beautiful, so full of life. So . . . glittering! I have always envied those other men and wanted to be like them. And I have been horribly jealous and tried to make your life a misery. But I have not meant to. And after Christmas you can go away with your parents, and no one will know that we are separated. There will be no stigma on your name. But you will be free of my taciturn and morose presence." He smiled fleetingly. "My marble-statue self. But perhaps the ring will help you to remember me a little more kindly. Will it?"

"Allan!" She whispered his name. And looked down at the ring on her finger, the ring that was not the Star of Bethlehem, but that she knew would be just as precious to her. And she noticed the parcel lying forgotten in her hands. She held it out to him. "Open yours."

He was disappointed that she said no more. He tried to keep his hands from trembling as he opened her gift.

He stood smiling down at the silver snuffbox with its turquoise-studded lid a moment later. "It is the very one I could not persuade Humber to sell me," he said. "You succeeded, Estelle? You remembered that I wanted it for my collection? Thank you, my dear. I will always treasure it."

But she was looking anxiously into his eyes. "Open it," she said. "There is something else inside. It is not really a present. I mean, it is not for you. It fits me. But I lost the other—yes, I did, Allan. I lost it all, though I have been afraid to tell you. But I wanted you to have this so that you would know that I did not do so carelessly."

He lifted the lid of the snuffbox and stood staring down at a diamond ring set with nine sapphires. He looked up at her, his eyes wide and questioning.

"I didn't mean to lose it," she said. "I have broken my heart over it, Allan. It was my most treasured possession. Because it was your first gift to me, and because at the time I thought it was a symbol of what our marriage would be. And because I spoiled that hope by going about a great deal with my friends when I might have stayed with you, and by flirting quite deliberately with other men when you were so quiet and never told me that I meant anything to you. Because I wanted you to know that my behavior has never shown my true sentiments. Those other men have meant nothing whatsoever to me. I have never allowed any of them to touch more than my fingers. You are the only person—the only one, Allan—who occupies the center of my world. The only one I can't bear to think of spending my life without.

"Because I wanted you to keep the ring when you send me away after Christmas, so that perhaps you will come to know that I love you and only you. And so that perhaps you will want to bring me home again someday and put it on my finger again." She flashed him a nervous smile. "I have given it to you, you see, in the hope that you will give it back to me one day. Now, is that not the perfect gift?"

He lifted the ring from the snuffbox, slipped the box into a pocket, and took her right hand in his. He slid the ring onto her third finger and looked up into her face. "Perfect," he said. "Now you have two gifts and I have one. I do not need to keep the ring for even one minute, you see, Estelle."

The look in his eyes paralyzed her and held her speechless.

"It is the most wonderful gift I have ever had," he said. "It is yourself you are giving me, is it not, Estelle?"

She nodded mutely.

"Come, then," he said. "Give me your second and most precious gift."

She moved into his arms and laid one cheek against his broad shoulder. She closed her eyes and relaxed all her weight against him.

"Do you understand that my gift is identical to yours in all ways?" he murmured against her ear.

"Yes." She did not open her eyes or raise her head. She lifted her hand to touch his cheek with the backs of her fingers. "Except that your ring has only eight sapphires."

He laughed softly.

"You love me, Allan?" She closed her eyes even more tightly.

"I always have," he said. "I knew it the moment I put the Star of Bethlehem on your finger two years ago. I am not good at showing it, am I?"

She raised her head suddenly and gazed into his eyes. "How is it possible," she said, "for two people to be married for almost two years and live close to each other all that time and really not know each other at all?"

He smiled ruefully. "It is rather frightening, is it not?" he said. "But think of what a wonderful time we have ahead of us, Estelle. I have so much to tell you, if I can find the words. And there is so much I want to know about you."

"I may find too many words," she said. "You know that I can't be stopped once I start, Allan."

"But always to other people before," he said. "Very rarely to me, because you must have thought that I did not want to hear. Oh, Estelle." He hugged her to him and rocked her.

Her arms were wrapped about his chest. She held up her two hands behind his back and giggled suddenly. "I love my two presents," she said. "One on each hand. But I love the third present even more, Allan. The one I hold in my arms."

"This was an inspired choice of location for mistletoe," he said, kissing her again. "Perhaps we should take it upstairs with us, Estelle, and hang it over the bed."

She flushed as she smiled back at him. "We have never needed any there," she said.

He took her right hand in his, smiled down in some amusement at his Christmas present, which he had placed there, and drew her in the direction of the door and the stairs and—for the first time in their married life—his own bedchamber.

The servants had been called into the drawing room to receive their Christmas gifts, the cook first, as she flatly refused to abandon her kitchen for longer than five minutes at the very most.

The Earl of Lisle allowed his wife to distribute the presents, contenting himself with shaking each servant's hand warmly and conversing briefly with each. He wondered if he was looking quite as glowingly happy as Estelle was looking this morning. But he doubted it. No one was capable of glowing quite like her.

Anyway, it was against his nature to show his feelings on the outside. He doubtless looked as humorless and taciturn as ever, he reflected somewhat ruefully, making a special effort to smile at one of the scullery maids, who clearly did not quite know where to put herself when it became clear that she was expected to place her hand into that of her employer, whom she rarely saw.

But, the earl thought, startling the girl by asking if she had quite recovered from the chill that had kept her in bed for two days the week before and so showing her that he knew very well who she was, it was impossible—quite impossible—for Estelle to be feeling any happier than he was feeling. He hoped that she was *as* happy as he, but she could not be more so.

For he knew that the glow and the sparkle in her that had caused all attention to be focused on her since she had appeared in the breakfast room before they all adjourned to the drawing room to open their gifts—he knew that he had been the cause of it all. She glowed because he loved her and had told her so and shown her so all through what had remained of the night when they had gone to bed.

Indeed, it was amazing that she was not yawning and that she did not have dark rings beneath her eyes to tell the world that she had scarce had one wink of sleep all night. When they had not been making love, they had been talking. They had both tried to cram a lifetime of thoughts and feelings and experiences into one short night of shared confidences. And when they had paused for breath, then they had used even more breath in making love to each other and continuing their conversation in the form of love murmurings and unremembered nonsense.

It seemed that the only time they had nodded off to sleep had been just before his valet had come into his room from the dressing room, as he always did, to pull back the curtains from the windows. It was fortunate that the time of year was such that the earl had covered Estelle up to the neck with blankets, because she did not have a stitch on beneath the covers any more than he did.

Poor Higgins had frozen to the spot when he had glanced to the bed and seen his master only barely conscious, his cheek resting on a riot of tumbled dark curls. The poor man had literally backed out of the room. Estelle, fortunately, had slept through the encounter until Allan woke her with his kisses a few minutes later. And he had gazed in amusement and wonder at the blush that had colored her face and neck—after two years of marriage.

Estelle had just given Nicky his present and, child that he was, he had to open it right there. She sat down close to where he stood, one arm about his thin waist, heedless of the presence of all her guests and many of the other servants. She looked into his face with a smile and watched his look of wide-eyed wonder and his dropped jaw as he saw his watch for the first time.

She laughed with delight. "It is a watch for you, Nicky," she said, "so that you will always know what time of day it is. Do you know how to tell time?"

"No, missus," he said in his treble voice, his eyes on his new treasure.

"Then I shall teach you," she said, hugging him and kissing his cheek. "And when you move to the country with your mama and your sister, you will know when it is time to come to the stables to groom the horses, and when it is time to go home from school. Happy Christmas, sweetheart."

He traced the silver frame of the watch with one finger, as if he were not quite sure that it was real.

"His lordship and I will be going into the country after Christmas too," she said. "We will meet your mama and your sister. What is her name?"

"Elsie," he said, and then added hastily, "missus."

"You will want to run along," she said, kissing his cheek again. "I hear that one of the footmen is to accompany you and carry a basket of food to your mama and then go back for you tonight. Do have a lovely day."

"But he don't need to come for me," the child said with some spirit, "I know the way."

Estelle smiled, and the earl held out his hand gravely. "Happy Christmas, Nicky," he said. "Her ladyship and I are very happy that you have come to us."

The child forced his eyes up to the dreaded ones of his master, but he saw nothing but a twinkling kindness there. He turned to leave, but at the last moment whisked a crumpled rag out from the band of his breeches and almost shoved it into Estelle's hands.

"For you," he said, and was gone from the room before she could react at all.

"Oh, Allan, he has given me his seashell," she said to her husband in some distress before being caught up again in the noise and bustle of the morning.

An hour passed before there was a lull enough that the Earl of Lisle could take his wife by the hand and suggest into her ear that they disappear for half an hour. She picked up the half-forgotten rag as they were leaving the room.

"I wished you a happy Christmas very early this morning under the mistletoe," he said with a smile when the study door was safely closed behind them, "and early this morning after I had quite finished waking you. But I feel the need to say it again. Happy Christmas, Estelle." He lifted her hands one at a time to his lips, kissing first the ring he had given her, and then the one she had given him. "We have established an undying reputation for eccentricity, I believe, with two almost identical rings, one on each of your hands."

"They are identical in meaning too," she said, gripping his hands and stretching up to kiss him on the lips. "Allan, what am I to do with this seashell? He has treasured it so much."

"He really wanted to give it to you," he said. "Let's have a look at it, shall we?"

They both stood speechless a few moments later, their foreheads almost touching as they gazed down at the Star of Bethlehem nestled on her palm inside the rag. And then their foreheads did touch and Estelle closed her eyes.

"Oh," she said, after a lengthy silence during which neither of them seemed able to find quite the right words to say, "was there ever such a Christmas, Allan?"

"What I am wondering," he said in a voice that sounded surprisingly normal considering the emotion that had held them speechless, "is where we are to find another finger to put it on."

"I see how it is," she said, clasping ring and rag in one hand and lifting both arms up about his neck. She made no attempt to suggest a solution to the problem he had posed. "The Wise Men lost the star too for a while, but when they found it again, it was over Bethlehem, and they found also everything they had ever been looking for. Oh, Allan, that has happened to us too. It has, hasn't it? What would we have ever done if Nicky had not come into our lives?"

He did not answer her. He kissed her instead.

She giggled suddenly after he had lifted his head. "I have just had a thought," she said. "A thoroughly silly thought.

Nicky came down a chimney and brought us a Christmas happier than any our dreams could have devised."

He laughed with her. "But I don't think even our wildest dreams could convey sainthood on Nicky," he said. "I don't think he can possibly be the real Saint Nicholas, Estelle. Would a real saint steal both a diamond and a ring, as Nicky of the sharp eyes obviously did, be smitten by a pretty lady who smells pretty, and have the ring mended by some devious means? I think it will be entirely better for my digestion if I don't investigate that last point too closely, though doubtless I will feel obliged to do just that tomorrow. The little imp. Perhaps he is Saint Nicholas after all. Now, do you suppose we should go back upstairs to our guests?"

She hesitated and brushed at an imaginary speck of lint on his shoulder and passed a nervous tongue over her lips.

"What is it?" he asked.

She flushed and kept her eyes on his shoulder. "I have another gift for you," she said. "At least, I am not sure about it, though I am almost sure. And I suppose I should not offer it as a gift until I am certain. But by that time Christmas will be over. And it is such a very special Christmas that I have become greedy and want to make it even more so."

He laughed softly. "Suppose you give it to me," he said, "and let me decide if it a worthy offering or not."

She raised her eyes to his and flushed a deeper shade. "I can't actually give it to you for a little more than seven months," she said. "That is, if I am right about it, anyway. But I think I must be, Allan, because it has been almost a whole month now."

"Estelle?" He was whispering.

"I think it must be right," she said, wrapping her arms about his neck again, "because I am never late except perhaps by a day or two. And I think I have felt a little dizzy and nauseated some mornings when getting out of bed, though that could, of course, be wishful thinking. I think I am with child, Allan. I think so. After almost two years. Can it be true, do you think?"

He did not even attempt to answer her question. He caught her up in a hug that seemed designed to crush every bone in her body, and in the body of their child too. He pressed his face to her neck. Hers was hidden against his shoulder.

For the next several minutes it was doubtful that Estelle was the only one without dry eyes. It seemed that men did sometimes cry—in very exceptional circumstances.

THE
BEST GIFT

"Christmas is an unutterable bore," Lady Enid Penn said with an affected sigh. "There is positively no one with whom to amuse oneself except parents and aunts and uncles and cousins by the score and nothing to do except feast and make merry—with one's own family!"

There was a murmur of sympathetic agreement from several other young ladies.

"I shall simply die," the Honorable Miss Elspeth Lynch informed her listeners, "if the Worsleys remain in town for the holiday, as they did last year, instead of returning home. Patricia Worsley is my dearest bosom friend, and Howard Worsley is . . . well, he is interesting." She looked around archly at her companions, who tittered on cue.

"If one were only sixteen instead of fifteen," the Honorable Miss Deborah Latimer said, adding her sigh to everyone else's. "One's parents and aunts and uncles and all their friends have a wonderful time dancing and partaking of the wassail bowl and staying up almost until dawn while one is banished to the nursery and to bed with the children."

"And what about you, Craggs?" Lady Enid turned her head to look at the lady who had sat silently writing at her desk while they talked. "Do you find Christmas a bore, too? Or do you have wonderfully exciting plans? You are older than sixteen, after all."

The other young ladies tittered again, though there was an edge of cruelty to their laughter this time.

"Do you have dozens of beaux, Craggs? *Do* tell," Miss Lynch said, widening her eyes.

Miss Jane Craggs looked up from the journal in which she was writing. Although it was homework hour and school rules stated quite categorically that it was to be a silent hour, she was not enforcing the rule this evening. It was the last day of school before Christmas. Tomorrow all the girls would be going home, most of them with their parents or with liveried servants in sumptuous carriages.

"I believe it would be something of an exaggeration, Elspeth, to count my beaux in the dozens," she said. "Besides, a lady never does tell, you know."

"But you are not a lady, Craggs," one of the younger girls said.

But she won only frowns for her witticism. Everyone knew that Jane Craggs was not a lady, that she had spent most of her life at Miss Phillpotts's school for young ladies, her board and education paid for by an unknown benefactor—undoubtedly her father—until she was seventeen, that she had stayed on afterward as a teacher, though Miss Phillpotts treated her more as a servant than as an instructor. All the girls took their cue from the headmistress. The names of all their teachers were preceded by "Miss" except for Craggs. They treated her with a condescension bordering sometimes on insolence. But there was an undefined borderline beyond which they would not go. It was unladylike to remind Craggs in words that she was no lady.

"I believe," Jane Craggs said, closing her journal and getting to her feet, "we will make a concession to the approaching holiday and end homework hour five minutes early. Would anyone care to argue the point?"

There was relieved laughter and some enthusiastic cheering from the young ladies, who jumped to their feet and made for the door.

"Happy Christmas, Craggs," Deborah Latimer said as she was leaving the room.

Jane Craggs smiled at her and returned the greeting.

She sat down again when she was alone and began deliberately to clean and mend the pen she had been using. And she tried to ignore the knowledge that Christmas was approaching—an impossibility, of course.

No one with whom to amuse oneself except aunts and uncles and cousins and parents. Nothing to do but feast and make merry with one's family members. Such a Christmas was unutterably boring? Jane felt rather like crying, and ruthlessly suppressed the feeling. If only she could once—just once in her life—experience such a Christmas.

She had always hated Christmas. As a child and as a young girl she had also dreaded it. Dreaded the aloneness, with which she had always lived every day of the year but that always assaulted her most cruelly at Christmas. Dreaded the emptiness. Dreaded the excitement of the other girls as they prepared to go home and waited for family members or servants to come and fetch them. Dreaded the departure of Miss Phillpotts and the teachers until she was quite alone in the school with the few servants who were kept on for the holidays—always, it seemed, the most humorless of the servants.

Now she was three-and-twenty years old. The dread had gone. But the aloneness, the loneliness, the emptiness had not. She had heard and read so much about Christmas. For her there had never been family—she understood that she had spent her early years in an orphanage, a rather expensive one. She believed, though she did not know for sure, that her mother had been a nobody, perhaps a whore, while her father had been a wealthy man who had agreed to support her until she was old enough to support herself. And so there had never been family for her and never Christmas gifts or Christmas parties.

Sometimes she had to remind herself that her name was Jane. A rather plain name, it was true, but her own. She heard it so rarely on anyone's lips that she could not remember the last time. It seemed singularly unfortunate to her that someone—her mother, she supposed—had blessed her with the surname of Craggs.

As a child she had dreamed of Christmas, and the dream had lingered even though she had passed the age of dreams. But did one ever pass the age of dreams? Would life be supportable if one could not dream?

She had dreamed of a large house with three stories in which every window blazed with light. It was always twilight and there was snow outside blanketing the ground and making of the trees and their branches magical creations. Inside there was a large hall, three stories high, with two large fireplaces crackling with log fires, the hall decked out in greenery and bows for the season. It was a house filled with people. Happy, beautiful people. All of whom loved her. All of whom she loved.

As a child she had even given names and faces and personalities to all those people. And in her imagination she had bought or made special gifts for each of them and had received gifts in return.

In her dream there was always a carved Nativity scene in the window of the drawing room, and it was always the focal point of family celebrations. The family always went to church on Christmas Eve, trudging through the snow to get there, filling a number of the pews. They always ran and laughed and ambushed one another with snowballs and rolled one another in the snow on the way home.

The contrast between dream and reality had been almost unbearable when she was a child. Now it was bearable. Jane tidied the already tidy teacher's desk, picked up her journal, her best friend, and clasped it with both hands against her bosom as she left the study room to climb the stairs to her small attic room. Now she was old enough to know that Christmas Day was just a day on the calendar like all others, that it would pass, that before she knew it the teachers and girls would be returning for the spring term. She had learned to be sensible.

She lit a candle in her room, shivered, and began to undress. Oh, no, she had not—she had not learned to be sensible. And it had not become bearable. It had not, it had not.

But she had learned to pretend to be sensible. And she

had learned to pretend that it was bearable. She had learned to hold on to her childish dreams.

To say that he was feeling annoyed was to understate the case. He disliked Christmas. He had disliked it for most of his adult years. It was all just a parcel of nonsense as far as he was concerned. He liked to remove himself from town and all other centers of merriment well before the collective madness set in and take himself off to Cosway, his country seat, where he could wait out the season in quietness and sanity.

The trouble was that his family knew it and saw him as being available to care for unwanted relatives. Not that it had ever happened before, it was true, but it was happening this year, and he knew that it would happen again, that he was setting a trend this year that he would regret forever after. His sister and brother-in-law had decided entirely on the spur of the moment to spend Christmas with friends in Italy and had disposed of the minor inconvenience of a fifteen-year-old daughter by informing him—yes, Susannah had told him, not asked him—that she would spend Christmas with him at Cosway.

What, in the name of all that was wonderful, was he going to do with a fifteen-year-old niece for a few weeks? And at Christmas, of all times?

What he would do, he had decided at once, having neglected the obvious solution of telling his elder sister that she must change her plans, that he just would not do it—what he would do was enlist the help of someone else. Some female who had no other plans for Christmas. Someone who would be pleased enough to spend it at Cosway, keeping Deborah out of mischief. And out of his way.

Agatha, in fact. But Agatha, his maiden aunt, had been invited to spend the week of Christmas with her dear friends, the Skinners, in Bath, and while she hated to inconvenience her dear nephew and great-niece, she really could not disappoint the Skinners this close to Christmas.

When Viscount Buckley descended from his carriage outside Miss Phillpotts's school and had himself announced to speak with the headmistress herself, he was scowling. And his mood matched his expression exactly.

"Deborah will be very delighted to learn that her uncle, the viscount, has come in person to convey her home for the holidays, my lord," Miss Phillpotts said to him, smiling graciously.

His lordship sincerely doubted it. Especially when the child discovered that her parents had taken themselves off to Italy without a word to her. He felt sorry for the girl, if the truth were known. But he felt sorrier for himself.

"I suppose, ma'am," he said, without allowing himself to feel even the faintest glimmering of hope, "that there is not another young lady at the school who has nowhere to go for the holiday? Someone who could come with my niece and be company for her over Christmas?"

"I am afraid not, my lord," the headmistress said. "All our girls will be leaving today."

The viscount sighed. "It was a faint hope," he said. "I am not much in practice as far as entertaining very young ladies is concerned, ma'am." Or as far as celebrating Christmas was concerned. And Deborah would doubtless want to celebrate it. *Damn!*

"It is indeed kind of you to be willing to extend your hospitality to another young lady," Miss Phillpotts said. "But the only person who will be remaining at the school apart from three servants is Miss Craggs."

Miss Craggs sounded like an elderly tyrant. But Viscount Buckley was somewhat desperate. "Miss Craggs?" he said.

"One of my teachers," Miss Phillpotts explained.

Undoubtedly a tyrant. Poor Deborah. She would probably hate him forever for asking the question he was about to ask.

"Is there any possibility," he asked, "that she would be willing to accompany us to Cosway?"

"I believe she would be delighted, my lord," the headmistress told him. "Shall I send her down to you? I see that Sir Humphrey Byrde's carriage has arrived." She glanced toward the window, which looked down onto a cobbled courtyard. "I should go to greet him."

The viscount bowed his acquiescence and wandered to the window while Miss Phillpotts left the room to see another of her pupils on her way. *Damn Susannah and Miles!* How could they think of going off to Italy for Christmas when they had a young daughter to care for? And how could they think of leaving her with him when they knew he did not celebrate Christmas? But then Susannah had always been the flighty, selfish one, quite different from their other two sisters. She was the youngest of the three and by far the most beautiful.

He had a suspicion that Susannah had never wanted children.

He thought briefly of his own child. Had he reminded his secretary to send her a gift? But then Aubrey would remember without a reminder. Part of his job was to remember what his employer was likely to forget.

He turned when the door opened behind him. She was not elderly, and despite her name, she did not look like a tyrant.

"Miss Craggs?" he said.

She inclined her head.

She was not elderly at all. She was probably five or six years younger than he, in fact. She was rather tall, and slender almost to the point of thinness. She had a rather thin, pale face, with fair hair smoothed back into a bun at her neck. Her gray dress was of cheap fabric and was high-waisted but made no other concession to fashion. Only her eyes saved her from being so nondescript that she might have faded entirely into her surroundings. Her eyes were dark gray and long-lashed. And they appeared to have such depth that he had the strange feeling that most of her living must be done very far within herself.

"Miss Craggs." He took a few steps toward her. "I understand that you will be staying here for Christmas?"

"Yes, my lord." Her voice was unexpectedly low and soft.

"You are expecting company?" he asked. "There would be someone to miss you if you were not here?"

Her face did not change expression. And yet he was given the impression that far within herself, where her living was done, she grimaced. "No, my lord," she said.

"I am Deborah Latimer's uncle," he said. "Warren Nash, Viscount Buckley, at your service, ma'am. Would it be possible to persuade you to come with us to my country seat in Hampshire? My sister and her husband, Deborah's parents, have gone to Italy and left her in my care. Frankly, I do not know what I am to do with a fifteen-year-old over Christmas. I need a female companion or chaperon for her. Will you come?"

There was the merest flicker in her eyes. Nothing more. He had never known a woman who was so impassive. He had always thought of women as open books, their emotions as clear to view as the words on a page. He had never had any problem knowing what his various mistresses felt or thought.

"Yes, my lord," she said.

He waited for more, for some questions or conditions. But she said nothing else. Her eyes, he noticed, were focused, not on his, but on his chin or thereabouts.

"I would guess that Deborah is eager to leave," he said. "How soon can you be ready, Miss Craggs?"

"Half an hour?" she said.

Half an hour! Good Lord, most women of his acquaintance would have asked for two or three days. He inclined his head to her. "Would you have Deborah sent to me?" he asked as she turned to leave the room.

Damn Susannah, he thought, too irritated to think of an original way mentally to censure his sister. How was he supposed to break the news to his niece?

Miss Craggs looked as if she had about as much joy in her as would half fill a thimble. A thimble for a small finger.

Damn!

* * *

She could not remember going farther from the school than could be accomplished on foot. She could not remember riding in a carriage. She could not remember being in company with a gentleman for longer than a minute or two at a time, except the dancing master who came in to teach the girls. She was usually chosen to partner him when he taught them the steps because he was not allowed to touch any of the girls, and none of the other teachers was willing to tolerate his lavishly insincere compliments and his moist hands.

She was not sure if she was glad or sorry to be where she was. At first she had been numbed with the strangeness and wonder of it. She was going on a holiday. She was going to spend Christmas at a private home in Hampshire. The home of Viscount Buckley. She was not going to be alone at the school, as she always had been for as far back as she could remember. And then she had been excited. Her teeth had chattered and her hands had shaken and her mind had whirled at dizzying speed as she had packed her few belongings into a valise she had had to borrow from Miss Phillpotts.

Now, after hours of travel, the luxury of a well-sprung, lavishly upholstered carriage was no longer able to mask the discomfort of the near silence that existed among its three occupants. An unnatural, uncomfortable silence. Deborah was sullen and unhappy. Jane did not blame her when she had discovered only this morning that her parents had gone away for Christmas and left her behind. But she feared that part of the sullenness was caused by the fact that she had been appointed the girl's companion. Craggs, the teacher who was not really a lady.

The viscount was merely silent. Jane doubted that he felt uncomfortable. But she did. Dreadfully so. She had had no experience with maleness. Viscount Buckley seemed suffocatingly male to her. He was dark, not much taller than she, elegant. She imagined he was handsome by any standards. She really had not seen many men. He seemed to her more handsome than any man she could possibly imagine. And very male.

She was uncomfortable and terrified.

"We are almost there," he said, turning his head and looking at Deborah. "You will feel better after a cup of tea."

"I will *not* feel better," his niece said sullenly. "I hate Christmas. And I hate Mama and Papa."

Jane looked at the girl. She wanted to take her hand and tell her that at least she had an uncle willing to take her in. At least she had someone to whom she belonged and somewhere to go. But such an assurance would not console, she supposed.

"If it is any consolation," the girl's uncle said, "they are not exactly my favorite people at this moment either, Deborah."

"Meaning that you do not want to be burdened with me, I suppose," the girl said, misery overlaying the sullenness. "Everyone knows you do not believe in Christmas, Uncle Warren."

"Well," he said with a sigh, "I shall have to see what I can do to exert myself on your behalf this year, Deborah. Ah, the house. It is always a relief to see it at the end of a long journey."

Jane did not hear the rest of the conversation if, indeed, there was more. She had seen the house. Built within the last century, it had a classical symmetry of line combined with a deceptive simplicity of design. Built of light gray stone, it was rectangular in shape, three stories high, with a domed central portion and a pillared portico with wide marble steps leading up to double doors. It was larger and more magnificent than the house of her dream. And there was no snow, only bare trees and flower beds and grass of faded green. But it was all like enough to the dream house to catch at her breathing.

This was Cosway? This was where she was to spend the holiday?

She was aware suddenly that she had leaned forward

and was gazing rather intently through the window. She was aware of the silence of her two companions. She turned her head and met the viscount's dark eyes. She sat back in her seat again and retreated within herself, into that secret place far inside where it never mattered that no one noticed her or respected her or loved her. A secret place she had discovered as a very young child.

"You admire my home, Miss Craggs?" the viscount asked her.

"Yes, my lord," she said. She felt the uncharacteristic urge to babble, to enthuse. She curbed it. "It is very beautiful."

"I think so too," he said.

She felt his eyes on her for a few moments longer. She kept her own eyes firmly on the hands she had clasped in her lap. And then the carriage lurched slightly as it stopped, and the door was being opened and the steps set down. She felt excitement ball in her stomach again.

Was this really happening? To her?

Always as he drove up to the house, and more especially when he stepped inside the great domed hall, he wondered why he did not spend more of his time here. There was always a special feeling of homecoming when returning to Cosway. He loved the hall, especially in the winter, when the log fires in the great twin fireplaces at opposite sides gave welcome and the illusion of warmth. The hall was too large and too high, of course, ever to be really warm in reality.

"Ah, Kemp," he said to his butler, rubbing his hands together as a footman took his hat and his gloves and waited for him to remove his greatcoat. "It is good to be home. I have brought my niece with me, as you see, and her companion, Miss Craggs. You will see that Mrs. Dexter assigns rooms to them? And that their bags are taken up? We will have tea served in the drawing room immediately."

Kemp cleared his throat. "There was a, ah, delivery for you earlier this afternoon, m'lord," he said, nodding his head significantly to one side. "I did not know quite what to do with it but knew you would be arriving yourself before the afternoon was out."

The viscount turned his head toward one of the fireplaces. Beside it, seated on a wooden settle, quite upright and quite still, sat a small child so bundled up inside a large coat and woolen scarf and mittens and so hidden beneath an absurdly large hat that she looked more like a bundle of abandoned laundry than a living child. To the left side of her chest was pinned a square sheet of paper.

"She would not, ah, remove her gloves or her hat, m'lord, or allow either Mrs. Dexter or myself to remove the label," the butler said. "The name on the label is Miss Veronica Weston, m'lord, care of yourself and this house."

Veronica Weston. Oh, good Lord. Viscount Buckley crossed the hall, his booted feet echoing on the marble tiles, and stopped a few feet in front of the child, who looked up at him with eyes that he supposed were very like his own.

He had never seen her before. He had known of her existence since before her birth and had never tried to deny paternity or to shirk the responsibility of providing for her financially. But he and Nancy had parted company before she discovered the pregnancy, and she had moved on to another protector soon after the birth. He himself had never felt any particular human interest in his daughter.

"Veronica?" he asked.

"Yes." She was looking very directly into his eyes. "Are you my papa? I am not to speak to anyone except my papa."

Papa! He had never thought of himself by any such name. He was a father. He had a daughter. He had never been a papa.

"This name is mine." He touched one finger lightly to the label she wore on her chest. "You may speak to me. Your mama sent you here?"

"Mama went away," the child said. "Mrs. Armstrong said I was to come to my papa."

"Mrs. Armstrong?" He raised his eyebrows.

"She looks after me," the child said. "But Mama went away and Mrs. Armstrong said there was no money. I was to come to my papa."

The label was thick. He guessed that there was a letter sealed up within it. Nancy had never neglected the child despite the demands of an acting career. Aubrey had assured him of that. But she had gone away? She had tired of the child?

"Do you have a letter for me, Veronica?" he asked, holding out one hand. He was only just beginning to realize what a coil he was in now. As if things were not bad enough as they were.

The child looked down and laboriously unpinned the label from her coat. She handed it to him. Sure enough, there was a letter. Nancy had been out of town for a weekend party, leaving her daughter with Mrs. Armstrong, a neighbor who frequently cared for the child. Nancy had fallen from an upper gallery in the house she was visiting to the hall below and had died instantly. Mrs. Armstrong, with six children of her own, could not afford to keep the child when there was no chance of payment. She respectfully sent her to her father. She had been to the expense of hiring someone to write the letter for her and of sending the child on the stagecoach. She hoped she would be reimbursed for her pains.

Poor Nancy, he thought. She had been beautiful and a talented actress. And a skilled lover. She had borne his child. And now she was dead. He folded the letter again and looked down at his daughter. She was gazing up at him, quiet and self-contained. And all of four years old.

Lord. Oh, dear Lord. What was he to do?

He turned his head to the two young ladies, who were still standing there, watching him. His eyes instinctively came to rest on Miss Craggs.

"She is my daughter," he said. "Her mother has d— Her mother has gone away and she has been sent here." He looked at her in mute appeal, like a child himself who did not know how to proceed.

"Uncle Warren!" Deborah said, shock in her voice.

Miss Craggs came closer, her eyes on the child. "She will want something to eat and a glass of milk," she said. "She will need to remove her hat and her coat and have them and her bag taken to a room that will be hers."

Of course! How practical and how simple. "Are you hungry, Veronica?" he asked.

"Yes, Papa," the child said.

"Come along, then," he said, clasping his hands awkwardly behind him. Good Lord, his illegitimate child, his by-blow, was in his own home with his niece. His servants would be scandalized. His neighbors would be shocked. "Will you give your hat and your coat to Kemp?"

"Will you let me help you, Veronica?" He watched as Miss Craggs went down on her knees before the child, who stood up and allowed her outer garments to be removed. "What a pretty color your scarf is. There—now you will be more comfortable. But we will need to comb those curls of yours before you sit down for your milk and your food." She touched the backs of two fingers to a tangled curl at the child's cheek and smiled at her.

The viscount felt jolted, first by the sight of his daughter without the heavy outer garments—she was little more than a baby—and then by the smile on the face of his niece's teacher. Good God, he thought, he had not noticed that the woman was beautiful. Though he knew even as he thought it that she was not beautiful, that it was merely something from deep within her that for the moment she had allowed to the surface of her face.

"Would you like to hold my hand?" she asked his daughter.

"Yes, please," the child said, looking up at her and suiting action to words.

"Uncle Warren?" Deborah asked faintly.

"She is my child," he told her. He felt almost as if he were realizing it for the first time. It was one thing to know one had fathered a child and to have accepted financial responsibility for her. It was another thing entirely to see

the child, tiny and dainty and quiet, her eyes and her hair
the color of his own.

"But—" Deborah said.

"She is my daughter," he said firmly. "Shall we go up for
tea and get warm again?" He offered her his arm.

"Is this Papa's very own house?" Veronica was asking
Miss Craggs.

Her own awkwardness and awe and even her excitement
had been forgotten. Although the great hall was the
hall of her dream with the addition of a painted and gilded
dome, and although the staircase was wide and magnificent
and the drawing room large and splendid, Jane noticed
them only with her eyes and not with her heart. And her
own bedchamber with a separate dressing room was large
and richly furnished and far surpassed anything she might
have dreamed for herself. But she merely glanced at it when
she hurried in to change her dress for dinner—to change
from one drab gray dress to another.

Her time and her attention and her heart were otherwise
engaged than in the perusal of a mere house and in the
recognition of a dream come true.

She had never had anything to do with very young children. The girls who came to Miss Phillpotts's school were
older and more independent and did not really need her for
anything outside her capacity as a teacher.

No one had ever needed her. The thought came without
any self-pity. It was simply the truth.

Until today. But today she had seen a small child bewildered and frightened by the loss of her mother and by her
arrival at the home of the father she had never seen before.
And her heart had lurched with all the love she had never
been called upon to give.

She had taken a comb from her own reticule in the drawing room and drawn it gently through the soft baby curls.
And she had sat by the child and helped her to food and
milk. And then she had taken her to the nursery, where a

bed had been made up, and had helped her unpack her little
bag, which had been full of surprisingly pretty dresses. She
had taken the child down to dinner, although she would
probably eat in the nursery on future days, and had helped
her wash and change into her nightgown afterward. She
had tucked her into bed.

A maid was to stay in the nursery next to the bedchamber and sleep on a truckle bed there.

"Good night, Veronica," Jane said as she was leaving.
Her heart ached with unfamiliar love and happiness. Someone had needed her for almost half a day and would need
her again tomorrow.

"Good night, Miss Craggs," the child said, peering at
her with wide eyes over the blanket that had been tucked
beneath her chin. "When will Mama be coming back?"

Ah, poor child. Poor child. "Mama had to go away for a
long time," she said, walking back to the bed and smoothing her hand over the child's head. "She did not want to
leave you, Veronica, but she had to go. She sent you here,
where you will be safe."

"Miss Craggs," the child said, "don't leave."

"I'll stay for a while," Jane said, seating herself on the
side of the bed. "You are quite safe, dear. My name is Jane.
It sounds a little nicer than 'Miss Craggs,' does it not?"

"Miss Jane," the child said, and closed her eyes.

There was a rather painful aching around the heart to
hear her name spoken aloud by another person. Jane sat
quietly on the side of the bed, waiting for the little girl to
fall asleep. But after a few moments the child's eyes opened
and she lay staring quietly upward.

And the door opened softly, and when Jane turned her
head it was to find Viscount Buckley standing there, his
hand on the doorknob.

"She is still awake?" he asked after a few moments.

"Yes," Jane said.

He came to stand beside her and gazed down at his
daughter. A daughter he had had with a mistress. A child

he had never seen until today. And a child he seemed not to know what to do with. What *would* he do with her? Jane felt fear for the defenseless baby who was still staring quietly upward.

"Veronica?" he said. "Is there anything you need?"

"No, thank you," the child said, not moving the direction of her gaze.

"You are tired?" he asked.

"Yes."

"Go to sleep, then." He leaned forward rather jerkily to lay the backs of his fingers against her cheek for a moment. "You are quite safe now. I will arrange something for you."

The child looked at him finally. "Good night, Papa," she said.

"Are you coming, Miss Craggs?" he asked, looking at Jane.

"I will stay until she falls asleep," Jane said.

He inclined his head to her. "Deborah is having an early night," he said. "Will you join me in the library as soon as you may? I need to talk with you."

Veronica was asleep no more than ten minutes later, not having spoken or moved since her father left the room. Jane got carefully to her feet, bent down after a moment's hesitation to kiss the child's forehead, and tiptoed from the room.

How wonderful it must be, she thought, how wonderful beyond imagining, to be a mother.

He sat in the library resisting the urge to refill his brandy glass for the second time. If he drank any more he would be foxed. The thought had its definite appeal, but getting drunk would solve nothing. He had learned that much in his almost thirty years of living.

Deborah was sullen and unhappy—and angry.

"How could you, Uncle Warren?" she had said just before going to bed. "How could you let her stay here and announce for all the world to hear that she is your daughter? Mama will be furious with you. Papa will kill you."

Yes, they would be a trifle annoyed, he conceded. But it served them right for foisting their daughter on him without so much as a by-your-leave.

What was he to do? How did one go about finding a good home for a young child? Aubrey would doubtless know, but Aubrey was in London, about to take a holiday with his family. Perhaps Miss Craggs would have some idea. He hoped so.

He was relieved when she was admitted to the library less than half an hour after he had left her in the nursery. He rose to his feet and motioned her to a chair. She sat straight-backed on the edge of it, he noticed, and clasped her hands in her lap. Her face had the impassive, empty look again now that Veronica was no longer present.

"These things happen, Miss Craggs," he said. He wondered how shocked this prim schoolteacher was beneath the calm exterior.

"Yes, my lord," she said. "I know."

"Can you blame me for taking her into my own home?" he asked. "What was I to do?"

She looked fully into his eyes but did not reply. He shifted uncomfortably. He had never encountered eyes quite like hers.

"Send her back where she came from?" he asked. "I could not do it, ma'am. She is my own flesh and blood."

"Yes, my lord," she said.

"What am I to do, then?" he asked. "How does one find a home for a child? A home in which one can be quite sure she will be well cared for. It is an infernally awkward time of year. Everything will be complicated by the fact that it is Christmas. What am I to do?"

"Perhaps, my lord," she said, "you should celebrate Christmas."

He frowned at her.

"You have a young niece," she said, "who is unhappy at being abandoned by her parents at this of all times. And you have a small child who is bewildered at the disappearance of her mother. Perhaps it is the very best time of year. Let Christmas bring some healing to them both."

He might have known it. For all her drab appearance and seemingly sensible manner and bearing, she was a sentimentalist. Christmas bringing healing, indeed! As if there was something inherently different in that day from all others. Besides, how could Christmas bring any sort of happiness to four such very different people—Deborah, Veronica, Miss Craggs, and himself?

"You believe in miracles, Miss Craggs?" he asked. "Do you have any suggestions as to how this healing can be effected?"

She leaned slightly forward in her chair, and there was a suggestion of eagerness in her face. "We could decorate the house," she said. "I have always dreamed of . . . There must be greenery outside that we can gather."

"Holly and such?" he asked, still frowning.

"And mistletoe," she said, and interestingly enough she blushed.

"And that will do it?" he asked, a note of sarcasm in his voice. "An instant miracle, Miss Craggs?"

"Deborah needs company," she said. "She is of an age at which it seems that life is passing her by unless she has company of her own age and activities to keep them busy and happy."

He grimaced. "Company of her own age?" he said. "From memory and experience I would say that young people of Deborah's age are usually ignored at Christmastime—and all other times of the year, for that matter. Adults want nothing to do with them, yet they are too old to enjoy being with the children. It is an unfortunate time of life that has to be endured until it passes."

"Perhaps," she said, "there are other young people in the neighborhood who would be only too happy to get together independently of either the adults or the children."

"Are you seriously suggesting that I visit all my neighbors within the next few days, seeking out the young and organizing a party here?" he asked, aghast.

"I think that a wonderful suggestion, my lord," she said.

He should have left the woman where she was, he thought. She was definitely dangerous.

"You would doubtless be left to organize and chaperon such an affair," he warned her. "I will be invited to join a sane adult party." And he would accept too, though he usually sent his excuses.

"I am accustomed to supervising young people, my lord," she reminded him.

"Very well, then," he said. "On your own head be it." He was feeling decidedly annoyed. Except that her suggestion made sense. And it would definitely solve the problem of Deborah. "I will have to postpone making a decision about Veronica until after Christmas. I suppose it will not matter greatly. She is a quiet and well-behaved child."

"She is hiding," Miss Craggs said quietly.

"Hiding?" he frowned.

"She suspects that something dreadful has happened to her mother," she said. "And she knows that you are a stranger, although you are her father. She is not at all sure that she is safe, despite your assurances to her and my own. She does not know what is going to happen to her. And so she has found a hiding place. The only one available. She is hiding inside herself."

The notion was thoroughly preposterous. Except that he recalled his impression that morning that Miss Craggs herself did most of her living far inside herself. What was her own story? he wondered briefly. But there was a topic of more pressing importance on which to focus his mind.

"But she must know," he said, "that I will care for her, that I will find her a good home. I always have cared for her."

"Why must she know any such thing?" Miss Craggs asked. "She is four years old, my lord. A baby. Financial care and the assurances of a good home mean nothing to her. Her world has rested firmly on one person, and that person is now gone."

"Miss Craggs," he asked quietly, though he already

knew what her answer was going to be, "you are not suggesting that I keep the child here, are you?"

She looked down at the hands in her lap. "I am suggesting nothing, my lord," she said.

But she was. She obviously knew nothing about life. She knew nothing about the types of relationships that might exist, between a man and his illegitimate offspring.

And yet, even as he thought it, he recalled the totally unfamiliar experience of standing in the nursery looking down at his own small child in the bed there, lying still and staring quietly upward, in a most unchildlike way. And he felt now, as he had felt then, an unidentifiable ache about his heart.

She was his child, the product of his own seed. She was his baby.

"Miss Craggs." He heard the irritability in his voice as he got to his feet. "I see clearly that nothing can be done and no decisions can be made until Christmas is over. It is looming ahead of us, a dark and gloomy obstacle, but one that must be lived through. Make of it what you will, then. Load the house with greenery if you must. Do whatever you will. And in the meantime I shall call upon my neighbors and try to organize that unheard-of phenomenon, a preadult party." He felt thoroughly out of sorts.

"Very well, my lord," she said, and looked up at him.

He felt almost as if he might fall into her eyes.

"Come," he said, extending an arm to her even though he had brought her here as more of a servant than a guest, "I will escort you to your room, Miss Craggs."

She got to her feet and looked at his arm with some misgiving before linking her own through it. Her arm was trembling quite noticeably though she did not feel cold, and she stood as far from him as their linked arms would allow.

Good Lord, he thought, had she been shut up inside that school for so long?

He stopped outside her dressing room and opened the door for her. "Thank you," he said, "for agreeing to accompany Deborah here. And thank you for showing kindness and gentleness to Veronica. Good night."

"Good night, my lord," she said, her eyes on a level with his neckcloth. And she moved hastily into the dressing room and closed the door behind her even as he prepared to take her hand to raise to his lips.

He was glad then that she had not given him a chance to do it. She was, after all, merely a servant. What was her first name? he wondered. He hoped it was something more fortunate than her surname. Though it was of no concern to him. He would never have reason either to know it or to use it.

J ane helped Veronica get dressed the following morning and brushed her curls into a pretty style while the child sat very still on a stool, her legs dangling over its edge. They were breakfasting together in the nursery when Mrs. Dexter, the viscount's housekeeper, arrived there to ask Miss Craggs what her orders were regarding the Christmas baking and cooking.

"What my orders are?" Jane asked, bewildered. "Should you not be consulting his lordship, Mrs. Dexter?"

"He said I should come to you, miss," the housekeeper said, looking somewhat dubious. "He said that whatever you wanted was to be supplied."

Oh, dear. He really meant what he had said last night, then. She was to do whatever she wanted to celebrate Christmas. The thought was dizzying when at the age of three-and-twenty she never had celebrated the season. She was to have a free hand?

"Where is his lordship?" she asked.

"He has gone visiting with Miss Deborah, miss," the housekeeper said. "He said you were to wait until this afternoon to gather greenery so that he can help you carry it."

"Oh, dear," Jane said. "What is usually cooked for Christmas, Mrs. Dexter?"

The housekeeper raised her eyebrows. "Anything that

will not remind his lordship that it is Christmas," she said. "The cook threatens every year to resign, miss, but she stays on. It is unnatural not to have a goose and mince pies, at the very least."

Goose and mince pies. The very thought of them was enough to set Jane's mouth to watering. "Perhaps," she said, "I should go down to the kitchen and consult the cook."

"Yes, miss," Mrs. Dexter said. But she paused as she was about to leave the room. "It is time Christmas came back to this house. It has been too long gone. And it needs to be celebrated when there is a child in the house, poor little mite." She nodded in Veronica's direction.

Jane wondered what had happened to banish Christmas from Cosway. She could not imagine anyone deliberately deciding not to celebrate it. She looked at Veronica and smiled.

"Shall we go down to the kitchen and talk to Cook?" she asked.

The child nodded and got down from her stool to hold out her hand for Jane's. Jane, taking it in hers and feeling its soft smallness, wondered if there could be a greater happiness in life.

The cook was so overjoyed at the prospect of Christmas baking that Jane found she did not need to make any suggestions at all. She merely sat at the kitchen table with a cup of tea and approved every suggestion made. The cook lifted Veronica to the table, placed a large, shiny apple in her hand, and clucked over her and talked about the delight of having a child in the house again.

"I do not care what side of the blanket she was born on, if you take my meaning, miss," she said to Jane. "She is a child, and children have a right to a home and a right to be loved. Chew carefully, ducky. You do not want to choke on a piece."

Veronica obediently chewed carefully.

"It will do his heart good to have her here," the cook said, jerking her head toward the ceiling. "He does not love easy, miss, and when he do, his heart is easy to break."

Jane could not resist. "Was his heart broken once?" she asked.

The cook clucked her tongue. "By his childhood sweetheart," she said. "You never saw a man so besotted, miss, though she were a flighty piece, if you was to ask me. Their betrothal was to be announced on Christmas Day here at a big party. A big secret it was supposed to be, but we all knew it, miss. And then halfway through the evening, just when his lordship were excited enough to burst, a stranger who had come home with her brother a month before stood up and announced *his* betrothal to her. And she smiled at him as sweet as you please without so much as a guilty glance at our boy—or at her papa, who was as weak as water, as far as she was concerned. Six years ago it was, miss. His heart don't heal easy. But this is one to mend any heart."

She nodded at Veronica, who had spotted a cat curled beside the fire and had wriggled off the table to go and kneel beside it and reach out gingerly to pat its fur. The cat purred with contentment.

"A blessed Christmas gift she is for any man," the cook said.

Yes. Jane remembered sitting alone with him in the library last evening. She alone with a man! And talking with him. Being consulted on what he should do with his daughter. And having the temerity to give her opinion and her suggestions. She would have expected to have been quite tongue-tied in a man's presence. But she had made a discovery about this particular man. He was not the infallible figure of authority she had thought all men were. He was an ordinary human being who did not have all of life's answers or even the most obvious of them.

He did not know that all his child needed—all!—was love. The love of her father. And he did not know that good, docile behavior in a child did not necessarily denote a happy child. He had turned to her, Jane, for help. Even a man could need her in some small way for one small moment of time.

It was the thought she had hugged to herself in bed. And

also the memory of how it had felt to touch him. To feel his strongly muscled, unmistakably male arm with her own. To smell the unfamiliar odor of male cologne. To feel the body heat of a man only inches away from her own body. And to know that the yearning she had suffered and suppressed in herself for years had a definite cause. It was the yearning for a man, for his approval and his support and companionship. And for something else, too. She did not know quite what that something else was except that outside her dressing room, when he had stopped and thanked her for coming and for giving her attention to Veronica, she had felt suffocated. She had felt that there was no air in the corridor.

She had felt the yearning for . . . for *him.* She still could not express the need less vaguely than that.

And so she had fled into her room like a frightened rabbit.

"And there." The cook's hand patting her shoulder felt strangely comforting. There had been so few physical touches in her life. "He would be a blessed Christmas gift for some lady too, missy."

But you are not a lady, Craggs. She heard again the words that had been spoken in the homework room just two days before. No, she was no lady. She smiled and got to her feet.

"You are going to be busy if you are to make everything you have suggested," she said. "Oh, I can hardly wait for all the smells and all the tastes. I can hardly wait for Christmas."

The cook chuckled. "It will come, miss, as it always does," she said.

But it had never come before. This would be her first-ever Christmas. She could scarcely wait. At the same time, she wanted to savor every moment as it came. They were to gather greenery during the afternoon, she and Veronica and perhaps Deborah. And Lord Buckley was to come to help carry the loads.

Veronica was sitting cross-legged on the stone floor, smoothing the cat's fur.

* * *

He could not quite believe that this was himself. Himself up a tree, balanced precariously on a branch, feeling hot and disheveled and dusty. His boots, he was sure, though he did not look down at them, must be in a condition to give his valet heart palpitations. Below him Miss Craggs stood with arms partly spread as if to catch him if he fell, Deborah had her hands to her mouth and was alternately squealing and giggling, and Veronica was gazing gravely upward.

"Miss Craggs believes that in addition to all the holly we have gathered and all the pine boughs we have cut down we need some mistletoe," he had said to his daughter a short while before. "What do you think, Veronica? Do we need mistletoe?"

"Yes, please, Papa," she had said.

And Deborah had giggled—she had started giggling during their morning visits and had scarcely stopped since—and had added her voice to everyone else's. It just would not be Christmas, it seemed, unless there was some mistletoe hanging in strategic places so that one might be caught beneath it accidentally on purpose.

So here he was up a tree.

And then down with a sizable armful of mistletoe and a tear on the back of one kid glove and a scrape so deep on the inside of his left boot that it would never be the same again.

And all in the name of Christmas.

"Do you know why I have risked life and limb just to gather this?" he asked Veronica, frowning.

"Because Miss Jane wanted it?" she asked.

Jane. He might have guessed that she would have such a name. And yet it suited her. It was quietly, discreetly pretty.

"Not at all," he said. "This is what it is used for." He held one sprig above the absurd hat, which Nancy had doubtless thought suitably flamboyant for the daughter of an actress,

stooped down, and kissed her soft, cold little cheek. And
took himself quite by surprise. Now why had he done that?

"Any gentleman has the right to kiss any lady he catches
beneath the mistletoe," he said, "without fear of having his
face slapped. It is a Christmas custom. You see?" And he
straightened up and repeated the action with Deborah, who
giggled. "Now we have to carry all this greenery back to
the house."

"What about Miss Jane?" a grave little voice asked him.

And he knew he was caught. Caught in the act of maneuvering. For when he had demonstrated the use of mistletoe on his daughter and his niece, he had really wanted
to use Miss Craggs as his model. Even though she was prim
and gray and every inch the schoolteacher. Though that was
not the whole truth this afternoon. Since they had left the
house there had been a light in her eyes that had touched
him. She was enjoying all this just like a child.

"Oh, it works with Miss Craggs too," he said, turning to
her and raising his sprig of mistletoe again. And he felt
suddenly and stupidly breathless. She was standing very
still and wide-eyed.

He kissed her lightly and briefly, as he had kissed the
other two. Except that foolishly he kissed her on the lips.
And ended up feeling even hotter than his excursion up the
tree had made him.

She turned hurriedly away before their eyes could meet
and began energetically arranging the heap of holly they
had gathered into three bundles.

"Here, Veronica," he said, "you may carry the mistletoe,
since it will not prick you all to pieces. Deborah, take that
bundle of holly. I'll take this one."

His hand brushed Miss Craggs's as he gathered up the
largest bundle and belatedly their eyes met. Her own were
still large and bright. Brighter. Was it the cold that had
brought the tears there? Or was it the kiss? Surely she had
been kissed before. Surely that had not been her first kiss.

Had it? Once again he wondered about her past, about
her life. Impoverished parents and the need to go out and

make her own living? But she had not been planning to go
home for Christmas.

"I will send someone back with a wagon for the pine
boughs," he said.

" 'Deck the halls with boughs of holly,' " Deborah sang
suddenly with loud enthusiasm and no musical talent whatsoever.

" 'Fa la la la la la la la la,' " Miss Craggs sang with her in
a rather lovely contralto voice.

" ' 'Tis the season to be jolly.' " He joined his tenor voice
to their singing and looked down at Veronica.

" 'Fa la la la la la la la la.' " She piped up with them, off-key.

" 'Don we now our gay apparel.' " Three of them sang
out lustily while the fourth continued with the fa-la-las.

And the damned thing was, Viscount Buckley thought,
that it could grab at one quite unawares. Christmas, that was.

Jane had never been very assertive, even as a teacher. She
had never been the type who liked to boss and organize
people. And yet over the next couple of days she seemed to
be transformed into a wholly different person.

It was she who directed the decorating of the house—of
drawing room, staircase, and hall. The viscount had suggested that the servants could do it, but she had exclaimed
in horror and disappointment before she could stop herself,
and he had meekly agreed that perhaps they could do it
themselves, the four of them.

"But I have no eye for design, Miss Craggs," he had told
her. "You will have to tell us what you want."

And she had told them. She stood in the middle of the
drawing room giving orders like a sergeant with a company
of soldiers. Boughs and sprigs and wreaths were hung exactly where and exactly how she directed, and if she did not
like the look of them when the deed was done, then she
directed their replacement. And everyone obeyed, even the
viscount, who was given all the climbing to do. He balanced on chairs and tables and ladders in his shirtsleeves,

decking out pictures and mirrors and door frames while she stood critically below him, head to one side, examining the effects of his handiwork and criticizing any slight error on his part.

She felt so happy by the time they were finished that she thought she might well burst with it. She was surrounded by Christmas—by the sights and smells of it. She could smell the pine boughs, and there were interesting smells wafting up from the kitchens. Particularly the smell of Christmas puddings.

"Oh, it is so very beautiful," she said, her hands clasped to her bosom when they were all finished and were all standing admiring their efforts. "If only we had some ribbons for bows."

"Oh, yes," Deborah said. "Red ones and green ones."

Viscount Buckley sighed. "Ribbons and bows," he said. "And bells, too, I suppose? Doubtless you will find what you need in the village, Miss Craggs. Go there if you must and purchase whatever you need and have the bill sent to me."

"Oh." She turned to him with glowing eyes. "May I? Oh, thank you, my lord."

He looked at her and made her a little mocking bow. And she remembered the earth-shattering feeling of his lips touching hers and wondered if he realized what an enormous treasure this Christmas was going to be to her in memory. The most precious treasure of her life.

Veronica was tugging at her skirt. "May I come too, Miss Jane?" she asked.

"Of course, sweetheart," she said, hearing in some surprise the unexpected endearment she had used. "I will need you to help me choose."

"And I will come too, Craggs," Deborah said. But she flushed suddenly and added, "*Miss* Craggs." And then she extended both arms and twirled into the steps of a waltz. "Uncle Warren," she said, "do you think we may dance on Christmas Day?"

Deborah had completely changed since the visits she had paid with her uncle during the morning. She had come rushing into the house on their return home to announce to Jane that she was to have a party of her very own on Christmas Day. Fifteen young people were to come during the afternoon for walks and games and were to stay for the evening while their parents—and her uncle—engaged in an adult party at the home of the Oxendens. Even the seventeen-year-old and very dashing George Oxenden had decided to come to Cosway, though his parents had agreed to allow him to attend the adult party if he wished.

Jane saw the viscount grimace. "A dance?" he said. "And who is to provide the music, pray?"

But Deborah made it instantly clear that the idea had not come to her on the spur of the moment. "Mr. George Oxenden told me that his aunt plays the pianoforte rather well," she said, "and that she would be only too pleased to be with the young people rather than with the adults on Christmas Day."

Her uncle looked skeptical. "I will have to see what can be arranged," he said.

"Oh, thank you, Uncle Warren," she said, darting back across the room to hug him. "This is going to be the best Christmas ever, after all, I just know it."

The viscount raised his eyebrows and looked at Jane.

Jane could only agree with his niece.

But there was work to be done. The village shop had to be visited and yards of the widest, brightest ribbon to be chosen and measured. Jane felt guilty when she was told the total cost, but she did not change her purchases. Viscount Buckley was a wealthy man, was he not? When Veronica gazed admiringly and rather longingly at some porcelain bells, she even added three to her purchases, a dreadful extravagance. But they would look lovely hanging from the holly on the mantel in the drawing room.

And then she discovered during a visit to the kitchens that the servants were murmuring over the fact that there was to be no Yule log. The head gardener was only too delighted to go in search of the largest one he could find when Jane insisted that they must have one. A Yule log!

She had not even thought of it. She knew so little about Christmas.

During the same visit she learned that one of the grooms was skilled with his hands and loved to whittle on wood whenever he had a few spare moments. When Jane admired a spoon he was carving for his girl in the village, he offered to carve a small crib for the drawing room. And that other detail of her dream returned to Jane. Time was short, but the groom agreed to try to carve a baby Jesus to go inside the crib, and a Mary and Joseph to kneel beside it, and perhaps even a shepherd or two and an animal or two to worship and adore.

The decorations would be complete, Jane decided, standing alone in the drawing room after the ribbons and bells had been added to all the greenery, if only there could be a Nativity scene in the window.

Oh, Christmas would be complete. She twirled around and around rather as Deborah had done and thought of the little bonnet and muff for Veronica and the small bottle of perfume for Deborah she had had set aside in the village shop as Christmas gifts. They would take all the meager hoard of money in her purse, but she could not resist. She had never bought Christmas presents before. She had nothing for Viscount Buckley, but it would be inappropriate anyway to give a gentleman a gift.

For Deborah's sake she was going to make this a wonderful Christmas. And for Veronica's sake. Veronica was quietly obedient, but Jane knew that the child was still hiding inside herself. And she knew from long experience how that felt. She was going to do her very best to see that Christmas brought the child out of herself again, even if it was only to a realization of her grief and her insecurity. At least then she could be properly comforted.

If there could be any meaningful comfort. Jane stopped twirling. Her heart chilled to the memory of the viscount's asking how he was to find his daughter a good home. He intended to send the child away again to be cared for by strangers. They would be strangers, no matter how kindly they might be.

Oh, for the viscount's sake too, this must be a wonderful Christmas. He must be made to see that love was everything, that family was everything. Why could people who had always had family not see that? Why could he not see that his daughter was his most priceless possession?

And for her own sake she was going to see that this Christmas was celebrated to the limit. It was her first and might well be her last. It was going to be a Christmas to remember for a lifetime.

Yes, it was. Oh, yes, indeed it was.

She twirled again.

Christmas Eve dawned gray and gloomy, and Viscount Buckley, surrounded by all the foolish sights of Christmas, his nostrils assailed by all the smells of it, felt his irritation return. Because she—Miss Jane Craggs, the tyrant—had persuaded him into the madness of allowing a party for young people to take place in his home tomorrow, he had been faced with the necessity of absenting himself from that home. And so he was facing the unspeakable monotony of a Christmas gathering at the Oxendens'. He was being forced to enjoy himself.

Well, it could not be done. Just look at the weather. He did just that, standing at the window of his bedchamber, gazing out at raw, cheerless December.

But one hour later he felt foolish. How was it he had recognized none of the signs when they had been as plain as the nose on his face? For of course the grayness and the gloom were harbingers of snow, and before the morning was even half over, it was falling so thickly that he could scarcely see six feet beyond the window. And it was settling too, just like a white blanket being spread.

Good Lord, snow! He could not remember when it had last fallen at Christmastime. Certainly not the year Elise had humiliated him and broken his foolish young heart. It had been raining that year and blowing a gale. Typical British winter weather. This was not typical at all. He wondered if Veronica had seen the snow, and was halfway up the stairs to the nursery before he realized how strange it was that he had thought of sharing the sight of snow with a child. But he continued on his way.

They were all in there, Veronica and Deborah kneeling on the window seat, their noses pressed against the glass, Miss Craggs standing behind them.

"Look, my lord." She was the only one who had glanced back to see who was coming through the door. "Snow. We are going to have a white Christmas. Can you conceive of anything more wonderful?"

Sometime before she returned to Miss Phillpotts's school he was going to have to sit down and have a good talk with Miss Jane Craggs. There was something deep inside the woman that could occasionally break through to her face and make her almost incredibly beautiful. She was beautiful now, flushed and wide-eyed and animated. And all over the fact that it was snowing for Christmas.

He found himself wondering quite inappropriately what her face would look like as he was making love to her. Totally inappropriately! He had a mistress waiting for him in London with whose services he was more than satisfied. He had had her for only two months. He had not even begun to tire of her yet.

"I am trying," he said in belated answer to her question. "And at the moment I can think of nothing."

She smiled at him and his heart and his stomach danced a pas de deux.

Good Lord, he wanted her, the gray and prim Miss Craggs.

"Look, Papa," his daughter was saying. "Look at the trees. They are magic."

He strolled over to the window and stood almost shoulder-to-shoulder with Jane Craggs, looking out on a Christmas wonderland.

"And so they are," he said, setting his hand on the child's

soft curls. "I have just had a thought. There used to be sleds when I was a boy. I wonder what happened to them."

"Sleds?" Deborah turned her attention to him, "Oh, Uncle Warren, could we go sledding tomorrow? A sledding party? Do you think so? How many are there?"

"Wait a minute," he said, holding up one hand. "I am not even sure they still exist. I suppose you are going to insist that I get on my greatcoat and my topboots and wade out to the stables without further delay."

Yes. Three pairs of eyes confirmed him in his suspicions. And then three voices informed him that they were coming with him, and Jane Craggs was bundling Veronica inside her coat and winding her inside her scarf and burying her beneath her hat while Deborah darted out to don her own outdoor clothes.

"I knew," Miss Craggs said, looking up at him with a face that was still beautiful, "that this was going to be a perfect Christmas. I just knew it."

How could it be perfect for her, he wondered, when she had been brought here merely as a glorified servant to chaperon a sullen girl and then had been saddled with the responsibility of caring for an illegitimate child, whose presence in the house might well have offended her sensibilities? How could it be perfect when she was away from her own family?

But there was that light in her eyes and that beauty in her face, and he knew that she was not lying.

And he knew suddenly that for the first time in many years there was hope in him. The hope that somehow she might be right, that somehow this might be the perfect Christmas.

That somehow the magic might come back.

There were four sleds, three of them somewhat dilapidated. But he was assured that by the morrow they would be in perfect condition.

"Well, Veronica," he said as they were wading back to the house with the snow falling thickly about them and onto them, "are you going to ride on a sled tomorrow too? Faster than lightning down a hill?"

"No, Papa," she said.

"With me?" he asked her. "If I ride with you and hold you tight?"

"Yes, Papa," she said gravely.

He could not ask for a more docile and obedient child. Nancy had brought her up well. And yet he could not help remembering what Jane Craggs had said about her—that she was hiding inside herself. And wondering how she could know such a thing, if it were so. But he was beginning to believe that perhaps it was true. Over the past few days the child had joined in all the activities, and she had made a great friend of the kitchen cat, whom he had found curled impertinently in his favorite chair in the drawing room, of all places, just the day before. But there had been no exuberance in her as there had been in Deborah and even in Miss Craggs.

He was beginning to worry about Veronica. The sooner he found her a good home to go to, the better it would be for her. She needed a mother and father to care for her. As soon as Christmas was over he must set Aubrey to work on it. It must take priority over all else.

"Look at me," Deborah shrieked suddenly, and she hurled herself backward into a smooth drift of snow, swished her arms and legs to the sides, and got up carefully. "Look. A perfect angel."

"Which you assuredly are not," he said, looking at the snow caked all over her back.

She giggled at him. "I dare you to try it, Uncle Warren," she said.

"It certainly does not behoove my dignity to be making snow angels," he said.

But he did it anyway because it had never been his way to resist a dare. And then they were all doing it until they had a whole army of angels fast disappearing beneath the still-falling snow. Like a parcel of children, he thought in some disgust, instead of two adults, one young person, and one child.

"This must be the multitude of the heavenly host that sang with the angel Gabriel to Mary," he said. "I do not know about the rest of you, but I have snow trickling down my neck and turning to water. It does not feel comfortable at all. I think hot drinks at the house are called for."

"Veronica has made the best angels," Deborah said generously. "Look how dainty they are."

It was the first time she had mentioned his daughter by name, the viscount thought.

"That is because she is a real little angel," he said, stooping down impulsively and sweeping the child up into his arms. "Are you cold, Veronica?"

"A little, Papa," she admitted.

She weighed almost nothing at all. He tightened his hold on her and realized something suddenly. He was going to miss her when she went away. He was always going to be wondering if she were happy, if she were being loved properly, if she were hiding inside herself.

"Snuggle close," he said. "I shall have you inside where it is warm before you know it."

Miss Craggs, he noticed, was watching him with shining eyes—and shining red nose. She looked more beautiful than ever. Which was a strange thought to have when, really, she was not beautiful at all.

At first she was going to go to church alone. It was something she had always done on Christmas Eve and something she wanted to do more than ever here. She had seen the picturesque stone church on her journeys to the village. And the thought of trudging through snow in order to reach it was somehow appealing. It would bring another part of her dream to life.

She asked Veronica at dinner—the child still ate in the dining room with the adults—if she would mind not being sat with tonight until she slept. Jane explained her reason.

"I promise to look in on you as soon as I return," she said.

But Veronica looked at her rather wistfully. "May I come too, Miss Jane?" she asked.

It would be very late for a child to be up, but Viscount Buckley immediately gave his permission and announced his intention of attending church, too. And then Deborah wondered aloud if Mr. George Oxenden would be at church, blushed, and declared that anyway she always enjoyed a Christmas service.

And so they walked together the mile to the church, the snow being rather too deep for the carriage wheels, Veronica between Jane and the viscount, holding to a hand of each, while Deborah half tripped along beside them. And they sat together in church, Veronica once again between the two adults until, after a series of yawns, she climbed onto Jane's lap and snuggled close. Jane was unable to stand for the final hymn, but she sat holding the child, thinking about the birth of the Christ child and understanding for the first time the ecstasy Mary must have felt to have her baby even though she had had to give birth far from home and inside a stable.

Christmas, Jane thought, was the most wonderful, wonderful time of the year.

They walked home after the viscount had greeted his neighbors and Deborah had chatted with her new friends, the Oxenden sisters, and had been rewarded with a nod and a smile and a Christmas greeting from their elder brother. Jane sat holding the sleeping child on her lap while she waited for them.

And then Viscount Buckley was bending over her in the pew and opening his greatcoat and lifting his daughter into his own arms and wrapping the coat about her. Jane smiled at him. Oh, he felt it too. What a tender paternal gesture! He loved the child and would keep her with him. Of course he would. It was something she, Jane, would be able to console herself with when she was back at Miss Phillpotts's. Though she would not think of that. Not yet. She was going to have her one wonderful Christmas first.

And wonderful it was too, she thought as they approached the house in a night that was curiously bright despite the fact that there were clouds overhead—more snow clouds. It was her dream come true, even though not every window in the house blazed with light. But close enough to her dream to make her believe for once in her life in miracles.

Deborah was yawning and ready for bed by the time they reached the house. She went straight to her room. Veronica stirred and grumbled in her father's arms as he carried her upstairs. Jane followed him and undressed the child in her bedchamber while he waited in the nursery. He came to stand in the doorway as he always did after Jane had tucked her up in bed. She was only half-awake.

"Good night, Mama," she said.

Jane could hardly speak past the ache in her throat. "Good night, sweetheart," she said softly.

"Good night, Papa."

"Good night, Veronica," he said.

Jane sat for a few minutes on the side of the bed, though it was obvious that the child had slipped back into sleep. She was too embarrassed to face the viscount. But when she rose and turned to leave the room, she found that he was still standing in the doorway.

"I ordered hot cider sent to the library," he said. "Come with me there?"

She longed to be able to escape to her room. Or a part of her did, anyway—that part that was flustered and even frightened at the thought of being alone with him. But the other part of herself, the part that was living and enjoying this Christmas to the full, leaped with gladness. She was going to sit and talk with him again? She only hoped that she would be able to think of something to say, that her mind would not turn blank.

When they reached the library, he motioned her to the chair she had occupied once before. He ladled hot cider into two glasses and handed her one before seating himself at the other side of the fire.

She had never drunk cider before. It was hot and tasted of cinnamon and other, unidentified spices. It was delicious. She looked into the glass and concentrated her attention on it. She could not think of anything to say. She wished she had made some excuse after all and gone to bed.

"You were going to spend Christmas alone at the school?" he asked her.

"Yes." She looked up at him unwillingly.

"Where does your family live?" he asked. "Was it too far for you to travel?"

She had never talked about herself. There was nothing to talk about. She could be of no possible interest to anyone except herself.

"I have no family," she said. She was not particularly given to self-pity, either. But the words sounded horribly forlorn. She looked down into her drink again.

"Ah," he said, "I am sorry. Have they been long deceased?"

"I believe," she said after rejecting her first impulse, which was to invent a mythical warm and loving family, "I was the product of a union much like yours and Veronica's mother's. I do not know who my mother was. I believe she must have died when I was very young. Or perhaps she merely did not want to be burdened with me. I do not know my father, either. He put me into an orphanage until I was old enough to go to Miss Phillpotts's school. He supported me there until I was seventeen. I have earned my way there since."

He said nothing for a long time. She kept her eyes on her drink, but she did not lift it to her mouth. She knew her hand would shake if she tried it.

"You have never known a family," he said very quietly at last.

"No." But she did not want him to think that she was trying to enlist his pity. "The orphanage was a good one. The school is an expensive one. He cared enough to make sure that my material needs were catered to and that I had a good enough education to make my way in the world."

"But you stayed at the school," he said. "Why?"

How could she explain that, cold and cheerless as it was, the school was the only home she had known, that it was the only anchor in her existence? How could she explain how the thought of being cast adrift in unfamiliar surroundings, without even the illusion of home and family, terrified her?

"I suppose," she said, "I drifted into staying there."

"In an environment that is wholly female," he said. "Have you never wanted to find yourself a husband and have a family of your own, Miss Craggs?"

Oh, it was a cruel question. How could she find a husband for herself? Even if she left Miss Phillpotts's, what could she hope to do except teach somewhere else or perhaps be someone's governess? There was no hope of matrimony for someone like her. And a family of her own? How could she even dream of a family when there was no possibility of a husband?

To her annoyance, she could think of no answer to make. And in her attempt to cover up her confusion, she lifted her glass to her lips, forgetting that her hand would shake. It did so and she had to lower the glass, the cider untasted. She wondered if he had noticed.

"How did you know," he asked, seeming to change the subject, "that Veronica hides inside herself? I begin to think you must be right, but how did you realize it?"

"She is too quiet, too docile, too obedient for a child," she said.

"Did you know it from experience?" he asked.

"I . . ." She swallowed. "Is this an interrogation, my lord? I am not accustomed to talking about myself."

"Why not?" he asked. "Does no one ever ask you about yourself? Does Miss Phillpotts believe she does you a favor by keeping you on at the school? And do the teachers and pupils take their cue from her? Do they all call you Craggs, as Deborah did until recently? Does no one call you Jane?"

For some reason she felt as if she had been stabbed to the heart. There was intense pain.

"Teachers are not usually called by their first names," she said.

"But teachers should have identities apart from their career," he said. "Should they not, Jane? For how long have you been in hiding?"

"Please." She set her hardly tasted cider on the small table beside her and got to her feet. "It is late, my lord. It is time for me to say good night."

"Have I been very impertinent, Jane?" He too stood, and somehow he possessed himself of both her hands. "No, you do not need to answer. I have been impertinent and it has been unpardonable of me when you are a guest in my home and when you have been very kind to both Deborah and my daughter and when you have brought Christmas to this house for the first time in years. Forgive me?"

"Of course," she said, trying to draw her hands free of his without jerking on them. She felt again as if she were suffocating. His closeness and his maleness were overpowering her. "It is nothing, my lord."

"It is something," he said. "It is just that you have intrigued me during the past few days, Jane. You are like two people. Much of the time you are a disciplined, prim and—forgive me—plain teacher. But sometimes you are eager and warm and quite incredibly beautiful. I have been given the impression that the latter person has come bubbling up from very deep within. Is she the real person, the one you hide from the world, the one you have never had a chance to share with anyone else?"

"Please." She dragged at her hands but was unable to free them. Her voice, she noticed in some dismay, sounded thin and distressed. She sounded on the verge of tears.

"He was a fool, your father," he said. "He had you to love and let opportunity pass him by."

She forgot herself instantly. She looked up into his face,

her eyes wide. "And are you going to make the same mistake?" she asked. "You too have a daughter to love."

"But the situation is different," he said. "I am not going to abandon her to an orphanage or a school. I am going to find her the very best parents I can."

"But she is four years old," Jane said. "Do you not think she will remember, however hazily? She will remember that her mother disappeared mysteriously and she will try to persuade herself that she died and did not merely abandon her. You need to tell her the truth. However cruel it seems now, she needs to know. And she will remember that her father was titled and wealthy and that he cared enough to provide for her physical needs but did not care enough to provide for the only need that mattered."

"And that is?" He was frowning and she thought that perhaps he was angry. But so was she. She would answer his question.

"The need for love," she said. "The need to know that to someone she means more than anything else in the world."

"But she is illegitimate." He was almost whispering. "She is the daughter I fathered on a mistress. Do you understand, Jane? Do you know anything about what is acceptable and what is not in polite society?"

"Yes," she said. "Oh, yes, I know, my lord. I am such a daughter too, remember. No one in my memory has ever wanted to know me as a person. No one has ever hugged me. Or kissed me. No one has ever loved me. I am three-and-twenty now, old enough to bear the burdens of life alone, but I would not want another child to have to live the life I have lived. Not Veronica. I hope she will remember that you have kissed her cheek and rubbed your hand in her hair and carried her home from church inside your greatcoat. I am not sure it will help a great deal, but I hope she remembers even so. I wish I had such memories."

"Jane," he said, his voice shaken. "Oh, my poor Jane."

And before she knew what was to happen or could do anything to prevent it, his hands had released hers and grasped her by the shoulders instead, and he had pulled her against him. And before her mind could cope with the shock of feeling a man's warm and firmly muscled body against her own, his mouth was on hers, warm and firm, his lips slightly parted.

For a moment—for a fleeting moment after her mind had recovered from its first shock—she surrendered to the heady physical sensation of being embraced by a man and to the realization that she was experiencing her first real kiss. And then she got her palms against his chest and pushed firmly away from him.

"No," she said. "No, my lord, it is not poor Jane. It is poor Veronica. She has a father who could love her, I believe, but who feels that the conventions of society are of greater importance than love."

She did not give him a chance to reply though he reached for her again. She whisked herself about and out of the room and fled upstairs to her bedchamber as if being pursued by a thousand devils.

It had snowed a little more during the night. The viscount stood at his window, eager to go downstairs to begin the day, yet wanting at the same time to stay where he was until he could safely escape to the Oxendens' house. He wanted to go downstairs because he had told her the truth last night. She had brought Christmas to his home for the first time in many years, and he found himself hungry for it. And yet he dreaded seeing her this morning after his unpardonable indiscretion of the night before. And he dreaded seeing Veronica. He dreaded being confronted with love. He had decided six years ago to the day that he must be incapable of loving enough to satisfy another person. He had confined his feelings since then to friendships and to lust.

She was wrong. It was not that he put the conventions of society before love as much as that he did not believe he could love his daughter as well as a carefully chosen couple would. He wanted Veronica to have a happy childhood. Because he loved her. He tested the thought in his mind, but he could not find fault with it. He did love her. The thought of giving her up to another couple was not a pleasant one. And that was an understatement.

He was the first one downstairs. Before going to the breakfast room he went into the drawing room to take the parcels he had bought in a visit to a nearby town two days before and a few he had brought home with him and to set them down beside the rudely carved but curiously lovely Nativity scene with its Mary and Joseph and babe in a manger and a single shepherd and lamb. They had been set up last night. He was seeing them for the first time.

He looked about the room. And he thought of his irritation at finding himself saddled with his niece for Christmas and of her sullenness at being abandoned by her parents and left to his care. And of the terrible aloneness of Veronica as she had sat in his hall, like a labeled parcel abandoned until someone could find time to open it.

Yes, Jane had transformed his home and the three of them who lived in it with her. Under the most unpromising of circumstances she had brought the warmth and joy of Christmas. He wondered if it was something she was accustomed to doing. But he knew even as he thought it that that was not it at all. If she had been about to spend Christmas alone at the school this year, then surely she must have spent it alone there last year and the year before. His heart chilled. Had she ever spent Christmas in company with others? Had she always been alone?

Was all the love of her heart, all the love of her life being poured out on this one Christmas she was spending with strangers? With three other waifs like herself? But she was so much stronger than they. Without her, he felt, the rest of them would have wallowed in gloom.

But his thoughts were interrupted. Deborah burst into the room, parcels in her hands. She set them beside his and turned to smile at him.

"Happy Christmas, Uncle Warren," she said. "Veronica is

up. Craggs—*Miss* Craggs—is dressing her and brushing her hair. They will be down soon. I wish they would hurry. I have presents for everyone. I bought them in the village shop. And you have presents too. Is there one for me?"

"Yes." He grinned at her. "Happy Christmas, Deborah."

And then they came into the room, hand in hand, Jane and Veronica, and his heart constricted at sight of them. His two ladies. Jane was carrying two parcels. Veronica was saucer-eyed.

And finally it was there again, full-grown—the glorious wonder of Christmas in a young child's eyes, which were fixed on the Nativity scene and on the parcels beside it. He hurried across the room to her and stooped down without thought to lift her into his arms.

"Happy Christmas, Veronica," he said, and kissed her on her soft little lips. "Someone brought the baby Jesus with his mama and papa during the night. And someone brought gifts, too. I will wager some of them are yours."

Jane, he saw, had hurried across the room to set down her parcels with the rest.

"For me?" Veronica asked, her eyes growing wider still.

He sat her on his knee close to the gifts, feeling absurdly excited himself, almost as if he were a boy again. And he watched her as she unwrapped the dainty lace-edged handkerchief Deborah had bought for her and held it against her cheek, and the pretty red bonnet and muff Jane had bought her, both of which she had to try on. And then he watched her, his heart beating almost with nervousness, as she unwrapped his exquisitely dressed porcelain doll.

"Oh!" she said after staring at it in silence for a few moments. "Look what I have, Papa. Look what I have, Miss Jane. Look, Deborah."

Viscount Buckley blinked several times, aware of the acute embarrassment of the fact that he had tears in his eyes. And yet when he sneaked a look at Jane, it was to find that her own eyes were brimming with tears.

"She is beautiful, Veronica," she said.

"Lovely," Deborah agreed with enthusiasm.

"Almost as beautiful as you," her father assured her. "What are you going to call her?"

"Jane," his daughter said without hesitation.

And then Deborah opened her gifts and exclaimed with delight over the perfume Jane had given her and with awe over the diamond-studded watch her parents had left for her and with warm appreciation over the evening gloves and fan her uncle had bought for her—because she was as close to being adult as made no difference, he explained. She declared that she would wear them to the dance that evening.

Viscount Buckley unwrapped a linen handkerchief from Deborah and a silver-backed brush and comb from his sister and brother-in-law.

And he watched as Jane unwrapped her own lace-edged handkerchief from Deborah and smiled rather teary-eyed at the girl. And then he watched more keenly as she took out his cashmere shawl from its wrapping and held it up in front of her, its folds falling free. She bit her lip and shut her eyes very tightly for a few moments.

"It is the most beautiful thing I have ever seen," she said before turning to him, her face looking almost agonized. "Thank you. But I have nothing for you. I did not think it would be seemly."

Veronica had wriggled off his lap and was gazing down with Deborah into the manger at the baby Jesus, her doll clutched in both arms. Deborah was explaining to her what swaddling clothes were.

"You have given me a gift beyond price, Jane," he said quietly, for her ears only. "You have opened my eyes to Christmas again and all its meanings. I thank you."

She gazed back at him, the shawl suspended in front of her from her raised arms.

But Deborah had decided it was time for breakfast and was assuring Veronica that she could bring her doll along and they would find it a chair to sit on and a bowl to eat from. His niece seemed to have quite got over her shock at being exposed to the company of his illegitimate daughter.

"Come," he said to Jane, getting to his feet and extending a hand to her, "let us eat and then we must have the servants up here for their gifts. They will doubtless be happy to see that I can do it without a frown this year."

He smiled at her and she smiled rather tremulously back.

Once, when she was seventeen, Miss Phillpotts had given her a porcelain thimble in recognition of her new status as a teacher. It was the only gift she had ever received—until today. Jane set down her handkerchief and her shawl carefully on her bed, as if they too were of porcelain and might break, smoothed a hand over each, and swallowed back her tears so that she would not have to display reddened eyes when she left her room.

But the best gift of all was what he had said to her. *You have given me a gift beyond price, Jane.* And he had smiled at her. And he had held Veronica on his knee and had looked at her with what was surely tenderness.

Going back to Miss Phillpotts's, being alone again, was going to be more painful than ever, she knew, now that she had had a taste of family life, now that she had fallen in—No, that was a silly idea. That she would have fallen in love with him was thoroughly predictable under the circumstances. It was not real love, of course. But however it was, she would put up with all the pain and all the dreariness, she felt, if only she could know that he would keep Veronica with him. She would give up all claim to future Christmases without a murmur if only she could be sure of that.

It was a busy day, a wonderfully busy day. There were the servants to greet in the drawing room while Viscount Buckley gave each of them a gift, and toasts to be drunk with them and rich dainties to eat. And there were gifts from almost all of them for Veronica to open. It was certainly clear that his staff had taken the viscount's young daughter to their hearts. And there were carols to sing.

After the Christmas dinner, taken *en famille* in the dining room very early in the afternoon, there were the young guests to prepare for. There was no containing Deborah's excitement. As soon as they had arrived, all of them bright and merry at the novel prospect of a party all to themselves without adults to spoil it and tell them to quieten down or to stay out of the way, they were whisked out-of-doors.

They engaged in an unruly snowball fight even before they reached the hill where the sledding was to take place. Deborah, Jane noticed with indulgent interest, was almost elbow-to-elbow with Mr. George Oxenden, the two of them fighting the common enemy, almost everyone else. But before she knew it, Jane was fighting for her own life, or at least for her own comfort. A soft snowball splattered against her shoulder, and she found that Viscount Buckley was grinning smugly at her from a few yards away. She shattered the grin when by some miracle her own snowball collided with the center of his face.

Jane found herself giggling quite as helplessly as Deborah was doing.

The sleds were much in demand when they reached the hill as the young people raced up the slope with reckless energy and then zoomed down two by two. Nobody complained about the cold even though there was a great deal of foot stamping and hand slapping against sides. And even though everyone sported fiery red cheeks and noses.

Veronica stood quietly watching, holding Jane's hand.

"Well, Veronica," her father said, coming to stand beside them, "what do you think? Shall we try it?"

"We will fall," she said, looking gravely up at him.

"What?" he said. "You do not trust my steering skills? If we fall, we will be covered with snow. Is that so bad?"

"No, Papa," she said, looking dubious.

"Well." He held out a hand for hers. "Shall we try?"

"Can Miss Jane come too?" Veronica asked.

Jane grimaced and found the viscount's eyes directed at her. They were twinkling. "It might be something of a squash," he said. "But I am willing if you two ladies are."

"I . . . I . . ." Jane said.

"What?" His eyebrows shot up. "Do we have a coward here? Shall we dare Miss Jane to ride on a sled with us, Veronica?"

"Yes, Papa," his daughter said.

And so less than five minutes later Jane found herself at the top of the hill, seating herself gingerly on one of the sleds, which suddenly looked alarmingly narrow and frail, and having to move back to make room for Veronica until her back was snug against the viscount's front. His arms came about her at either side to arrange the steering rope. And suddenly, too, it no longer seemed like a cold winter day. She was only half aware of the giggles of the young ladies and the whistles and jeers and cheers of the young gentlemen. She set her arms tightly about Veronica.

And then they were off, hurtling down a slope that seemed ten times steeper than it had looked from the bottom, at a speed that seemed more than ten times faster than that of the other sledders when she had watched them. Two people were shrieking, Veronica and herself. And then they were at the bottom and the sled performed a complete turn, flirted with the idea of tipping over and dumping its load into the snow, and slid safely to a halt.

Veronica's shrieks had turned to laughter—helpless, joyful, childish laughter. The viscount, the first to rise to his feet, scooped her up and held her close and met Jane's eyes over her shoulder. Perhaps it was the wind and the cold that had made his eyes so bright, but Jane did not think so.

Oh, how good it was—it was the best moment so far of a wonderful Christmas—how very good it was to hear the child laugh. And beg to be taken up again. And wriggle to get down and grab at her father's hand and tug him impatiently in the direction of the slope. And to watch her ride down again with him, shrieking and laughing once more.

And how good it was—how achingly good—to see him laughing and happy with the little child he had fathered almost five years before but had not even seen until a few days ago.

Chilly as she was—her hands and her feet were aching

with the cold—Jane willed the afternoon to last forever. He
was to go to the Oxendens' for dinner and he was to spend
the evening there and perhaps half the night too. Once he
had gone she would be the lone chaperon of the group,
apart from the lady who was coming to play the pianoforte.
She was going to feel lonely.

But she quelled the thought. She had had so much, more
than she had ever dreamed. She must not be greedy. This
evening was for the young people.

And then, just before it was mutually agreed that it was
time to return to the house to thaw out and partake of some
of Cook's hot Christmas drinks and mince pies, Veronica
was borne off by Deborah to ride a sled with her and Mr.
Oxenden, and Viscount Buckley took Jane firmly by one
hand and led her toward the slope.

"If you stand there any longer," he said, "you may well
become frozen to the spot. Come and sled with me now that
I have relearned the knack of doing it safely."

She savored the moment, this final moment of her very
own Christmas. But alas, this time they were not so fortunate. Perhaps the constant passing of the sleds had made
the surface over which they sped just too slippery for successful navigation. Or perhaps there was some other cause.
However it was, something went very wrong when they
were halfway down the slope. The sled went quite out of
control, and its two riders were unceremoniously dumped
into a bank of soft, cold snow. They rolled into it, arms and
legs all tangled together.

They finally came to rest with Jane on the bottom, flat
on her back, and Viscount Buckley on top of her. They
were both laughing and then both self-conscious. His eyes
slid to her mouth at the same moment as hers slid to his.
But for a moment only. The delighted laughter of the young
people brought them to their senses and their feet, and they
both brushed vigorously at themselves and joined in the
laughter.

Jane was tingling with warmth again. If only, she
thought shamelessly. If only there had been no one else in

sight. If only he had kissed her again. Just once more. One more kiss to hug to herself for the rest of her life.

Oh, she really had become greedy, she told herself severely. Would she never be satisfied?

An unwanted inner voice answered her. No, not any longer. She never would.

But it was time to take Veronica by the hand again. It was time to go back to the house.

Viscount Buckley went upstairs to change into his evening clothes while the young people played charades in the drawing room and Jane played unobtrusively in one corner with Veronica and her new doll, the kitchen cat curled beside them, apparently oblivious to the loud mirth proceeding all about it. He had lingered in the room himself, reluctant to leave despite the squeals from the girls and loud laughter from the boys that just a few days before he had welcomed the thought of escaping. But he could delay no longer if he were to arrive at the Oxendens' in good time for dinner.

Yet despite the fact that he was pressed for time, he wandered to the window of his bedchamber after his valet had exercised all his artistic skills on the tying of his neckcloth and had helped him into his blue evening coat, as tight as a second skin, according to fashion. He stood gazing out at twilight and snow, not really seeing either.

He was seeing Veronica in her red Christmas bonnet, her muff on a ribbon about her neck. He was seeing her rosy-cheeked with the cold, bright-eyed and laughing, and tugging impatiently at his hand. Looking and sounding like a four-year-old. And he was thinking of her next week or the week after or the week after that, going away to settle with her new family.

He was going to be lonely. He was going to grieve for her for the rest of his life. And if Jane was correct, he was not even doing what was best for Veronica.

Jane! He could see her too, animated and giggling—yes,

giggling!—and beautiful. Ah, so beautiful, his prim, plain Jane. And he thought of her the week after next, returning to Miss Phillpotts's school with Deborah, returning to her life of drudgery and utter aloneness. She had never been hugged or kissed or loved, she had said—not out of self-pity but in an attempt to save Veronica from such a fate.

He was going to be lonely without Jane. He thought of his mistress, waiting for him in London with her luscious, perfumed body, and of the skills she used to match his own in bed. But he could feel no desire, no longing for her. He wanted Jane with her inevitable gray dress and her nondescript figure and her face that was plain except when she stopped hiding inside herself. Jane, who did not even know how to kiss—she pursed her lips and kept them rigidly closed. She probably did not know what happened between a man and a woman in bed.

He wanted her.

And he wanted to keep Veronica.

His valet cleared his throat from the doorway into his dressing room and informed him that the carriage was waiting. The viscount knew it was waiting. He had been aware of it below him on the terrace for at least the past ten minutes. The horses, he saw now when he looked down, were stamping and snorting, impatient to be in motion.

"Have it returned to the carriage house," he heard himself say, "and brought up again after dinner. I had better stay here and help Miss Craggs with the young people at dinner. They are rather exuberant and unruly."

That last word was unfair. And what the devil was he doing explaining himself to his valet?

"Yes, m'lord," the man said, and withdrew.

Well, that was the excuse he would give the Oxendens later, he thought, as he hurried from the room and downstairs to the drawing room, lightness in his step. It would seem an eminently believable excuse.

And so he sat at the head of the table during dinner, the second of the day, while Jane sat at the foot, Veronica beside her, and the young people were ranged along the two long sides. And he listened indulgently to all their silly chatter and laughter without once wincing with distaste. And he feasted his stomach on rich foods, which it just did not need, and feasted his eyes on his two ladies, who were both making sure that the doll Jane was having her fair share of each course.

And then it was time for the young people and their chaperon to adjourn to the drawing room. The servants had rolled back the carpet during dinner, and Mrs. Carpenter had arrived to provide music for the dancing. Vernoica was to be allowed to stay up and watch until she was sleepy. And he was to go to the Oxendens'. The carriage was waiting for him again.

But what if any of the silly children decided to imitate their elders and disappear in couples to more remote locations? What if young George Oxenden, in particular, decided to become amorous with Deborah? They had been flirting quite outrageously with each other all afternoon. He had even spotted the young man kissing her beneath the mistletoe she had deliberately stood under. How could Jane handle all that alone when she had Veronica to look after too?

No, he could not leave her alone. It would be grossly unfair when he was the master of the house—and when Susannah and Miles had entrusted Deborah to his care.

"Have the carriage sent away," he told his butler. "I will not be needing it this evening after all." He smiled fleetingly in self-mockery. This was the most blatant example of rationalization he had ever been involved in. And he must have windmills in the brain. He was choosing to party with young people rather than with sane adults?

No, actually he was choosing to party with his lady and his daughter.

They had danced a quadrille and numerous country dances. All the young people danced every set. They were clearly enjoying the novelty of being able to use the skills they had learned from dancing masters in the setting of a real ball—or what was almost a real ball.

Jane was feeling wonderfully happy as she watched and as she played with an increasingly tired Veronica. The child did not want to give in to suggestions that she be taken up to bed. At the moment she was seated cross-legged on the floor beside the Nativity scene, rocking her doll to sleep in her arms and looking as if she was not far from sleep herself.

But what completed Jane's happiness was the fact that for some reason Viscount Buckley had not gone to the Oxendens' after all but had stayed at the house. He had mingled with the company and chatted with Mrs. Carpenter between dances and had not been near Jane and Veronica. But it did not matter. Just having him in the room, just being able to feast her eyes on him, was enough. He looked even more splendidly handsome than usual in a pale blue evening coat with gray knee breeches and white linen and lace.

She thought with secret, guilty wonder of the fact that she had been kissed by this man. And that she had his gift, the lovely shawl, to hug about her—literally—for the rest of her life.

He was bending over Mrs. Carpenter, speaking to her, and she was nodding and smiling. He turned to his young guests and clapped his hands to gain their attention.

"This is to be a waltz, ladies and gentlemen," he said. "Do you all know the steps?"

They all did. But the young ladies in particular had not expected to be able to dance them in public for many years, until they had made their come-outs and had been approved by the patronesses of Almack's in London. There was a buzz of excitement.

Jane knew the steps of the waltz too. She remembered with an inward shudder demonstrating it for the girls at school with the dancing master, whose hands had always seemed too hot and too moist, and who had always tried to cause her to stumble against him. But it was a wonderful dance. Wonderfully romantic—a couple dancing face-to-face, their hands touching each other.

"Jane?" Suddenly he was there before her, bowing elegantly as if she were the Duchess of Somewhere, and extending a hand toward her. "Will you do me the honor?"

"Me?" she said foolishly, spreading a hand over her chest.

He smiled at her and something strange happened to her knees and someone had sucked half the air out of the room.

"Thank you." She set her hand in his and he looked down at Veronica.

"Do you mind if I steal Miss Jane for a few minutes?" he asked. "Will you watch us dance?"

Veronica yawned.

Jane had dreamed of happiness and romance and pleasure. But never until this ten-minute period had she had even the glimmering of a notion of what any of the three might really feel like. They were almost an agony. She danced—he was an exquisite dancer—and felt that her feet scarcely touched the floor. She danced and did not even have to think about the steps. She danced and was unaware that the room held anyone else but the two of them and the music. She was too happy even to wish that time would stop so that forever she would be caught up in the waltz with the man she had so foolishly fallen in love with.

To say it was the happiest ten minutes of her life was so grossly to understate the case that the words would be meaningless.

"Thank you," she said when it was over, coolly, as if it really had not meant a great deal to her at all. "I think I should take Veronica up to bed, my lord. She is very tired."

"Yes," he said, glancing down at his child. "Take her up, then. I will come in ten minutes or so to say good night to her."

And so the magic was gone and the day was almost over. She took the sleepy child by the hand and led her up to the nursery, undressed her and washed her quickly, helped her into her nightgown, and tucked her into bed beside her doll.

"Good night, sweetheart," she said, smoothing back the child's curls with one gentle hand. "Has it been a happy Christmas?"

Veronica nodded, though she did not open her eyes and she did not speak. And then Jane's heart lurched with alarm. Two tears had squeezed themselves from between the child's eyelids and were rolling diagonally across her cheeks.

Jane turned instinctively toward the door. He was standing there, as he did each night. When he saw her face, he looked more closely at his daughter. Jane could tell that he could see the tears. His face paled and he came walking across the room toward the bed.

He did not know what to do for a moment. She had seemed so happy for most of the day. She had been laughing and excited during the afternoon. What had happened to upset her? And how could he cope with whatever it was?

"Veronica?" He touched his fingers to her cheek. "What is it?"

She kept her eyes closed and did not answer him for a while. But more tears followed the first. There was something horrifying about a child crying silently. Jane had got up from the bed to stand behind him.

"Why did Mama not come?" his daughter asked finally. "Why was there no present from Mama?"

Oh, God. Oh, dear Lord God, he could not handle this. He sat down on the bed in the spot just vacated by Jane. "Mama had to go far away," he said, cupping the little face with his hands and wiping the tears away with his thumbs. "She would be here if she could, dear. She loves you dearly." He rejected the idea of telling her that the doll was from her mother. Children were usually more intelligent than adults gave them credit for.

His daughter was looking at him suddenly. "Is she dead?" she asked.

A denial was on his lips. And then Jane's words came back to him. She needed to know. Ultimately it would be worse for her not to know, for her to grow up believing that her mother had just tired of her and abandoned her. He stood up for a moment, drew back the bedclothes, scooped up his daughter in his arms, and sat down again, cradling her against him.

"Yes," he said. "She died, Veronica. But she sent you to Papa. And Papa loves you more than anyone or anything else in this world."

She was sobbing then with all of a child's abandoned woe. And he, rocking her in his arms, was crying too. Crying over his daughter's loss and grief. Crying over the truth of the words he had just spoken, and over the treasure he had so very nearly given carelessly away.

She stopped crying eventually and lay quietly in his arms. "You are not going to send me away, Papa?" she whispered.

"Send you away?" he said. "How could I do that? What would I do without my little girl? Who would there be to make me happy?"

She looked up at him with a wet and swollen face so that he was reaching into his pocket for a handkerchief even as she spoke. "Do you really love me, Papa?"

"You are my little Christmas treasure," he said, drying her eyes and her cheeks. "The best gift I ever had. I love you, dear."

She reached up to set one soft little hand against his lips. He held it there and kissed it and smiled at her. She yawned hugely and noisily. "Is Miss Jane going to stay too?" she asked.

He felt Jane shift position behind him.

"Yes," he said, "if I can persuade her to. Would you like that?"

"Yes, Papa," she said.

And in the way of children she was asleep. Asleep and safe and loved in her father's arms. He held her there for a few minutes until he was quite sure she would not wake and then stood to set her down carefully in her bed. Jane held the bedclothes back for him and then stepped aside again.

By the time he had tucked the blankets snugly about his daughter and bent to kiss her little mouth, Jane had disappeared.

It had been agreed that the young people could stay at Cosway until midnight. It was no surprise to anyone, then, when they did not actually leave until thirty minutes after the hour. After all, there had to be just one more dance to follow the last and then one more to follow that.

It was the best, the very best Christmas she had ever known, Deborah declared, dancing before her uncle and Jane in the hall after everyone had finally gone.

"But do not tell Mama and Papa," she said to the viscount, giggling, "or they will be hurt."

"It will be our secret," he said dryly. "Upstairs with you, now. It is long past your bedtime."

She pulled a face at him before kissing his cheek and dancing in the direction of the stairs. But she came back again and kissed Jane's cheek too, a little self-consciously. "I am glad you came here with me, Miss Craggs," she said. "Thank you."

"Good night." Jane smiled at her. And then, when the girl was only halfway up the stairs, Jane turned, fixed her eyes on the diamond pin Viscount Buckley wore in his neckcloth, and wished him a hasty good night too.

She was already on her way to the stairs when she felt her hand caught in his.

"Coward!" he said. "You really are a coward, Jane."

"I am tired," she said.

"And a liar," he said.

She looked at him indignantly. He was smiling.

"Into the library," he said, giving her no chance to protest. He was leading her there by the hand. "I have a job to offer you."

As Veronica's nurse? She was too afraid to hope for it, though he had assured his daughter that he would try to persuade her to stay. Oh, would he offer her the job? Could life have such wonder in store for her? After the child no longer needed a nurse, perhaps he would keep her on as a governess. But it was too soon to dream of the future when she was not even sure of the present.

"Jane." He closed the library door behind him and leaned against it. He was still holding her hand. Someone had lit the branch of candles in there.

"You really do not have to persuade me to stay," she said breathlessly. "Veronica will not even remember in the morning that you promised to do so. If you think me unsuitable for the job of nurse, I will understand. I have had no experience with young children. But I do love her, and I would do my very best if you would consider hiring me. But you must not feel obliged to do so." She stopped talking abruptly and looked down in some confusion.

"A nurse," he said. "I do indeed consider you unsuitable for the job, Jane. It was not what I had in mind at all."

She bit her upper lip, chagrined and shamed. Why, oh, why had she not kept her mouth shut?

"I was hoping you would take on the job of mother," he said. "Mother of Veronica and mother of my other children. My future children, that is."

She looked up at him sharply.

"And wife," he added. "My wife, Jane."

Oh. She gaped at him. "Me?" she said foolishly. "You want *me* to be your wife? But you cannot marry me. You know who and what I am."

"You and my daughter both," he said, smiling. "Two treasures. I love you, Jane. I have Veronica, thanks to your words of admonition and advice, and she is a priceless possession. But you can make my happiness complete by marrying me. Will you? I cannot blame you if you do not trust me. I am new to love. I have not trusted it for a long time. But I—"

"Oh," she said, her eyes wide, her heart beating wildly. "You *love* me? You love *me*? How can that be?"

"Because," he said, still smiling, "I have been playing hide-and-seek, Jane. I have not yet discovered all of you there is to discover. You have done an admirable job over the years of hiding yourself. But what I have seen dazzles me. You are beautiful, inside and out, and I want you for myself. Yes, I love you. Could you ever feel anything for me?"

"Yes," she said without hesitation. "Oh, yes. Oh, yes, my lord. I love you with all my heart."

Somehow his arms were clasped behind her waist and hers behind his neck. Only a part of her mind had grasped what he was saying to her and what he was asking of her. She knew that it would take a long time before the rest of her brain caught up to the knowledge.

"It is going to have to be Warren," he said. "Say it before I kiss you."

"Warren," she said.

It was a kiss that lasted a scandalous length of time. Before it was over she had allowed him to bend the whole of her body against his and she had responded to the coaxing of his lips and softened her own and even parted them. Before it was over she had allowed his tongue into her mouth and his hands on parts of her body she would have thought horrifyingly embarrassing to have touched. Before it was over she was weak with unfamiliar aches of desire.

"My love," he was saying against her mouth, "forgive me. I would not have you for the first time on the library floor. It will be on my bed upstairs on our wedding night. If . . ." He drew his head back and gazed at her with eyes that were heavy with passion and love—for her. "If there is to be a wedding night. Is there? Will you marry me?"

"Yes," she said, stunned. Had she not already said it? "Warren—"

But whatever she was about to say was soon forgotten as his mouth covered hers again and they moved perilously close after all to anticipating their wedding night.

After all, it was Christmas and they had both just discovered love and joy and romance. And the treasure of a child to love and nurture together.

It was Christmas. Christmas after a long, long time for him. The first Christmas ever for her.

It was Christmas.

PLAYING
HOUSE

The logs in the fireplace were crackling and shooting sparks up into the chimney. The fire's warmth felt good to the young lady who had just come in from the cold and the wind and rain. She held her hands out to the blaze.

But she could not draw a great deal of comfort from the fire. She caught sight of the hem of her wool dress. It was heavy with wetness and streaked with mud. Her half boots looked no better. And she wished she had not removed her bonnet and handed it to the footman with her cloak. Her hair was hopelessly damp and flattened to her head. And she knew that her nose as well as her cheeks must be glowing red.

It was cold outside, and the mile-and-a-half walk across the park to Bedford Hall had been taken into the teeth of the wind and into the driving force of the rain and had seemed more like five miles.

Lilias lowered her hands from the blaze and brushed nervously at her dress. The darned patch near the hem was more noticeable now that the fabric was wet. She looked down at her right wrist and twisted her sleeve so that the darn there would be out of sight.

She should not have come. She had known that as soon as the footman had opened the front doors and asked her, after she stepped inside, if he could take her to Mrs. Morgan. But no, she had replied with a firmness that had been fast deserting her, she was not calling on the housekeeper today. She wished to speak with his lordship, if it was convenient.

She should not have come, a single lady, alone, to speak with a single gentleman. She knew she would never have dared to do so if she were in London or some other fashionable center. Even here in the country it was not at all the thing. She should have brought someone with her, though there was no one to bring except the children. And she did not want them to know she was paying this call.

And who was she, even if she had had a respectable companion, to be paying a call on the Marquess of Bedford? She was wearing her best day dress, yet it was patched in three places. She had had to walk from the village because she owned no conveyance or even a horse or pony. In two weeks' time she was to be a servant.

She should have come to the kitchen entrance, not to the main doors.

Lilias took one step back from the fireplace, suddenly feeling uncomfortably warm. If she hurried, she could grab her cloak and bonnet from the hallway and be outside and on her way home before any more harm was done. The rain and wind would be at her back on the return journey.

But she was too late. The door to the salon in which she had been asked to wait opened even before she could take one more step toward it, and he stepped inside. Someone closed the door quietly behind him.

The Marquess of Bedford.

Lilias swallowed and unconsciously raised her chin. She clasped her hands before her and dropped into a curtsy. She would scarcely have known him. He looked taller, and he was certainly broader. He bore himself very straight, like a soldier, though he had never been one. He was immaculately and fashionably dressed. His hair was as thick as it had ever been, but its darkness was highlighted now by the suggestion of silver at the temples. But he was not thirty yet.

His face was what had changed most. It looked as if carved out of marble, his jaw firm and hard, his lips thin and straight, his blue eyes above the aquiline nose heavy-lidded and cold. One eyebrow was arched somewhat higher than the other.

He made her a stiff half bow. "Well, Miss Angove," he said in a voice that was softer, colder than the voice she remembered, "what an unexpected pleasure. You are the first of my neighbors to call upon me. All alone?"

"Yes, my lord," she said, clasping her hands more firmly before her and consciously resisting the impulse to allow them to fidget. "This is not a social call. I have a favor to ask."

One eyebrow rose even higher and his lips curved into the suggestion of a sneer. "Indeed?" he said, advancing farther into the room. "Well, at least you are honest about it. Have a seat, ma'am, and tell me how I may be of service to you."

She sat on the very edge of the chair closest to her and clasped her hands in her lap. Someone had tamed his hair, she thought irrelevantly. It had always waved in a quite unruly manner and had forever fallen across his forehead. It had been a habit of his to toss it back with a jerk of the head.

"It is not precisely a favor," she said, "but more in the way of the calling in of a debt."

He seated himself opposite her and looked at her inquiringly. His eyes had never used to be like this. They had been wide and sparkling eyes, mesmerizing even. But then, they were compelling now too. They regarded her with cynical contempt. Lilias glanced down nervously at her sleeve to find that the darned patch was staring accusingly up at her. But she did not twist the sleeve again. Perhaps he would not notice if she kept her hands still. Except that she felt that those eyes saw everything, even the larger darned patch beneath her left arm.

"When you were at school," she said, "and found your Latin lessons difficult, Papa helped you during your holidays. You used to come to the rectory every morning for two successive summers. Do you remember?" She did not wait for a reply. "You would not tell your own papa for fear that he would be disappointed in you. And Papa would accept no payment for your tuition. You told him—I was there when you said it—that you would always consider yourself in his debt, that you would repay him one day."

"And so I did say," he said in that quiet, cold voice. His expression did not change at all. "Your father has been dead for well over a year, has he not, Miss Angove? But I take it that the day of reckoning has come. What may I do for you?"

"I think less than the tuition for two summers would have cost you," she said hastily, wishing that she could keep her voice as cool as his. "I would not put myself in your debt."

His eyelids appeared to droop even lower over his eyes. "What may I do for you, ma'am?" he asked again.

"I want a Christmas for my brother and sister," she said raising her chin and looking very directly into his face. She could feel herself flushing.

Both his eyebrows rose. "An admirable wish," he said. "But it would seem that if you wait patiently for one more week, Christmas will come without my having to do anything about the matter."

"They are still children," she said. "My parents' second family, people have always called them. Philip and I were two years apart, and then there were eleven years before Andrew was born. And Megan came two years after that. They are only eleven and nine years old now. Just children. This is our last Christmas together. In two weeks' time we will all be separated. Perhaps we will never be together again. I want it to be a memorable Christmas." She was leaning forward in her chair. Her fingers were twining about one another.

"And how am I to help create this memorable Christmas?" he asked. His mouth was definitely formed into a sneer now. "Host a grand party? Grand parties are not in my style."

"No," she said, speaking quickly and distinctly. "I want a goose for Christmas dinner."

There was a short silence.

"Papa was not a careful manager," she continued. "There was very little money left when he died and now there is none left, or at least only enough to pay for our journeys in two weeks' time. The people of the village would help, of course, but they were so used to finding that Papa would not accept charity in any form that they now do not even offer. And perhaps they are right." Her chin rose again. "I have some of his pride."

"So," he said, "instead of asking charity, you have found someone who is in your debt."

"Yes," she said, and swallowed awkwardly again.

"And you want a goose for Christmas," he said. "Your needs are modest, ma'am. That is all?"

"And a doll for Megan," she said recklessly. "There is the most glorious one in Miss Pierce's window—all porcelain and satin and lace. I want that for Megan. She has never had a doll, except the rag one Mama made for her when she was a baby. I want her to have something really lovely and valuable to take with her."

"And for your brother?" he asked softly.

"Oh." She gazed at him wistfully. "A watch. A silver watch. But there are none in the village, and I would not know how to go about purchasing one for him. But it does not matter. Andrew is eleven and almost not a child any longer. He will understand, and he will be happy with the scarf and gloves I am knitting for him. The cost of a goose and the doll will not exceed the cost of tuition for two summers, I don't believe. Will it?"

"And for yourself?" he asked even more softly.

Lilias gazed down at her hands and reached out to twist the offending sleeve. "I don't want anything that will cost money," she said. "I want only the memory of one Christmas to take with me."

"Where are you going?" he asked.

She looked up at him. "Into Yorkshire," she said. "I have a post as a governess with a family there."

"Ah," he said. "And your brother and sister?"

"I have persuaded my grandfather to take Andrew," she said. "It took several letters, but finally he agreed to take him and send him to school. Sir Percy Angove, that is, Papa's father. The two of them never communicated after Papa's marriage."

The marquess nodded curtly.

"And Megan is going to Great-aunt Hetty in Bath," Lilias said. "I am afraid I pestered her with letters too. But it will be only until I can earn enough money to bring us all together again."

Bedford got to his feet and looked down at her from cold and cynical eyes. "Ah, yes," he said. "A suitably affecting story, Miss Angove. I must congratulate you on the manner in which you have presented it."

Lilias looked up at him in some bewilderment.

His bearing was military again, his manner curt, his eyes like chips of ice. "You will have your goose, ma'am," he said, "and your sister her doll. Your brother will have his watch too—I shall see to it. You will have your Christmas and the memory of it to take into Yorkshire with you. I shall wish you good day now."

Victory? Was it to be so easy? Was she to have more than a Christmas dinner to give the children? Was Megan to have her doll? And Andrew his watch? Andrew was going to have a watch! All without any struggle, any persuasion, any groveling?

Was this victory?

Lilias scrambled to her feet and looked up at the tall, austere figure of the Marquess of Bedford. She curtsied. "What can I say?" she said breathlessly. "Thank you sounds so tame."

"You need not say even that," he said. "I am merely repaying a debt, after all. You will wait here, ma'am, if you please. I shall have tea sent to you while you await the arrival of my carriage to take you home. I take it you walked here?"

He would not take no for an answer, although there was no apparent kindness at all in his manner. Lilias found herself gazing once more into the fire a few minutes later, having been left to take her refreshments alone. And after drinking her tea, she was to have a warm and comfortable— and dry—ride home.

She should be feeling elated. She *was* feeling elated. But uncomfortable and humiliated too. As if, after all, she were taking charity. She blinked back tears and stared defiantly into the flames. She was not taking charity. She was merely accepting what was hers by right.

He seemed to be made of stone to the very heart. Not once had he smiled. Not once had he given any indication that theirs was no new acquaintance. And he had called her explanation an affecting story. He had said so with a sneer, as if he thought it contrived and untrue.

It did not matter. She had got what she had set out to get. More. She had not even been sure she was going to ask for the doll. But as well as that, Andrew was to have a watch. It did not matter that Bedford had not smiled at her or wished her a happy Christmas.

It was at Christmastime he had first kissed her. It had been one of those magical and rare Christmases when it had snowed and there was ice on the lake. They had been sledding down a hill, he and she the last of a long line of young people, all of whom had been trekking back up again by the time they had had their turn. And she had overturned into the snow, shrieking and laughing, and giggling even harder when he had come over to help her up and brush the snow from her face and hair.

He had kissed her swiftly and warmly and openmouthed, stilling both her laughter and his own until he had made some light remark and broken the tension of the moment. It had been Christmastime. Christmas Eve, to be exact. She had been fifteen, he one-and-twenty.

It did not matter. That had been a long time ago, almost exactly seven years, in fact. He was not the same man, not by any means. But then, she was not the same, either. She had been a girl then, a foolish girl who had believed that Christmas and life were synonymous.

She turned and smiled at Mrs. Morgan, who was carrying a tray into the salon.

He had a daughter somewhere in the house, Lilias thought for the first time since her arrival.

The child tugged at her father's hand, trying to free her own.

"The water is running down my arm, Papa," she complained. A few minutes before she had told him that the rain was running down the back of her neck. "I want to go home now. Pick me up."

The Marquess of Bedford stooped down and took his daughter up in his arms. She circled his neck with her own arms and burrowed her head against the heavy capes of his coat.

"We'll be home in a twinkling, poppet," he said, admitting to himself finally that he was not enjoying tramping around his own grounds any more than she, being buffeted by winds and a heavy drizzle that seemed to drip into one's very bones. "The snow will come before Christmas, and we will build snowmen and skate on the lake and sled on the hill."

"Your coat is wet, Papa," she said petulantly, moving her head about as if in the hope of finding a spot that the rain had not attacked. "I'm cold."

He was clearly fooling only himself, Bedford thought, unbuttoning the top two buttons of his coat so that his daughter might burrow her damp head inside. Christmas would not come. Not this year or ever again. December the twenty-fifth would come and go, of course, this year and every year, but it would not be Christmas for all that.

Christmas had come for the last time six years before, when his father had still been alive, and Claude too. When he had been a younger son. When Philip Angove had still been alive. Before Spain had taken Claude and Waterloo, Philip. When life had been full of hope and promise.

Christmas in that year and in all the years preceding it had invariably been white. Always snow and skating and sledding and snowball fights. And Yule logs and holly and mistletoe. And family and laughter and the security of love. And food and company and song.

Christmas had always been white and innocent. How could there ever be Christmas again?

His brother—his great hero—had died at Badajoz. And his father less than a year later. And soon after that he had discovered that the world was not an innocent or a pleasant place in which to do one's living. Suddenly he had had friends by the score. And suddenly women found him irresistibly attractive and enormously witty. And suddenly relatives he had hardly known he had developed a deep fondness for him.

In his innocence he had been flattered by it all. In his innocence he had fallen for the most beautiful and most sought-after beauty of the London Season. He had married her before the Season was out.

Lorraine. Beautiful, charming, and witty. The only thing she had lacked—and she had lacked it utterly—was a heart. She had made no secret of her affairs right from the beginning of their marriage and had merely laughed at him and called him rustic when he had raged at her.

"Papa, open another button so that I can get my arms in," his child said, her voice muffled by the folds of his cravat.

He kissed one wet curl as he complied with her demand. He was not even sure that she was his, though Lorraine had always insisted that she was.

"Darling," she had said to him once, when she was very pregnant and fretful at being confined to home, "do you think I would go through all this boredom and discomfort for any other reason than to give you your precious heir?"

She had been very angry when Dora was born.

Lorraine had drowned two years later in Italy, where she had been traveling with a group of friends, among whom was her latest lover.

And the lures had been out for him again for almost all of the two years since. Women gazed at him with adoration in their eyes. Women cooed over a frequently petulant and rather plain-faced Dora.

The Marquess of Bedford ran thankfully up the marble steps in front of his house and through the double doors, which a footman had opened for him.

"Let's see if there is a fire in the nursery, poppet, shall we?" he asked, setting his daughter's feet on the tiled floor and removing her bonnet and cloak. "And buttered muffins and scones?"

"Yes, if you please, Papa," she said, raising a hand for his. But her tone was petulant again as they climbed the stairs side by side. "When will Christmas come? You said there would be lots of people here and lots to do. You said it would be fun."

"And so I did," he said, his heart aching for her as he looked down at her wet and untidy head. "But Christmas is still five days away. It will be wonderful when it comes. It always is here. You will see."

But he was lying to her. The dolls and the frilled dresses and the bows would not make a happy Christmas for her. The only real gift he would be able to give her was his company. The choice had been between any of a number of house parties to which he had been invited alone, and Christmas spent, for the first time ever, with his child. He had chosen the latter. But he was not at all sure that that was not more a gift to himself than to her.

Where was the snow? And the young people? And the laughter and song?

"When will the rain end, Papa?" the child asked, echoing his own thoughts.

"Soon," he said. "Tomorrow, probably."

"But it has rained forever," she said.

Yes it had. For all of a week, at least.

He should not have come. He had not been home for almost six years. Not since leaving in a hurry with his father when the news about Claude had come. He should have kept that memory of home intact, at least. That memory of something perfect. Something pure and innocent. Something beyond the dreariness and the corruption of real life.

But he had been fool enough to come back, only to discover that there was no such place. And perhaps there never had been. Only a young and innocent fool who had not yet had his eyes opened.

The rain was bad enough when he had been expecting the magic of his childhood Christmases. Worse by far had been that visit two days before.

Even Lilias.

She had been his first real love. Oh, he had lost his virginity at university and had competed quite lustily with his fellow students for the favors of all the prettiest barmaids of Oxford. But Lilias had been his first love.

A sweet and innocent love. Begun that Christmas when he had first become aware of her as a woman and not just as the fun-loving and rather pretty sister of his friend, Philip Angove. And continued through the following summer and the Christmas after that.

It had been an innocent love. They had never shared more than kisses. Sweet and brief and chaste kisses. He had been very aware of her youth—only sixteen even during that second Christmas. But they had talked and shared confidences and dreamed together.

A sweet and uncomplicated love.

He wished he had kept that memory untainted. But the world had come to her too. He had wondered about her when he had decided to come home, wondered if he would see her, wondered what it would be like to see her again. He had been amazed to be told on his second day home that she was waiting downstairs in the salon for him. And he had hoped with every stair he took that it would not be as he suspected it would.

It had been worse.

The wet and muddy hem of her gown; the darned patches on the hem and sleeve—the second brought to his attention by the artful design to conceal it; the damp and untidy hair; the thin, pale face; the sad, brave story; the modest appeal for assistance; the ridiculous mention of a debt unpaid. He had seen worse actresses at Drury Lane.

He had been furious enough to do her physical harm. She had come to his home to arouse his pity and his chivalry, and in the process she had destroyed one of his few remaining dreams.

Could she find no more honest way of finding herself a husband? Did she really imagine he was so naive? She had not even had the decency to wait awhile. She had been the first to come.

"Papa," Dora was saying. She had climbed unnoticed onto his lap beside the fire in the nursery and was playing with the chain of his watch, "it is so dull here. I want to go somewhere."

"Tomorrow, poppet," he said. "Mr. Crawford has two little boys, who will surely be pleased to see you. And the rector has a family of five. Maybe there are some little ones among them. We will call on them tomorrow, shall we?"

"Yes, please, Papa," she said.

"And I have another errand to run in the village," he said, staring down at his watch, which she had pulled from his pocket. "To see a little boy and girl, though they are not quite as little as you, Dora."

"Tomorrow?" she said. "Promise, Papa?"

"I promise," he said, kissing her cheek. "Now, Nurse wants to dry and comb your hair again. And I need to change my clothes and dry my own hair."

Lilias set three pairs of mud-caked boots down outside the door of her cottage and looked down at them ruefully. Would it be better to tackle the job of cleaning them now, when the mud was still fresh and wet, or later, when it had dried? She glanced up at the sky. The clouds hung heavy and promised that the rain was not yet at an end, but for the moment it had stopped. The boots would not get wet inside just yet.

She was closing the door when her eye was caught by the approach of a carriage along the village street. The very one she had ridden in just three days before. She closed the door hastily. She did not want to be caught peeping out at him as he rode past. But she could not prevent herself from crossing to the window and standing back from it so that she could see without being seen.

"Ugh," Megan said from the small kitchen beyond the parlor. "It is all soaking wet, Lilias."

"Ouch," Andrew said. "Is there any way to pick up holly, Lilias, without pricking oneself to death?"

"Oh, mercy on us," Lilias said, one hand straying to her throat, "he is stopping here. And descending too. One of the postilions is putting down the steps."

The dripping bundles of holly, which they had all just been gathering at great cost to fingers and boots, were abandoned. Megan and Andrew flew across the room to watch the splendid drama unfolding outside their window.

"The marquess?" Megan asked, big-eyed. "And is that his daughter, Lilias? What a very splendid velvet bonnet and cloak she is wearing."

Andrew whistled, an accomplishment he had perfected in the past few months. "Look at those horses," he said. "What prime goers!"

Lilias licked her lips and passed her hands over hair that was hopelessly flattened and untidy from her recent excursion outdoors. The watch? Had he come to bring the watch in person? The doll had been delivered by a footman the day before, fortunately at a time when the children had gone over to the rectory to play with the children there. It had been carefully hidden away after she had smoothed wondering fingers over the lace and the soft golden hair. And the butcher had informed her that she might pick up a goose on Christmas Eve.

She wished she were wearing her best day dress again. She crossed to the door and opened it before anyone had time to knock. And she saw with some dismay the row of muddy boots standing to one side of the doorstep. She curt-sied.

"How do you do, ma'am?" the Marquess of Bedford said. He looked even larger and more formidable than he had looked three mornings before, clad as he was in a many-caped greatcoat. He held a beaver hat in one hand. "I have been taking my daughter about to meet some of the children of the neighborhood."

"Oh," Lilias said, and looked down at the small girl standing beside him, one hand clutched in his. She was handsomely dressed in dark red velvet, though she was not a pretty child. "I am pleased to make your acquaintance, my lady."

"This is Miss Angove, Dora," the marquess said.

The child was looking candidly up at Lilias. "We have brought you a basket of food from the house," she said, tossing her head back in the direction of the postilion, who was holding a large basket covered with a white cloth.

"Won't you come inside, my lord?" Lilias asked, stand-ing hastily to one side when she realized that she had been keeping them standing on the doorstep. "And there really was no need." She glanced at the basket and took it reluc-tantly from the servant's hand.

"We have taken one to each of the houses we have called at," he said. "A Christmas offering, ma'am." He looked at her with the hooded blue eyes and the marble expression that she had found so disconcerting a few days before. "Not charity," he added softly for her ears only.

His daughter was eyeing Megan and Andrew with cau-tious curiosity.

"Do you think girls are silly?" she asked Andrew after the introductions had been made and Lilias was ushering the marquess to a seat close to the fire.

Andrew looked taken aback. "Not all of them," he said. "Only some. But then, there are some silly boys too."

"Mrs. Crawford's sons think girls are silly," Dora said.

"They would," Andrew said with undisguised contempt.

"And do you squeal and quarrel all the time and run to your mama with tales?" Dora asked Megan.

Megan giggled.

"Dora," her father said sharply, "watch your manners."

"Because the children at the rectory do," Dora added.

"We have no mama to run to," Megan said. "And when Drew and I quarrel, we go outside and fight it out where Lilias cannot hear us and interfere." She giggled again. "We have been gathering holly. It is all wet and prickly. But there are so many berries! Do you want to see it? You may take your coat off and put on one of my pinafores if you wish."

"Megan," Lilias said, her voice agonized. One of Megan's faded pinafores on Lady Dora West?

"What is the holly for?" Dora asked. "And, yes, please." She looked at her father on an afterthought. "May I, Papa? Where did you find it? I wish I could have come with you."

"No, you don't," Andrew said. "My fingers look like one of Miss Pierce's pincushions. We found some mistletoe too. It is in the kitchen. Come and look."

Lilias found herself suddenly seated opposite the marquess in the small and empty parlor, the object of his silent scrutiny. She jumped to her feet again.

"May I offer you tea?" she asked.

"No," he said. "That is not necessary. We had tea at the rectory not half an hour since."

She flushed. "I am afraid I have nothing else to offer," she said.

"Sit down," he said. He looked over his shoulder into the kitchen, where the voices of the children mingled. "One of my men has been sent into town for your brother's watch, among other things. I shall have it delivered tomorrow."

Lilias felt herself flush even more deeply. "You are kind," she said. "And thank you for the other things."

More than ever she felt that she had begged from him and had been given charity. There was no unbending in his manner, not the merest hint of a smile on his lips or in his eyes. He was regarding her with what looked uncomfortably like scorn.

"Dora is lonely," he said. "She has never had children to play with. Until less than a year ago she lived with her grandparents."

Lilias did not reply. She could think of nothing to say.

"Unfortunately," he said, "when she does find playmates, she demands perfection. She wants them to be the sort of friends she would like to have. I am afraid our visits this afternoon have not been a great success."

Lilias smiled fleetingly.

"Look, Papa." Dora was back in the room, holding up one small index finger for her father's inspection. A tiny globe of blood formed on its tip. "I pricked myself." She put the finger in her mouth even as the marquess reached into a pocket for a handkerchief. "Megan and Andrew are going to put the holly all about the house for Christmas. May I stay and watch?"

"It is time to go home," he said.

"But I don't want to go home," she said, her lower lip protruding beyond the upper one. "I want to stay and watch."

"We shall gather holly too, shall we?" he asked. "And decorate our house with it?"

"But it will be no fun," she said mulishly, "just you and me. I want to watch Megan and Andrew. And I want to watch Andrew carve the Bativity scene he is making. We don't have a Bativity scene, do we?"

"No," he said, getting to his feet, impatience showing itself in every line of his body, Lilias thought as she too rose from her chair, "we don't have a Nativity scene, Dora. Take off the pinafore now. I shall help you on with your cloak and bonnet."

"They have mistletoe, Papa," Dora said, making no attempt to undo the strings of her pinafore. "They hang it up and kiss under it. Is that not silly?"

"Yes," he said, undoing the strings for her, "very silly."

"Can we have some, Papa?" she asked.

"Yes," he said. "We will find some tomorrow."

"But it will be no fun," she said again.

"We will come with you," Megan offered, glancing at her brother. "Won't we, Drew? We know all the best places to look. Or rather, Lilias does, and she showed us today. Shall we come with you?"

The child looked almost pretty for a moment, Lilias thought, as her face lit up with eagerness. "Yes, you come too," she said. "We will need ever so much holly because our house is much bigger than yours. Isn't it, Papa? And mistletoe for every room. And Andrew can carve a Bativity scene just for me."

"No," Andrew said, "there will not be time. But I will bring the shepherd with me to show you. It will be finished by tomorrow."

Lilias found herself suddenly gazing into the marquess's eyes across the heads of the children and feeling decidedly uncomfortable. His eyes were cold and penetrating. And for the first time there was a half smile on his lips. But she wanted to shiver. The smile had nothing to do with either amusement or friendship.

"Well, Miss Angove," he said, "it would be quite too bad if you were the only one to miss this merry outing. I shall send my carriage for the three of you after luncheon tomorrow and we will all go holly gathering together. You will do us the honor of taking tea with us afterward."

He did not ask questions, Lilias noticed. He did not even make statements. He gave commands. Commands that she would dearly have liked to refuse to comply with, for if one thing was becoming clear to her mind, it was that he disliked her. Quite intensely. Perhaps it was her temerity in reminding him of a long-forgotten debt that had done it. She could think of no other reason for his hostility. But it was there nonetheless.

And she was glad suddenly that he had come home, glad that she had seen what he had become, glad that she could put to rest finally a dream and an attachment that had clung stubbornly long after he had left in such a hurry the very day after they had spent two hours together strolling the grounds of his home, hand in hand, looking at the flowers of spring and planning what they would do during the summer.

She was glad he had come back, for he no longer lived, that gentle and sunny-natured young man whom she had loved. He was dead as surely as his older brother was dead. As surely as Philip was dead. He had died six years before. She had just not known it.

He was holding her eyes with his own. He was obviously waiting for an answer, though he had asked no question. And how could she answer as she wished to do when there were three children standing between them, all eagerly anticipating the treat that the morrow would bring?

"Thank you, my lord," she said. "That would be very pleasant."

Very pleasant indeed, the Marquess of Bedford was thinking the following afternoon as the five of them descended the steps of his house and set off past the formal gardens and the lawns and orchards to the trees and the lake and the hill and eventually the holly bushes.

She was wearing a cloak that looked altogether too thin for the weather. And beneath it he could see the same wool dress she had worn for her first interview with him. Except that he had realized the day before that it could not, after all, be her oldest gown. The cotton dress she had worn when he and Dora had called upon her was so faded that it was difficult to tell exactly what its original color had been.

The children were striding along ahead, one Angove on each side of Dora, Megan holding her hand. Dora had had a hard time getting to sleep the night before. He had sat with her, as he had each night since their coming into the country, until she fell asleep. He had sat there for almost an hour.

"We won't forget the mistletoe, Papa?" she had asked after he had tucked her comfortably into her bed.

"No," he had assured her, "we won't forget the mistle-toe."

"Will you kiss me, Papa?" she had asked.

He had leaned over her again and kissed her.

"Under the mistletoe, silly," she had said, chuckling uncontrollably for all of two minutes.

"Yes, I will kiss you, poppet," he had said. "Go to sleep now."

But she had opened her eyes several minutes later. "Do you think Andrew will remember the shepherd, Papa?" she had asked.

"I expect so," he had said.

He had thought her asleep ten minutes after that. He had been considering getting up from his chair, tiptoeing out of the room, and leaving her to the care of her nurse.

"Papa," she had said suddenly, frowning up at him, "what is a Bativity scene?"

"A Nativity scene," he had said. "I'll tell you some other time. It is time to sleep now."

"It won't rain tomorrow, Papa, will it?" she had asked plaintively.

She had been excited about the promised outing with the Angoves. More excited than he had seen her since taking her from Lorraine's parents early the previous spring, a thin and listless and bad-tempered child.

Damnation! he thought now, and offered his arm to Lilias. Events could not have turned more to her advantage if she really had planned them. The afternoon before he had thought she had, but he had been forced to admit to himself later that she could not have done so. Too much had depended upon chance. She had not even known that he and Dora were going to call on her.

But she would take full advantage of the cozy family outing. He supposed he would be forced to listen to patient cheerfulness about the prospective post as governess and tender lamentations on the fact that the family was about to be broken up. Doubtless she would confide again her intention of reuniting them when she had made her fortune as a governess.

Lilias. He had not expected her to come to this. He looked down at her as she walked silently at his side. She had not grown since the age of sixteen. Her head still barely passed his shoulder. Her hair was still smooth and fair beneath her bonnet. But she was thinner. Her hand, even inside its glove, was too slender on his arm. Her face was thin and pale. Her dark-lashed gray eyes seemed larger in contrast. She really did look as if she were half-starved.

Damnation!

"I wanted Christmas for my daughter," he told her, realizing with a jolt as he heard his own words that that was exactly what she had said to him four days before about her brother and sister. "Christmas as I remembered it. I thought I would find it here. But I chose just the year when there is no snow. Only this infernal cold and damp."

"But it did not always snow," she said, looking up at him. "Just very rarely, I think. It was especially lovely when it did. But Christmas was always wonderful anyway."

"Was it?" He frowned.

She drew breath as if to speak, but she seemed to change her mind. "Yes," she said.

"I have your watch," he said. "It is at the house. I shall see that you have it before you leave after tea."

She looked up at him again, bright-eyed. "Thank you," she said.

Here we go, he thought. He had supplied her with the perfect opportunity to heap upon his head reflections on how happy the boy would be during the coming years and how he would be able to remember his sisters and their life together every time he pulled the watch from his pocket. He clamped his teeth together and felt his jaw tighten.

He felt guilty suddenly. She so obviously *was* very poor, and it was so obviously true that the three of them were to be separated after Christmas. He just wished she had not decided to use the pathos of her situation to win herself a rich and gullible husband.

Except that he was not gullible. Not any longer.

She half smiled at him and shifted her gaze to the three children, who were now quite a distance ahead of them. She said nothing.

Dora was skipping along, he was surprised to notice when he followed the direction of Lilias's eyes.

"This is where we got the holly yesterday," Megan announced a while later when they came up to the thicket. And then she looked at Lilias, a hand over her mouth, and giggled.

Andrew was laughing too. "We were not supposed to say," he said, darting a mischievous look at the marquess. "We were trespassing."

Lilias was blushing very rosily, Bedford saw when he glanced at her. She looked far more as she had looked as a girl.

"But these ones don't have as many berries as yours," Dora complained.

"All the good branches are high up," Andrew said. "We could not reach them yesterday. Even Lilias."

"It seems that I am elected," the marquess said. "Thank goodness for leather gloves. This looks like certain self-destruction."

Megan giggled as he stepped forward and his coat caught on the lower branches of holly. He had to disengage himself several times before he could reach up to cut the branches that were loaded with berries. His upturned face was showered with water. Dora was giggling too.

Lilias had stepped in behind him to take the holly as he handed it down. Her gloves and cloak were not heavy enough to protect her from hurt, he thought, and clamped his lips together as he was about to voice the thought.

"Ouch," Dora cried excitedly, and giggled even more loudly. "I have almost as big an armful as you, Andrew. I have more than Megan. Oh, ouch!"

"You must not clutch them," Andrew said. "Just hold them enough that they do not drop."

"Well," the Marquess of Bedford said when he paused

and looked behind him. "You look like four walking holly bushes. Do you think you can stagger back to the house with that load? Only now does it strike me that we should have had a wagon sent after us."

"Oh, no," Andrew said. "That would spoil the fun."

"This is such fun, Papa," Dora said.

"Let me take some of this load," Bedford said, reaching out to take some from Lilias's arms, "before you disappear entirely behind it."

Her eyes were sparkling up at him.

"But, Papa," Dora wailed. "The mistletoe."

"Oh, Lord," he said, "the mistletoe. I shall go and get some. You all start back to the house." But she was loaded down. She would never get back without being scratched to death. "Better still, drop your load, Lilias, and show me where this mistletoe is. You children, on your way. We will catch up to you."

God, he thought, turning cold as she did what she had been told—considering her load, she had had little choice—he had called her Lilias. *The witch!* Her wiles were working themselves beneath his guard despite himself. His jaw hardened again.

She led him around past the thicket of holly bushes, past the old oaks, to the mistletoe, which he had forgotten about. The old oaks! He had climbed them with her, to sit in the lower branches, staring at the sky and dreaming aloud with her. He could remember lifting her down from the lowest branch of one—he could not remember which—and kissing her, her body pressed against the great old trunk, her hands spread on either side of her head, palm to palm against his. He could remember laughing at her confusion because he had traced the line of her lips with his tongue.

"It was all a long time ago," he said abruptly, and felt remarkably foolish as soon as the words were spoken. As if he had expected her to follow his train of thought.

"Yes," she said quietly.

He gave her the mistletoe to carry, being very careful not to lift it above the level of her head as he handed it to her. And on the way back he took the large bundle of holly into his own arms, against her protests, to carry to the house.

"My coat and my gloves are heavier than yours," he said.

She brushed her face against the mistletoe as they walked.

"I suppose," he said harshly after a few silent minutes, "you do not get enough to eat."

She looked up at him, startled. "My lord?" she said.

"Your brother and sister do not look undernourished," he said. "I suppose you give all your food to them."

Her flush was noticeable even beneath the rosiness that the wind and cold had whipped into her cheeks.

"What a ridiculous notion," she said. "I would have starved to death."

"And have been doing almost that, by the look of you," he said, appalled at his own lack of breeding and good manners.

"What I do is my own business, I thank you, my lord," she said. Her voice was as chill as his own, he realized. "I do not choose to discuss either my appetite or my means with you."

"You were quite willing to do so a few days ago," he said.

"Only enough to explain why I had to bring up the matter of that old debt," she said. "And I take it unkindly in you to refer again to a topic I confided only with embarrassment and reluctance."

He strode on, knowing that he was walking too fast for her, but doing nothing to slacken his pace.

"Stephen," she said. She sounded close to tears. "Why do you hate me?"

Stephen. No one had called him by his given name for years, it seemed. Lorraine had never called him anything but Bedford. He slackened his pace so that she was no longer forced almost to run at his side.

It was clever. Very clever. It almost unnerved him. It was too clever. She had overplayed her hand.

"I do not hate you, ma'am," he said, thankful to see the house close by. The children must be inside already. "What possible reason would I have to hate you?"

"I don't know," she said.

He gritted his teeth against the trembling of her voice. It was too overdone. Too contrived.

Lilias, he thought, and remembered the oak trees. And remembered Lorraine and dozens of admiring female eyes and more dozens of obsequious hangers-on. All with their various wiles and arts, and not a few of them with their sad stories and their outstretched hands.

Life might have been so different if only Claude had not died, he thought bitterly, standing aside so that Lilias might precede him up the steps and through the doors into the hallway of his home.

Lilias was putting the final stitches in a strip of faded blue cloth for Mary's robe while Megan was painstakingly lining the manger with straw. Andrew was whittling away at a sheep that insisted on looking more like a fox, he complained, a deep frown between his eyes.

"But Joseph is quite splendid, Drew," Megan said loyally. "He looks quite like a real man."

"And how lovely it will be," Lilias said, "to have our own Nativity scene when everyone else has to go to church to see one. What shall we sing?"

" 'Lully, lulla, thou little tiny child,' " Megan began to sing, and Lilias joined her, while Andrew held his sheep at arm's length and regarded it with half-closed eyes.

They all stopped what they were doing when there was a knock at the door. Lilias rose to answer it.

Lady Dora West was dressed in dark blue velvet this time, in a small but dashing riding outfit. Her eyes shone and her cheeks were flushed with color. She was clutching her father's hand as she had two days before.

"We rode here on Pegasus," she announced as soon as the door was opened, and Lilias could see beyond her a magnificent black stallion tethered to the fence. "Papa said we might call and see your decorations and see Joseph if he is finished."

"I do beg your pardon if you are busy." The Marquess of Bedford was looking at her with hooded and wary eyes, Lilias saw when she lifted her own reluctantly to his face.

Why had he come? The afternoon before had been unspeakably embarrassing, especially after her outburst, when she had called him by his given name and asked him such a foolish question. Instead of sitting in the drawing room after tea while the children ran excitedly about first that room and then the nursery, placing the holly, and giggling over where to hang the mistletoe, they had trailed almost silently after. Afraid to be alone together.

She had not expected to see him again.

"Dora has quite taken to your brother and sister," he said. "She can derive no excitement from her nurse's company or from mine. She will be satisfied with ten minutes, I believe."

But by the time he entered the cottage, Dora had already thrown aside her hat and riding jacket and had run into the kitchen to lift from a hook behind the door the pinafore she had worn the last time.

"Oh, the holly," she cried. "It looks so lovely in here because the room is small. And the mistletoe is right in the center." She stood beneath it and chuckled. "Kiss me, Papa."

He did so, bending from his great height to take the upturned face between his hands and kiss the puckered mouth. Lilias turned away, a curious churning in her stomach.

"But that is supposed to be just for Christmas," he said. "Not for another two days, poppet."

Listening to his voice as he spoke to the child, not seeing him, she thought he sounded like Stephen. But no, she would not think that. It was not true.

Dora was soon exclaiming over Joseph and laughing delightedly over the sheep when Andrew told her that it looked like a fox. She noticed Mary, who was already dressed in her blue robe.

"Oh, pretty," she said, fingering it.

Bedford seated himself, uninvited, his eyes on his daughter.

"We were singing when you came," Megan said, and began singing the same carol that had been interrupted by the arrival of their guests. Dora smiled and stroked Mary's robe. "You sing too, Lilias."

Lilias flushed. "Later, Megan," she said, and glanced in some embarrassment at the marquess, whose eyes had shifted to her. His expression was unfathomable.

"You used to sing," he said. "All the time."

She smiled fleetingly and wished she still had Mary's robe to stitch at. She had not yet started Joseph's.

"You used to go caroling," he said, frowning as if the memory had only just come back to him. "On Christmas Eve. We all used to go—Claude, Philip, Susan and Henrietta Price, the Hendays. But you used to lead the singing."

Lilias bit her lip. "We still go," she said. "Some of the villagers and I. The children too. We go around the village before church at eleven, and out to some of the cottages too if we know that someone is too unwell to come to church."

"Tomorrow night," Andrew said, looking up briefly from his work. "We had great fun last year. Mr. Campbell gave us all hot cider before he realized that some of us were children and ought not to be drinking it."

Megan giggled. Then she looked up, arrested by some bright thought. "You ought to come too this year," she said. "Dora can come. I will hold her hand. And you too, sir," she added magnanimously.

"May I, Papa?" Dora had leaped to her feet. She looked definitely pretty, Lilias thought, untidy hair and faded pinafore notwithstanding. "May we?" She danced up and down on the spot in an agony when he did not answer immediately. "Oh, please, please, Papa, may we?"

"You do not know any of the carols, poppet," he said. "And it will be too late for you. It will be past your bedtime."

"But Megan will teach me," she said. "Won't you, Megan? And Miss Angove. Won't you, Miss Angove? And I will go to sleep tomorrow afternoon, Papa, and sleep all afternoon and be very good. Oh, may we go too? Please."

"We will have to talk about it further," he said stiffly. He looked almost angry, Lilias saw at a glance. "Right now we are interrupting work, Dora. And I have some errands to run in the village."

"But I don't want to go," she said. "You will stop to talk to people, Papa, and I will be dull. You go and do your errands and I will stay here. Miss Angove will teach me the carols."

The marquess stood up resolutely. "Put your pinafore away where you found it, now," he said, "and I shall help you on with your coat."

She stared at him, her lower lip protruding beyond the upper.

"We will be very happy to have her stay, if you will agree," Lilias said softly. "It is good to have children here at Christmastime."

His eyes turned on her, hooded, inscrutable. He inclined his head. "Very well, then, ma'am," he said. He turned back to his daughter. "You may stay for an hour, Dora," he said. "But you must come without protest when I return."

Megan and Dora clapped their hands. Even Andrew looked pleased.

Lilias, standing at the door a minute later, watching the marquess swing himself into the saddle of his horse and proceed along the village street, was not sure if she had done the right thing or not, interfering between a father and his daughter. He had paused in the doorway and looked down at her.

"Another debt to call in?" he had said softly and icily.

She had not comprehended his meaning until he was riding down the pathway to the gate, and even then she was not sure he had meant what she thought he had meant. She hoped he had not. And she wondered again, though she wished with all her heart that she had not asked it, why he hated her.

They sang for almost the whole hour, sometimes the same carol over and over, while Andrew tackled the final feature of the Nativity scene, the baby Jesus, and Megan arranged and rearranged the items already completed. Dora first helped and then stood at Lilias's elbow, staring fascinated at the tiny robe for Joseph that she was making.

Lilias smiled at her after a few minutes, when they were between carols. "Why don't you pull up that stool?" she said.

"Papa told me the story," Dora said when she was seated. "About the baby and the stable and the manger and the smothering clothes."

"The swaddling clothes," Lilias said with a smile. "That is what I will be making next."

"He is going to tell me again tonight," Dora said. "I like that story. I am going to learn to sew next year when I am five."

"Are you?" Lilias smiled again. "Will you like that?"

"Nurse is to teach me," Dora said. "But I am going to ask Papa if you can teach me instead. It would be fun with you."

Megan began singing another carol.

The caroling was not the only part of Christmas he had forgotten, Bedford discovered the following morning. And he really had forgotten that. He had always remembered Christmas as a white and outdoor affair. Everything else had become hazy in memory.

But there had always been the caroling and the lanterns and the rosy cheeks and laughter, and the glasses of cider and wassail until not one of them had been quite sober by the time they got to church. None of them had ever been precisely drunk—just smiling and warm and happy. How could he have forgotten? And how everyone had wanted to stand next to Lilias because she had such a sweet voice and such perfect pitch. He had won almost all of those battles.

Dora, restless in the morning because it seemed such a

long wait until the evening—he had promised her the night before, much against his better judgment, that they would join the carolers—wandered down to the kitchen to watch the cook roll the pastry for the mince pies. And she fell into conversation with Mrs. Morgan, who was delighted to have a child in the house again.

And that encounter led, unknown to Bedford until later, to a visit to the attic to find the relics of Christmases past.

"Papa!" Dora burst into the library, where Bedford was trying to read, though it was hard to bring his thoughts to bear on the book opened before him. She was moving at a run past the footman who held the door open for her, and her face was flushed and pretty with an excitement that she could barely contain. "Papa, come to the attic with me. We have been looking at Christmas. The dearest bells. And the star! May we have an evergreen bough, Papa? Mrs. Morgan says there were always evergreens. May we? Do put down the silly book and come."

He put down the silly book and came. Or rather was dragged by an insistent little hand and a voice brimming with an excitement he had thought her incapable of.

And of course, he thought as soon as he looked into the opened boxes in the attic and dismissed a rather uncomfortable and apologetic Mrs. Morgan . . . Of course. How could he have forgotten? The evergreen boughs, decorated with crystal balls and bells that tinkled and twinkled every time a door was opened or a draft blew down a chimney. The evergreen boughs that had brought the smell of Christmas right inside the house.

And one year the candles on the boughs, until they had been forbidden forever after . . . after the great fire, when the branch had been singed black and a whole circle of carpet ruined, for he had collided with the bough during blindman's buff and tipped it over . . . They must be only thankful that he had not burned too, his mother had said, hugging him while his father had scolded. And someone had been smothering hysterical giggles through it all. Lilias.

"May we have an evergreen bough, Papa? May we?"
Dora's voice was almost a wail, there was so much anxiety
in her tone.

"There are enough decorations here for a whole forest of
boughs," he said with a laugh. "There used to be some in
the nursery and dining room as well as a whole great tree
in the drawing room."

"A tree, Papa. Just one whole tree in the nursery," she
said, and reached up her arms to be picked up when he
smiled down at her.

"Just one, then," he said. "We will go out and find one
ourselves and cut it down, shall we? I think the rain stopped
about an hour ago."

"Yes," she said, hugging his neck and kissing his cheek.

It was only when they were outside and she was tripping
along at his side, her gloved hand firmly clasped in his,
that she had her great idea. Though to her it seemed quite
natural.

"We will take one for Megan and Andrew and Miss
Angove as well," she announced. "Just a little one because
they have such a small room. But there are so many bells
and balls. We will take them before luncheon, Papa, so that
I may still have my sleep ready for tonight. They will be
happy, won't they?"

"I think they have enough, poppet," he said. "They are
making their own Christmas. They will not want our offerings."

"Oh, yes, they will," she said happily. "You said Christmas is for giving, Papa. They will be happy if we give them
a whole evergreen tree. Besides, I want to see the baby Jesus. He was not finished yesterday. Such a dear little manger, Papa. Miss Angove was going to make the smoth—the
swathering clothes."

"Was she?" he said, his heart sinking. Christmas was for
giving, he had told her, and she had just thrown it back in
his teeth. How could he refuse to give his daughter happiness?

"Just a little tree, then," he said. "Papa has only two hands, you know."

She chuckled. "But they are big hands, Papa," she said. "Miss Angove is going to teach me to sew when I am five."

"Is she?" he said, his lips tightening.

"Yes," she said. "It will be more fun with her than with Nurse."

And so little more than an hour later they were yet again knocking on the door of the cottage, Bedford found, Dora at his side, jumping up and down.

"I want to tell, Papa," she told him. The evergreen and the box of decorations, including the great star, were still inside the carriage.

And she did tell, rushing through the door, tearing at her cloak, and whisking herself behind the kitchen door for the pinafore just as if she had lived there all her life. And soon Megan was squealing and giggling and Andrew was exclaiming in delight and offering to accompany the marquess into the garden to fetch a pail of earth to set the tree in—a whole tree, and not just a bough!—and Lilias was clearing a small table and covering it with a worn lace cloth close to the window.

And there he was, Bedford discovered half an hour later, his coat discarded, his shirtsleeves rolled up, his neckcloth askew, balanced on a kitchen chair and pounding a nail into the ceiling. For the great star, it seemed, had not been brought for the Christmas tree at all—"How silly, Papa," Dora had said with a giggle. "It would be too big"—but to hang over the Nativity scene.

"Just look at the darling baby Jesus," Dora was saying in a voice of wonder while everyone else was gazing upward at the star Bedford was suspending from the nail.

And then they were all standing in the room, gazing about them at all the splendor and wonder of Christmas, just as if it had come already: the holly boughs and the tree hung with bells and crystal balls, all catching the light from the outdoors and from the fire and the rudely carved Nativity scene with its bright and outsize star and its minute baby wrapped in swaddling clothes.

"Lilias is standing beneath the mistletoe," Megan said suddenly and in great delight.

Dora clapped her hands and laughed.

And he met her eyes from three feet away and saw the dismay in them and the flush of color that rose to her cheeks, and he was no longer sure that it was all artifice. It was a thin and large-eyed face. It was beautiful.

"Then I had better kiss her," Andrew said in a tone of some resignation. "Again." He pecked her noisily on the cheek and she moved swiftly to the window to still a bell that was swaying and tinkling.

"Time to go, poppet," the Marquess of Bedford said.

There was a chorus of protests.

"All right, then," he said. "Dora may stay for another half hour. But no caroling and no church tonight."

Five minutes later he sank thankfully back against the velvet upholstery of his carriage. He had thought himself hardened to all feeling. He had thought that he could never be deceived again, never caught out in trusting where he should not trust. He would never be caught because he would never trust anyone ever again. It was safer that way.

His saner, more rational, more cautious, more hardened self told him that it was all a ruse, that she was an opportunist who was using all her feminine wiles to trap him and save herself and her brother and sister from a dreary and impoverished future.

His madder, more irrational, more incautious, more gullible self saw a mental image of her eyes lighting up when she saw the tree and the ornaments and their effect on the two children in her charge. And saw her below him as he stood on the chair, her arms half raised as if she expected to be able to catch him if he fell. And saw the look of Christmas in her eyes as she stood in the middle of her living room looking about her. And the flustered look of pure beauty when she realized that she was standing beneath the mistletoe.

Had she known that she stood there? It was impossible to tell. And it made all the difference in the world. Had she known or had she not?

Even more important, did he care either way? Did he still regret that it had been her brother who had stepped forward to kiss her?

No, he must not, he thought, closing his eyes. He must not. He must not.

"Must I sleep all afternoon?" Dora asked him. "May we decorate our evergreen first, Papa?"

"We will do it immediately after luncheon," he said, opening his eyes and looking at her sternly. "And then you are going to sleep all afternoon."

"Yes, Papa," she said.

For the past few years Lilias had been the oldest of the carol singers. But none of the others had been willing for her to retire.

"But, Miss Angove," Christina Simmonds had protested when she had suggested it two years before, "what would we do without you? You are the only one who can really sing."

"Besides," Henry Hammett had added, with a wink for his friend, Leonard Small, "if one of the other girls were to start the carols, Miss Angove, the rest of us would have to either dig a trench to reach the low notes or carry a ladder around with us to hit the high ones."

A deal of giggling from the girls and rib-digging from the young men had followed his words, and Lilias had agreed to stay.

She was not to be the oldest this year, though. Most of the young people were inclined to be intimidated when they first saw the Marquess of Bedford as one of their number. Most of them had only glimpsed him from a distance since his return home, and most of them were too young to remember that during his youth he had joined in all the village activities.

However, after singing at a few houses and consuming a few mince pies and a couple of mugs of wassail, they no longer found him such a forbidding and remote figure. And the usual jokes and laughter accompanied them around the village.

The younger children formed their own group, Dora firmly in the middle of them, clinging to Megan's hand. The marquess carried one of the lanterns and held it each time they sang, as he had always used to do, above Lilias's shoulder so that she could see her music.

She was very aware of him and wished she were not. Apart from the fact that the other faces around them had changed, there was a strange, disturbing feeling of having gone back in time. There was Stephen's gloved hand holding the lantern above her, and Stephen's voice singing the carols at her right ear, and Stephen's hand at the small of her back once as they crossed the threshold into one home.

She had to make a conscious effort to remember that he was not Stephen, that he was the Marquess of Bedford. She had to look at him deliberately to note the broadness of his shoulders and chest beneath the capes of his coat, showing her that he was no longer the slender young man of her memories. And she had to look into his face to see the harsh lines and the cynical eyes—though not as cynical as they had been a week before, surely.

She brought her reactions under control and bent over a very elderly gentleman in a parlor they had been invited into who had grasped her wrist with one gnarled hand.

"Miss Lilias," he said, beaming up at her with toothless gums, "and Lord Stephen." He shook her arm up and down and was obviously so pleased with what he had said that he said it again. "Miss Lilias and Lord Stephen."

Lilias smiled and kissed his cheek and wished him a happy Christmas. And the marquess, whom she had not realized was quite so close, took the old man's free hand between both of his and spoke to him by name.

In the voice of Stephen, Lilias thought, straightening up.

The children were all very tired by the time they had finished their calls and the church bells had begun to ring. But not a single one of them was prepared to admit the fact and be taken home to the comfort of a bed.

Dora was yawning loudly and clutching Lilias's cloak.

"I'll take you home, poppet," Bedford said, leaning down to pick her up. "Enough for one day."

But she whisked herself behind a fold of Lilias's cloak and evaded her father's arms. "But you promised, Papa," she said. "And I slept all afternoon. I was good."

"Yes, you were good," he said, reaching out a hand to take one of hers. "You may see the day out to its very end, then."

And somehow, Lilias found, the child's other hand made its way into hers and they climbed the steps to the church together, the three of them, just as if they were a family. People turned from their pews to look at the marquess, and nodded and smiled at them. Megan and Andrew were already sitting in their usual pew, two seats from the front.

Lilias smiled down at Dora when they reached the padded pew that had always belonged to the marquess's family, and released her hand. She proceeded on her way to join her brother and sister.

"But, Papa," she heard the child say aloud behind her, "I want to sit by Megan."

A few moments after Lilias had knelt down on her kneeler, she felt a small figure push past her from behind and heard the sounds of shuffling as Megan and Andrew moved farther along the pew. And when she rose to sit on the pew herself, it was to find Dora sitting between her and Megan, and the Marquess of Bedford on her other side. She picked up her Psalter and thumbed through its pages.

There were candles and evergreen branches and the Nativity scene before the altar. And the church bells before the service, and the organ and the singing during it, and the Christmas readings. And the sermon. And the church

packed with neighbors and friends and family. There were
love and joy and peace.

It was Christmas.

Christmas as it had always been—and as it would never
be again. She had to concentrate all her attention on her
Psalter and swallow several times. And a hand moved
toward her so that she almost lifted her own to meet it halfway. But it came to rest on his leg and the fingers drummed
a few times before falling still.

She was saved by a loud and lengthy yawn and a small
head burrowing itself between her arm and the back of the
pew. She turned and smiled down at Dora and slipped one
arm behind her and the other under her knees so that she
could lift her onto her lap and pillow the tired head against
her breast. The child was asleep almost instantly.

The marquess's eyes, when Lilias turned her head to
look into them, were very blue and wide open. And quite,
quite inscrutable. When the organ began to play the closing
hymn, and before the bells began to peal out again the good
news of a child's birth, he stood and took his child into his
own arms so that Lilias could stand and sing.

His carriage was waiting outside the church, but Lilias
refused a ride for herself and her brother and sister.

"It is such a short distance to walk," she said.

He set the still-sleeping Dora down on the carriage seat
and turned back to them. "I shall say good night, then," he
said. He held out a hand for Megan's. "Thank you for inviting Dora. I don't think you know how happy you have made
a small child." He took Andrew's hand. "You may come to
the house the day after tomorrow, if your sister approves,
and we will take that ride I have promised you."

"Oh, ripping," Andrew said excitedly.

Bedford turned to Lilias and took her hand in his. He
searched her face with his eyes and seemed about to say
something. But he merely clasped her hand more tightly.

"Happy Christmas, Lilias," he said.

"Happy Christmas, Stephen."

She had said the words and heard them a hundred times

that evening, Lilias thought as she turned away and made her way along the street with the two tired children. But the last two times burned themselves on her mind, and she felt herself smiling and happy . . . and swallowing back tears.

Christmas Day. Chill and dry but heavy with gray clouds out-of-doors. Warm with the glow and the smells and the goodwill of the season indoors. It did not matter that there was no soft white snow to trudge through, no snow to form into snowballs to hurl at shrieking relatives, no hills of snow to slide down and fall into, no ice to skate on. It did not matter. Christmas was indoors.

The goose was cooking, and the vegetables, saved from the summer's garden, were simmering. The plum pudding, part of the contents of the basket that had come from the hall, was warming. The light from the fire and the window was glinting off the crystal balls on the tree and off the star suspended from the ceiling. The bells occasionally tinkled when someone walked by and created a draft. And the baby Jesus, wrapped warmly in swaddling clothes in his manger, was being adored by Mary and Joseph, the Three Kings, an angel with one wing larger than the other, one shepherd, and one sheep, which might as easily have passed for a fox.

Megan was seated cross-legged on the floor close to the fire, rocking her new doll to sleep and gazing in wonder at the porcelain perfection of its face. Andrew was jerking his new watch from a pocket every five minutes to make sure that the goose was not being overcooked. And Lilias sat watching them, a smile on her face.

It was their last Christmas together, at least for a very long time. And their best for several years. She did not regret for a moment the humiliation she had had to suffer in going to the hall to beg for what she had needed to make it a memorable Christmas. And she did not regret that he had come to despise her and even hate her for that begging.

It did not matter. For now it was Christmas, and she had

one week left in this cottage and with these children. And she had seen the wonder in their eyes when they had seen their presents that morning. They would have a day together that she would hug to herself in memory for many long months to come.

If there was a restlessness, an emptiness, a strange sense of something missing, then she would not think of it. For she could not bring back Papa or Philip, or Mama from even longer ago. She could not bring back the Christmases at the hall with their charades and blindman's buff and forfeits and sometimes their dancing. She could not bring back those rare and magical white Christmases when they had all spilled outdoors and been reluctant to go back inside even for the foods of Christmas.

And she could not bring Stephen back. For though he had stood beside her last evening when they had gone caroling and sat beside her at church, and though he had taken her hand in his at the end of the evening and wished her a happy Christmas and called her by her name, he was not Stephen. He was the Marquess of Bedford, serious and aloof. And he disliked her, even hated her, perhaps.

She must count her blessings—so many of them—and keep all her attention and all her love and hope within these four walls for today. She would not think of either the past or the future today.

She glanced across the room to the small table where the evergreen stood, and beneath it the box with the ill-fitting lid that Andrew had carved for her, and the carefully hemmed cotton handkerchief with the embroidered forget-me-not that Megan had made for her during stolen private moments over the past few weeks. She smiled again.

"I wish Dora could see my doll," Megan said. "Do you think she has had anything as grand, Lilias?"

"I can hardly wait for tomorrow," Andrew said, consulting his watch once more. "Do you think his lordship will let me ride one of his prime goers, Lilias?"

* * *

Dora was playing quietly with her own new doll. Indeed, she looked almost like a doll herself, her father thought, glancing across the nursery at her. She was dressed all in her Christmas finery with quantities of satin and lace, and large pink satin bows in her hair, which her nurse had dressed painstakingly in masses of shining dark ringlets.

The child was singing one of her newly learned carols to the doll.

They had opened their own gifts and distributed gifts to the servants, but it was still barely midmorning. Bedford turned to stare out the window. A gray world met his eyes. Those were surely snow clouds overhead, but they were stubbornly retaining their load. If only it had snowed, he thought. He could have taken Dora outside. He could have played in the snow with her all day long and seen that flush of color in her cheeks and that light of pleasure in her eyes that he had not seen a great deal during her short life.

Perhaps he should, after all, have organized some sort of party at the house. There had always used to be a large gathering there for Christmas. But he had come late and without a great deal of warning. Most of the neighbors had made their plans for the day already.

Perhaps he should have accepted one of the numerous invitations he had received since his arrival. But none of them had seemed to be for family gatherings. It would have meant packing Dora off upstairs to someone's nursery with other children while he was entertained by the other adults. With cards, doubtless, or dancing. He had been greedy for a Christmas spent with his daughter. He loved her with an almost fierce ache, he had discovered when he had finally taken her from her grandparents' home the previous spring.

But perhaps he should have accepted one of those invitations. Perhaps Dora would have enjoyed being with other children instead of with him or her nurse all day long. Perhaps he had been selfish.

Christmas Day suddenly seemed to stretch for many long hours ahead of him. What were they to do for the rest of the day? Their Christmas dinner was not to be served until the evening.

"Papa," Dora said from beside him. She was still cradling her doll in her arms. "Will you tell me a story?"

"Yes, I will," he said. "What will it be?" He leaned down and swung both child and doll up into his arms. "Shall we go for a walk or a drive afterward? Perhaps take your doll for some fresh air?"

"To Megan's?" she asked eagerly.

"It is Christmas Day," he said. "We must not disturb them today, poppet. Tomorrow Andrew is coming to ride with me. We shall have Megan come over to play with you, shall we?"

"But I want to see her today," she said. "I want to go now. I want to show Miss Angove my doll."

"Tomorrow," he said, hugging her. "You still have not told me which story you want."

"I want to go now," she said petulantly. "I want to see the holly and the tree and the baby Jesus and the star."

"But we have our own decorations and our own evergreen," he said, sitting down with her and settling her on his lap.

"But it's not the same," she said. "They are so much more cozy, Papa. Please may we go. Please!"

One thing he had discovered about himself in the past year, Bedford thought ruefully: He was incapable of exercising the proper control over his child. He knew that it was not good always to give in to her whims; he knew that he must stand up against her, for her own good as much as for his. But he could not bear to see pleading in her eyes and dash it to pieces.

He had so much to atone for: almost four years when he had scarcely seen her but had left her to the not-so-tender care of her grandparents. Lorraine had not wanted her; she had had no use for a daughter. Now he had to be both mother and father to her. There was no soft, motherly presence to bring her the love and security so necessary to a small child. He had to provide that care himself. But he knew that he was allowing her to rule him, that eventually she would suffer from having no one to take a firm stand with her.

He sighed as he looked down into the pleading eyes of his child. Perhaps it would be easier to say no if he did not wish so desperately to go himself. This house was altogether too large and cheerless for two people, especially at Christmas. The cottage in the village was like a magnet to him.

Lilias was like a magnet. But he put the thought ruthlessly from his mind.

"We will take the carriage, then," he said, "and go immediately. Just for half an hour, to wish them a happy Christmas. No longer, poppet, because they will be busy preparing their dinner, and they will want to enjoy one another's company."

Dora's face lit up and she slid from his knee. "May I take my new muff?" she said. "May I, Papa? And may we take them gifts? I am going to give Megan my little pearls and Miss Angove my diamond brooch. What shall we take for Andrew?"

The marquess laughed. "Slow down," he said. "Gifts are a good idea, Dora, but nothing too valuable, or we will embarrass them."

She looked crestfallen, but her brow puckered in thought. "May I give Megan the new blue ribbon you bought for my bonnet?" she asked.

"I think that is a splendid idea," he said.

"And I could give Miss Angove the painting I did of you on your horse," she said. "Is it good enough, Papa?"

"I am sure she will be pleased," he said, hoping that his daughter would forget to identify the horseman when she presented the gift.

"But what can we give Andrew?" She was frowning.

"I'll wager he would like that seashell we found at Brighton," he said. "The one you can hold to your ear to hear the tide. Can you bear to part with it?"

Dora's face lit up again, and she darted off to find the three treasures. Bedford watched her go.

He really should not have given in on this occasion, should he? He must be the last person Lilias would want to see on this of all days. But just for half an hour. It would not quite ruin her day, surely. And it would make Dora's day.

It was Christmas morning, too early for the carriages of those going visiting for the afternoon. The street had been silent all morning. But it was no longer silent. It was Andrew who first remarked on the sound of horses and who crossed to the window to look out. Megan joined him there when it became clear that there was also a carriage approaching.

"It is Lord Bedford's carriage," Andrew cried. "And it is stopping here, Lilias. Oh, ripping! He will see that I have a watch, just like a man."

"Dora is with him," Megan cried. "How pretty she looks. And she has a doll with her. Do come and look, Lilias."

"I think one of us should think of opening the door," Lilias said, getting to her feet with a smile. And she passed nervous hands over her apron, realized she was wearing it, and removed it hastily. She was pleased that she was wearing her blue silk. It was true that it was no longer fashionable, but it had been worn so sparingly in the last few years that it was barely faded and not patched at all. She was wearing the lace collar that had been Mama's. And she had taken special care with her hair that morning because it was Christmas.

He was holding himself very straight. His expression was wooden. She would have said he was embarrassed if she had thought him capable of such feelings. But she had little time in which to stare.

"We have called for half an hour to wish you all a merry Christmas," he said stiffly.

But Dora was jumping up and down at his side and then

pushing her way through the door. "We have brought you presents," she said in a voice that seemed designed to be heard by someone at the other end of the street. "And I have a new doll, Megan. Oh, and you do too. Ooh, she is pretty. What is her name? And see my new muff, Miss Angove? Papa bought it in London for me, though I did not know until this morning. I wanted to see the star again. Oh, it does look lovely. What smells so good? Does it not smell delicious, Papa? And here are your gifts. Open them. Oh, open them."

"Quieten down, poppet," the marquess said, bending down to remove her muff and undo her coat. He kissed her on the cheek, and Lilias felt that churning in her stomach she had felt before.

Megan and Andrew were soon exclaiming over their gifts while Dora shouted them both down, explaining that the ribbon had been meant for her but she had wanted to give it to Megan. And the shell she and Papa had found their very own selves on the beach at Brighton. And couldn't Andrew just hear the tide at Brighton when he held it to his ear?

Lilias sat down before removing the ribbon from the paper and unrolling her painting.

"Ah," she said. "How lovely. And you painted it yourself."

"Yes, I did," Dora said, climbing up onto Lilias's lap so that she could see the picture too. "That is Papa, but he does not look very much like him, does he? Papa is more handsome, isn't he? That is Papa's horse. His one leg is white, you see? Really he is not quite black, but I had to paint him black because my brown paint was not dark enough. I painted a sun, see?"

"It is beautiful," Lilias said, burying her face in the child's ringlets for a moment. "Quite the loveliest painting I have ever owned. I shall treasure it."

"Will you?" Dora looked up at her. "This is pretty." She laid one small forefinger against the lace collar. "Do you like my muff?"

But she did not wait for an answer. She wriggled down to the floor again in order to exchange exclamations of delight with Megan over their dolls.

The marquess was bent over Andrew, meticulously examining his watch, for all the world as if he had never seen it before, Lilias thought.

Dora accepted a mince pie, another of the offerings from the hall; the marquess did not. Dora sat very straight on a chair close to the Nativity scene, her usual pinafore protecting her dress from crumbs, her feet dangling above the floor.

"I like Christmas in your house," she told Lilias and Megan after telling them all about the distributing of gifts to the servants that morning. "I wish we could stay here all day."

The marquess, Lilias could hear with some delight, was telling Andrew about Tattersall's. He would make a friend for life. Andrew had a passion for horses.

"You *can* stay all day," Megan said. "Can't they, Lilias? Our goose is ever so big and there are enough vegetables to feed the five thousand. Lilias said so just a short while ago. We could play house all day. I could be mother and you could be elder sister. And the two dolls can be the babies. Andrew could be the father, but I don't suppose he will want to be. But that does not matter, does it?"

"I am sure his lordship must have other plans for the day," Lilias said quietly to Megan, but Dora had already slipped from her chair and crossed the room to stand beside her father's. She stood there, pulling at his sleeve.

"Papa," she said, "Miss Angove and Megan want us to stay for the rest of the day. There is lots of food, Miss Angove says, and Megan and I are going to play house all day. May we, Papa? Please, may we?"

"Yes," Andrew said with some enthusiasm.

Wide-open blue eyes were turned on her, Lilias saw. Accusing? Assessing? Hostile? Incredulous? It was impossible to tell. She felt herself flushing.

"Impossible, Dora," the marquess said, getting to his

feet. "We could not so impose. You agreed to half an hour, and that must be just about up."

There was a chorus of disappointed protests from the three children.

"You would be very welcome," Lilias found herself saying. "There really is plenty of food, and it would be such a treat for the children to have company."

His eyes burned into hers from across the room. *And for me too,* she told him silently. For suddenly there was no longer that elusive sense of something missing. There was excitement in the house and happiness. And Christmas was somehow complete.

And *he* was there. And there was a chance—she clasped her hands in front of her very tightly—that he would be there for the whole day. Her memorable Christmas would be memorable indeed, for she would remember him as Stephen. No matter how much he was this withdrawn and austere and even hostile marquess, in memory she knew she would erase all facts except the essential one: He was Stephen. And she had never stopped loving him. Maybe she never would.

If he stayed, she would be able to carry him with her in memory with all the other memories of this last Christmas with her family. It would all be complete.

"This is preposterous," he said, sitting back down again and looking distinctly uncomfortable. "Whatever will Miss Angove think of us, Dora?"

"Hurrah," Andrew shouted out. "He is going to say yes."

The girls squealed and jumped up and down on the spot. And when Dora climbed onto her father's lap to hug him and kiss him, Megan climbed onto his other knee and smiled adoringly into his face.

"Thank you," she said. "Oh, thank you, sir."

"Your sister is going to throttle me, little imp," he said, and to Lilias's amazement, he hugged the child close with one arm and kissed her cheek. "I had better go outside and dismiss my coachman. He might die of boredom and cold if we leave him out there for the rest of the day."

The children were enjoying themselves quite noisily. Even Andrew had been prevailed upon to join in the game of house and was currently sitting on a stool having his hair combed and parted down the wrong side by Dora.

They were having a good time, and that was what really mattered, Bedford thought. But what on earth must Lilias think of him for agreeing so weakly to stay for dinner and even for the rest of the day? He had instructed his coachman to return for him and Dora at eight o'clock.

Or perhaps he should not be feeling guilty, but angry. A few days before he would have been angry and suspicious. It would have been very easy for her to set the children to trapping him into this domestic situation and leading him on to making her an offer.

But he found it hard to believe still that her every action since his homecoming had been conniving. And if it were, was it so despicable? She and the children really were in a desperate situation, and they really were facing a bleak future. Would it be so wrong of her to scheme to win for herself a husband who could lift the burden from her shoulders?

"I have never done this before, you know," he said now, looking rather dubiously at the goose she had asked him to carve. "The meat seems to want to come away in clumps rather than in neat slices."

Lilias laughed. "I have never done it either," she said. "That is why I asked you." She was stirring the gravy. But she paused and looked at him in some concern. "If any of that grease gets on your shirt, it will be ruined."

He looked down at his white shirt. He had already removed his coat and waistcoat and rolled up his sleeves to the elbow.

"What you need is an apron," she said, and crossed to the hook on the kitchen door to fetch one.

"But my hands are greasy," he protested when she held it out to him.

"Lower your head, then," she said with a giggle he had not heard for years, and she slipped the neck strap over his head. She moved behind him, and there was a moment when her arms came around his waist to grasp the ties of the apron so that she could secure it behind him.

"There," she said, coming around to the front of him again to survey her handiwork. His hands were greasy, and he held them suspended in the air. "The Marquess of Bedford in heavy disguise." She laughed. "Oh, you do look funny, Stephen."

But the smile froze on her face and faded, and color rose up her neck and into her cheeks, and he watched her swallow. The children's voices seemed very distant, even though they were just beyond the open door between the kitchen and the parlor. His eyes strayed to her lips.

"The goose awaits," he said lightly.

"The gravy will be lumpy," she said simultaneously.

They worked together in the small kitchen in an awkward silence.

The tension eased when they all sat down to dinner. But there was a heightened awareness that Bedford did not find altogether unpleasant. They sat at either end of the table, Andrew on one side of them and Megan and Dora on the other. Just like a family, all of them playing house in the warm and cozy little cottage. He met Lilias's eyes across the table and smiled. She looked down hastily and then back at him.

"Will you say grace, my lord?" she asked.

He had never in his life washed dishes. But when the plum pudding was finally eaten and they were all groaning with the good foods they had stuffed into themselves, he rolled up his sleeves and put on the apron again. The children giggled.

"Oh, you must not," Lilias said, flustered. "Please sit down in the parlor, my lord. The children and I will see to the dishes."

"No, this is famous," Andrew exclaimed. "You wash, sir, and Megan and I will dry."

"My thoughts entirely," the marquess said. "Your sister thinks I am incapable, you see, Andrew. We will show her, won't we? You may clear away the food, ma'am, and then we will all have something to do."

"I want to dry too." Dora had climbed onto a chair to make herself noticed.

"Oh, sweetheart," Lilias said, "you may help me put away. I really need assistance with that. Will you?"

Doing dishes had never been so much fun, Andrew declared half an hour later when the wet towels were being hung up to dry. Megan and Dora were still giggling over the cup that had slipped from the marquess's wet hand and smashed on the floor.

"Let's play house again," Megan said.

"Let's go for a walk," Andrew said.

"Yes." Dora jumped up and down on the spot. "Go for a walk."

"I am sure we all need a brisk walk of at least five miles," the marquess said, patting his stomach. He turned to Lilias. "You have been busy all morning, ma'am. Would you care to have a rest while I take the children walking?" He looked down at her hopefully. "Or would you care to join us?"

"I shall join you," she said. "Fresh air sounds wonderful."

Steady, Bedford told himself as he buttoned Dora's coat a few minutes later and pulled on his own greatcoat. He must not become too mesmerized by the feeling of family he had had for the past few hours. Only Dora was his family. The other children belonged to Lilias, and she was not his family at all.

Perhaps she should have refused, Lilias thought as she drew her cloak about her and tied the strings of her bonnet. Perhaps she needed an hour alone in which to clear her head of this seductive feeling of warmth and belonging she had had in the past few hours. Perhaps she should not go walking with him, just as if they were one close and happy family.

But there was so little time left. Less than a week, and

then a long and lonely life as someone's governess. And the long illusion that one day she would earn enough money to gather her family back around her again. Less than a week left with Megan and Andrew. Less than a week with Stephen and Dora.

No, she thought, pulling her gloves on resolutely, she was not doing the wrong thing. He had ordered the carriage for eight. That left them with six hours. Six hours. It was not long. She was going to enjoy every minute of it, even if to do so was only to invite future pain. She did not care about the future. Only the present mattered.

Dora attached herself to one of her hands, Megan to the other. Dora skipped rather than walked, and entertained her companions with stories of all that her papa had shown her in London and Brighton. Andrew and the marquess were striding along ahead, deep in conversation—doubtless about horses, Lilias thought with a smile. She was glad for Andrew. He needed more male company than he had had in the past two years. But then, of course, soon he would have nothing but male company, their grandfather during holidays, other boys of his own age during term time. She shut the thought from her mind.

They walked to the lake on the grounds of Bedford Hall. It was looking very bleak and even had a thin layer of ice covering it.

"Yes," Andrew was saying excitedly as Lilias and the girls came up to him and the marquess. "If it stays cold like this, we will be able to slide on the ice in a few days' time."

The children were soon running around the bank, gazing eagerly at the film of ice.

Lilias had not realized how cold it was until she stopped walking. The wind cut at her like a knife. She glanced up at the heavy clouds.

"Snow clouds," the marquess said. "Are they just teasing, do you suppose? But I think not. I believe we are going to have our snow yet."

"Yes," Lilias said, "I think you are right." Her teeth were chattering. She shivered. She could feel him looking at her.

She sought in her mind for something to say. There was an awkwardness when they were alone. They needed the presence of the children to create an atmosphere of ease between them.

"Lilias," he said. His voice was tight and withdrawn, the voice of the Marquess of Bedford again, despite his use of her given name, "your cloak is too thin. It must be quite threadbare. When did you last have a new one?"

She looked jerkily up at him. "It is quite adequate, I thank you," she said. "It is just this standing still that is making me cold."

"When did you last buy yourself anything?" he asked. His voice sounded angry. "Has everything been for the children in the last few years? Your lips are quite blue."

"Don't," she said. His face had that shuttered look it had had the first few times she had seen him. "It is none of your concern."

"Your dress," he said. "It was quite fashionable six years ago when it was new. You wore it for Christmas then. Had you forgotten?"

She stared at him, though she did not see him at all. She was blinded by hurt and humiliation. She *had* forgotten. She had felt pretty that morning. Pretty for him. She turned quickly away.

"It is none of your business," she said. "What I wear and what I spend on myself and the children is none of your concern at all. I am not answerable to you."

"No, you are not," he said, moving closer to her so that he stood between her and the wind. He lifted his head and his voice suddenly. "Andrew," he called, "your sister and I are going to begin the walk home. You may bring the girls along behind us. Don't let anyone set even a single toe on that ice."

"No, I won't, sir," Andrew called back.

He took her arm through his and hugged it close to his side. He walked at a brisk pace. And he plied her the whole way home with questions about her governess post: where it was and who the family were and how many charges she would have and how arduous the duties were likely to be. And he asked about Andrew, about what school he was to attend, how well he was likely to be treated by his grandfather, how much he looked forward to being away from home. He wanted to know about Great-aunt Hetty in Bath and how suitable a home she would be able to offer a nine-year-old child.

Lilias answered as briefly as she could.

"Why would your grandfather not take all of you?" he asked as they entered the village again.

"Papa defied him when he married Mama," she said. "He has never recognized us. I was fortunate to be able to persuade him to take Andrew."

"You are his grandchildren," he said. "He ought to have taken you. Did you ask him to?"

She shook her head. "I will not answer any more questions," she said. "I have arranged everything to my own satisfaction, my lord."

"In other words, it is none of my business, again," he said, his voice still angry. "You are right. But those children need you, Lilias. They are still very much children."

She stared stonily ahead to the cottage. The temptation to tip her head sideways to rest against his shoulder, to sag against the strength of his arm, to close her eyes and pour out all her pain to him was almost overwhelming. She was only thankful that for the return walk he had chosen to be the Marquess of Bedford rather than Stephen. She might not have been able to resist letting down her guard with Stephen.

He put fresh logs on the fire when they went indoors while she filled the kettle. By the time they were ready to settle into an uncomfortable silence, the children were home, and they brought with them again all the joy and laughter of Christmas—and, yes, the warmth too, despite rosy cheeks and reddened fingers and noses.

"Tell the Nativity story again, Papa," Dora begged when all outdoor garments had been removed and put away, climbing onto his knee.

"Again?" he said. "You have heard it three times already, poppet."

"Tell it again," she said, fingering the diamond pin in his neckcloth.

Megan was standing beside them. The marquess smiled at her—Lilias's heart did a complete somersault—and reached out his free arm to draw her onto his other knee. He told both girls the story, and Andrew too, who was sitting at his feet whittling away at the sheep again, trying to improve its appearance. Lilias busied herself getting tea.

The time went too fast. He willed it to hold still; he willed eight o'clock never to come. But of course it did come. Stories and singing and charades and forfeits had passed the time merrily. Megan and Dora were bright-cheeked and bright-eyed and very giggly long before eight o'clock came, a sure sign that they were very tired.

"But I don't want to go, Papa," Dora said, yawning very loudly. "One more hour?"

"One more?" Megan pleaded.

Lilias was sitting in a chair opposite his own, her feet resting on the hearth. She was smiling. She looked very beautiful. Why had he not told her that out at the lake? Why had he not told her that she looked even lovelier this year in the unfashionable blue gown than she had looked six years before? Why had he allowed himself to get angry instead? Angry at a fate that could treat her so? He wanted her to have everything in the world, and instead, she had almost nothing. Why had he not told her she looked beautiful?

"Not even one more minute," he told the girls. "And, as it is, that coach of ours is late. Wherever can it be?"

He got up from his chair and crossed the room to the window. He pulled back the curtains, which they had closed as soon as they had returned from their walk, and leaned past the evergreen in order to peer out into the darkness. Not that he had really needed to lean forward, he realized immediately. It was not completely dark outside.

"Good Lord," he said. "Snow."

It must have started in great earnest the moment they had pulled the curtains. And it must have been snowing ever since. There were several inches of it out there.

"Snow!" There were three identical shrieks, and three human missiles hurled themselves against him and past him in order to see the spectacle. "Snow!" There was a loud babble of excitement.

"Well," he said, "at least we know what has delayed the coach. It is still in the coach house and the horses in the stable, if Giles has any sense whatsoever."

Dora shrieked and bounced at his side. "We can stay, then, Papa?" she asked. "We can stay all night?"

He turned to see Lilias standing before the fireplace.

"She can share Megan's bed," she said hastily. "There will be room for the two of them. You must not think of taking her out if the snow really is too deep for your carriage."

"And you can share mine," Andrew said brightly.

The marquess laughed. "Thank you, Andrew," he said, "but I shall walk home. For days I have been longing to set my feet in snow. But I will be grateful to leave Dora here until morning. Thank you, ma'am." He looked at Lilias.

She went upstairs almost immediately with Megan to get all ready. He took Dora onto his lap to explain to her that he would go home alone and return for her in the morning. But he need not have worried. She was so tired and so excited at the prospect of spending the night with Megan that she seemed not at all upset at being separated from him. He took her upstairs.

The door to one small bedroom was open. Megan was crying. The marquess stood still on the stairs and held his daughter's hand more tightly.

"Hush," Lilias was saying. "Oh, hush, sweetheart. You know we had a pact not to talk of it or even think of it until Christmas was well and truly over. Hush now. It has been a lovely Christmas, has it not?"

"Ye-e-es," Megan wailed, her voice muffled. "But I don't want to go, Lilias."

"Sh," Lilias said. "Dora will be here in a minute. You don't want her to see you cry, do you?"

"No-o-o."

The marquess looked down into the large eyes of his daughter and held a finger to his lips. He frowned. Then he stepped firmly on the next stair. "Here we are," he said cheerfully. "Two little girls to squash into one little bed."

Megan giggled.

"Four little girls," Dora corrected him, indicating the doll clutched in her own arms and pointing to Megan's, which was lying at the foot of the bed.

Both girls giggled.

"Four, then," he said. "In you get."

Andrew was no less tired than the girls. He went to bed only ten minutes later. Ten minutes after that the giggling and whisperings stopped. It seemed that all were asleep.

The marquess was standing at the window, looking out into the curiously lightened world of freshly falling snow. Lilias was seated silently at the fire.

"Lilias," he said. He could no more think of the right words to say than he had been able to twenty minutes before. He continued to look out the window. "You must marry me. It is the only way. I cannot let you take on the life of a governess. And Andrew and Megan must not be separated from each other, or from you. You must marry me. Will you?" He turned finally to look across the room at her. And knew immediately that he had done it all wrong, after all.

She was quite pale. She stared up at him, all large eyes in her thin face. "No," she said, and her voice was trembling. "No, I will not accept charity. No."

But she must be made to accept. Did she not realize that? He felt his jaw harden. He retreated behind the mask that had become almost habitual with him in the past few years.

"I don't think you have any choice," he said. "Do you seriously think that, as a governess, you will ever again have a chance to see your brother and sister? Do you imagine that you will be able to save even enough money to travel to where they are to visit? It will not happen. When you leave here, you will see them for perhaps the last time."

She was sitting on the very edge of her chair, her back straight, her hands clasped tightly in her lap.

"Do you think I do not know that?" she said.

"Andrew will not even be allowed to see you again," he said. "He will be taken back into the fold, and he will be taught to despise you. Do you realize that?"

"Yes."

He saw the word forming itself on her lips. He did not hear it. "Megan will be an old woman's slave," he said. "She will have a dreary girlhood. She will probably end up like you, a governess or a paid companion. Have you thought of that?"

"Yes," she said.

"Then you must marry me," he said. "For their sakes, if not for your own. You will be able to stay together." His eyes strayed down her body. "And you will be able to have some new clothes at last."

He ached to buy her those new garments, to see the pleasure in her eyes as he clothed her in silks and lace and warm wool. He wanted to hang jewels about her neck and at her ears. He wanted to put rings on her fingers.

"You *must* marry me," he said.

She rose to her feet. He knew as soon as she did so that she was very angry. "Must I?" she said softly. "Must I, my lord? Is this what your title and wealth have done for you? Do you talk to your servants so? Do you talk to everyone so? And does everyone kiss the ground at your feet and do what they must do? Is this how you persuaded your first wife to marry you? And did she instantly obey? Well, not me, my lord. I do not have to marry you, or anyone else. And if it is true that my brother and sister will live less than perfect lives according to the arrangements I have made for them, then at least we will all be able to retain our pride and hold our heads high. I will not sell myself even for their sakes."

The Marquess of Bedford had trained himself not to flinch outwardly under such scathing attacks. He merely stared at her from half-closed eyelids, his teeth and lips firmly pressed together.

"Pride can be a lonely companion," he said.

"Perhaps so," she said. "But charity would be an unbearable companion, my lord."

He nodded. "I will wish you good night, then," he said. "Thank you for giving Dora a bed. And thank you for giving her the loveliest day of her life. I know I do not exaggerate. I hope we have not spoiled your day."

"No," she said. The fire of battle had died in her eyes. She looked smaller and thinner even than usual. "You have not spoiled our day. The children have been very happy."

The children. Not she. The marquess half smiled, though he feared that his expression must look more like a sneer. He picked up his greatcoat and pulled it on.

"Good night," he said again, pulling his collar up about his ears. "Don't stand at the door. You will get cold."

He did not look at her again. He concentrated his mind on wading through the soft snow without either falling or losing his way.

She sat back down on the edge of her chair and stared into the fire. She would not think. She would not remember . . . or look ahead. She would not think. She would not. She would sit until some warmth seeped into her bones, and then she would go to bed and sleep. She felt bone-weary. But she would not think at all. Tomorrow she would work things out.

She would sit there until she was warm and until she could be sure that her legs would support her when she stood up. And until she could see to climb the stairs. She blinked her eyes determinedly and swallowed several times.

But she would not think.

She sat there for perhaps fifteen minutes before leaping to her feet suddenly and flying to the door to answer a loud hammering there. She pulled it open, letting in cold and snow. And she closed it again, setting her back to it, and watching in a kind of stupor as Bedford stamped the snow from his boots and tore off his coat and hat and threw them carelessly aside.

"Listen to me, Lilias," the marquess said fiercely, turning to her. But he stopped talking and looked at her in exasperation. He reached out and took one of her hands in a firm clasp. "No, don't listen to me. Come with me."

He did not take her far, only to the middle of the parlor. She looked up at him in mute inquiry.

"You will not even be able to slap my face," he said, drawing her against him with his free arm. He glanced upward at the mistletoe. "It is a Christmas tradition, you see." He bent his head and kissed her.

She stood still, rigid with shock. It was a hard and fierce kiss.

"Don't," he said against her lips. His very blue eyes were gazing into hers. "Don't, Lilias. Don't shut me out."

And then she could only cling to him and sag against him and eventually reach up to hold him more firmly by the shoulders and about the neck. He was no longer a slender boy, kissing her with the eager kisses of a very young man. He had a man's body, hard and firmly muscled. And his kisses were a man's kisses, deep and experienced and full of a knee-weakening promise.

But he was the same, nonetheless. He was Stephen as she remembered him, as she had dreamed of him and cried for him, and as she had consigned to the most treasured memories of her young life. He was Stephen as she had longed for him and yearned for him through six years when she might have married any of several other worthy men. Stephen, whom she had loved at the age of fifteen, and whom she would love at the age of ninety, if she lived that long.

She did as he asked. She did not shut him out. At long last, she lowered her guard and did not shut him out.

"Lilias." He held her head against his shoulder and looked down into her face. "I said it all wrong. I did it all wrong. Right from the start. Six years ago. How could I ever have left you? After Claude died, my father impressed upon me that I was now his heir, that I must put behind me all that was humble and beneath the dignity of a future marquess. And when he died soon after, I was dazzled by my own importance and popularity. I forgot you. I married Lorraine."

"I understood," she said, reaching up a hand and touching his cheek with her fingertips. "I did not expect any different. Even before you left, I never expected more from you. Only friendship and an innocent romance. I was very young. Too young to have any expectations of anything beyond the moment."

"I never allowed myself to think of you," he said. "You just became part of the dream of a perfect childhood and boyhood."

"I know," she said. "You became my dream, too."

"I did only one good and worthy thing in all those years," he said, "and had only one claim to happiness: I begot Dora."

"Yes," she said. "I know."

"I have had her only since last spring," he said. "And as Christmas approached, I knew I had to bring her here. I remembered that Christmases here were always perfect. I thought it was the snow and the sledding and skating. Memory can sometimes be so defective. I was wrong about that. But not wrong in the main. Christmas *was* always perfect here, and it has been perfect this year, even though the snow has only just come. It was because of you, Lilias. Because you were always there. And because you were here this year."

She turned her face to his shoulder. "I wanted Christmas for the children," she said. "I did not know how I was to do it. But when I heard that you had come, I knew that you would be able to provide it. Not just with money, though that is what I ended up asking for and remembering that ridiculous incident of the Latin lessons. I just felt that I had to go to you and that you would make everything all right. But you had changed. I was frightened when I saw you."

"Lilias," he said, and held her head more firmly against his shoulder. "How can I say it this time without saying quite the wrong words again? If not for your own sake and your brother's and sister's, will you do it for mine? Marry me, I mean. Though I don't deserve it. I left you without a word. For Dora's, then? She needs a mother. You would not believe what a sullen and bad-tempered child she was when I first took her, and how petulant she can still be when she does not have her way. And I cannot say no to her, though I know I must learn how. She needs you, Lilias. And she loves you already. Have you seen that? I want you to be her mother. Will you? Will you marry me?"

She pulled her head free of his hand and looked up into a face that was anxious and vulnerable.

"No," she said, shaking her head. "Not for Dora's sake, Stephen. It would not be enough. And not for Andrew's and Megan's. That would not be enough either. And not for my need. Somehow I will survive as a governess."

He opened his mouth to protest. She set one finger lightly over his lips.

"For one reason only," she said. "For the only reason that would make it work. Only if we love each other. Both of us."

Wide blue eyes looked down into hers. "You have been there for six long and unhappy years," he said. "The dream of you. I brought my child to you this Christmas, though I did not realize when we left London quite why I was bringing her here. The dream has come alive again. Like a greedy child, I have Christmas and want to keep it forever here in my arms. I don't want it to disappear tomorrow or the next day. I don't want that dreary world back, Lilias. I don't want to live without you. Yes, I love you. I always have, but like a fool, I have repressed the knowledge for six years. Will you have me?"

"So many times," she said, "I have told myself how foolish I was not to let go the memory of you. I had the well-being of two children to see to, and my own, and I have had two offers since Papa died. We could have been comfortable, the three of us. But I could not let you go, even though I was so very young when you left. Now I know I was not foolish, after all. For whether you marry me or leave me forever tomorrow, Stephen, you will always be a part of me. I will never love any other man. There is only you."

He was quite the old Stephen suddenly, his eyes dancing, his mouth curved into a grin. "Now, let me get this straight," he said. "Was that yes or no?"

She laughed back into his eyes. "It was yes," she said.

"Was it?" He stooped down suddenly and she found herself swung up into his arms. He carried her over to the fire and sat down on a chair with her. "God, Lilias, you weigh no more than a feather. The first thing I am going to do with you, my girl, is fatten you up."

She clung to his neck and laughed.

"And the next thing I am going to do," he said, "is take you to London and buy you so many clothes it will take you a year to wear them all. And so many jewels that it will take two footmen to lift you from the ground."

Her laughter turned to giggles.

"But there," he said, shrugging his shoulder so that her face was turned to his again, "I was always a fool, wasn't I, love? The costliest gown in London could not look lovelier on you than this blue silk. And anyway, those things are going to have to come second and third. A very distant second and third. There is something else I must do first."

"What?" she asked, reaching up to touch the silver hairs at his temples.

"I'll show you in just a moment," he said. "But first you had better tell me what time you are planning to kick me out of here."

"Mm," she said. "Give me time to think about it. What were you going to show me, Stephen?"

He rubbed his nose against hers. "How to play house properly," he said, grinning at her once more before seeking her mouth with his own again.

NO ROOM
AT THE INN

The White Hart Inn, somewhere in Wiltshire—it had never been important enough for anyone to map its exact location on any fashionable map or in any guidebook, fashionable or otherwise—was neither large nor picturesque nor thriving. It was not a posting inn and had no compensating claim to fame—not its location, nor the quality of its ale or cuisine, nor the geniality of its host, nor anything, in short. It was certainly not the type of place in which one would wish to be stranded unexpectedly for any length of time.

Especially at Christmastime.

And more especially when the cause was not a heavy snowfall, which might have added beauty to the surroundings and romance to the adventure, but rain. Torrential, incessant rain, which poured down from a leaden sky and made a quagmire of even the best-kept roads. The road past the White Hart was not one of the best-kept.

The inn presented a picture of squatness and ugliness and gloom to those who were forced to put up there rather than slither on along the road and risk bogging down completely and having to spend Christmas inside a damp and chill carriage—or risk overturning and celebrating the festive season amidst mud and injuries and even possibly death.

None of the travelers who arrived at the inn during the course of the late afternoon of the day preceding Christmas

Eve did so by design. None of them did so with any pleasure. Most of them were in low spirits, and that was an optimistic description of the mood of a few of them. Even the landlord and his good lady were not as ecstatic as one might have expected them to be under the circumstances that they had rarely had more than one of their rooms filled during any one night for the past two years and more. Before nightfall all six of their rooms were occupied, and it was altogether possible that someone else might arrive after dark.

"What are we going to give 'em to eat?" Letty Palmer asked her husband, frowning at the thought of the modest-size goose and the even more modest ham on which the two of them had planned to feast on Christmas Day. "And what are we going to give 'em to drink, Joe? There is only ale, and all of 'em are quality. Not to mention the coachmen what brought 'em 'ere."

"It'll 'ave to be ale or the rainwater outside," Joseph Palmer said, a note of belligerence in his voice, as if his guests had already begun to complain about the plain fare at the White Hart. "And as far as vittles is concerned, they'll 'ave to eat what we 'as and be thankful for it too."

But the guests had not yet begun to complain about the food and drink, perhaps because they had not yet had an opportunity to sample the fare on which it seemed likely they would have to celebrate Christmas.

Edward Riddings, Marquess of Lytton, cursed his luck. He had been fully intending to spend the holiday season in London as he usually did, entertaining himself by moving from party to party. The ladies were always at their most amorous at Christmastime, he had found from experience. Yes, even the ladies. There was always pleasure to be derived from a sampling of their charms.

But this year he had been persuaded to accept one of the invitations that he always received in abundance to a private party in the country. Lady Frazer, the delectable widow, was to be at the Whittakers' and had given him an unmistakable signal that at last she would be his there. He had been laying determined siege to her heart, or rather to her body, since she had emerged from her year of mourning during the previous spring. She had the sort of body for which a man would be willing to traverse England.

Yet now it was evident that he was neither to reach that body in time for Christmas nor to return to London in time to console himself with the more numerous but perhaps less enticing pleasures of town. Even if the rain were to stop at this very instant, he thought, looking out of the low window of the small and shabby room to which he had been assigned at the White Hart, it was doubtful that the road would be passable before Christmas Day at the earliest. And there were still twenty miles to go.

The rain showed no sign of abating. If anything it was pounding down with greater enthusiasm than ever.

If he were fortunate—but events were not shaping up to bring any good fortune with them—there would be a beautiful and unattached lady of not quite impeccable virtue also stranded at this infernal inn. But he would not allow himself to hope. There could not be more than five or six guest rooms, and he had already seen five or six of his fellow strandees, none of whom appeared even remotely bedworthy.

It was going to be some Christmas, he thought, gritting his teeth and pounding one fist against the windowsill.

Miss Pamela Wilder gazed from the window of her room and felt all the misery of utter despair. She could not even cry. She could not even feel all the awkwardness of her situation, stranded as she was at a public inn without either maid or chaperon. It did not matter. Nothing mattered except that her first holiday in more than a year was to be spent here at this inn, alone. She thought of her parents and of her brothers and sisters, and she thought of Christmas as she had always known it—except last year—at the rectory and in the small church next to it. There was warmth and light and wonder in the thought, until nostalgia stabbed at her so painfully that the memories could no longer bring any comfort.

They did not know she was coming. It was to be a surprise. Lawrence, one of Sir Howard Raven's coachmen, had been given a few days off for Christmas and had even been granted permission to take the old and shabby carriage that was scheduled for destruction as soon as the new one was delivered. And his home was not ten miles from the rectory where Mama and Papa lived. Pamela had broached the subject very tentatively and quite without hope, first with Lawrence and then with Lady Raven, and wonder of wonders, no one had raised any objection. It seemed that a governess was not particularly needed at Christmastime, when young Hortense would have cousins with whom to play and greater freedom to mingle with the adults.

Pamela was free until two days after Christmas. Free to go home. Free to be with her family and spend that most wonderful time of the year with them. Free to see Wesley and hope that finally he felt himself well enough established on his farm to offer for her. Free to hope that perhaps he would at least ask her to betroth herself to him even if the wedding must be postponed for a long time. Having an unspoken understanding with him had not soothed her loneliness since she had been forced to take her present post more than a year before. She craved some more definite hope for the future.

Yet now she was to spend Christmas at the White Hart, eight miles—eight impossible miles—from home. Even if the rain were to stop now, there seemed little chance that she would make it home for Christmas Day. But the rain was not going to stop now or before the night was over at the very earliest. There was no point in even hoping otherwise.

She was hungry, Pamela realized suddenly, even though she was not at all sure she would be able to eat. How could she do so, anyway? How could she go downstairs alone to the dining room? And yet she must. She was not of any importance at all. There seemed little hope of persuading anyone to bring up her dinner on a tray.

What a Christmas it was going to be, she thought. Even last year had been better—that dreadful Christmas, her first away from home, her first in the status of a servant and yet not quite a servant. She had been able to celebrate the coming of Christ with neither the family nor the servants. Perhaps after all she would be no more alone this year than last, she thought in a final effort to console herself.

Lord Birkin stood at the window of his room, his lips compressed, his hands clasped behind him and beating a rhythmic tattoo against his back. What a confounded turn of events.

"We should have come a week ago, like everyone else," Lady Birkin said, "instead of staying in London until the last possible minute."

She was seated on the edge of the bed behind him. He knew that if he turned and looked at her, he would see her the picture of dejection, all her beauty and animation marred by the rain and the poverty of her surroundings. She would hate having to spend Christmas here when they had been on their way to spend it with the Middletons and more than twenty of their relatives and friends.

"You would have missed the opera and the Stebbins' ball," he said without turning.

"And you would have missed a few days at your club," she said, a note of bitterness in her voice.

"We could not have predicted the rain," he said. "Not in this quantity anyway. I am sorry that you will miss all the Christmas entertainments, Sally."

"And you will miss the shooting," she said, that edge still in her voice. "And the billiards."

He turned to look at her at last, broodingly. Marriage had turned out to be nothing like what he had expected. They were two people living their separate lives, he and

Sally, with the encumbrance of the fact that they were legally bound together for life.

Were things quite as bad as that? They had been fond of each other when they had married, even though their parents on both sides had urged the match on them. He still was fond of her, wasn't he? Yes, he was still fond of her. But somehow marriage had not drawn them closer together. The occasional couplings, now no more frequent than once or twice a month, though they had not been married much longer than three years, brought with them no emotional bond. They both behaved on the mornings after the couplings as if they had never happened.

"I am sorry about the sparsity of rooms," he said. "I am sorry we must share."

His wife flushed and looked about the room rather than at him. It was going to be dreadful, she thought. Dreadful to be alone with him for what would probably be several days. Dreadful to have to share a room with him and a bed for that time. They had never shared a bed for longer than ten minutes at a time, and even those occasions had become rarer during the past year.

She had married him because she loved him and because she had thought he loved her, though he had never said so. *Foolish girl.* She must have appeared quite mousy to such a blond and beautiful man. He had married her because it was expected of him, because the connection was an eligible one. She knew now that she had never attracted him and never could. He rarely spent time with her. Their marital encounters were a bitter disappointment, and so rare that she did not even have the consolation of having conceived his child.

She knew about his mistresses, though he did not know that she knew. She had even seen his latest one, a creature of exquisite beauty and voluptuous charms. She herself had come to feel quite without beauty or charm or allure.

Except that she had not allowed herself to give in to self-pity. She had had a choice early in her marriage. Either she could retreat into herself and become the mousy, uninteresting thing he saw her as, or she could put her unhappiness and disappointment behind her and live a life of busy gaiety, as so many married ladies of her acquaintance did. She had chosen the latter course. He would never know for what foolish reason she had married him or what foolish hopes had been dashed early in their marriage.

"There is no point in apologizing for what cannot be helped, Henry," she said. "Under the circumstances I suppose we are fortunate to have a roof over our heads. Though I could wish that it had happened at some other time of the year. It is going to be an unimaginably dull Christmas."

She wondered what it would be like to lie all night in the large and rather lumpy bed with him beside her. Her breathing quickened at the thought, and she looked up at him with an unreasonable resentment.

"Yes," he said. "Whoever heard of Christmas spent at an inn?"

"It would not have happened," she said, hearing the irritability in her voice and knowing that she was being unfair, "if we had come a week ago, like everyone else."

"As you keep reminding me," he said. "Next year we will do things differently, Sally. Next year we will see to it that you are surrounded by friends and admirers well before Christmas itself comes along."

"And that you have plenty of other gentlemen and gentlemen's sports with which to amuse yourself," she said. "Perhaps there will be some gentlemen here, Henry. Perhaps you will find some congenial companions with whom to talk the night away and forget the inconvenience of such congested quarters."

"I can sleep in the taproom if you so wish," he said, his voice cold.

They did not often quarrel. One or the other of them usually left the room when a disagreement was imminent, as it was now.

"That would be foolish," she said.

He was leaving the room now. He paused, with his hand on the doorknob. "I doubt there is such a luxury as a private parlor in this apology for an inn," he said. "We will have to eat in the public dining room, Sally. I shall go and see when dinner will be ready."

An excuse to get away from her, Lady Birkin thought as the door closed behind him. She concentrated on not crying and succeeded. She had perfected the skill over the years.

It was an excuse to get away from her, Lord Birkin thought as he descended the stairs. Away from her accusing voice and the knowledge that the worst aspect of the situation for her was being forced to spend a few days in his dull company. She did not sleep with any of her numerous admirers. He did not know quite how he could be sure of that, since he had never spied on her, but he did know it. She was faithful to him, or to their marriage, at least, as he was not. But he knew equally that she would prefer the company of any one of her admirers to his.

But she was stuck with it for several days. And at Christmas, of all times.

The Misses Amelia and Eugenia Horn, unmarried ladies of indeterminate years, had left their room in order to seek out the innkeeper. The sheets on their beds were damp, Miss Amelia Horn declared in a strident voice.

"Perhaps they are only cold, dear," Miss Eugenia Horn suggested in a near whisper, embarrassed by the indelicate mention of bedsheets in the hearing of two gentlemen, not counting the innkeeper himself.

But her elder sister was made of sterner stuff and argued on. They were bitterly disappointed, Miss Eugenia Horn reflected, leaving the argument to her sister. They would not make it to dear Dickie's house fifteen miles away and would not have the pleasure of their annual visit with their brother and sister-in-law and the dear children, though the youngest of Dickie's offspring was now seventeen years old. How time did fly. They would all be made quite despondent by her absence and dear Amelia's. Dickie was always too busy, the poor dear, to have them visit at any other time of the year.

Miss Eugenia Horn sighed.

Colonel Forbes, a large, florid-faced, white-haired gentleman of advanced years, was complaining to Lord Birkin, the innkeeper's attention being otherwise occupied at the time. He deplored the absence of a private parlor for the convenience of his wife and himself.

"General Hardinge himself has invited us for Christmas," the colonel explained. "A singular honor and distinguished company. And now this blasted rain. A fine Christmas this is going to be."

"We all seem to be agreed on that point, at least," Lord Birkin said politely, and waited his turn to ask about dinner.

Sometimes the most dreaded moments turned out not to be so dreadful after all, Pamela realized when the emptiness of her stomach drove her downstairs in search of dinner. Although the dining room appeared alarmingly full with fellow guests and she felt doubly alone, she did not long remain so. Two middle-aged ladies looked up at her from their table, as did all the other occupants of the room, saw her lone state, and took her beneath their wing. Soon she was tucked safely into a chair at their table.

"Doubtless you expected to be at your destination all within one day, my dear," Miss Eugenia Horn said in explanation of Pamela's lack of a companion.

"Yes, ma'am," she said. "I did not expect the rain."

"But it is always wiser to expect the unexpected and go nowhere without a chaperon," Miss Amelia Horn added. "You would not wish to give anyone the impression that you were fast."

"No, ma'am." Pamela was too grateful for their company to feel offended.

The Misses Horn proceeded to complain about the dampness of their bedsheets and their threadbare state.

"I suppose," Miss Amelia Horn said, "that we should have expected the unexpected, Eugenia, and brought our own. It is never wise to travel without."

The rain and all being stranded at the very worst time of the year had appeared to draw the other occupants of the room together, Pamela noticed. Conversation was becoming general. She looked about her with some curiosity, careful not to stare at anyone. A quiet gentleman of somewhat less than middle years sat at the table next to hers. He said very little, but listened to everyone, a smile in his eyes and lurking about his mouth. He was perhaps the only member of the party to look as if he did not particularly resent being where he was.

An elderly couple sat at another table, the man loudly and firmly condemning England as a place to live and declaring darkly that if the government did not do something about it soon, all sensible Englishmen would take themselves off to live on the Continent or in America. He did not make it clear whether he expected the government to do something about the excessive amount of rainfall to which England was susceptible or whether he was referring to something else. Whatever the cause, he was very flushed and very angry. His wife sat across the table from him, quietly nodding. Pamela realized after a while that the nodding was involuntary. They were Colonel and Mrs. Forbes, she learned in the course of dinner.

A young and handsome couple sat at another table, perhaps the most handsome pair Pamela had ever seen. The lady was brown-haired and brown-eyed and had a proud and beautiful face and the sort of shapely figure that always made Pamela sigh with envy. Her husband, Lord Birkin, was like a blond Greek god, the kind of man she had always found rather intimidating. They were clearly unhappy both with each other and with a ruined Christmas. Apparently they were on their way to a large country party. They were the sort of people who had everything and nothing, though that was a flash judgment, Pamela admitted to herself, and perhaps unfair.

There was another gentleman in the room. Pamela's eyes skirted about him whenever she looked up. On the few occasions when she looked directly at him, her uncomfortable impression that he was staring at her was confirmed. He was not handsome. Oh, yes, he was, of course, but not in the way of the blond god. He was more attractive than handsome, with his dark hair and hooded eyes—they might be blue, she thought—and a cynical curl to his lip. She had met his like a few times since becoming a governess. He was undressing her with his eyes and probably doing other things to her with his mind. She had to concentrate on keeping her hands steady on her knife and fork.

"Oh. On my way home, ma'am," she said in answer to a question Mrs. Forbes had asked her. "To my parents' home for Christmas. Eight miles from here."

Everyone was listening to her. They were sharing stories, commiserating with one another for the unhappy turn of events that had brought them all to the White Hart. Only the quiet gentleman seemed to have had no Christmas destination to lament.

"I am a governess, ma'am," she said when Miss Eugenia Horn asked her the question. "My father is a clergyman." The gentleman of the lazy eyelids—the innkeeper had addressed him as "my lord"—was still staring at her, one hand turning his glass of ale.

The conversation turned to the food and a spirited discussion of whether it was beef or veal or pork they were eating. There was no unanimous agreement.

A governess, the Marquess of Lytton was thinking, daughter of a clergyman. A shame. A decided shame. Governesses were of two kinds, of course. There were the virtuous governesses, the unassailable ones, and there were the governesses starved for pleasures of the sexual variety and quite delightfully voracious in their appetites when one had finally maneuvered them between bedsheets or into some other satisfactory location. He judged that Miss

Pamela Wilder was of the former variety, though one never knew for sure until one had made careful overtures. Perhaps she would live up to her name.

She was certainly the only possibility at the inn. There had not appeared to be even any chambermaids or barmaids with whom to warm his bed. He had the uncomfortable feeling that he might be facing an alarmingly celibate Christmas if Miss Wilder were saving herself for a future and probably illusory husband. There was the delectable Lady Birkin, of course, but then he had never made a practice of bedding other men's wives or even flirting with them, whether the husband was in tow or not.

Miss Pamela Wilder was the only possibility then. And a distinct possibility she was, provided she was assailable. She was slim, perhaps a little slimmer than he liked his women when there was a choice, but there was a grace about her figure and movements that he found intriguingly feminine and that stirred his loins, though he had drunk only two tankards of the landlord's indescribably bad ale. Her face was lovely—wide-eyed, long-lashed, with a straight nose and a soft, thoroughly kissable mouth. Her hair was smooth and tied in a simple knot at her neck, as one would expect of a governess, but no simplicity of style could dim its blond sheen.

Two nights, probably three, at this inn, he thought, if they were fortunate. She could help Christmas pass with relative comfort, perhaps with enormous comfort. She might console him for the fact that the consummation of his lust with Lady Frazer must be postponed beyond the festive season.

The innkeeper and his wife did not seem to feel it would be diplomatic to discuss private business in private. Mr. Joe Palmer was refilling the gentlemen's glasses with ale when the inevitable new arrivals came to the inn, looking for a room. Mrs. Letty Palmer came and stood in the doorway to discuss the matter with him just as if the room were not full of guests who had their own conversations to conduct.

"We don't 'ave no room for 'em," Mr. Palmer said with firm decision. "They'll 'ave to go somewhere else, Letty."

"There's nowhere else for 'em to go," Mrs. Palmer said. "We're full with quality and their servants. They aren't quality, Joe. I thought p'raps the taproom?"

"And 'ave 'em rob us blind as soon as we goes to bed?" Mr. Palmer said contemptuously, earning a roar of fury from Colonel Forbes when he slopped ale onto the cloth beside that gentleman's glass. "We don't 'ave no room, Letty."

"The woman's in the fambly way," Mrs. Palmer said. "Looks as if she's about to drop 'er load any day, Joe."

"Oh, dear," Miss Eugenia Horn said, a hand to her mouth. Such matters were not to be spoken aloud in genteel and mixed company.

Mr. Palmer put his jug of ale down on the cloth and set his hands on his hips. "I didn't arsk 'er to get in the fambly way, now, did I, Letty?" he said. "Am I 'er keeper? What are they doin' out in this weather anyway if she's close to 'er time?"

"'Er man's in search of work," Mrs. Palmer said. "What shall we do with 'em, Joe? We can't turn 'em away. They'll be drowned."

Joe puffed out his cheeks, practicality warring with compassion.

"I won't 'ave 'em in 'ere, Letty," he said. "There's no room for 'em and I won't risk 'aving 'em steal all our valuables. And all these qualities' valuables. They'll 'ave to move on or stay in the stable. There's an empty stall."

"It's cold in the stable," she said.

"Not with all 'em extra 'orses," the innkeeper said. "It's there or nowhere, Letty." He picked up his jug and turned determinedly to the quiet gentleman. "They comes 'ere expectin' a body to snap 'is fingers and make new rooms appear." His voice was aggrieved. "And they probly don't 'ave two 'a'pennies to rub together."

The quiet gentleman merely smiled at him. Poor *devils,* the marquess thought, *having to sleep in the stable.* But it was probably preferable to the muddy road. He would not think of it. It was not as if the inn itself offered luxury or even basic comfort. The dinner they had just eaten was disgusting, to put the matter into plain English.

"Poor people," Lady Birkin said quietly to her husband. "Imagine having to sleep in a stable, Henry. And she is with child."

"They will probably be thankful even for that," he said. "They will be out of the rain, at least, and the animals will keep them warm."

She stared at him from her dark eyes with an expression that never failed to turn his insides over. She had a tender heart and carried out numerous works of charity, though she always fretted that she could do so little. She was going to worry now about the two poor travelers who had arrived at safety only to find that there was no room at the inn. He wanted to reach across the table to take her hand. He did not do so, only partly because they were in a public place.

"Will they?" she said. "Be warm, I mean? The landlord was not just saying that? But it will smell in there, Henry, and be dirty."

"There is no alternative," he said, "except for them to move on. They will be all right, Sally. They will be safe and dry, at least. They will be able to keep each other warm."

Her cheeks flushed slightly, and he felt a stabbing of desire for her—the sort of feeling that usually sent him off in search of his mistress and an acceptable outlet for his lust.

"I am going back upstairs," she said, getting to her feet. He walked around the table to pull back her chair. "Are you coming?"

And impose his company on her for the rest of the evening? "I'll escort you up," he said, "and return to the taproom for a while."

She nodded coolly, indifferently.

Her movement was the signal for everyone to get up except the quiet gentleman, who continued to sit and sip on the bad ale. But Lord Birkin did not wait for everyone else.

He escorted his wife to their room and looked about it with a frown.

"You will be all right here, Sally?" he asked. "There is not much to do except lie down and sleep, is there?"

"I am tired after the journey," she said.

He looked at the bed. It did not look as if it were going to be comfortable. He was to share it with her that night. For the first time in over three years they were to sleep together, literally sleep together. The thought brought another tightening to his groin. He should have slept with her from the start, he thought. He should have made it the pattern of their marriage. Perhaps the physical side of their marriage and every other aspect of it would have developed more satisfactorily if he had. Perhaps they would not have drifted apart.

He did not know quite why they had done so, or even if *drifted* were the right word. Somehow their marriage had never got properly started. He did not know whose fault it was. Perhaps neither of them was to blame. Perhaps both of them were. Perhaps she had really been as fond of him as he was of her at the beginning. Perhaps they should have put their feelings into words. Perhaps he should not have given in to the fear that she found him dull and his touch distasteful. Perhaps he should not have treated her with sexual restraint, as his father and other men had advised, because she was a lady and ladies were supposed to find sex distasteful. Perhaps he should have taken her with the desire he felt—surely it was not disrespectful to show pleasure in one's wife's body.

Perhaps. Perhaps and perhaps.

"I'll be up later," he told her. "Don't wait up for me." *You may sleep. I'll not be demanding my conjugal rights.* He might as well have said those words too.

She nodded and turned away to the window, waiting for the sound of the door closing behind her and the feeling of emptiness it would bring. And the familiar urge to cry. It was Christmas, and he preferred being downstairs drinking with strangers to being alone with her.

She looked down into wet darkness and shivered. Those poor people—trying to get warm and comfortable in a dirty and drafty stable, trying to sleep there. She wondered if the man loved his wife, if she loved him. If he would hold her close to keep her warm. If he would offer his arm as her pillow. If he would kiss her before she slept so that she would feel warm and loved even in such appalling surroundings.

She wiped impatiently at a tear. She did not normally give in to the urge to weep. She did not usually give in to self-pity.

The Misses Horn were busy agreeing with Mrs. Forbes that indeed it was dreadful that those poor people had to find shelter in a stable on such a wet and chilly night. But what could the husband be thinking of, dragging his poor wife off in search of work when she was in a, ah, delicate situation? There was a deal of embarrassed coughing over the expression of this idea and furtive glances at the gentlemen to make sure that none of them was listening. She would give the man a piece of her mind if she had a chance, Miss Amelia Horn declared.

The Marquess of Lytton got to his feet.

"Allow me to escort you to your room, Miss Wilder," he said, offering her his arm and noting with approval that the top of her head reached his chin. She was taller than she had appeared when she entered the dining room.

She looked calmly and steadily at him. At least she was not going to throw a fit of the vapors at the very idea of being conducted to her bedchamber by a rake. He wondered if she knew enough about the world to recognize him as a rake, and if she realized that all through dinner he had been compensating for the appallingly unappetizing meal by mentally unclothing her and putting her to bed—with himself.

"Thank you," she said, and rested her hand on his arm, a narrow, long-fingered hand. An artist's hand. Either she was a total innocent or she had accepted the first step of seduction. He hoped for the latter. He hoped she was not an innocent. It was Christmas, for God's sake. A man was entitled to his pleasures at that season of the year above all others.

"This is an annoyance and a discomfort that none of us could have forseen this morning," he said.

"Yes." Her voice was low and sweet. Seductive, though whether intentionally so or not he had not yet decided. "Do you suppose they are dreadfully cold out there? Was there anything we could have done?"

"The couple in the stable?" he said. "Very little, I suppose, unless one of us were willing to give up his room and share with someone else."

She looked up into his eyes. Hers had a greenish hue, though they had looked entirely gray from a farther distance. "I suppose that was a possibility," she said. "Alas, none of us thought of it."

He had, though he did not say so. Of course, if they did share a room that night, they could hardly go and advertise the fact to the Palmers. The poor devils were doomed to their night in the stables regardless. A governess. A quiet, grave girl instead of Lady Frazer. A poor exchange, perhaps, though not necessarily so. The quiet ones were often the hottest in bed. And this one was definitely stirring his blood.

She knew that he had offered his escort not out of motives of chivalry, but for other reasons. Her employers entertained a great deal. She had learned something about men during the year of her service. She might have had half a dozen lovers during that time. She had never been tempted.

She was tempted now. She was twenty-three years old, eldest daughter of an impoverished clergyman, a governess. In all probability she was headed for a life of drudgery and humiliation and spinsterhood. She did not believe in her heart that Wesley would ever feel himself in a secure enough position to take her as a wife. Or perhaps he used insecurity as an excuse to avoid a final commitment. The hope of marriage with him was just the frail dream with which she sustained her spirits. It was in truth a dreary life to which she looked forward.

And now even the promised brief joy of this Christmas was to be taken away from her. Except that she could spend it with this incredibly attractive man. She did not doubt that he wanted her and that he would waste no time in sounding out her availability. She had even less doubt that he knew well how to give pleasure to a woman. She could have a Christmas of unimagined pleasure, a Christmas to look back upon with nostalgia for the rest of her life. Now, within the next few minutes, without any chance for her mind and her conscience to brood upon the decision, she could discover what it was like to be with a man, what it was like to be desired and pleasured.

She was tempted. The realization amazed her—she did not even know him. She did not know his name. But she was tempted.

She stopped outside her door and looked up at him. "Thank you, sir," she said. "The innkeeper called you 'my lord'?"

"Lytton," he said. "The marquess of. Green eyes, gray—which are they?"

"A little of both, my lord," she said. *A marquess. Oh, goodness.* He was tall, broad-shouldered. "Thank you," she said again.

He opened the door for her, but when she stepped inside he followed her in and closed the door behind his back. She had been expecting it, she realized. And she realized at the same instant that this was the moment of decision. She did not have any time in which to think, not even a minute.

"It is likely to be a lonely Christmas," he said. "You away from your family, me from my friends."

"Yes." One of his hands had come up so that he could touch her cheek with light fingertips. She felt his touch all the way to her toes. His eyes—yes, they were blue—were keen beneath the lazy lids. She looked into them.

"Perhaps," he said, "we can make it less lonely together."

"Yes." But no sound came out with the word.

She had been kissed before—twice, both times by Wesley. But the experience had not prepared her at all for the Marquess of Lytton's kiss. It was not that it was hard or demanding. Quite the opposite, in fact. His lips rested as lightly against hers as his fingertips had against her cheek a few moments before. But they were parted, warm and moist, and they moved over hers, feeling them, caressing them, softening them, even licking at them. When his hands came to her waist to bring her against him, she allowed herself to be embraced and rested her body against his—against this hard, muscled, warm male.

He felt wonderful. He smelled wonderful. And he was doing wonderful things to her body, though his hands were still at her waist and his lips still light on hers. Then his hands moved up to her breasts and she knew that now—now, not one moment later—was the point of no return. Now she must stop it or move on to new experiences, to a new state of being.

She would be a fallen woman.

She was incredibly sweet. He had never known innocence, had never imagined how arousing it could be. She was yielding without being in any way aggressive. She held still to his touch without being in any way cringing. She was his, he knew, with a little skill and a little care. And yet he knew equally that she was an innocent despite having allowed him inside her room and having allowed his kiss without any hesitation or coyness.

Her waist was soft, warm, small, with the promise of feminine hips below. He slid his hands up to her breasts. They were not large, but they were firm and soft all at the same time. Her nipples, he found when he tested them with his thumbs, were already peaked. She was his, he knew, despite the almost imperceptible stiffening he felt when his hands moved. He felt her indecision, but knew what that decision would be. He raised his head and looked down at her. She gazed back, wide-eyed.

"I had better say good night," he said, "before I go too far and get my face slapped. Yes, perhaps we can make each other less lonely for Christmas, Miss Wilder. I look forward to conversing with you tomorrow."

"Yes," she said, but he could not tell from her expression if she had been fooled. Did she really believe that he had meant nothing more than pleasant conversation and almost chaste good-night kisses as the means of soothing their loneliness at Christmas? Did she believe that he had not entered this room to bed her?

"Good night," he said, inclining his head to her and letting himself out of her room. Fortunately there was no one to witness his leaving it.

Fool! he thought, his lip curling into a cynical half smile. He had been issued the sort of invitation he had never before in his life refused, and yet he had done just that. He had wanted her. He still did. And yet he had put her from him and pretended that he had meant nothing more than a good-night kiss. He did not believe he had ever kissed a woman good night and not expected more.

She would have had him, too. And she would have been sweet despite her innocence and inexperience. Of course, there would have been her virginity to take—he would wager his fortune that she was a virgin. Perhaps that had been the problem, he thought, shrugging and turning in the direction of the staircase and the taproom. The thought of taking someone's virginity frankly terrified him. He might be a rake, but he was not a corrupter of innocence. Especially when the girl was lonely and unhappy and incapable of making a rational decision.

All the men were in the taproom, though it seemed likely that they were seeking out one another's company rather than their landlord's ale, the marquess thought, grimacing as he tasted it again. Christmas would be beginning now at the Whittakers', with all its rich and tasty foods and drinks and with all its congenial company. He pictured Lady Frazer and put the image from his mind with a mental sigh.

* * *

Lord Birkin did not stay long. He could not concentrate on the conversation. It was true that she did not seem to find his company of any interest, and equally true that she must be horrified at the thought of sharing a bed with him all night. But even so it seemed somehow wrong to sit belowstairs, making conversation with the other gentlemen guests while she was forced to be alone in their small and shabby bedchamber.

A candle still burned in their room, though she was lying far to one side of the bed with her eyes closed. He could not tell if she slept or not. He undressed, wondering if she would open her eyes, finding it strange to think that they had never allowed themselves to become familiar with each other physically. They had never seen each other unclothed. He wished again that it were possible to go back to the beginning of their marriage. He would do so many things differently. Now it seemed too late. How did one change things when patterns had been set and habits had become ingrained?

He blew out the candle and climbed into bed, keeping close to the edge. But it was impossible to sleep and impossible to believe that she slept. She was too still, too quiet. He almost laughed out loud. They had been married for longer than three years and yet were behaving like a couple of strangers thrown together in embarrassing proximity. But he did not laugh; he was not really amused.

"Sally?" He spoke softly and reached out a hand to touch her arm.

"Yes?"

But what was there to say when one had been married to a woman for so long and had never spoken from the heart? Patterns could not so easily be broken. Instead of speaking he moved closer and began the familiar and dispassionate ritual of raising her nightgown and positioning himself on top of her.

All their actions, hers and his, were as they always were. There were never variations. She allowed him to spread her legs, though she did not do it for him, and she lifted herself slightly for his hands to slide beneath. He put himself firmly inside her, settled his face in her hair, felt her hands come to his shoulders, and worked in her with firm, rhythmic strokes until his seed sprang. He was always careful not to indulge himself by prolonging the intercourse. She never gave the slightest sign of either pleasure or distaste. She was a dutiful wife.

And yet he wondered, after he had disengaged himself from her and settled at her side, why he carried out the ritual at all, since it brought neither of them any great pleasure and was not performed frequently enough for there to be any realistic expectation that she would conceive. Why did he do it at all when his desires and energies could be worked out on women who were well paid to suffer the indignity?

Perhaps because he needed her? Because he loved her? But of what use was his love when he had never been able to tell her and when he had never taken the opportunity to cultivate her love at the beginning, when she had perhaps been fond of him?

Lady Birkin lay still, willing sleep to come. Were they reasonably warm and comfortable in the stable? she wondered. Did the man care for his wife? Was she lying in his arms? Was he murmuring words of love to her to put her to sleep? Did her pregnancy bring her discomfort? What did it feel like to be heavy with child—with one's husband's child? She burrowed her head into the hard pillow, imagining as she often did at night to put herself to sleep that it was an arm, that there was a warm chest against her forehead and the steady beat of a heart against her ear. Her hand, moving up to pull the pillow against her face, brushed a real arm and moved hastily away from it.

Breakfast was late. It was not that the night before had been busy and exciting enough to necessitate their sleeping on in the morning. And it was certainly not that the beds were comfortable enough or the rooms warm and cozy enough to invite late sleeping. It was more, perhaps, lethargy, and the knowledge that there was not a great deal to get up for. Even if the rain had stopped, travel would have been impossible. But the rain had not stopped. Each guest awoke to the sound of it beating against the windows, only marginally lighter than it had been the day before.

And so breakfast was late. When the guests emerged from their rooms and gathered in the dining room, it seemed that only the quiet gentleman had been sitting there for some time, patiently awaiting the arrival of his meal.

Greasy eggs and burned toast accompanied complaints about other matters. Eugenia was sure to have taken a chill, Miss Amelia Horn declared, having been forced to sleep between damp sheets. Miss Eugenia Horn flushed at the indecorous mention of sleep and sheets in the hearing of gentlemen. Colonel Forbes complained about the lumps in his bed and swore there were coals in the mattress. Mrs. Forbes nodded her agreement. The Marquess of Lytton lamented the fact that the coal fire in his room had been allowed to die a natural death the night before and had not been resuscitated in the morning. Lord Birkin wondered if they would be expected to make up their own beds. Lady Birkin declared that the ladies could not possibly be expected to sit in their rooms all day long. In the absence of any private parlors, the gentlemen must expect their company in the taproom and the dining room. The other ladies agreed. Even Pamela Wilder nodded her head.

"That is the most sensible suggestion anyone has made yet this morning," the Marquess of Lytton said, nodding his approval to Lady Birkin and fixing his eyes on Pamela.

The innkeeper's wife was pouring muddy coffee for those foolish enough or bored enough to require a second cup. The innkeeper appeared in the doorway.

"You'd best come, Letty," he said. "I told yer we should 'ave nothing to do with 'em. Now look at what's gone and 'appened."

"What 'as 'appened?" The coffee urn paused over the

quiet gentleman's cup as Mrs. Palmer looked up at her husband. "'Ave they gone and stole an 'orse, Joe?"

"I wish they 'ad," Mr. Palmer said fervently. "I wish they 'ad, Letty. But no such luck. 'E's in the taproom." He jerked a thumb over his shoulder. "She's 'aving 'er pains. In our stable, mind."

"Oh, Lord love us," Mrs. Palmer said. The quiet gentleman was still waiting for his coffee. "She can't 'ave it there, Joe. Who ever 'eard of anyone 'aving a baby in a stable?"

The quiet gentleman smiled and appeared to resign himself to going without his coffee.

"Oh." Lady Birkin was on her feet. "The poor woman. How dreadful." She looked at her husband in some distress. "She must be taken extra blankets."

"There ain't no extra blankets," Mrs. Palmer said tartly. "We 'ave a full 'ouse, my lady."

Lady Birkin looked appealingly at her husband. "Then she must have the blankets from our bed," she said. "We will manage without, won't we, Henry?" She reached out a hand to him and he took it.

"Perhaps one from your bed and one from ours, Lady Birkin," Mrs. Forbes said. "Then we will both have something left."

"I have a shawl," Miss Eugenia Horn said. "A warm woolen one that I knitted myself. I shall send it out. Perhaps it will do for wrapping the baby when it is, ah, born." She flushed.

"And I will send out my smelling salts," Miss Amelia Horn said. "The poor woman will probably need them."

"I have a room," Pamela said quietly. "She must be carried up there."

"We don't 'ave no other room to put you in, miss," Mrs. Palmer said.

"And I won't 'ave no one in the taproom," Mr. Palmer added firmly.

"Then I shall sleep in the stable tonight," Pamela said.

The Marquess of Lytton got to his feet. "Is the husband

large and strong?" he asked the innkeeper. "If not, I shall carry the woman in from the stable myself. To *my* room. Miss Wilder may keep hers. And you will, my good man, have someone in the taproom. Tonight. Me."

Mr. Palmer did not argue.

"I'll lend a hand," Lord Birkin said, and the two gentlemen left the room together, followed by Mr. Palmer.

"Perhaps," Lady Birkin said, looking at the innkeeper's wife, who appeared to have been struck with paralysis, "you should have coals sent up to Lord Lytton's room to warm it."

"Lord love us," Mrs. Palmer said, "I 'ave breakfast to clear away, my lady, and dishes to wash before I gets to the rooms."

Colonel Forbes puffed to his feet. "I have never heard the like," he said. "I never have. An inn with no help. Where are the coals, ma'am? I shall carry some up myself."

Mrs. Forbes nodded her approval as her husband strode from the room.

"I shall go up and get the bed ready," Pamela said, "if you will tell me which room is Lord Lytton's, ma'am." She flushed rosily.

"That would be improper, dear," Miss Eugenia Horn said. "Though, of course, it is not his lordship's room any longer, is it? I shall come with you nevertheless."

"Thank you," Pamela said.

"And I shall go and fetch your shawl, Eugenia, and my smelling salts," Miss Amelia Horn said.

"You will send for a midwife?" Lady Birkin said to Mrs. Palmer.

"Oh, Lord, my lady," Mrs. Palmer said. "There is no midwife for five miles, and she wouldn't come 'ere anyhow for no woman what can't pay as like as not."

"I see," Lady Birkin said. "So we are on our own. Have you ever assisted at a birth, Mrs. Palmer?"

The woman's eyes widened. "Not me, my lady," she said. "Nor never 'ad none of my own neither."

Lady Birkin's eyes moved past the Misses Horn and Pamela to Mrs. Forbes. "Ma'am?" she said hopefully.

Mrs. Forbes ceased her nodding in order to shake her head. "I was forty when I married Colonel Forbes," she said. "There was no issue of our marriage."

"Oh," Lady Birkin said. She looked around at the other ladies rather helplessly. "Then I suppose we will have to proceed according to common sense. Will it be enough, I wonder?"

Pamela smiled at her ruefully and left the dining room so that Lord Lytton's former room would be ready by the time he carried up the woman from the stable. Pamela had been surprised by his offer both to give up his room and to carry the woman up to it. She would not have expected compassion of him.

The quiet gentleman picked up the urn, which Mrs. Palmer had abandoned on his table, and poured himself a second cup of coffee.

Lisa Curtis's baby did not come quickly. It was her first and it was large and it appeared determined both to take its time in coming into the world and to give its mother as much grief as possible while doing so. Tom Suffield, the father, was beside himself with anxiety and was no help to anyone. Big, strapping young man as he was, he made no objection to the marquess's carrying his woman into the inn and up the stairs, Lord Birkin hovering close to share the load if necessary. Tom was rather incoherent, accounting perhaps for his lack of wisdom in admitting to his unwed state.

"We was going to get married," he said, hurrying along behind the two gentlemen while Lisa moaned, having had the misfortune to suffer a contraction after the marquess had picked her up. "But we couldn't afford to."

And yet, Lord Lytton thought, wincing at the girl's obvious agony, they could afford a child. An unfair judgment, perhaps. Even the poor were entitled to their pleasures, and children had a habit of not waiting for a convenient moment to get themselves conceived.

A strange scene greeted them at the entrance to his former inn room—had he really given it up in a chivalrous gesture to counter Miss Wilder's brave offer to sleep in the stable? Miss Amelia Horn was hovering at one side of the doorway, a woolen shawl of hideous and multicolored stripes clutched in one hand and a vinaigrette in the other. Mrs. Forbes was hovering and nodding at the other side. The room itself was crowded. He had not realized that it was large enough to accommodate so many persons.

Colonel Forbes was kneeling before the grate, blowing on some freshly laid coals and coaxing a fire into life. Both his hands and his face were liberally daubed with coal dust. He was looking as angry and out of sorts as he always did. Miss Eugenia Horn was at the window, closing the curtains to keep out some draft and a great deal of gloom. Lady Birkin was in the act of setting down a large bowl of steaming water on the washstand. Pamela Wilder was bent over the tidied bed, plumping up lumpy pillows and turning back the sheets to receive its new occupant. Lord Lytton, despite the weight of his burden, which he had just carried from the stable into the inn and up the stairs, pursed his lips at the sight of a slim but well-rounded derriere nicely outlined against the wool of her dress.

What a fool and an idiot he had been the night before! He might by now be well familiar with the feel of that derriere. She turned and smiled warmly at the woman in his arms. He found himself wishing that her eyes were focused a little higher.

"The bed is ready for you," she said. "In a moment we will have you comfortable and warm. The fire will be giving off some heat soon. How are you feeling?"

"Oh, thank you," Lisa said, her voice weak and weary as the marquess set her gently down. "Where's Tom?"

"Here I am, Leez," the young man said from the doorway. His face was chalky white. "How are you?"

"It's so wonderfully warm in here," the girl said plaintively, but then she gasped and clasped a hand over her swollen abdomen. She opened her mouth and panted loudly, moaning with each outward breath so that all the occupants of the room froze.

"Who is in charge?" the marquess asked when it appeared that the pain was subsiding again. He had felt his own color draining away. "Who is going to deliver the child?"

The one Miss Horn, he noticed, had disappeared from the doorway, while the other had turned firmly to face the curtained window. Obviously not them, and obviously not Miss Wilder. He must take her downstairs, away from there. But it was she who answered him.

"There is no one with any experience," she said. She flushed. "And no one who has given birth. We will have to do the best we can."

Hell, he thought. *Hell and damnation! No one with any experience. A thousand devils!*

"Sally," Lord Birkin said, "let me take you back to our room. Mrs. Palmer is doubtless the best qualified to cope."

"Mrs. Palmer," she said, her eyes flashing briefly at him, "has the breakfast to clear away and the dishes to wash and the rooms to see to. I'll stay here, Henry." She turned to the girl, who was sitting awkwardly on the side of the bed, and her expression softened. "The stable must have been dreadfully dirty," she said. "I have brought up some warm water. I will help you wash yourself and change into something clean. I have a loose-fitting nightgown that I believe will fit you." She looked up. "Will you fetch it, Henry? It is the one with the lace at the throat and cuffs."

He looked at her, speechless. She, the Baroness Birkin, was going to wash a young girl of low birth who at present smelled of rankly uncleaned stable? She was going to give the girl one of her costly nightgowns? But yes, of course she was going to. It was just like Sally to do such things, and with such kindness in her face. He turned to leave the room.

"I'll help you, my lady," Pamela said. She stooped over the girl on the bed. "Here, I'll help you off with your dress once the gentlemen have withdrawn. What is your name?"

"Lisa," the girl said. "Lisa Curtis, miss."

"We will make you comfortable as soon as we possibly can, Lisa," Pamela said.

Miss Eugenia Horn coughed. "You must come with me away from this room, my dear Miss Wilder," she said. "It is not fitting that we be here. We will leave Lisa to the care of Lady Birkin and Mrs. Forbes, who are married ladies."

The Marquess of Lytton watched Pamela's face with keen interest from beneath drooped eyelids. She smiled. "I grew up at a rectory, ma'am," she said. "I learned at an early age to help my fellow human beings under even the most difficult of circumstances if my assistance could be of some value."

It was a do-gooder sentiment that might have made him want to vomit, the marquess thought, if it had not been uttered so matter-of-factly and if her tone had not been so totally devoid of piety and sentiment.

"I think it will survive without your further help, Forbes," the marquess said, looking critically at the crackling fire. "Let us see if our landlord can supply us with some of that superior ale we had last night, shall we? Join us, Suffield."

He was rewarded with a grateful smile from Pamela Wilder. Lady Birkin was squeezing out a cloth over the bowl of water and rubbing soap on it. Miss Eugenia Horn was preparing to leave the room and sights so unbecoming to maiden eyes.

It was strange, perhaps, that for the rest of the day all the guests at the White Hart Inn could not keep their minds away from the room upstairs in which a girl of a social class far beneath their own, and a girl moreover who was about to bear a bastard child, labored painfully though relatively quietly. Her moans could be heard only when one of them went upstairs to his own room.

"They should have stayed at home," Colonel Forbes said gruffly. "Damn fool thing to be wandering about the countryside at this time of year and with the girl in this condition."

"Perhaps they could not afford to stay at home," Lord Birkin said.

Tom could not answer for himself. He had returned to the stable despite the offer of ale and a share of the fire in the taproom. He was pacing.

"The poor child," Miss Eugenia Horn said, having decided that it was unexceptionable to talk about the child, provided she ignored all reference to its birth. She was sitting in the taproom, knitting a pair of baby boots. "One cannot help but wonder what will become of it."

"Tom will doubtless find employment and make an honest woman of Lisa, and they and the child will live happily ever after," the marquess said.

Mrs. Forbes nodded her agreement.

"It would be comforting to think so," Lord Birkin said.

Mrs. Palmer, looking harried, was emerging from the kitchen, where she had given the guests' servants their breakfast and washed the dishes, and was making her way upstairs to tidy rooms.

They were all increasingly aware as the day dragged on that it was Christmas Eve and that they were beginning to live through the strangest Christmas they had ever experienced.

"We might decorate the inn with some greenery," Miss Amelia Horn said at one point, "but who would be foolhardy enough to go outside to gather any? Besides, even if some were brought inside, it would be dripping wet."

"As far as I am concerned," Colonel Forbes said, "there is enough rain outside. We do not need to admit any to the indoors." No one argued with him.

They all began to think of what they would have been

doing on that day if only they had had the fortune or wisdom to travel earlier and had reached their destinations. But the images of elegant and comfortable homes and of relatives and friends and all the sights and sounds and smells of Christmas did not bear dwelling upon.

Lord Birkin went back upstairs with his wife when she appeared briefly early in the afternoon to fetch more water from the kitchen. She had reported to all the gathered guests that there was no further progress upstairs. Poor Lisa was suffering cruelly, but appeared no nearer to being delivered than she had done that morning.

Lord Birkin took his wife by the arm when they reached the top of the stairs and steered her past Lisa's room and into their own.

"Sally," he said, "you are going to tire yourself out. Do you not think you have done enough? Should it not be Mrs. Palmer's turn? Or Mrs. Forbes's?"

She sat down on the edge of the bed and he seated himself beside her.

"Mrs. Palmer is frightened by the very thought of becoming involved," she said. "I can tell. That is why she is keeping so busy with other things. And Mrs. Forbes is quite inept. Well-meaning but inept. The few times she has come inside the room she has stood close to the door and nodded sweetly and clearly not known what she should do."

"And you *do* know?" he said.

She smiled. "Some things come by instinct," she said. "Don't worry about me, Henry."

"But I do worry," he said, taking her hand and holding it in both of his. "And I blame myself for not bringing you from London sooner than I did. This is Christmas Eve, Sally. Have you realized that? You should be with Lady Middleton and all your friends and acquaintances now. You should be in comfort. The partying should have begun— the feasting and caroling and dancing. Instead we are stuck here. Not only stuck, but somehow involved with a girl who is giving birth. This is no Christmas for you."

"Or for you," she said. "It really does not seem like

Christmas at all, does it? But we cannot do anything about it. Here we are and here Lisa is. I must return to her."

"What is going to happen when it comes time for her to deliver?" he asked.

He had struck a nerve. There was fear in her eyes for a brief unguarded moment. "We will jump that hurdle when we come to it," she said.

"You are afraid, Sally?" he asked.

"No, of course not," she said briskly. But then she looked down at their clasped hands and nodded quickly. Her voice was breathless when she spoke again. "I am afraid that in my ignorance I will cause her death or the baby's."

He released her hand, set an arm about her shoulders, and drew her toward him. She sagged against him in grateful surprise and set her head on his shoulder.

"Without you and Miss Wilder," he said, "she would be alone in the stable with the hysterical Tom. You are being very good to her, Sally. You must remember that, whatever happens. I wish I could take you away from here. I wish I had not got you into this predicament."

She nestled her head on his shoulder and felt wonderfully comforted. If this had not happened, they would be caught up in the gaiety of Christmas at this very moment, surrounded by friends. Except that they would not be together. As like as not, he would be off somewhere with some of the other gentlemen, playing billiards, probably, since the weather would not permit shooting.

"Don't blame yourself," she said. "Besides, it is not so very bad, is it? If we were not here, I fear that Pamela would have to cope alone. That would be too heavy a burden on her shoulders. She is wonderful, Henry. So calm and brave, so kind to Lisa. Just as if she knew exactly what she was doing."

"You sound like two of a kind, then," he said.

She looked up at him in further surprise. His face was very close. "Do you think so?" she said. "What a lovely thing to say—and very reassuring. I feel quite inadequate, you see."

He dipped his head and kissed her—swiftly and firmly and almost fiercely. And then raised his head and looked into her eyes as she nestled her head against his shoulder again. He very rarely kissed her. She ached with a sudden longing and put it from her.

"I must go back," she said. "Pamela will be alone with Lisa."

"If there is anything I can do," he said, "call me. Will you?"

Her eyes sparkled with amusement suddenly. "You will spend the rest of the day in fear and trembling that perhaps I will take you at your word," she said.

He chuckled, and she realized how rarely he did so these days. She had almost forgotten that it was his smile and the way his eyes crinkled at the corners when he laughed that had first attracted her to him. "You are probably right," he said.

He escorted her back to Lisa's room, though he did not go inside with her. She felt refreshed, almost as if she had lain down and slept for a few hours. Pamela was leaning over a moaning Lisa, dabbing at her brow with a cool, damp cloth. She looked around at Lady Birkin.

"Two minutes," she said. "The pains have been two minutes apart for more than an hour now. It must be close, don't you think, Sally?"

But it was not really close at all. There were several more hours of closely paced contractions and pain to live through.

E veryone moved from the taproom into the dining room for afternoon tea, just so that they might have a welcome change of scenery, Colonel Forbes said with a short bark of laughter. Lord Birkin, strolling to the window, announced that the rain appeared to be easing and that he hesitated to say it aloud but the western horizon looked almost bright.

"But it is happening too late, my lord," Miss Amelia Horn said. "Christmas has been ruined already."

Mrs. Forbes sighed and nodded her agreement.

And yet they were all making an effort to put aside their own personal disappointments over a lost Christmas. They were all thinking of the baby who was about to be born and of the child's destitute parents. Miss Eugenia Horn was still busy knitting baby boots. Mrs. Forbes, having recalled that she had no fewer than eight flannel nightgowns in her trunk, flannel being the only sensible fabric to be worn during winter nights, declared that she did not need nearly as many. She was cutting up four of them into squares and hemming them so that the baby would have warm and comfortable nappies to wear. Miss Amelia Horn was cutting up a fifth to make into small nightshirts. She had already painstakingly unpicked the lace from one of her favorite caps to trim the tiny garments.

Even the gentlemen were not unaffected by the impending event. Colonel Forbes was thinking of a certain shirt of which he had never been overly fond. It would surely fit Tom and keep him warm too. By good fortune the garment was in the trunk upstairs—for the simple reason that it was one of his wife's favorites. Lord Birkin thought of the staff at his London house and on his country estate. There really was no room for an extra worker. His wife had already foisted some strays upon him. He was definitely over-staffed. Perhaps some banknotes would help, though giving money in charity always seemed rather too easy. The Marquess of Lytton turned a gold signet ring on his little finger. It was no heirloom. He had bought it himself in Madrid. But it had some sentimental value. Not that he was a sentimentalist, of course. He drew it slowly from his finger and dropped it into a pocket. Sold or pawned, it would provide a family of three with a goodly number of meals. The quiet gentleman withdrew to the stable after tea to stretch his legs and breathe some fresh air into his lungs.

Pamela Wilder appeared in the dining room doorway when tea was over and immediately became the focus of attention. But she could give no news other than that Lisa was very tired and finding it harder to bear the pains. Miss Wilder looked tired too, the Marquess of Lytton thought, gazing at her pale and lovely face and her rather untidy hair. Lady Birkin had sent her downstairs for a half-hour break, having had one herself earlier.

"The tea is cold, dear," Miss Eugenia Horn said. "Let me get you a fresh pot. There is no point in ringing for service. One might wait all day and all night too if one did that."

But Pamela would not hear of anyone else's waiting on her. She went to the kitchen herself. The marquess was sitting in the taproom when she came out again, carrying a tray.

"Come and sit down," he said, indicating the chair next to his own, between him and the fire, which he had just built up himself. "It is quieter in here."

She hesitated, but he got to his feet and took the tray from her hands. She sighed as she sat down and then looked at him in some surprise as he picked up the teapot and poured her cup of tea.

"Is she going to deliver?" he asked. "Or is there some complication?"

He liked watching her blush. Color added vibrancy to her face. "I hope not," she said. "Oh, I do hope not."

"Do you have any idea what to do?" he asked. "Or does Lady Birkin?"

"No," she said, and she closed her eyes briefly. "None at all. We can only hope that nature will take care of itself."

Oh, Lord. There was a faint buzzing in his head.

"You are a clergyman's daughter," he said. "You were never involved with such, er, acts of nature?"

"No," she said. "My mother made sure that I had a very proper upbringing. I wish I knew more." She looked down at her hands. "I hope she does not die. Or the baby. I will always blame myself if they die."

A thousand hells and a million damnations! He reached out and took one of her hands in his. "If they die—and probably they will not," he said, "they will die in a warm and reasonably comfortable inn room instead of in a stable, and tended by two ladies who have given them unfailingly diligent and gentle care instead of by a hysterical boy."

She smiled at him rather wanly. "You are kind," she said.

He looked down at her hand and spread her fingers along his. "You have artists' hands," he said. "You must play the pianoforte. Do you?"

"Whenever I can." She looked wistful. "We always had a pianoforte at the rectory. I played it constantly, even when I should have been doing other things. I was often scolded."

"But there is no instrument at your place of employment?" he asked.

"Oh, yes," she said. "A beautiful one with the loveliest tone I have ever heard. I give my pupil lessons and try to steal a few minutes for myself whenever I can."

He felt angry suddenly. "They have to be stolen?" he asked. "They are not granted?"

She smiled. "Mrs. Raven, my employer, suffers from migraine headaches," she said. "She cannot stand the sound of the pianoforte."

His jaw tightened. "It is not a good life, is it," he said, "being a governess?"

She stiffened and withdrew her hand from his. She reached out to pick up her cup and raised it to her lips. "It is a living, my lord," she said, "and a reasonably comfortable one. There are many women, and men too, far worse off than I. We cannot all choose the life we would live. You do not need to pity me."

He looked at her broodingly. Her hand was shaking slightly, though she drank determinedly on. Did he pity her? He was not in the habit of pitying other mortals. No, he did not think it was pity. It was more admiration for her and anger against employers who evidently did not appreciate her. It was more the desire to protect her and see happiness replace the quiet discipline in her face—the desire to give her a pianoforte for Christmas, all wrapped about with red ribbons. His lip curled in self-derision. Was this unspeakably dull Christmas making him sentimental over a governess?

"What would you be doing now," he asked her, "if it had not rained?"

She set her cup down in its saucer and smiled down into it, her eyes dreamy. "Decorating the house with the children," she said. "Helping my mother and our cook with the baking. Finishing making gifts. Delivering baskets to the poor. Helping my father arrange the Nativity scene in the church. Getting ready to go caroling. Looking forward to the church service. Running around in circles wishing I could divide myself into about twelve pieces. Christmas is always very busy and very special at home. The coming of Christ—it is a wonderful festival."

He took her hand again, almost absently, and smoothed his fingers over hers. He was the Marquess of Lytton, she reminded herself, and she a mere clergyman's daughter and a governess. Last night he had held her and kissed her, and she had almost gone to bed with him. She was still not sure if she would have allowed the ultimate intimacy or if she would have drawn back at the last moment. But he had drawn back, and now they were sitting together in the taproom, talking, her hand in his. This was a strange, unreal Christmas.

"What would *you* be doing?" she asked. "If it had not rained, I mean."

He raised his gaze from their hands, and she was struck again by the keenness of his blue eyes beneath the lazy lids. They caused a strange somersaulting feeling in her stomach. "Stuffing myself with rich foods," he said. "Getting myself inebriated. Preparing to make merry and to drink even more. Flirting with a lady I have had my eye on for some time past and wondering if I would be spending tonight with her or if she would keep me waiting until tomorrow night." One corner of his mouth lifted in an expression that was not quite a smile. "A wonderful way to celebrate the coming of Christ, would you not agree?"

Pamela found herself wondering irrelevantly what the lady looked like. "I cannot judge," she said. "We all have our own way of enjoying ourselves."

"Yours is a large family?" he asked.

"I have three brothers and four sisters," she said, "all younger than myself. It is a very noisy household and frequently an untidy one, I'm afraid."

"I envy you," he said. "I have no one except a few aunts and uncles and cousins with whom I have never been close." He raised one hand and touched the back of a finger to her cheek. "I am sorry you have not been able to get home for Christmas."

"I believe that everything that happens does so for a purpose," she said. "Perhaps I was meant to be trapped here for Lisa's sake."

"And perhaps I was meant to be trapped here with you for . . . for what purpose?" he asked.

His eyes were looking very intently into hers. She could not withdraw her own. "I don't know," she said.

"Perhaps," he said, and his voice was very soft, "to discover that innocence can be more enticing than experience. And far more warming to the heart."

He raised her hand while she watched him with widening eyes and warming cheeks, and set his lips to it.

"I must be going back upstairs," she said.

"Yes." He lowered her hand. "You must."

But the next moment they were both on their feet. Lady Birkin had appeared at the top of the stairs. She was looking distraught and was beckoning urgently.

"Pamela," she called. "Oh, thank heaven you are there. Something is happening. Oh, please come." And she turned and hurried out of sight again.

Pamela could feel the color draining from her face as she rushed across the room toward the staircase. She scarcely heard the quite improper expletive that was the marquess's sole comment.

"Bloody hell!" he said.

* * *

The bed was soaked. Fortunately Mrs. Palmer had given them a pile of old rags and told them to spread some over the sheets. There was something about waters breaking, she had mumbled before scurrying away about some real or imagined chore. Pamela and Lady Birkin stripped away the wet rags and replaced them with dry ones. But Lisa was in severe distress. She was panting loudly and thrashing about on the bed. Her moans were threatening to turn into screams.

"Hot water," Lady Birkin said, trying to keep her voice calm. "I have heard that hot water is needed."

"Lisa," Pamela had a cool cloth to the girl's brow. "What may we do for you? How may we help?"

But there was a feeling of dreadful helplessness, an almost overpowering urge to become hysterical or simply to rush from the room.

And then the door opened. Both Lady Birkin and Pamela looked in some surprise at the Marquess of Lytton, who stood in the doorway, his face pale. Perhaps they would have felt consternation too, if they had not been feeling so frightened and helpless.

"I think I can help," he surprised them both by saying. And he grimaced and turned even paler as Lisa began to moan and thrash again. He strode over to the bed. "I think she should be pushing," he said. "The pain will subside soon, will it not? Next time we must have her in position and she must push down. Perhaps the two of you can help her by lifting her shoulders as she pushes."

The two ladies merely stared at him. Lisa screamed.

"The Peninsula," he said. "I was a cavalry officer. There was a peasant woman. There was a surgeon too, but he had just been shot through the right hand. He instructed a private soldier and me. The private held her and I delivered."

Lisa was quiet again, and the marquess turned grimly back to the bed. "Raise your knees," he told her, "and brace your feet wide apart on the bed. The next time the pain comes, I want you to bear down against it with all your strength. This little fellow wants to come out. Do you understand me?"

Through the fog of weakness and pain, the girl seemed to turn instinctively to the note of authority and assurance in his voice. She looked up at him and nodded, positioning herself according to his instructions. And then the fright came back into her eyes and she began to pant again.

"Now!" he commanded, and he pushed his hands forward against her knees through the sheet that still covered her to the waist while Lady Birkin and Pamela, one on each side of her, lifted her shoulders from the bed and pushed forward. Lisa drew a giant breath and bore down with all her might, pausing only to gasp in more air before the pain subsided again.

"Send down for hot water," Lord Lytton said while Lisa relaxed for a few moments. "Go and give the instruction yourself, Pamela, but come right back. Someone else can bring it. But wait a moment. She needs us again."

He was going to forget something, he thought as he pushed upward on the girl's knees. He would forget something and either she or the child was going to bleed to death. Or there was going to be a complication, as there had not been with the Spanish peasant girl. This girl was already weak from a long and hard labor. Soon—perhaps after the next contraction—he was going to have to take a look and pray fervently that it was the child's head he would see. He could recall the surgeon's talking about breech births, though he had given no details.

And then between contractions, as he was about to draw the sheet back, there was a quiet voice from the doorway. It almost did not register on his mind, but he looked over his shoulder. He had not been mistaken. The quiet gentleman was standing there.

"I am a physician," he repeated. "I will be happy to deliver the child and tend the mother."

Anger was the Marquess of Lytton's first reaction. "You are a physician," he said. "Why the hell have you waited this long to admit the fact? Do you realize what terrors your silence has caused Lady Birkin and Miss Wilder in the course of the day?"

"And you too, my lord?" The quiet gentleman was smiling. He had strolled into the room and taken one of Lisa's limp hands in his. He spoke very gently. "It will soon be over, my dear, I promise. Then the joy you will have in your child will make you forget all this."

She looked calmly back at him. There was even a suggestion of a smile in her eyes.

But the marquess was not mollified. Relief—overwhelming, knee-weakening relief—was whipping his anger into fury. "What the hell do you mean," he said, "putting us through all this?" He remembered too late the presence in the room of three women, two of them gently born.

The quiet gentleman smiled and touched a cool hand to Lisa's brow as she began to gasp again. "How could I spoil a Christmas that had promised to be so dismal for everyone?" he asked, and he moved to draw the sheet down over the girl's knees. "The blood will probably return to your head faster, my lord, if you remove yourself. The ladies will assist me. Have some hot water brought up to us, if you will be so good."

Lord Lytton removed himself, frowning over the physician's strange answer to his question. Lady Birkin and Pamela, moving back to their posts, puzzled over it too. What had he meant? Christmas might have been dismal but was not? Because of what was happening?

"Set an arm each about her back to support her as you lift her," the quiet gentleman said. "Your labors too, will soon be at an end, ladies, and you will experience all the wonder of being present at a birth. Ah. I can see the head, my dear. With plenty of dark hair."

"Ohhh!" Lisa was almost crying with excitement and exhaustion and pain.

But all sense of panic had gone from the room. Both

Lady Birkin and Pamela were aware of that as the physician went quietly and efficiently about his work and Lisa responded to his gentleness. Her son was born, large and healthy and perfect—and crying lustily—early in the evening. They were all crying, in fact. All except the doctor, who smiled sweetly at each of them in turn and made them feel as if it were not at all the most foolish thing in the world to cry just because one more mouth to be fed had been born into it.

Lisa was exhausted and could scarcely raise her arms to Tom when he came into the room several minutes later, wide-eyed and awed, while Lady Birkin was washing the baby and Pamela was disposing of bloodstained rags. Lisa accepted the baby from Lady Birkin and looked up with shining eyes into Tom's face while he reached out one trembling finger to touch his son. But she had no energy left.

"I'll take him," Lady Birkin said, "while you get some sleep, Lisa. You have earned it."

"Thank you, mum." Lisa looked up at her wearily. "I'll always remember you, mum, and the other lady." Her eyes found Pamela and smiled. "Thank you, miss."

And so Lady Birkin found herself holding the child and feeling a welling of happiness and tenderness and . . . and longing. *Ah, how wonderful,* she thought. How very wonderful. She acted from instinct. She must find Henry. She must show him. Oh, if only the child were hers. Theirs.

Word had spread. Everyone was hovering in the hallway outside Lisa's room. The birth of a little bastard baby was the focus of attention on this Christmas Eve. The ladies oohed and aahed at the mere sight of the bright stripes of the shawl in which it was wrapped. But Lady Birkin had eyes for no one except her husband, standing at the top of the stairs close to the Marquess of Lytton and gazing anxiously at her.

"Henry," she said. "Oh, look at him. Have you ever seen anything so perfect?" She could hear herself laughing and yet his face had blurred before her vision. "Look at him, Henry."

He looked and smiled back up at her. "Sally," he whispered.

"He weighs nothing at all," she said. "How could any human being be so small and so light and so perfect and still live and breathe? What a miracle life is. Hold him, Henry."

She gave him no choice. She laid the bundle in his arms and watched the fear in his eyes soften to wonder as he smiled down at the baby. The child was not quite sleeping. He was looking quietly about him with unfocused eyes.

Lord Birkin smiled. What would it be like, he wondered, to look down like this at his own child? To have the baby placed in his arms by its mother? By his wife?

"Sally," he said, "you must be so tired." She was pale and disheveled. He had a sudden image of how she should be looking now, early in the evening of Christmas Eve, immaculate and fashionable and sparkling with jewels and excitement and ready to mingle with their friends far into the night. And yet he saw happiness now in her tired eyes— and breathtaking beauty.

The ladies wanted to hold the baby. And so he was passed from one to another, quiet and unprotesting. He was cooed over and clucked over and even sung to, by Miss Amelia Horn. The occasion had made even the Palmers magnanimous.

"Well," Mr. Palmer said, rubbing his hands together and looking not unpleased. "I never did in all my born days."

"I mean to tell Mr. Suffield," Mrs. Palmer said in a voice loud enough for all to hear, "that we are not even going to charge 'im for the room."

No one saw fit to comment on this outpouring of incredible generosity.

The Marquess of Lytton reached out both hands to Pamela when she came from the room. She set her own in them without thought and smiled at him. "Have you seen him?" she asked. "Is he not the most beautiful child you have ever set eyes on?"

"I'm sorry," he said to her, squeezing her hands until

they hurt. "I ripped up at the physician for keeping quiet so long, and yet that is exactly what I had been doing all day. You and Lady Birkin were wonderfully brave. I am sorry my own cowardice made me hide a fact that might have made your day less anxious."

"I don't think," she said, gazing up into his eyes, her own filling with sudden tears, "that I would change one detail of this day even if I could. How glad I am that it rained!"

His eyes searched hers. "And so am I," he said, raising both hands to his lips and continuing to regard her over them. "More glad than I have been of anything else in my life."

"Anyway," Colonel Forbes's voice was declaring gruffly over the babble of voices in the hallway; it seemed that Mrs. Forbes had been trying to force him to hold the baby. "Anyway, this was a damned inconvenient thing to happen. What would have been the outcome if one of our number had not turned out to be a doctor, eh? Whoever heard of any woman having a baby at Christmas?"

The babble of voices stopped entirely.

The Marquess of Lytton's eyes smiled slowly into Pamela's. "Good Lord," he said, and everyone kept quiet to listen to his words, "a crowd of marvelous Christians we all are. Did any of us realize before this moment, I wonder? We have, in fact, been presented with the perfect Christmas, have we not? Almost a reenactment of the original."

" 'How could I spoil a Christmas that had promised to be so dismal for everyone?' " Pamela said quietly. "I think someone realized, my lord."

"The child was very nearly born in a stable," Lady Birkin said.

"It is uncanny enough to send shivers up one's spine," Miss Eugenia Horn said.

"I hope you have not caught a chill from the damp sheets, Eugenia," Miss Amelia Horn said.

"I wonder," Lord Birkin said, "if above the heavy rain clouds a star is shining brightly."

"Fanciful nonsense," Colonel Forbes said. "I am ready for my dinner. When will it be ready, landlord, eh? Don't just stand there, man. I would like to eat before midnight—if it is all the same to you, of course."

Lady Birkin took the baby from Mrs. Forbes's arms. "I'll take him back to his mother," she said, tenderness and wistfulness mingled in her voice.

"Back to his manger," Lord Birkin said, laughing softly.

"Well, anyway," Mrs. Palmer said to the gathered company as she cleared away the plates after dinner, "we didn't keep 'em in the stable like them innkeepers did in the Bible. We gave 'em one of our best rooms and aren't charging 'em for it neither."

"For which deeds you will surely find a place awaiting you in heaven," the Marquess of Lytton said.

"And yet it give me quite a turn, it did, when the colonel said what 'e did and we all thought of that other babe what was born at Christmas," Mr. Palmer said. He was standing in the doorway of the dining room, busy about nothing in particular. "I was all over shivers for a minute."

"I am sure in Bethlehem there was not all this infernal rain," Colonel Forbes commented.

"The kings would have arrived in horribly soggy robes and dripping crowns," the marquess said. "And the heavenly host would have had drooping wings."

"I am quite sure their wings were more sturdy than to be weakened by rain, my lord," Miss Amelia Horn said. "They were angels, after all."

Mrs. Forbes nodded her agreement.

"I think it would be altogether fitting to the occasion," Miss Eugenia Horn said, "if we read the Bible story together this evening."

"And perhaps sang some carols afterward," Lady Birkin said. "Does everyone feel Christmas as strongly as I do tonight despite all the usual trappings being absent?"

There were murmurings of assent. Mrs. Forbes nodded. The quiet gentleman smiled.

"Does anyone have a Bible?" Lord Birkin asked.

There was a lengthy pause. No one, it seemed, was in the habit of traveling about with a Bible in a trunk.

"I do," the quiet gentleman said at last, and he got to his feet to fetch it from his room.

And so they all spent a further hour in the dining room, far away from friends and families and parties, far from any church, far away from Christmas as any of them had ever known it. There were no decorations, no fruit cake or mince pies, no cider or punch or wassail. Nothing except a plain and shabby inn and the company of strangers become acquaintances. Nothing except a newborn baby and his mother asleep upstairs, cozy and warm because they had been taken from the stable and given a room and showered with care and with gifts.

The quiet gentleman himself read the story of the birth of another baby in Bethlehem, and they all listened to words they had heard so many times before that the wonder of it all had ceased to mean a great deal. They listened with a new understanding, with a new recognition of the joy of birth. Even the one man who rarely entered a church, Lord Lytton, was touched by the story and realized that perhaps Christmas had not been meant to be an orgy of personal gratification.

Singing that might have been self-conscious, since there was no instrument to provide accompaniment, was, in fact, not self-conscious at all. Lady Birkin, Pamela Wilder, Colonel Forbes and, surprisingly, Miss Amelia Horn all had good voices and could hold a tune. Everyone else joined in lustily, even the tone-deaf Mrs. Forbes.

Lord Birkin left the room after a while. He found Tom Suffield in the kitchen, where he had been eating with the guests' coachmen. Lisa and the baby were asleep, Tom explained, scrambling to his feet, and he did not want to disturb them. Lord Birkin took Tom through into the taproom.

"I don't know what you are good at, Tom," he said. "I

can't offer much in the way of employment, I'm afraid, but I can send you to my estate in Kent and instruct my housekeeper to find you work in the stables or in the gardens. I doubt there will be an empty cottage, but we will find somewhere where you and Lisa can stay for a while, at least."

Tom shifted his weight awkwardly from one foot to the other. "That be awf'ly good of ye, sir," he said, "but Mr. Cornwallis needs a cook and a handyman and have offered the jobs to me and Lisa."

"Mr. Cornwallis?" Lord Birkin raised his eyebrows.

"The doctor, sir," Tom said.

"Ah." It was strange, Lord Birkin thought, that even though they had all introduced themselves the evening before, he had thought of Mr. Cornwallis ever since only as the quiet gentleman. "I am glad, Tom. I hated to think of your taking Lisa and your baby to one of the industrial towns with no job waiting for you there."

"Aye, sir," Tom said. "Everyone is right kind. Thanks again for the money, sir. We will buy new clothes for the baby with it."

Lord Birkin nodded and returned to the dining room.

The Marquess of Lytton found Tom just ten minutes later. "Having a woman and child and no home or employment is a burdensome situation to find yourself in, Tom," he said.

"Aye, that it is, sir," Tom said. "But I feels like a wealthy man, sir, with all the gifts. And with your gold ring, sir. And a home and a job from Mr. Cornwallis." He told his tale again.

"Ah," the marquess said. "I am glad to hear it, Tom. I was prepared to give you a letter of introduction to a friend of mine, but now I see you will not need it. I would like to give you a small sum of money, though. Call it a Christmas gift to you personally, if you will. It is the price of a license. You must marry her, Tom. Such things are important to women, you know. And you would not wish to hear anyone calling your son a bastard."

"Bless you, sir," Tom said, flushing, "but Mr. Cornwallis is to marry us, sir, as soon as we gets to his home."

"The physician?" the marquess raised his eyebrows.

"He's a clergyman, sir," Tom said.

"Ah." The marquess nodded pleasantly to him and returned to the dining room. The quiet gentleman, he thought, was becoming more intriguing by the moment. Was he a physician or a clergyman? Or both? Or neither?

Lord Lytton seated himself beside the quiet gentleman and spoke to him while everyone else was singing. "You are a clergyman, sir?" he asked.

The quiet gentleman smiled. "I am, my lord," he said.

"And a physician too?" The marquess frowned.

"It is possible to be both," the quiet gentleman said. "I am a clergyman, but not of a large and fashionable parish, you see. My time is not taken up by the sometimes tedious and meaningless duties I would have if I belonged to a large parish, and certainly not by the social commitments I would have if I had a wealthy patron. I am fortunate. My time is free to be devoted to the service of others. I am not distracted by the trappings of the established faith." He chuckled. "I have learned to deliver babies. It is the greatest delight and the greatest privilege a man could experience. You discovered that once upon a time, I believe."

"And the greatest terror," the marquess said fervently. "I dreaded facing it again today. There was the terror of becoming the instrument of death rather than of life."

"Ah," the quiet gentleman said, "but we must learn to accept our limitations as part of the human condition. It is our Lord who controls life and death."

The marquess was quiet for a while. "Yes," he said. "We are all of us too busy, aren't we? Especially at Christmastime. Too busy enjoying ourselves and surrounding ourselves with the perfect atmosphere to remember what it is all about. This unexpected rainstorm has forced us to remember. And you have helped too, sir, by sitting back and allowing us to face all the terror of imminent birth."

"Without suffering there can never be the fullness of joy," the quiet gentleman said.

The Misses Horn were rising to retire for the night, and everyone else followed suit. But they did not part to go to their separate rooms without a great deal of handshaking and hugging first.

"Happy Christmas," they each said a dozen times to one another. But the words were not the automatic greeting they had all uttered during all their previous Christmases, but heartfelt wishes for one another's joy. Suddenly this Christmas—this dull, rainy disaster of a Christmas—seemed very happy indeed. Perhaps the happiest any of them had ever known.

And so Christmas Eve drew to an end. A baby had been born.

It was a little different when they were alone together in their room. Some of the magic went from the evening. It was all right for her, Lady Birkin thought. She had been busy all day and directly involved in the wonder of the baby's birth. Men were not so concerned about such matters. It must have been a dreadfully dull day for him.

"Henry," she said, looking at him apologetically, as if everything were her fault, "I am so sorry that this is such a dull Christmas for you."

"Dull?" He looked at her intently and took a step toward her so that he was very close. "I don't think I have ever celebrated Christmas until this year, Sally. I am very proud of you, you know."

Her eyes widened. "You are?" He so rarely paid her compliments.

"You worked tirelessly all day to help that girl," he said. "You and Miss Wilder. I don't know how Lisa would have managed without you."

"But there was a physician in the house, after all," she said. "What we did was nothing."

He framed her face with his hands. "What you did was everything," he said. "The doctor gave his skills. You gave yourself, Sally, despite being frightened and inexperienced."

"Oh," she said. She felt like crying. She had tried so hard to impress him since their marriage, dressing to please him, talking and smiling to please him. And losing him with every day that passed. And yet now he was looking at her with unmistakable admiration and . . . love?

"Henry," she said, and on impulse she put her arms up about his neck. "What is it about this Christmas? It is not just me, is it? Everyone has been feeling it. You too? What is so wonderful about it? This inn is not *the* inn, after all, and the baby is not Jesus, not even born in the stable."

He slipped his hands to her waist. "We have all seen to the core of Christmas this year," he said. "We are very fortunate, Sally. We might so easily have never had the chance. We have no gifts for each other. They are somewhere with our baggage coach. And this inn has provided us with nothing that is usually associated with the season. We had all come to believe that Christmas could not possibly be celebrated without those things. But this year we have been forced to see that Christmas is about birth and life and love and giving of whatever one has to give, even if it is only one's time and compassion."

She should not say it, she thought. She might spoil everything. They never said such things to each other. There seemed to be a great embarrassment between them where personal matters were concerned. But she was going to say it. She was going to take a chance. That was what the whole day seemed to have been about.

"Henry," she said. She was whispering, she found. "I love you so very much."

He gazed into her eyes, a look of hunger in his own. He drew breath but seemed to change his mind. Instead of speaking he lowered his head and kissed her—an open-mouthed kiss of raw need that drew an instant response of surprise and desire. She tightened her arms and arched herself to him. There was shock for a moment as she felt his hands working at the buttons down the back of her dress, and then a surge of happiness.

"I always have," she said against his mouth. "Since the first moment I saw you. I have always worshiped you."

She gasped when he lowered her bodice and her chemise to her waist, and her naked breasts came back against his coat. And then his hands were on them, cupping them and stroking them, and his thumbs and forefingers were squeezing her nipples, rolling them lightly until she felt such a sharp stab of desire that she moaned into his mouth.

"Henry," she begged him, her eyes tightly closed, her mouth still against his, "make love to me. I have always wanted you to make love to me. Please, for this special day. Make love to me."

She would die, she thought if he merely coupled with her as he had the night before and all those other nights since their marriage. She should not have said what she just had. She should not have given in to the temptation to hope. She should not have begged for what he had never freely given.

But she was on the bed before she could get her thoughts straight, before she could feel shame for her wanton words. She was flat on her back, and he was stripping away her clothes from the waist down, looking at her from eyes heavy with desire as he straightened up and began to remove his own clothes. She was surprised to find that she felt no embarrassment though the candles burned and those passion-heavy eyes were devouring her nakedness. She lifted her arms to him.

She had asked for it, begged for it, wanted it. He would not feel guilt. This was not the way a gentleman used his wife, but they both wanted it. They both needed it. He resisted the urge to douse the candles so that she would be saved from embarrassment. And as he joined her naked on the bed, he rejected the idea of somehow restraining his passion. She wanted him as much as he wanted her. For this one occasion, she had said. So be it, then.

He worked on her mouth with his lips and his tongue

and on her breasts with his hands and his fingers. She fenced his tongue with her own and sucked on it. She pushed her breasts up against his hands and gasped when he pinched her nipples, hardening them before rubbing his palms lightly over them. Her own hands explored his back and his shoulders. She wanted him. He felt a fierce exultation. She wanted him. This was not a mistress. This was his wife. This was Sally. And she wanted him.

He moved one hand down to caress her and ready her for penetration. She was hot and wet to his touch, something she had never been before. His temperature soared and his arousal became almost painful.

"Please," she was moaning into his mouth. "Please. Henry, please."

And so he moved on top of her, felt her legs twine tightly about his, lifted his head to look down into her face—her eyes were wide-open and gazing back—and mounted her, sliding deeply into wet heat. *God. Oh, my God. Sally.*

"Love me," she whispered to him. "Oh, please, Henry. There is such an ache."

She was going to come with him, he thought, the realization hammering through his temples with the blood. She was going to climax. He had heard that it was possible with some women.

"Tell me when." He lowered himself on his elbows until his mouth was an inch from hers and he began to move slowly and deeply in her. "I'll wait as long as you need."

But she did not have to tell him. He felt the gradual clenching of her inner muscles, the building tension of her whole body. He heard her deep breaths gradually turn to gasps. And he watched the concentration in her face as her eyes closed and her mouth opened in the agony of the final moments before she looked up at him, stillness and wonder in her eyes, and began to tremble.

He lowered himself onto her, held her tightly, held himself still and deep in her, and let himself experience the marvel of his woman shuddering into release beneath him and crying out his name. Only when he was sure that she had experienced the full joy of the moment did he move again to his own climax.

It was the most wonderful night of her life. She did not care if it was never repeated. She had this to hug to herself in memory for the rest of her days, the most wonderful Christmas that anyone could hope to have. She was nestled in his arms, watching him sleep. After more than three years of marriage she felt like a new bride. She felt . . . oh, she felt wonderful. And she would be satisfied, she swore to herself. She would not demand the moon and the stars. She had the Christmas star, the brightest and best of them all. She would be satisfied with that. Things could never be quite as bad between them now that they had had this night—or this part of a night.

He had opened his eyes and was looking at her. She smiled. *Don't remove your arm,* she begged him with her eyes. *Let's lie like this, just for tonight.*

"You said it," he said. "It seemed to come so easily, though I know it did not. You have not been able to say it in three years, have you? Why have we found it so hard? Why is it so difficult to talk from the heart with those closest to us?"

"Because with them there is most fear of rejection?" she said. "Because we have to protect our hearts from those who have the power to break them every day for the rest of our lives?"

"I do not have your courage," he said, one hand stroking lightly over her cheek. "I still don't. Sally, my love . . . Ah, just that. My love. Did I hurt you? Did I disgust you?"

"Say it again," she said, smiling at him. "Again and again. And do it again and again. I want to be as close to you as I can be, Henry. Close to your body, close to your heart, close to your mind. Not just for tonight. I am greedy."

"My love." He drew her closer to him, set his lips against hers. "It is what I have always wanted, what I have always yearned for. But I have wanted to treat you with respect. Foolish, wasn't I?"

"To think that being respectful meant holding me at

arm's length?" she said. "And giving much of what I have longed for to mistresses? Have I made you flush? Did you think I did not know? Yes, you have been foolish, Henry. And I have been foolish not to fight for your love and not to put you straight on this ridiculous notion that gentlemen seem to have about women."

"Would this be happening if we had reached the Middletons' before the rain came?" he asked her.

"No," she said. "No, it would not. Perhaps it never would have happened. We would have kept drifting until perhaps we would have lived apart. Henry . . ." There was pain in her voice.

He rubbed his lips against hers and drew back his head to smile at her. "But it did happen," he said. "Christmas happened almost two thousand years ago, and it has happened this year for us. Love always seems to blossom at the most unexpected times and in the most unexpected places. This was meant to happen, Sally. We must not shudder at the thought of how nearly it did not happen. It was meant to be."

"Do you think we will ever have a child?" she asked him wistfully, snuggling closer to the warmth and safety of him. "I wanted so much today for that baby to be mine, Henry. Ours. Do you think we ever will?"

"If we don't," he said, and he chuckled as he drew her closer still, "it won't be for lack of trying."

"Oh," she said.

"Shall we try now?" he said to her. "And perhaps again later?"

"And again later still?" she asked.

He laughed. "After all," he said, "dawn comes late in December. And there does not seem to be a great deal to get up early for at this apology for an inn, does there? Especially not on Christmas morning."

"Christmas morning is for babies," she said.

"The making of them as well as the birthing of them," he said, turning her onto her back and moving over her.

She smiled up at him.

"Sally," he said, serious again as he lowered his mouth and his body to hers, "my most wonderful Christmas gift. I love you."

It did not seem quite the same once everyone had gone to bed and he was left alone in the taproom. Even though he built up the fire and sat on a settle close to the heat, the place felt cheerless again. Christmas had fled again.

He thought of the Whittakers' large and fashionable mansion and of Lady Frazer's enticing beauty. He felt a moment's pang of regret but no more. He did not want to be there, he realized with a wry smile directed at the fire. He wanted to be exactly where he was. Well, not exactly, perhaps. There was a room upstairs and a bed where he would rather be. But perhaps not. He could no longer think of her in terms of simple lust. There was a warmer feeling and a nameless yearning when he thought of her. Also a regret for wasted years, for years of senseless debauchery that had brought no real happiness with them.

They would not be able to travel during the coming day, Christmas Day. Probably they would the day after. The rain had finally stopped, and the sky had cleared before darkness fell. He would have one more day in which to enjoy looking at her and in which to maneuver to engage her in conversation. One day—a Christmas to remember.

And then he looked up from his contemplation of the flames in the hearth to find her standing before him, looking at him gravely. She held a blanket and a pillow in her arms.

"I thought you might be cold and uncomfortable," she said, holding them out to him. "It was very kind of you to give up your room for Lisa. You are a kind man."

"I gave up my room," he said, taking the pillow and blanket from her and setting them down beside him, "because you had tried to give up yours and I wanted to impress you with a show of chivalry. Kindness had nothing to do with it. I am not renowned for my kindness."

"Perhaps because you sometimes try not to show it," she said. "But I have seen it in other ways. You came to help Lisa give birth though it terrified you to do so."

He shrugged. "I came for your sake," he said. "And I did not help all day long, while you were exhausting yourself. In the event I did not help at all."

"But you would have," she said. "The intention was there. Tom showed me the ring you gave as a gift for the baby."

He shrugged again. "I am very wealthy," he said. "It was nothing."

"No," she said, still looking at him with her grave eyes, "it was something."

"Ah," he said, "then I have impressed you. I have achieved my goal."

She stared at him silently. He expected her to turn to leave, but she did not do so.

"Do you know how you have affected me?" he asked. "I do not believe I have ever before refused an invitation to bed. That *was* an invitation you were issuing last night?"

She lowered her eyes for a moment, but she lifted them again and looked at him calmly. "Yes," she said. "I suppose so."

"Why?" he asked. "You are not in the habit of issuing such invitations, are you?"

She shook her head. "Sometimes," she said, "I grow tired of the grayness of life. It was so full of color until a little more than a year ago, but there has been nothing but grayness since and nothing but grayness to look forward to. It is wrong of me to be dissatisfied with my lot, and normally I am not. But I thought this was going to be a disappointing Christmas."

"And it has not been?" he asked.

"No." She smiled slowly. "It has been the most wonderful Christmas of all."

"Because of the baby," he said.

"Yes," she said, "because of him. And for other reasons too."

He reached out a hand. "Come and sit beside me," he said.

She looked at his hand and set her own in it. She sat down beside him and set her head on his shoulder when he put an arm about her.

"I wanted you last night," he said. "You know that, don't you? And why I left you, the deed undone?"

"Because you knew I was inexperienced," she said. "Because you knew me to be incapable of giving you the pleasure you are accustomed to. I understood. It is all right."

"Because I realized the immensity of the gift you were offering," he said. "Because I knew I could not take momentary pleasure from you. Because any greater commitment than that terrified me."

"I expected no more," she said.

"I know," he said. "That was the greatness of your gift."

She sighed and set an arm across his waist. "I am going to remember this Christmas for the rest of my life," she said. "It will seem quite unreal when I get back to my post, but I will remember that it really did happen."

He turned his head, found her lips with his own, and kissed her long and lingeringly. Her lips were soft and warm and willing to part for him. He nibbled at them, licked them, stroked them with his tongue. But he would not allow passion to grow. It was neither the time nor the place for passion.

"I am a dreadful rake, Pamela," he said. "My debauched behavior has been notorious for several years. Decent women give me a wide berth."

She raised one hand and touched her fingertips to his cheek.

"But I have never debauched a married woman," he said. "I have always held marriage sacred. I have always known that if I ever married, it would have to be to a woman I loved more than life itself, for I could never be unfaithful to her."

Her finger touched his lips and he kissed it.

"Would you find such a man trustworthy?" he asked her.

"Such a man?" she said. "I don't know. You? Yes. I have seen today, and last night, too, that you are a man of conscience and compassion."

He took her hand in his and brought her palm against his mouth. "How do you think your father would react," he asked, "to the idea of his daughter marrying a rake? Would my title and fortune dazzle his judgment?"

Her eyes grew luminous. "No," she said. "But he would be swayed by kindness and compassion—and by his daughter's happiness."

"Would you be happy, Pamela?" he asked. "Would you take a chance on me?"

She closed her eyes and turned her face to his shoulder.

"It is absurd, isn't it?" he said. "How long have we known each other? Forever, is it? I have known you forever, Pamela. I have just been waiting for you to appear in my life. I have loved you forever."

Her face appeared again, smiling. "I would be happy," she said. "I would take a chance, my lord."

"Edward," he said.

"Edward."

"Will you marry me, my love?" he asked her.

She laughed softly and buried her face again. She hugged his waist tightly. "Yes," she said.

He held her wordless for a while. Then he slid one hand beneath her knees and lifted her legs across his. He reached beside him, shook out the blanket, and spread it over both of them. He settled the pillow behind his head, against the high wooden backrest of the settle.

"Stay with me tonight?" he murmured into her ear. "Just like this, Pamela? It is not the most comfortable of beds, but I will not suggest taking you to your room. I would want to stay with you, you see, and if we were there, I would want to possess you. I want that to wait until our wedding night. I want our bodies to unite for the first time as a marriage commitment. Are these words coming from my mouth?" He chuckled softly. "Are these the words of a rake?"

"No." She turned her face up to his, her eyes bright with merriment. "They are the words of a former rake, Edward—and never to be again. Does that sound dreadfully dull to you?"

He grinned down at her. "It sounds dazzlingly wonderful actually," he said. "Pamela and only Pamela forever after. Are you comfortable?"

"Mm," she said and snuggled against him. "And you?"

"A feather bed could not compete with this settle for softness and ease," he said. He kissed her again, his lips lingering on hers. "Happy Christmas, my love."

"Happy Christmas, Edward," she said, closing her eyes and sighing with warm contentment.

Upstairs, in the room the Marquess of Lytton had occupied the night before, Tom kept watch over the mother of his child, who slept peacefully, and over his newborn son, who fussed in his sleep but did not wake. Tom stood at the window, gazing upward.

A single star almost directly overhead bathed the inn with soft light and glistened off acres of mud. It was not a pretty scene. Not a noticeably Christmas-like scene. The inn, somewhere in Wiltshire, was neither large nor picturesque nor thriving. No one has ever mapped its exact location.

There was nothing like a family Christmas to make a person feel warm about the heart—oh, and a little wistful too. And perhaps just a bit melancholy.

Brambledean Court in Wiltshire was the scene of just such a gathering for the first time in many years. All the Westcotts were gathered there, from Eugenia, the seventy-one-year-old Dowager Countess of Riverdale, on down to her newest great-grandson, Jacob Cunningham, the three-month-old child of the former Camille Westcott and her husband, Joel. They had all been invited by Alexander Westcott, the present Earl of Riverdale and head of the family, and Wren, his wife of six months.

The house hadn't been lived in for more than twenty years before Alexander inherited the title, and it had been shabby even back then. By the time he arrived it had grown shabbier, and the park surrounding it had acquired a sad air of general neglect. It had been a formidable challenge for Alexander, who took his responsibilities seriously but did not have the fortune with which to carry them out. That problem had been solved by his marriage, since Wren was vastly wealthy. The fortune she had brought to their union enabled them to repair the damage of the years and restore the house and park on the one hand and the farms on the other to their former prosperity and glory. But Rome was not built in a day, as the dowager countess was not hesitant to remark after her arrival. There was still a great deal to be done. A very great deal. But at least the house now had a lived-in air.

There were a few other guests besides the Westcotts and their spouses and children. There were Mrs. Kingsley from Bath and her son and daughter-in-law, the Reverend Michael and Mary Kingsley from Dorsetshire. They were the mother, brother, and sister-in-law of Viola, a former Countess of Riverdale, whose marriage of upward of twenty years to the late earl had been exposed as bigamous spectacularly after his death. There had been many complications surrounding that whole ugly episode. But all had ended happily for Viola. For on this very day, Christmas Eve, she had married Marcel Lamarr, Marquess of Dorchester, in the village church. The newlyweds were at the house now, as were Dorchester's eighteen-year-old twin son and daughter.

And Colin Handrich, Baron Hodges, Wren's brother, was here too. For the first time in his twenty-six years he was experiencing a real family Christmas, and after some feeling of awkwardness yesterday despite a warm welcome from everyone, he was now enjoying it greatly.

The house was abuzz with activity. There had been the wedding that morning—a totally unexpected event, it must be added. The marquess had burst in upon them without any prior warning last evening, armed with a special license and an urgent proposal of marriage for Viola a mere couple of months after he had broken off their engagement in spectacularly scandalous fashion during their betrothal party at his own home. But that was another story, and Colin had not been there to experience it firsthand. The wedding had been followed by a wedding breakfast hastily and impressively thrown together by Riverdale's already overworked staff, under Wren's supervision.

This afternoon had been one of laughter-filled attempts to add to yesterday's decorations. Fragrant pine boughs and holly and ivy and mistletoe, not to mention ribbons and bells and bows and all the other paraphernalia associated with the season were everywhere, it seemed—in the drawing room, on the stairs, in the hall, in the dining room. A kissing bough, fashioned under the guidance of Lady Matilda Westcott, unmarried eldest daughter of the dowager countess, hung in the place of honor from the center of the drawing room ceiling and had been causing laughter and whistles and blushes ever since yesterday as it was put to use. There had been the Yule log to haul in today and position in the great hall's large hearth, ready to be lit in the evening.

And all the while as they moved about and climbed and perched, pinned and balanced, pricked fingers and kissed and blushed, tantalizing smells had been wafting up from the kitchens below of Christmas puddings and gingerbread and mince pies and the Christmas ham, among other mouth-watering delights.

And there had been the snow as a constant wonder and distraction, drawing them to every available window far more often than was necessary to assure themselves that it had not stopped falling and was not melting as fast as it came down. It had been threatening for days and had finally begun during the wedding that morning. It had continued in earnest all day since then, until by now it must be knee deep.

Snow, and such copious amounts of it, was a rarity in England, especially for Christmas. They did not stop telling one another so all afternoon.

And now, in the evening, the village carolers had waded up the driveway to sing for them. The Yule log had been lit and the family had gathered and the carolers had come against all expectation, exclaiming and stamping boots and shaking mufflers and slapping mittens and rubbing at red noses to make them redder—and then quieting down and growing self-conscious as they looked around at the family and friends gathered in the great hall to listen to them.

They sang for half an hour, and their audience listened and occasionally joined in. The dowager countess and Mrs. Kingsley were seated in ornately carved and padded wooden chairs close to the great fireplace to benefit from the logs that flamed and crackled around the Yule log in the hearth.

It gave more the effect of cheerfulness than actual warmth
to the rest of the hall, but everyone else was happy to stand
until the carolers came to the end of their repertoire and
everyone applauded. Alexander gave a short speech wishing everyone a happy and healthy New Year. Then they all
moved about, mingling and chatting and laughing merrily
as glasses of spiced wassail and trays of warm mince pies
were brought up from belowstairs and offered first to the
carolers and then to the house guests.

After a while Colin found himself standing in the midst
of it all, alone for the moment, consciously enjoying the
warm, festive atmosphere of the scene around him. From
what he could observe, there appeared to be not one discor-
dant note among the happy crowd—if one ignored the impatience with which the dowager was batting away the
heavy shawl Lady Matilda was attempting to wrap about
her shoulders.

This was what family should be like.

This was what Christmas should always be like.

It was an ideal of perfection, of course, and ideals were
not often attained and were not sustainable for long even
when they were. Life could never be unalloyed happiness,
even for a close-knit family such as this one. But sometimes
there were moments when it was, and this was surely one
of them. It deserved to be recognized and enjoyed and savored.

And envied.

He smiled at the three young ladies across the hall who
had their heads together, chattering and laughing and stealing glances his way. It was not altogether surprising. He was
not unduly conceited, but he *was* a young, single gentleman
in possession of a title and fortune. Single gentlemen above
the age of twenty were in short supply here at Brambledean.
Indeed, he was it, with the exception of Captain Harry Westcott, Viola's son, who had arrived back from the wars in the
Peninsula two days ago—also unexpectedly—on recruit-
ment business for his regiment. Unfortunately for the three
ladies, however, the captain was the brother of one of them

and the first cousin of another. Only Lady Estelle Lamarr, the Marquess of Dorchester's daughter, was unrelated to him by blood, though she had become his stepsister this morning.

When they saw Colin smile, they all ducked their heads while above the general hubbub he could hear one of them giggling. But why would he not look and be pleased with what he saw—and flattered by their attention? They were all remarkably pretty in differing ways, younger than he and unattached, as far as he knew. They were all eligible, even Abigail Westcott, Viola and the late Earl of Riverdale's daughter, whose birth had been declared illegitimate after the disastrous revelation concerning her father's bigamy almost three years ago. Colin did not care a fig for that supposed stigma upon her name. Lady Jessica Archer was half sister of the Duke of Netherby and daughter of the former duke and his second wife, the youngest of the Westcott sisters.

It had not been easy during the six months since Wren married Alexander to sort out the complex relationships within this family, but Colin believed he had finally mastered them, even the step and half connections.

He was about to stroll across the hall to ask the three young ladies how they had enjoyed the carol singing when his sister appeared at his side and handed him a glass of wassail.

"You are going to have to stay here tonight after all, thanks to the snow, Colin," she said, sounding smug.

"But you already have a houseful, Roe," he protested, though in truth he knew it would be impossible to go home tonight and even more impossible to return tomorrow. Home was Withington House, nine miles away, where he had been living since the summer. It belonged to Wren, but he had gladly moved in there when she had offered it, rather than stay in London, where he had lived throughout the year for the past five years.

"*Roe,*" she said softly and fondly. She had been christened Rowena as a baby. *Roe* had been Colin's childhood name for her, and he still called her that when in conversation with her, even though her name had been legally changed to Wren. "One more guest will cause no upheaval, and it will make us all a lot happier. Me in particular. Was not the carol singing wonderful?"

"Wonderful," he agreed, though the singers had been more hearty than musical.

"And the wedding this morning was perfect," she said with a happy sigh. "And the wedding breakfast after it. And the snow and putting up more decorations and . . . Oh, and *everything*. Have you ever lived through a happier day?"

He pretended to think about it, his eyes raised to the high ceiling of the great hall, his forefinger tapping his chin. He raised the finger. "Yes, I have actually," he said. "The day Alexander came to call at my rooms in London and I discovered that you were still alive, and I went with him to meet you for the first time in almost twenty years."

"Ah. Yes." She beamed at him, her eyes luminous with memory. "Oh yes, indeed, Colin, you are right. When I looked at you, and you spoke my name, and I realized you were that little mop-haired boy I remembered . . . It was indeed an unforgettable day."

He had been told when he was six years old that ten-year-old Rowena had died shortly after their aunt took her away from Roxingley, supposedly to consult a physician about the great strawberry birthmark that swelled over one side of her face, disfiguring her quite horribly. In reality there had been no physician and no death. Aunt Megan had taken Rowena from a home in which she had been isolated and frequently locked in her room so that no one would have to look at her. Aunt Megan had married Reginald Heyden, a wealthy gentleman of her acquaintance, soon after, and the two of them had adopted Rowena Handrich, changed her name to Wren Heyden, and raised her as their own. Colin meanwhile had grieved deeply for his beloved sister and playmate. He had discovered the truth only this year, when Alexander had sought him out soon after marrying her.

Wren was lovely despite the purple marks down the left side of her face where the strawberry swelling had been when she was a child. And she was looking more beautiful than ever these days. Alexander had lost no time in getting her with child.

"Was Christmas a happy time for you when you were a boy, Colin?" Her face turned a little wistful as she gazed into his.

He had grown up as part of a family—there were his mother and father, an elder brother, and three older sisters. Roxingley Park was a grand property where there had always been an abundance of the good things in life. The material things, that was. His father had been a wealthy man, just as Colin was now. Christmases had come and gone, even after the supposed death of Rowena, the youngest of his sisters, and the real death of his brother Justin nine years later. But he did not remember them as warm family occasions. Not like this one. Not even close.

"I am sorry," she said. "You are looking suddenly melancholy. Aunt Megan and Uncle Reggie always made Christmas very special for me and for each other. Not like this, of course. There were just the three of us. But very lovely nevertheless and abounding with love. Life will get better for you, Colin. I promise. And you will be staying tonight. You will be here all day tomorrow and probably all of Boxing Day too. *Definitely*, in fact, for we will press ahead with the plans for our Boxing Day evening party even if some of our invited guests find it impossible to get here. This is going to be the best Christmas ever. I have decided, and I will not take no for an answer. It already is the best, in fact, though I do wish Aunt Megan and Uncle Reggie were still alive to be a part of it. You would have loved them, and they would have loved you."

He opened his mouth to reply, but Alexander had caught Wren's eye from his position behind the refreshments and she excused herself to weave her way back toward him in order to distribute more of the wassail to the carolers before they left.

Colin looked about the hall again, still feeling warm and happy—and a bit melancholy at having been reminded of the brokenness that was and always had been his own family. And perhaps too at the admission that, though he was now Baron Hodges himself and therefore head of his family, and though he was twenty-six years old and no longer had the excuse of being a mere boy, he had done nothing to draw its remaining members together—his mother and his three sisters and their spouses and children. He had not been to Roxingley since he was eighteen, when he had gone for his father's funeral. He had done nothing to perpetuate his line, to create his own family, something more like this one. The Westcotts had suffered troubles enough in the last few years and no doubt before that too. Life was like that. But their troubles had seemed to strengthen rather than loosen the bonds that held them.

Not so with the Handrich family.

Could it be done? Was it possible? Was he ready at least to try? To do something positive with his life instead of just drifting from day to day and more or less hiding from the enormity of what doing something would entail? His eyes alit again upon the group across the hall. The young ladies had been joined by the three schoolboy sons of Lord and Lady Molenor. Winifred Cunningham, Abigail's young niece, was with them too, as were a couple of the younger carolers. They were all merrily chatting and laughing and behaving as though this Christmas Eve was the very happiest of days—as indeed it was.

Colin felt suddenly as though he were a hundred years older than the oldest of them.

"A penny for them," a voice said from close by, and he turned toward the speaker.

Ah. Lady Overfield.

Just the sight of her lifted his mood and brought a smile to his face. He liked and admired her more than any other woman of his acquaintance, perhaps more than any other person of either gender. For him she lived on a sort of pedestal, above the level of other mortals. He might have been quite in love with her if she had been of an age with him or younger. Though even then it would have seemed somehow disrespectful. She was his ideal of womanhood.

She was Alexander's elder sister, Wren's sister-in-law, and beautiful through and through. He was well aware that other people might not agree. She was fair haired and trim of figure and had a face that was amiable more than it was obviously lovely. But his life experiences had taught him to look deeper than surface appearances to discover beauty or its lack. Lady Overfield was perhaps the most beautiful woman he had ever met. There was something about her manner that exuded a seemingly unshakable tranquility combined with a twinkling eye. But she did not hoard it. Rather, she turned it outward to touch other people. She did not draw attention to herself but bestowed it upon others. She was everyone's best friend in the family, the one with whom all felt appreciated and comfortable, the one who would always listen and never judge. She had been Wren's first friend ever—Wren had been close to thirty at the time—and had remained steadfast. Colin would have loved her for that alone.

He had liked her since his rediscovery of his sister, but he had felt particularly warm toward her since yesterday. He had felt a bit awkward being among the members of a close family, though everyone had made him welcome. Lady Overfield had singled him out, though, for special attention. She had talked with him all evening from her perch on the window seat in the room where they were all gathered, drawing him out on topics he would not normally have raised with a woman, talking just enough herself to make it a conversation. He had soon relaxed. He had also felt honored, for to her he must appear little more than a gauche boy. He guessed she must be somewhere in her mid-thirties to his twenty-six. He did not know how long she had been a widow, but she must have been quite young when she lost her husband, poor lady. She had no children. She lived with Mrs. Westcott, her mother, at Alexander's former home in Kent.

She had asked him a question.

"I was trying to decide," he said, nodding in the direction of the group of young people, "which of the three ladies I should marry."

She looked startled for a moment and then laughed with him as she glanced across the room.

"Oh, indeed?" she said. "But have you not heard, Lord Hodges, that when one gazes across a crowded room at the one and only person destined to be the love of one's life, one feels no doubt whatsoever? If you look and see *three* possible candidates for the position, then it is highly probable that none of them is the right choice."

"Alas," he said. "Are you quite sure?"

"Well, not *quite*," she admitted. "They are all remarkably pretty, are they not? I must applaud your taste. I have observed too that they are not indifferent to your charms. They have been stealing glances at you and exchanging nudges and giggles since yesterday—at least Abby and Jessica have. Estelle came only today after the wedding, but she seems equally struck by you. But Lord Hodges, *are* you in search of a wife?"

"No," he said after a slight hesitation. "Not really. I am not, but I am beginning to feel that perhaps I ought to be. Sometime. Maybe soon. Maybe not for a few years yet. And how is that for a firm, decisive answer?"

"Admirable," she said, and laughed again. "I expect the young female world and that of its mamas will go into raptures when you do begin the search in earnest. You must know that you are one of England's most eligible bachelors and not at all hard on the eyes either. Wren is over the moon with delight that you will be staying here tonight, by the way. She was disappointed last evening when you insisted upon returning home."

"I believe the snow is still coming down out there, Lady Overfield," he said. "If I tried to get home, there might be nothing more than my eyebrows showing above the snow when someone came in search of me. It would appear that I am stuck here for at least a couple of days."

"Better here than there even if you could get safely home," she said. "You would be stuck there and all alone for Christmas. The very thought makes me want to weep. But will you call me Elizabeth? Or even Lizzie? My brother is, after all, married to your sister, which fact makes us virtually brother and sister, does it not? May I call you Colin?"

"Please do, Elizabeth," he said, feeling a bit awkward at saying her name. It seemed an imposition. But she had requested it, a particular mark of acceptance. What a very happy Christmas this was turning out to be—and it was not even Christmas Day yet. How could he even consider feeling melancholy?

"You ought to be very thankful for the snow," she said. "Now you will not have to waste part of the morning in travel. Christmas morning is always one of my favorites of the year, if not my *very* favorite. Is it not a rare treat indeed to have a white Christmas? And has that been remarked upon a time or two already today? But I cannot remember the last time it happened. And it is not even a light dusting to tease the hopes of children everywhere, but a massive fall. I would wager upon the sudden appearance of an army of snowmen and perhaps snowladies tomorrow, as well as a heavenly host of snow angels. And snowball fights and sleigh rides—there is an ancient sleigh in the carriage house, apparently. And sledding down the hill. There are sleds too, which really ought to be in a museum somewhere, according to Alex, but which will doubtless work just as well as new ones would. There is even a hill, though not a very mountainous one, alas. It will do, however. You will not be sorry you stayed."

"Perhaps," he said, "I will choose to spend a more traditional Christmas in a comfortable chair by the fire, eating rich foods and imbibing spiced wine and napping."

She looked at him, startled again. "Oh, you could not possibly be so poor-spirited," she said, noticing the twinkle in his eye. "You would be the laughingstock. A pariah. Expelled from Brambledean in deep disgrace, never to be admitted within its portals again even if you *are* Wren's brother."

"Does that also mean none of your young cousins would be willing to marry me?" he asked.

"It absolutely means just that," she assured him. "Even I would not."

"Ah," he said, slapping a hand to the left side of his chest. "My heart would be broken."

"I would have no pity on you," she said, "even if you came to me with the pieces in your hand."

"Cruel." He sighed. "Then I had better be prepared to go out tomorrow and make a few snow angels and hurl a few snowballs, preferably at you. I warn you, though, that I was the star bowler on my cricket team at school."

"What modesty," she said. "Not to mention gallantry. But I see that two of the footmen are lighting the carolers' lanterns. They are about to leave. Shall we go and see them on their way?"

She took the arm he offered and they joined the throng about the great doors. The noise level escalated as everyone thanked the carolers again and the carolers thanked everyone in return and everyone wished everyone else a happy Christmas.

He *was* happy, Colin decided. He was a part of all this. He was an accepted member of the Westcott family, even if merely an extended member. Lady Overfield—Elizabeth— had remarked that they were virtually brother and sister. She had joked and laughed with him. Her hand was still tucked through his arm. There was surely no greater happiness.

There were a snowball fight and sledding to look forward to tomorrow.

And gifts to exchange.

And goose and stuffing and Christmas pudding.

Yes, it felt very good to belong.

To a family that was not really his own.